THE OLDE
Towen Buffet

(Or "Don't Eat the Calamari")

By Wesley Critchfield

PROLOGUE:

He stood there in the darkness. The sound of chanting voices filling the chamber. He could feel the power pulsing through him, the same power that held him in place and made him unable to move, like a painless, paralyzing, electricity.

This was it.

This was what he had longed for all his life.

He wanted this.

When the time came he would do anything for it. The changes had already begun to take place in him, and oh how wonderful they were. There had been no resistance. When the work was begun in him he hardly knew anything was happening at all... But soon it had been undeniable.

Now he stood in the darkness as the flames danced before him casting his shadow on the wall.

From somewhere off to his left, he heard the distant wailing cries of the woman he had once thought of as his wife; the woman who he once thought the most important thing in his puny existence. But now he understood so much more. Now he was part of something bigger. Something... cosmic.

She was nothing.

Her sobbing would soon be silenced and no longer of any account.

She cried his name over and over; pleading with him to break free, to come away with her, but freedom was an illusion, and it meant nothing without power.

And this was power.

Her face was beaten and bloody, and seeing that might

have once elicited some emotion from him, but now he was beyond such things.

Let it happen. Let it come now. No more waiting.

He wanted it to be over.

He wanted it to begin.

He wanted the power; the strength. All the might which had been conveyed upon him this night was but a taste of what was to come. When he had fully given himself over, when the darkness was embraced, then he would know this strength a thousand-fold. He would do anything, give anything; be anything that was required of him, so long as he could have this.

He had always thought that if somehow this boon was bestowed upon him, that his first goal would be vengeance. He had been sure that he would hunt down all those who had wounded him every day of his life; his father first and foremost of all.

He remembered the plans he had for the boss at the job he had so recently been fired from; Mr. Williams. The man for whom he had worked for nearly fifteen years and who now had ruined him. His life and career were over, not only at his law office, but for all legal work.

He thought of hunting down the girls who had rejected him in High School and even the bullies of the playground. Yes! How they would have all paid for what they had done. Anyone who had ever laughed at him, or made him feel small. He would grind their bones to meal.

He remembered when he was a child how nearly every day, they had circled him chanting, "Stubby Stanley! Stubby Stanley!" and "Fatty fatty, two by four, can't fit through the kitchen door." and the perennial favorite, "U-G-L-Y, you ain't got no alibi!"

How they had guffawed when he couldn't reach the monkey bars from the highest of the supports, let alone hold himself up as he tried to make his way from one bar to the next. Every time he would flop down in the hard-packed dirt below like a sack of moldy potatoes.

Then his memories swirled round to the girls who had rejected him because he was shorter than they, and the slow agony he would have extracted from them. Even now when he was becoming something beyond any of their understanding, their words echoed and raced through his mind, solidifying his choice:

"What girl wants a guy they have to get down on one knee to kiss? Tony, now there's a real man! Six-foot, two and he might get even taller!"

"Maybe I'll let you take me out when the school has a "Date a Hobbit Dance!"

"Do I look like my name is Esmeralda? 'Cause I sure ain't walking around on the arm of no Quasimodo!"

"Hey, short stuff! Get that ball from off the wall rack!" The coach had shouted at him, knowing he would have to climb up the rack to reach the only ball that was left at the very top. And when the rack had tipped over, as he knew it would, smashing him to the floor bruising his ribs, the coach had called out as the other boys laughed, *"If you can't get hold of a ball when it's sitting on a rack, how do you ever expect to play on my team? Get off the field, and don't come back Short Stuff!"*

Then there had been his father:

"Look at him Natalie, he's sixteen and he barely comes up to my chest! He'll never bee any good at sports! He's too small and weak for football. He's far too short for basketball and he's got zero hand-eye coordination! My only son is a runt! He's not even good at academics! And here you are, mollycoddling him! He's never going to amount to anything!"

All this and more swirled about in his head, but now he had no thought for revenge, it was all behind him. So small and petty.

Now he had worlds to conquer, soon all would bow before the might that was flowing into him. He could feel it coiling through him like a plant; like a vine, it was wrapping around his limbs and sinking into them, imbuing them with a virility he had never known, never could have known, but for the events of this strange night.

The sound of chanting in the darkness had ceased. Had it only stopped now, or was it some time ago? Trapped in a delicious trance of power and haze of remembrance he couldn't be sure. But now the shadows on the wall were changing, were different, undulating with a light far stranger than any fire could produce.

He knew, at last, the time had come.

He was about to gaze upon his new master for the first time. He would joyfully submit. He would accept any contract, make any deal. This was all he had ever wanted.

He felt the restraining power lift from him, and he could move once again. He lifted his eyes to see a sight that might have driven others mad. But to him it was beautiful. It was this one who had made a new life possible, and from somewhere deep inside himself, he heard his master's voice speak his name for the first time.

1

"Doggone it!" Ally cursed, straining, stretching as high as she could, "Who built this place! Andre the Giant?"

"No, it just wasn't built for Gnomes." Said her husband, effortlessly reaching up and taking down the suitcase, he had placed on the rack the night before, the handle of which had just evaded his wife's grasp.

He handed it over to her as she huffed a begrudging, "Thanks." And then mumbled, *"For nothing."* Under her breath.

Mark laughed, "Hey don't hold it against me, I didn't write your genetic code." He flopped on to the bed, making the suitcase wobble, as his wife reloaded it with all of her do-dads and whatnots that seemed so necessary for the care of her appearance. The trip was only going to last a week, but she seemed to have brought enough clothes for three. Then there were the two extra, small suitcases, full of nothing but beauty care. The total of four suitcases had taken up all the space that was leftover in the trunk of Marks Chevy Malibu, once the small toolbox, jack, and four-way lug wrench were pushed to the side. Mark had to put his one small suitcase in the back seat.

Now, three days later, they were on their way back from California to Chicago. They had spent the night in Aurora, about thirty-five miles south of Boulder. They were now only seventeen hours from home.

It would have been fifteen hours, but a major road construction project had begun just after they had passed through on Route 76, on the way to California.

Already at 9 am, traffic was backed up. According to the Mapping app on their phones, going back that way would have added nearly five hours to their trip. Mark had asked his wife to remind him to take route 70, in the morning so they could avoid that nightmare.

It came to her mind as she fit her curling iron and hairdryer back into the already cramped suitcase.

"I wish we didn't have to go around the construction, I hate Kansas."

"What's the matter with Kansas?" asked Mark, "I love all that farmland, especially this time of year, just before the harvest. All those fields of green. It's beautiful."

"It's boring. Flat straight and goes on for what feels like forever! Did you know there are more single-vehicle accidents in Kansas per-capita than any other state? People get hypnotized out there driving on the roads alone, and when the road turns, they don't. They go flying off into a ditch somewhere, and drown in a creek bed."

"Where did you read that?" Mark asked laughing to himself.

"Oh on the internet somewhere.... Which reminds me I better check my phone while we still have service, I just know we're going to get out there and lose signal."

"Our service plan covers 95% of the landmass of the continental US, according to the commercials."

"Yeah, and we are going to be driving right through that remaining 5%." She said snapping the clasps on the suitcase into place, "I guess that's everything."

"Don't forget your make-up kit, Shawty," Mark said, affecting an accent.

Ally looked up and groaned. There, on top of the rack was her black plastic make up kit, with all her various blushes and brushes.

"I'm never going to reach that. Why did you put it up there?"

"Why did you even unpack it?" Mark replied, not moving

from the bed, "When we were in LA, that made sense, you were getting all gussied up for the dinner. That made sense." He repeated. "But last night you were getting ready for bed, and you took it out of your suitcase. There's nobody here but me, and you know you shouldn't wear makeup to bed. And then, you didn't even use it."

"I was setting it out for the morning, I was planning to put my face on before we left, but I couldn't find it. I figured it had gotten buried in the clothes and I didn't want to dig it out." Ally said, annoyed.

"Put your face on? For what? The drive home? You and me and miles and miles of corn?" He got up off the bed and moved toward her. "Besides I think my wittle munchkin looks so much better without her make-up." He said affecting a "baby-talk" voice.

She punched him in the bicep, hard enough to sting but not to truly hurt.

"Ouch!" he said, playing it up.

"Stop picking on my height. You know I'm sensitive about it."

"But you are just so cude!" He said, still in baby-talk, wrapping her in his arms, which from fingertip to fingertip of the opposite hand, were exactly 5 feet, 11 inches, perfectly proportionate to his height, "I wuv my Widdle Baby Wifey!"

He picked her up and spun her around.

"Stop that!" She said half laughing, "Put me down!" she said, even though he already had. "I may be only 5 feet tall but I'll kick your butt anyway."

He laughed and reached up for the make-up kit, handing it to her. "Here you go Smurfette."

She ignored the jibe and reopened her make up suitcase, "Why'd you put it up so high?"

"Because you had it on the sink and I needed to shave. I didn't want to ruin anything, with drops of water flying everywhere.... And I did that so you'd need me to get it down for you later... I have to remind you how much you need me every once in a while... Just in case you get complacent, or think you can do better."

Ally laughed, snapping the suitcase closed again, "I know I can do better, I've just grown accustomed to you."

"You know, that's right." Mark said with a toothy grin.

2

As the car bounced along the road Ally sighed. Though the Air conditioner was working, it could barely cope with the sweltering summer heat.

"I told you that the AC needs to be recharged on this thing. It hasn't been working like it used to for months."

"Well Ally, if I get this job you won't have to worry about this car's AC working any more… I won't just get the car fixed; I'll get you a car of your own! A little bitty clown car that you can drive where ever you want. *Toot! Toot!*"

"You're the clown." Ally said rolling down the window, and letting the breeze blow in as the car bounced along Route 70.

"Well at least turn off the A. C., if you are going to roll down a window," Mark said, reaching up to the dial on the dashboard.

As they drove Mark put in an old audio cassette of songs he seemed to have prepared for driving through miles and miles of nothing. Mostly comprised of what Ally thought of as "Hippie Folk Songs", John Denver, Three Dog Night, Maureen McGovern, The Carpenters, and Paul Williams.

"Where's the Credence Clear Water Revival, or Steppenwolf, or at least The Who?" Ally asked, reaching into the glove compartment and putting on her oversized sunglasses to block out the glaring light of the sun, turning the whole world a yellow-brown, that while ugly, made the brightness easier to handle. She sighed as miles and miles of nothing much at all, rolled by.

"I think there's some of those on the other side," Mark said, annoyed, "Be patient."

"I don't see why we couldn't have spent one day at the hotel. That pool they had was magnificent. It was like three or four square pools pushed together to make one, and with all those little fountains. And it would have been so nice on a day like this."

"Had to have the room cleared by noon. I wasn't about to pay for an extra day at that place, the company was paying for it the last couple nights but after noon, it would have been on our dime."

"Doesn't mean we couldn't have put everything in the car and checked out and then used the pool for a while. Most places don't mind, as long as you paid for the night before, and you get out before sundown. And it's sooo hot!"

Mark sighed as he steered, "Yeah... Who would have thought it'd still be so hot this late in September?"

The miles rolled by. Eventually, Ally got annoyed with the music and asked Mark to put on something else. Mark paired his phone to the car's stereo and put on an audiobook he had been listening to, but after a while, the subject began to bore Ally.

She pushed a button and the audio cassette started playing again. It was that spooky one about being *"Out in the Country."* She had always found the music between verses to be kind of eerie, but the chorus was what really unnerved her.

"Before the breathing air is gone,
Before the sun is just a bright spot in the night time.
Out where the rivers like to run, I stand alone,
I take back something worth remembering."

The singer was probably talking about pollution, smog, and the ever-spreading "urban sprawl" and had simply written a song about getting away from it all. They were probably influenced by that book *"The Silent Spring"* a book that had caused panic in the sixties and seventies over the damage man was doing to the environment. But to her, it had always seemed like there was more to it. Something she didn't like to think about. To Ally it always made her think the protagonist was aware of some imminent disaster. An Apocalypse that would, in a single day turn the *"breathing air"* into a poisonous haze, and block out the sun, making it a *"Just a bright spot in the night time."* Something he couldn't do anything about, like an asteroid or comet or a nuclear war. She imagined him looking out of the same spot a few days later, *"Out where the rivers liked to run"* and seeing only a blasted landscape, of dust and ash. Sitting in the car she shuddered to think of it, despite the summer heat.

"Don't you have something a little more interesting?" Ally asked, referring to the book they had been listening too and to take her mind off the song, "Like... I don't know, a treasure hunt or a time-traveler in the Scottish Highlands?"

It had been about forty-five minutes of listening to the bad reader drone on about some incident during the Second World War, and it seemed like half of that had been a catalog of expensive dinnerware and cutlery.

"How can you not find this interesting?" Mark asked, truly astonished, "Erik Larson is the best!"

"This is even more boring than the one he wrote about the Lusitania. At least that one had a ship blowing up in it."

"*Dead Wake*, and I thought you liked that one." "No the one I liked was the one they made that movie out of with Leo... *Devil of the White City* or something."

"In."

"In what?"

"*Devil in the White City*."

"Whatever. And then it wasn't nearly as good as the movie, he focused way too much on the making of the World's Fair, and not nearly enough on the killer, Hounds."

"Hounds?" Mark asked laughing.

"Hounds, really?"

"Yeah, that was his name wasn't it? H. H. Hounds."

"Holmes. Like Sherlock."

"Ok fine. You knew what I meant."

They sat in silence for a moment, but then Mark started to laugh to himself. First a chuckle, then a small snort, and a chuckle, with a shake of the head... A moment passed and then he was in a full out belly laugh.

"What?" Ally asked, trying not to laugh herself. She didn't know what was so funny but Mark's laughter was always contagious to her. The only other person who had ever been able to make her laugh just by hearing them laugh had been Tom Hanks, particularly when the tub fell through the floor in "The Money Pit." "What's so funny?" she repeated.

"H. H. Hounds." Mark said, "I just had this picture in my head of a dog walking about in a bowler cap singing with a bloody knife in his hands."

Ally tisked, but then the mental image made her snort a little as well... It might have been forgotten but then Mark started to hum, then whistle and before long he was caterwauling in a "hicktown" voice, *"Oh, my darlin' Oh, my Darlin'! Oh, my Darlin' Clementine! You are lost and gone forever, dreadful sorry Clementine!"*

Soon Ally was laughing and singing along, the two of them trying to outdo each other on how badly they sang, without losing some semblance of the tune.

Then Mark started singing a verse from the Andy Griffith show, that Barney the Cop had once sung about himself, *"But Fife was tricky, a dead-eye Dickie, now they're locked up in the tank!"*

The two of them were laughing so hard, that neither of them spotted the remnant of 18 Wheeler tire lying in the road until it was too late.

"Look out!" Ally cried, and Mark tried to swerve to miss it, but still caught the rear passenger tire on a splinter of wire that stuck out of the discarded tire. From the rear of the Malibu there came a sickening pop and followed quickly by the *"womp womp womp"* of a busted tire.

Mark cursed fecal matter as he targeted the side of the road with the front end of the car.

Ally sat in the passenger seat quietly, knowing that anything she said at the moment could only make things worse.

The car thumped to a stop and the grind of the metal rim on blacktop came from the back of the vehicle. Mark turned off the engine and sighed deeply.

"You okay?" he asked.

"Yeah... I'm fine."

"I'm sorry I should have been watching more closely."

"It's alright... We were having fun." She took his hand. They sat there for a moment, and finally, she said, "Are you going to get out and put on the spare?"

"I would, if we had one... The spare is on the front driver's side... It popped a week ago and I replaced it... I kept meaning to buy a new one."

"Well... that's just great." Ally said, with as little venom in her voice as possible.

"Yep," Mark said, smacking his lips, looking out at the road in front of them.

"We're going to have to call the Auto Club." Ally said, taking her hand out of Mark's so she could reach for her phone, which sat on the charger.

The words she had expected lit up when she pushed the button. *"No Signal."*

"You got anything?" Mark asked, with no hope in his voice.

"Not a bar." She said, "You?"

"Nope... Same Network... or lack thereof."

"So..." She said, "... What do we do?"

"Well..." He said, flicking his finger across his screen, "While I don't have GPS, we passed a mile marker about two minutes ago, and if that was right, there is an exit about half a mile, in that direction." Mark pointed out ahead of them. "I think I can see the sign for it... If we get out and walk down the road a piece, and down that exit, and if we are lucky, we'll find a gas station or a restaurant with a telephone."

"You honestly expect me to walk half a mile in heels?"

"Why did you wear heels? We are in the car!?" Mark asked, sounding more like a distressed Tom Hanks than ever before.

Ally suppressed a small laugh, "Well if you hadn't been making all those "short" wisecracks earlier... Besides, heels was all I brought because I thought we would be spending most of our time in the restaurant and you would be in meetings while I swam in the pool... and until now I was right."

"I have some boots I keep in the trunk for the winter." Mark said, "They are meant to support your ankle, we can tie them down tight as possible for you."

"Great, so I have to go clomping down the road with my size 5 feet in your size 12 combat boots."

"We'll stuff them with dirty socks or something," Mark said dismissively.

"Oh great so my feet will be smelly and huge!" Ally said truly raising her voice for the first time.

"So we'll stuff them with clean socks! Will you give me a break! Come on!!" Mark said shouting back.

3

Nearly an hour later, the two of them were walking down the road together in silence. Just as Mark had said, they had stuffed the inside of his boots with extra socks and small clothes to tighten up the space inside, and while this made the shoes less likely to slide around on Ally's feet, it also made them very hot and sweaty.

While Mark had stuffed the shoes, Ally had shoved the bare essentials of a few extra clothes for both of them, into her makeup suitcases, after placing the make up in one of the bigger suitcases they would leave behind them.

Ally had been upset at the very idea, but Mark didn't want to haul anything big along with them, and insisted.

He took four bottles of water and put them in each suitcase as well. He had no idea how far they might need to walk but he figured it would be quite some time before they found a farmhouse or a village.

The added weight in her suitcase didn't make Ally any happier, but it soon diminished by twenty ounces as she cracked open her first bottle. Mark had always kept a small cooler in the trunk with ten bottles of water in it, (the maximum it could hold) for emergencies. While he didn't keep ice in it, (What would have been the point?) the Cooler helped to keep the heat of the day out, and thus prevent the bottles from decaying and releasing CFCs into the water contained within.

Now as they approached the end of the exit ramp, they saw two signs, both with large arrows pointing to their right. The first was a green, state sign which read:

**Carter Hill 2
Gieger's Rest 6
Valley Lodge 10**

The second sign was one of those cheaply made signs you could have made for just about any occasion, from supporting a political candidate to your kid's graduation party. It was stuck into the ground on a weak, two-post, wire framework, which had long ago turned to rust. The sign was nearly covered by the tall grass, and read: The Olde Towen Buffet:

**3 MILES THAT WAY! ▶
Carter's Hill, KS Overnight Accommodations
for the Weary Traveler
Free Continental Breakfast**

Mark had to push down some of the Grass to read the bottom half of the sign, "Well, it looks like there's a restaurant three miles in that direction." He said pointing, "Where there's a restaurant, there's usually a phone, to make orders... Hopefully, a gas station too, though I don't see a sign for that."

"What I don't understand is why we haven't seen any other cars for nearly an hour since the tire popped." Ally said, sitting down on her suitcase. The case was well made and supported her barely 110-pound frame easily, if not exactly comfortably. "If 76 had a five hour back up, shouldn't we have been seeing a lot more people do what we did and take route 70?"

"It's a good question, I guess," Mark said, stretching. "There were a lot of people on the road as we were leaving Aurora, but it thinned out pretty quickly, especially once we got solidly into Kansas."

"If there had been other cars around we might have noticed the tire tread before we hit it, and never even been in this situation."

"That's true enough I guess..." Mark replied, placing his hands on his lower back and stretching, "We did see that Eighteen wheeler pass us by, remember? ... Tried to flag him down, but he just blew right through like a bat out of..." Mark drifted off. Looking down the road in the direction the signs pointed.

"What's the matter?" Ally asked, placing her right foot on her left knee, and starting to pick at the zipper and Velcro strap that opened up the boot without untying it.

"Don't take your shoe off." Mark instructed, "It was hard enough to get everything packed around your foot properly the first time. Ally threw up her hands, and slapped her thighs in disgust, "My feet are sweating like a pig in heat." She continued, "My feet are aching! I'm going to have to ring out my socks and everything else you packed into these shoes... There's so much sweat sloshing around in here, we'll be lucky if we don't flood the county."

"They could use the water... Look down there." Mark pointed.

Up until now, most of the land around them had been green and lush, as grass and crops can only be just before Fall sets in. Farmland lined most of the highway and what wasn't exactly farmable was full of tall prairie grass leaning against the wind... But just down the road from where they stood, there was an almost immediate die-off. The grass went from green to black.

Not to brown or beige, as you might see in the winter when the snow had melted away, or not yet fallen, but a thick over-saturated rotten green-black. It looked as if the grass and weeds had been contaminated by used motor oil, but instead of killing them outright, the plants had sucked it up and put forth into their greenery, rotting from the inside out.

This blackness only progressed for about 100 feet before giving way to complete bareness... Not dead grass, but dirt, in which nothing living grew. If there had once been dead grass in that place, it was now long gone, blown away by the wind.

"Ew." Said Ally, looking down the road, at the desolation. "I know..." Said Mark, "What do you think is causing that? Some sort of acidity in the soil? Maybe an oil leak of some kind?"

"What do I look like, a botanist?" Ally said, standing and stretching her ankles.

"No, but you do look like a navigator. Which way Miss Daisy?"

"What do you mean?"

"I mean we can go left under the overpass, or we can go right, toward Carter's Hill. Left doesn't seem to have anything in that direction, and Right seems to have at least two towns within walking distance, as well as the possibility of a restaurant and a gas station."

"Yeah, if the podunky little place didn't close up years ago from lack of business. Did you see how roached that sign is? It could have been there for years."

"Right." He said nodding, "To me its pretty obvious, but I wanted to include you on the decision." Ally picked up her suitcase and began to walk alongside him, "Lead on, MacDuff."

They walked down the road, into the midst of the deadening greenery.

The color of the plants looked so unhealthy and unnatural, to begin with, but when they got closer Ally noticed something even more disturbing.

"No aphids."

"What's that?"

"The dying plants, there are no holes in them. No places were the bugs have chewed threw them. Look at this..." She said plucking a frond from the side of the road.

"Don't touch it!" Mark said. Something about the greenery gave him the willies and he was sure that the feel of them would not be the stiff and crispy feel of dead, dried out plants, but the wet half-digested slime of rotting meat or fish.

"Don't be such a baby." She said bringing the plant near to show him the leaf. "It's pristine. Only a fake plastic leaf should ever be that free of bug holes. And look at this..."

She squeezed the bottom of the plant stem, and her hand was covered with black fluid, the consistency of water, she held her hand so that it would puddle just a bit in her hand, "No living plant should have water coming out of it that looks like this... At first, it looks like its black but if you look closer, its more of a suspension, than a fluid itself... It looks like there's something in it, like... I don't know... coal dust?"

"Wipe it on your pants, and be sure to wash your hands before you eat anything." Mark said, "In fact, here. Put your hand out."

She did it, and Mark dumped a little water on her hand, "Rub the water in your hand and shake it off. The last thing I need is for you to get an infection out here."

"It would only infect me if I had a cut on my hand... Probably not even then." Ally said with a roll of her eyes, "I'd have to eat some of it before it would make me sick.

"I thought you said you weren't a botanist." Mark laughed.

"I'm not. But I know when a thing is dangerous and when it's not."

"Says the woman who wanted to go swimming with sharks two years ago."

"They were baby whale sharks, in an aquarium. It would have been perfectly safe. They had experts there to guide you."

"I wouldn't swim with anything that had the word "Shark" in its name, I don't care what the experts say."

They walked on, past the rotting plants to the place were the grass ceased to grow, and on to the barren prairie. There were a few trees that they could now see more clearly, but they too were dead and devoid of leaf or fruit. For the most part, it looked as if they had all died some time ago, and been eaten or rotted out from the inside, and now we're barely being held up by much more than their bark. One tree lay in pieces about 10 yards from the road, and Mark walked over to examine it.

"Don't go off the road!" Ally said, "We've got to stay near it in case someone drives by!"

"I'm just going over there!" He called back, not stopping, "Keep moving, I'll catch up to you, if you see someone flag him down, see if he'll stop."

"I'll get too far ahead of you." She said, standing by the road.

"Hardly." He said, "The way you move on those little Marvin The Martian legs, I only need one stride for every ten steps you take."

Ally, clenched both her fists and held them by her side and grunted, setting her head between her shoulders. Then she continued walking.

Just as he had suspected, the inside of the tree was hollowed out, but not by termites or the natural rotting away of the wood, but the interior was coded with a black fungusy looking substance. He brushed it and came away with black juice in his hand, not unlike the black water which Ally had crushed out of the plant. Taking the same precaution, he dumped some water on his own hands.

It looked not unlike the black mold that he had seen in multiple houses when he was a kid living in the sticks, he knew what too much of that could do to your lungs... When they got into town he wanted to wash both his and Ally's hands in bleach, just to be sure.

"Mark!" Ally called from just a little further down the road, "There's a truck coming!"

"On the way!" He replied, standing up from his kneeling position and walking back toward the road.

Mark could hear the sound of the engine now, and Ally walked out into the middle of the road to wave down the truck. While he knew she was safe enough and could tell from the sound of the truck's old motor that it was not traveling very fast, something in Mark still seized up at the sight of her standing in the middle of the road, waving her arms at an approaching vehicle.

He'd picked on her a lot, for a million different things daily, but this was his way of showing affection to her ... (his "Love Language" she had called it,) as the old song said, "...with all your faults, I love you still." ...Not that her height could be considered a "fault"... but it was an easy target. But the thought of his wife in danger turned his heart into stone and brought ice into his veins.

The truck came into view and was already slowing down. The truck had once been blue, but now it was hard to say what color it was at all. Multiple splotches of color lay all over it. Some of it was spray paint, while other parts were body filler that had never been colored in and a lot more of it was the scabby brown and orange of rust. He was pretty sure that just making contact with the truck was enough to contract Tetanus and that it hadn't passed any inspection in years, and certainly never would again... But, *"any port in a storm."*

The truck came to a stop, without the expected squeal of rusted and worn-out brakes, its stainless steel protective grille gleamed in the sunlight.

It was the only part of the car not covered in rust, although a few large brown spots were only just becoming visible. The motor was chugging along happily, it did not have the expected sound of a major backfire or rumble of an uncared for engine.

The man in the truck was a young person, not much older than twenty, and he was dressed in a light blue dress shirt and clean overalls, he looked more like *"John Boy Walton"* than *"Cletus the Shade Tree Mechanic."*

"Hey there folks." The boy called out from inside the cabin of the truck, "You alright?"

"We're not," Mark said as he approached, making sure his presence was known and... yes to say in effect, *"She's with me."*

Ally seemed to sense this and gave him a withering look, as if to say, *"Really?"*

"Was that your Chevy I saw back on the highway?" The boy said, "The one with the white tee-shirt hanging out the window on the driver's side?"

"That's right," Ally said, "How did you know that was us?"

The boy laughed, "I've been described as having keen insight into the obvious."

Ally twitched her nose slightly, which was something she always did when she realized she'd not thought out a question before opening her mouth to state it.

But the boy didn't seem to mind, "Well I'm sorry to say I don't have a spare tire that will fit your car, or else I'd have put it on for you already, but if you'll let me give you a ride into town, I'm sure we can call someone for you at my father's convenience store."

"I'm glad to know someone has a phone... I haven't seen so much as a telephone pole around here." Mark said, drawing closer to the truck, "Usually they follow the road, but I haven't seen a telephone poll for hours."

"Oh yes, we have one, but it comes in from the south. You folks are North of town. They put one in coming up from Giger's Rest about fifteen years ago. It has about twelve connections on it from here to there... We even had a payphone up until about two years ago, but the telephone company came and took that out. Hardly ever got used anyway."

"I'd think they'd have left it up considering there's no cell phone towers out here." Ally said.

"Oh, we have a tower. Built right on the South edge of town, it just doesn't work, never did." The young man said.

"Well, that doesn't make sense." Ally said, puzzled, "Why would they build a Cell tower, and then leave it before it was working?"

"Couldn't ever get it to work. Said all the equipment was in working order. The boxes were giving off all the right signals, plenty of power, but it just couldn't make contact with the network. Tried and tried, but said it just wouldn't connect and the only thing that might fix it was building another tower or two between here and Dubuque."

"Iowa?" Ally said, concerned. "Kansas," the Boy laughed, "though the confusion is natural. My name is Aaron by the way. Pleased to meet you!"

"Mark Thurston." Mark said, raising his hand to a level where the boy could reach down and take it, "and this is my wife, Ally."

"Well climb on back Mr. Thurston, I assume you'll be wanting your wife to have the seat of honor, up in the passenger seat."

Ally seemed to flinch with trepidation at the thought of being in the cab of the rusted out hulk with the boy, and Aaron seemed to have noticed it.

"Don't worry, Miss the outside of the truck is nothing but rust, but the cab is as smooth as can be, Ma wouldn't have had it any other way."

"This is your mother's truck?" Ally said slightly taken aback.

"Was, until about 3 years ago, when she went home," Aaron explained.

"Oh... I'm so sorry." Ally said, with a slight frown. "I didn't say she died. She went home. Back to Topeka. She and Daddy had a fallin' out. She hated this place. And Dad.... Well..." The boy seemed to think about how to put it, "Daddy felt like he still had work to do here. Not to mention his running the Grocery store. The only place to get supplies for miles around."

"Oh... I see." Ally said as Mark helped her get into the cabin of the truck, practically picking her up so she could reach the rusty spot welded on pipe that acted as a step.

Mark closed the door of the truck, being careful not to slice his hand on the rust, and then climbed up the side of the truck into the bed, next to some supplies meant for the grocery store. Aaron opened the rear porthole window between the cabin and the bed, "Hey reach back there and get us all a Coke." He said, "Should be right there beside you."

"I don't see it," Mark said, looking for the familiar red and white plastic bottles.

"Sure you do." Aaron said, "The Glass bottles."

"Oh," Mark said, reaching into the open-topped wooden

case, lined with straw. Not some fake decorative plastic that looked like straw, but actual straw from the earth, which dead as it was, looked healthier and more alive than anything touched by the blight around them. Mark passed the bottle through the opening, his hand brushing the cold steel of the single-round shotgun that lined the rear cab of the truck.

"That a real gun?" Mark asked, the bottles hissing as Aaron popped the tin caps off all three bottles.

"Yep, not much point in carrying a fake one around. Don't worry, I just use it on deer, when they get hit by a passing car and need to be put out of their misery... Most of the time." Aaron said with a fake sinister sound to his voice, that left no question that he was kidding. He passed one of the bottles back to Mark through the window.

Ally meanwhile was gulping down the brown liquid as quickly as she could.

"Hey take it easy!" Aaron said, with a laugh, "you'll hurt yourself doing that!"

Ally gasped a little for air as she pulled the bottle away from her lips, "It's just really good, and it's still cold... The water we had was old and warm."

"Yup, hay holds in the cold, really well." Aaron started, "People don't realize-"

Aaron was cut off in mid-sentence by Ally as she let out an almighty belch so loud that no one would have believed it came from the petite little thing.

"Wow," Mark said from the back.

"I'm so sorry." Ally said putting a fist up under her nose.

"Don't be!" Aaron said, "That was awesome."

Mark laughed heartily as the Truck started off again, kicking up small stones and dust.

4

The convenience store was only about a mile and a half down the road, so at nearly 50 miles an hour, they were there in less than three minutes.

But as anyone who has walked a long distance in 90-degree heat and humidity will tell you, the prospect of having to walk even further being lifted from you is always welcome.

Had it not been for the strange mirage-like quality the air had taken on that day, they might have been able to see the store from the highway, let alone the short distance they had left to travel, the land being flat as it was. But the shimmer of the earth returning the heat from its surface, and the lack of hills caused the land to be reflective. Only thin ghosts of what lay beyond could be spotted through the haze.

To Mark it felt like they were chasing some invisible mirror wall, which seemed to retreat, revealing that which it had hidden as you approached.

Aaron turned the engine off and opened his door, as Mark started to stand to climb down, Aaron asked him to stay there for a moment, "I was hoping you could help me unload the truck. I'll get the hand cart and we can get this done faster... If your wife doesn't mind sitting in the cab a few moments longer."

"Don't mind me." Ally said rubbing her bare feet, having taken off the boots inside the cabin, almost as soon as the door had been closed, "I'm perfectly happy not to be on my feet."

"Yeah that should be fine, and more than worth it for the ride, and the Coke."

"Thanks!" Aaron shouted, already moving toward the

Grocery store, "Be right back!"

Within moments the truck was unloaded and the three of them were walking into the store. An older man sat behind the counter, reading a magazine, a national Geographic that must have been printed in the '50s or '60s, it was tattered but still in reasonably good condition.

"Howdy folks!" the man said leaning forward, placing all four feet of his chair back on the ground, which landed with an audible clack on the cracked black and white chessboard that was the convenience store's floor. "So you're the folks this old knucklehead son of mine picked up on the way in?"

"That'd be us." Mark said, "I was wondering if I could use your phone?"

"Sure thing, son!" The Man behind the counter said with a mischievous grin, "That is if you can figure out how to use it."

He reached under the counter and brought out a large gilded rotary style phone, which he placed in front of them.

Its receiver was large and ornate, with large brass sections near the earpiece and microphone, with plastic molded to look like mother of pearl in the connecting centerpiece. The base was heavy and made completely of Brass, with what was little better than a white sticker with black numbers on it, (no letters at all) and brass dialer wheel.

"Umm... Wow..." Mark said, "Okay."

Mark approached the phone with trepidation, as he might have approached a dead rat under other circumstances. He lifted the receiver and the metal cradle lifted with a slow scrape of metal, a spritz of WD-40 would have taken care of.

He tried putting his fingers through the holes in the dialer, to punch the number below, but there was no button or sensor beneath it.

"Oh for pity sake." Said Ally, "Give me that."

She took the receiver from his hand and placed her pointer finger in the hole for the number four, rotated her finger down to the metal hook, which was meant to be a stopper, released it, and dialed in three more numbers before realizing the phone receiver had not been making any noise in her hand.

"I think your phone is busted." Ally said, to the man behind the counter, "There's no dial tone or clicking or anything."

The man behind the counter laughed to himself, "I know. That phone hasn't worked for twenty-five years!" He laughed again, "I just wanted to see what you'd do with it! Most young people your age have never seen a rotary-style telephone before."

In spite of herself, Ally laughed too, as first at herself, and then at her husband when she looked up and saw the confused look on his face.

"How did you even know how to use that thing?" Mark asked, still confused.

"Honestly if you'd even watch a movie made before the year you were born, you might know a little something." Ally said, placing the hook back on the receiver. "I've tried to get you to watch Downton with me and you wouldn't even do that."

"Oh yes, I have time to waste watching posh British People in the 1900s order the servants about." Mark affected a snooty upper-class voice, that never would have passed for British *"Clean upstairs Squire, Clean downstairs, maid."* No thank you."

"Yes. Why would you ever want to improve yourself?" Ally said, looking back at the man behind the counter.

"Why should I? You know I'm perfect... That's why you married me."

"That's just too good!" The man said, "Can I have your permission to share that on the internet?"

"The internet?" Mark said, "You don't even seem to have phone service out here."

"Yeah but every couple weeks or so I go into town and upload everything to the net at the library. I've been filming you since you came in! Say 'Hi' and wave to the camera!"

The man pointed down the counter and there sat a small handheld camera, with a red light blinking on top of it.

Mark and Ally both waved at it, Mark with slightly less enthusiasm. "I'll edit it down later, just say something like *"We give our permission to show this online"* and that should be good enough."

Ally looked at the camera and repeated cheerfully. "We give our permission for this to be shown online. My husband's name is Mark and he's an idiot!

"My wife's name is Ally and I'm an idiot. But I was smart enough to marry her, even though she doesn't quite come up to my standards."

He placed his hand about four inches over his wife's head to demonstrate.

The Man laughed, "That's a great ending right there!" Bet you it will get a thousand likes.

"Well fun's fun, but we really need to use that phone now." Ally said, sweetly but insistently.

"Sure, sure! Absolutely, and no more practical jokes neither, I promise!" He said, reaching down to pick up the real phone, which was an old touchtone phone from the 1990s that didn't look nearly as impressive as the rotary phone had been, nor half as clean. It was smudged with oily dirt, (and probably dead skin,) blocking out half the numbers. Mark pulled out a tissue, fixed it over the end of his index finger and started to punch in the numbers for the Auto Club's towing service.

"Name's Hap, by the way," said the man behind the counter to Ally, "Real name is Howard, but folks always called me Happy when I was a young boy, and that kinda just became Hap over the years."

"Like Pip in Great Expectations." Said Ally.

"Oh a reader!" said Hap, "I knew I liked you."

"Yes. My Name is Mark Thurston, and my account number is 8-7-3...5-0-8..." Mark said into the phone, clearly talking to something automated.

"So," Hap continued, in a lower register, so as not to interfere with Mark's phone call, "What brought you out here to the middle of nowhere?"

"Mark was trying to get a new job." Ally said, matching his tone, "Trying to get out of Chicago and into LA... well, east of LA.. lots of opportunities to rise."

"You don't say, well I wish him luck. Is that what you want?" Hap asked. "I don't know what you-" Ally started.

"Eight hours?!" Mark shouted at the phone, "What in the world?"

"I'm sorry sir, that's the soonest we can get someone to you," Ally heard, the voice on the other side of the line say, "We've got a lot of back up because of the construction on 76, lots of fender benders."

"Alright... When you get someone headed my way, tell them all I need is a new tire, the key is in the gas cap door, along with a tip.... Hang on."

Mark looked at Hap, "Sir, would it be alright for me to give them your number so they can contact us when the job is done?"

"That'd be fine son, and you can count on me and Junior to let you know, the number's on the phone base." Mark started reading off the phone number to the Customer Service Representative.

"I asked if that is what you want. Do you want to move to LA?" Hap explained turning back to Ally. "I want what's best for him... What's best for us... And a better job with more money would be the best thing. We're barely making it in Chicago. I just hope LA will be better."

Clearly, Hap was used to reading faces and saw something hiding behind Ally's eyes, "But there's something in Chicago you don't want to leave. Am I right?"

Ally thought about how to frame it, "I'll miss the places I grew up around, but my parents moved to Florida years ago. Maybe I'll miss a couple of my girlfriends but... that's what marriage is all about right? You leave your parents and cleave to your spouse. Right?"

Hap looked her in the eye, "I like the way you said that.

It's a rare thing nowadays for a young person to have that attitude... Older people too, for that matter. What about Mark, does he *cleave*, to you?"

"Sometimes a little too much." Ally laughed, "he still hasn't figured out that I'm not going to be his mother, but I'll work that out of him."

"Typical," Hap said with a grin. "He's a pain in the neck and picks on my height a little too much. But I wouldn't trade him for all the tea in Japan."

"China." Hap corrected.

"Oh no, you offer me all the Tea in China and he's gone! That's a LOT of tea!" Ally said with a wink.

Hap laughed, "Fair enough, fair enough."

Mark hung up the phone a little too forcefully, making the bells within tinkle as he did it. "Well, they figure it's going to be at least eight hours before they can get a tow truck out here with a new tire. I gave them the size we need and the car model, and they said they have it. It will just be a while before they can get it done."

"Great." Ally said, annoyed, "So what are we going to do for eight hours, plus?"

"I suppose we should go get something to eat, look for a room for the night. If they get it done in eight hours, and it will probably be longer, I don't want to be walking three miles at night, at 2 or 3 in the morning. Best to just get a room and wait until morning, at that point." Mark turned to Hap, "Is there any place around here like that?"

"Well... uh..." Hap said hesitantly, all of his cheerful demeanor gone in an expression of pure apprehension, "I'll tell you what... you folks can stay here at my place tonight, it's just down the road a bit, less than 3 miles in fact, first on the right."

"Oh no, we couldn't do that." Mark said, "you and your son have already done enough."

"It wouldn't be no trouble." Hap said, "We've got an extra room with a double bed. It might be a little dusty. We only use it when the in-laws come to stay the night, but I could have Junior tidy it right up for you."

"What about that place on the sign we saw back at the road, "The Old Town Buffet" sign said something about rooms."

Hap looked crestfallen, "Oh... You... You saw that did you?"

"Yeah, there's no need for you to put us up when there's a hotel nearby," Mark said.

"Though we certainly appreciate the offer." Ally interjected, clearly annoyed by Mark's rudeness.

"I'll tell you, one friend to another... The food and lodgings up there aren't exactly the best. They'll overcharge you. While I could have Aaron rustle us up a fine meal. And in the meantime, you could take anything you like from the store here... I'll even give you half off... You can't ask for a better deal than that."

"That's far too kind of you." Ally started, but Mark interrupted. "I'm sure Ally'd rather go get something warm now and just tuck into bed. We've had a long day... So if you could just direct us to the place, we'll be out of your hair."

"Well if that's how you feel about it," Hap said with no malice, but something like disappointment and regret in his voice and demeanor, "Did you see that lone hill about two hundred yards down the way?"

"The one with the cottage looking place on top of it?" Ally said, remembering.

"That's the place. Carter's Hill, place the town is named for. It's really more of a mound than it is a hill... But around here it's about as close as we get. They say the Indians made that as a burial mound years and years ago, but then Mr. Carter built his house on top of it some hundred and fifty years ago. Practically a mansion for these parts. The bottom floor was four big rooms and a kitchen, the top floor had nearly ten bedrooms. But there were some strange doings up there and eventually, no one but Carter and his wife was living in the house, and I think she only stayed because she had nowhere else to go."

"Strange things?" Ally asked, "Like what?"

"Well, its all legend you see because until about ten years ago no one lived up in the big house at all.. and I haven't seen much myself... I've never been inside the place. But folk about here say there were a lot of noises around the house that no one could explain. Sounds like rats traipsing up and down the beams of the attic, but nary a rat was ever seen, rooms taking on, what one fella called "Strange Geometry"... Like there were angles to the room that you couldn't see, from one side but could from the other as if the walls were folding in on themselves. People said that they lost hours, sometimes days inside the walls of that place... They'd go inside at two in the afternoon and feel like they'd only been inside for an hour or so, and when they'd come out again it would be the dead of night, or the same time of day, only two days later. And then there are the colors."

"Colors." Ally said, "That sounds like something you've seen yourself."

"That we have. Me and Aaron. Elizabeth too if she were here to tell you. That's the one thing we can truly claim to have seen, every once in a while, with no real pattern that I could point out, but often on the Full or New moon, there have been strange lights come up out of that place and you can see it for miles. I've never been close enough to see if it was coming from the house itself or just from nearby on the hill... But mostly we see them up in the sky above it, more than on the ground... It looks... I've never seen it myself, except on Television of course, but it looks kind of like the Northern Lights, the *A-Rab Arbolius*."

"*Aurora Borealis*." Ally corrected.

"Yeah, that." Hap said pointing at Ally as if to give her a point on the scoreboard, "But the colors aren't exactly what you would call normal, they don't look like the northern lights, they look... Sicker, darker and more reddish than they should be... I don't know, all I can tell you is you won't find names to describe them in a box of crayons, or on those paint swatches they use at those big modern Hardware stores... And if they did manage to put them into paint or crayons they'd never sell... Ugly stuff, not beautiful at all."

"Well, now I have to go check it out! Maybe we'll get a light show tonight." Mark said, half-joking, "Sounds like its an electrical disturbance, like Foo Fighters, or St. Elmo's Fire."

"Something tells me you don't want that, son. Even if it's just some kind of natural electrical disturbance, it's liable to fry your cell phone. But if you ask me there ain't nothing natural about it."

"Do you think Aaron would mind giving us a ride up there?" Hap looked at them seriously, "He might not, but I do. I don't allow him to drive up there, and I won't do it myself neither... I don't even like that I have to drive past it to get to home and work each day... Listen, the offer is still open... Even if you go up there and don't like the accommodations, you're welcome to come and stay the night at our place. But I'd much prefer you to stay. We haven't had company in a long time."

"Thanks but we really can't impose upon you like that." Ally said, putting her husband's oversized shoes back on her dainty feet.

Hap looked at the floor, reminding Ally of a little heartbroken kid, who's ice cream scoop had just flopped off the cone and on to the floor, "I understand. Sometimes the pull of something like that place just can't be denied. But do me, and yourselves one big favor."

Mark stopped at the screen door to turn and look back at Hap, "What's that?"

"Don't eat the Calamari."

There was something about the way that he said it that made Mark and Ally pause. It wasn't like most times when a person who knows the local cuisine makes a comment like, *"Stay away from the Tuna."* Or *"The Pastrami at Noah's Deli is always a little off."* He said it like a man telling a child not to put his hand in the fire, or to stay away from the neighbor's barking dog, or a mother telling her child to stay off the road where semi-trucks come barreling through at twice the speed limit.

It was not a piece of good advice. It was a warning.

"Yeah..." Mark said hesitating, "We'll make sure not to do that. Thanks."

"Thank you." Ally said, "We'll be back in the morning to check if the Auto Club called."

"I hope to see you." Hap said as the screen door closed behind them, "I truly do."

"Did we just lose another two, Dad?" Aaron asked, walking up to the counter, with a few loaves of bread he meant to put on the shelves.

"I hope not, son." Hap said, looking out after them, as they crossed the street, walking toward Carter's Hill, "I hope not."

5

Ally and Mark trooped along the empty blacktop road, black no longer. Bleached by the sun and the weather, the blacktop was old and looked gray in most places, almost white in others. It was mostly unbroken, not littered with potholes. Here and there a few thin dark lines of tar and pitch marked where the road had been repaired from what amounted to little more than hairline cracks.

"I don't see why we couldn't have spent the night with them." Ally said, walking along the road.

Mark laughed, "That's how you end up in the middle of one of those horror movies you hate so much, like the Texas Chainsaw Massacre or The Hills Have Eyes." He kicked a stone that had gotten under his shoe, "First it's oh sure you can stay the night we'll even have you to dinner! Then, tomorrow night, you'll be dinner!"

Ally scoffed, "I hardly think the boy and the old man were cannibals."

"You never know," Mark said, affecting a perfectly awful Boris Karloff, "We don't know what really happened to the mothaahh!"

Ally shook her head and rolled her eyes.

"Maybe," he continued, not letting the gag go, "she's up-staaairs in the att-ic, just waiting for her fav-or-ite dishhh, Ally Thurston Su-preeze!"

"Stop it," Ally said, punching him in the shoulder, "They were nice people and they don't deserve that."

"Eh. Won't hurt 'em, neither." Mark said, sounding like

Bugs Bunny, a voice he was actually quite good at, "All the same," Mark continued speaking normally, "I'd rather go somewhere where we can get a meal now. I'm hungry, and if we'd stayed with them we would have had to wait until they were ready for dinner. And even if we'd gone over there right away it would have taken them an hour or two to prepare something. Meanwhile, there's a nice little restaurant and hotel, practically right across the street, where we can get something fresh... and leave a paper trail with a credit card in case we get dragged off by the Sawyers."

"Yes, because we can afford another $150 on our credit card." Ally said, "You know I hate those things, they always charge you way too much interest, and then they trick you into spending more than you can afford, so you end up paying them the minimum payment for all of eternity."

"I'd rather be alive long enough to get the bill." Mark quipped, "Besides, when I get this job-"

"If you get this job." Ally corrected.

"If. Thank you." Mark said, "If I get this job, we won't have to worry about a fee for a two-night stay at a nice hotel."

The two of them started up the long, but thankfully not too steep hillside that led to the Olde Towen Buffet.

"Do you really think this will be the best thing for us?" Ally said, "Leaving Chicago, going to LA."

"I think leaving Chicago is always the best thing you can do," Mark said, snidely. "It's not like it used to be when you and I were growing up, there's crime everywhere. You can hardly walk on the streets, especially at night, and the seats on the L always smell like... the elevators in the train stations."

"Chicago was crime city in the 1930s," Ally pointed out, "Al Capone. It hasn't changed that much in nearly a hundred years."

"Oh yes, it has," Mark replied, "in the 1930s if you weren't involving yourself with the gangsters you had a pretty good chance of survival. Oh sure, you might get caught in the crossfire, like anywhere, but they weren't after you specifically. Now if you wear a pair of shoes that are too nice, you could end up as street pizza."

"And you think Los Angeles will be much better?" Ally asked incredulously.

"Probably not, but if I get this job we won't be living in LA we'll be near it. As in more than an hour away. It's like living in Oswego, and it will be in a very nice neighborhood. A gated community with other people who live and work at the office, a place where we can raise a family if we decide that's something we want to do... At least in a couple of years or so."

"Is that what this is really about?" Ally asked as they approached the small parking lot in front of the Buffet, "You beating that old horse?"

"No." Mark said, mildly offended, "I don't want kids right now anymore than you do. But I'd like to get to a place where I feel comfortable having them if they come along."

"No need to worry about that." Ally said, "There won't be any children for a long time. I may have been too short and not pretty enough to be a model, but the one good asset I do have is my figure and the last thing I want, at this point, is to go through five or six months of bizarre cravings and morning sickness, and then spend the rest of my life trying to get back to the way I am now, and not succeeding."

"Would you stop it?" Mark said more quietly and sharply than he had perhaps intended, "Lower your voice, you are shouting. It didn't matter out on the road, but there are people around now."

"People? What people?" Ally asked. "There's not a single car in the parking lot. Not one. Are we sure this place is even open? If the restaurant is in operation, shouldn't there at least be a couple of cars? The workers? The cooks and waiters? The Owner?"

"It's a small place," Mark said, thoughtfully. "They might all live here. It could just be a family thing. Mom and Pop, bed and breakfast…. Or Bed and Dinner." He corrected himself.

The Olde Towen Buffet, read the sign above the door. But it looked very little like any buffet either of them had seen before, true to Hap's word the place was more like a big beautiful cottage than it was a restaurant.

Mark had seen homes and bed and breakfasts and other spaces made into small restaurants before. He had seen both the industrial "Box" store reformatted as a restaurant, and the "Corporate Conglomerate" buildings that looked almost the same no matter which one you went to in every state, but this place was "Original".

That was the best word he could think of for it. It had once been a virtual mansion; built like a Tudor Style Cottage. All around the foundation of the house were authentic off-colored stones. Not a façade, but honest to goodness plates of stone, broken off and mortared into the side of the building. This continued up to the top of the second floor, where it was replaced, (or at least covered,) with white stucco, broken up by thick wooden beams of a dark rich Oak, clearly very old, but still very strong.

"Wow." Ally said, placing her hand on the archway, and feeling the grain of the wood, "This place must be over a hundred years old."

"It would have to be if we are standing on an Old Indian Burial Mound," Mark observed, "Even in Kansas, I doubt they would have let you get away with that much later than 1920. They might let you do something with the land, maybe a park or something, but not a mansion like this. Not something you would have to dig down more than a couple of feet to lay a foundation for."

Mark was about to lay his hand on the big wooden handle to open the door when it flew back away from his hand and out stepped the last thing either of them would have expected to see. A little person. A dwarf. But he would, perhaps, be best described as a midget.

He seemed perfectly proportioned, and unlike some so afflicted, he did not "waddle" about as some do. His gate was perfectly normal and were it not for certain markers, he might have been mistaken for a small child, but his voice and demeanor left no question that this was a man well over the age of thirty. He stood a little more than three feet tall, a fact that Mark observed by the way his petite little "baby wifey" seemed to tower over the man, by comparison.

"Welcome! Welcome! My dear friends! Please! Please come in! We are so glad to see you!" His voice had that high pitched yet simultaneous deep tone that one might expect from a dwarf, but his accent was strange, and though Ally couldn't quite nail it down, it sounded like a mix of Gallic and Arabic.

Though he looked Caucasian, it was a dark Caucasian as though someone in his family had been from the Middle East.

"Welcome to the Olde Towen Buffet!" He said in his piping voice. "We are having a special today on the steak! A 10 ounce Sirloin! Only $9.99 and of course you get the buffet for free! On the Buffet, we are featuring Pork and Chicken and as always our delicious Calamari, specialty of the house! Always very fresh! Straight from the Ocean, every day, directly to us! Just the two?"

Everything he'd said had gone by so fast, and in his strange accent, it was difficult for either of them to catch every word, but Mark sputtered, "Yes... Two please."

"Very good! So good! This way Please! Please!"

He led them into a large open dining space, with black steel furniture and large wire framed chairs. There were a few booths lining the left side wall, while on the right was a long beautiful buffet, overflowing with all kinds of delicious foods.

"Soup today is Corn Clam Chowder and our special recipe, Spicy Calimari Stew, fantastic with Garlic Toast! And then we have the Chili but it is not very good today!"

He led them to a small table in the middle of the dining area, "Here is good?" he asked, and they said that it was.

He rushed around to the one side and pulled out the chair for Ally, "Sit lady, please sit!" he said, cordially.

Ally took the seat and allowed him to help her move it in.

"Can I start you off with drinks?" He asked, pulling out a small note pad, nearly twice the size of his hand.

"Do you have Coke or Pepsi products?" Ally asked.

"Pepsi, no Coke." Said the little man.

Mark, who had been relatively well behaved until now, snorted trying to hold in his laughter and then tried to cover it up by making it seem like he had choked.

"Sorry." He said, purposely making his voice sound horse, and clearing it again, "Just very thirsty, our car broke down back on the Highway, and we've been walking all afternoon."

"Oh, then I get drinks immediately!" he said, asking again what flavors of soda they wanted and then quickly walking away to a soda fountain that was exactly at his height and had been placed with his diminutive stature in mind.

"What were you laughing at?" Ally asked disdainfully.

"Pepsi, no Coke." Said Mark, trying not to laugh again, "That's an old bit from Saturday Night Live in the 1970s. We used to watch those old reruns all the time. It just struck me funny. The way he said it."

"As usual, you are the only one who understands your jokes." She said annoyed, "And don't think I don't hear all those little snide references playing in the back of your head."

"What? Me?" He said handing her a menu from the caddy at the end of the table, and affecting a Southern Belle accent, *"Why, I'm as innocent as the day is long! Butta wouldn't melt in my mouth!"*

"Sure." She replied in a way that left no doubt she didn't believe it for a second.

They both looked down at their menus, and read the lists before them.

The little man was coming back with a tray loaded down with their drinks and just before he could have been in earshot,

Mark spoke just loud enough for Ally to hear, *"De Plane Boss, De Plane!"* causing Ally to let off a similarly repressed snort, to the one Mark had given off not moments before.

"Oh, here are your drinks!" The little man cried, coming up behind her, and placing the cups of soda and ice on the table, "Please! Please! Drink! Do not worry I'll get you refills immediately!"

Trying to hide her embarrassment at laughing at Mark's inappropriate reference, all took the paper off the pre-placed straw and took a long pull on the soda. "Very good!" said the Little Man, "That's very good, I get you both another, then I'll take your order."

And off he ran, spit-spot, to get two more glasses.

"I tell you, that guy violates like fifteen stereotypes," Mark said, taking a sip at his straw.

"You are positively Primeval, do you know that?"

"Why thank you, Belle!" Mark shot back, quickly referencing one of Ally's favorite movies.

"Do you think they know that they have "Town" misspelled? Ally asked ignoring him and changing the subject.

"It's not uncommon for "Town" to have an E on the end. It's an old-timey spelling. Like putting an E on the end of "Old" or "Shop", they usually add a second P to that as well. Shoppe."

He said over pronouncing it *"Shop-ey."*

"I know but that's just the thing, they add the E to the end of the word. This has it in the middle, which makes it *"Towen"* not *"Towne."*

Ally exaggerated the word to make it *"Tow-when."*

"That's my last name." The little man said approaching them, "Everyone notices, is kind of joke. Everyone says, "You misspelled it!" and I tell them, its meant to be that way, I am Maru Towen, at your service."

He made a little bow.

"Is that... Middle Eastern?" Mark asked, not sure if he had gone too far, but Maru smiled back at him.

"No, but good guess! My mother was Arab, my father was

Irish. It is a Gallic name."

Mark thought to ask what it meant but figured he had pried into the man's life too much as it was, but then Maru said, "So are we ready to order?"

"I know I am." Ally said, "I'll just take the buffet please."

"Very good." Maru said making a note, "And you sir?"

"I'll have that steak deal you mentioned; I haven't had a good steak in a while."

"Wonderful, wonderful!" Maru said, making two quick little marks in his book, presumably making two little quotation marks to represent the same thing again, and then adding the sirloin to the order, "Help yourself to the buffet! Take all you want! Eat all you take!"

Mark snorted, again but this time Maru was far enough away that it didn't draw a reaction.

"The Simpsons!" Mark said, all but pounding the table, "He quoted the first Halloween episode of the Simpsons. I swear he's doing it on purpose."

"You've been lying to me about who the woman was who used to live with your father." Ally said, standing up. "You didn't have a mother, you were raised by a television set."

"Hey!" Mark said in mock offense, "Don't talk about Maggie like that, she loved me very much!"

"Maggie?" Ally asked confused, "Your mother's name was Bernice."

"Magnavox, we called her Maggie for short."

Ally closed her eyes, looked at the floor, and walked away toward the ladies' room.

Mark realized he should do the same, he was still dusty all over from their long walk down the highway, which while he hadn't mentioned it to Ally, had actually been closer to two miles, than the half-mile he had thought it was, and then the extra mile plus, across the blasted landscape leading to the place were they had been picked up along the road by Aaron.

Plus, both he and Ally had touched the diseased looking plants and rotted out tree, respectively.

He got up and went to the Men's room which was marked with a strange symbol he couldn't place. If it had been the only marking on the door, he would have had no idea where it led, but the word "Men" was written beneath it in large friendly letters.

He glanced over at the women's room door Ally had passed through only moments before and there was a similar, but different symbol on hers. Was it Arabic? Maru had mentioned having both Celtic and Arab in his background... No, the symbol definitely looked more Celtic than Arab, but it also seemed to be a strange amalgam of the two... as if it were from something far older, that both cultures had extrapolated from.

He noticed a very Celtic symbol of the "*Triskelion*" adorning one of the walls, but it seemed to have taken some liberty with the design forming a six-pointed "Double Triskelion". Six spirals were connecting to a center mass. And around it was all manner of small markings which added the Arabic flavor to the designs. The door itself was made to look like something you might see on the door of an old pub, four or five thick planks of wood held together by two crossbeams with a large metal bolt, penetrating through the crossbeam, into the door itself, and another matching crossbeam on the other side. It looked more like something meant to hold off an advancing horde rather than simply partition off a restroom from a dining area.

Pushing through the door, he saw the motif continued into the men's room. The walls of the room were lined with beige porcelain tiles forming columns. At the top of every sixth tile was a symbol, all of them strange, and just barely unrecognizable. They were decidedly Celtic looking with all the ropes and knots and twists, overlapping and under-lapping each other, but they lacked anything that could be called angular, as if, had they been real, and not just carved figures, they would have been made entirely out of rope, wrapping and writhing around itself.

Mark used the facilities, (something he hadn't realized

he'd needed to do so badly until he sat down,) cleaned up after himself, exited the stall and washed his hands.

The entire time he'd been in the stall, he'd had an uneasy feeling.

The voice of Bugs Bunny was ringing in his mind's ear, *"Hey Doc, did you ever have the feelin' you was being... watched?"* And that feeling did not leave him as he stood there, washing his hands.

Twice he looked up at the mirror before him and thought he saw something move along the wall behind him, as though one of the carved symbols had begun to wriggle and writhe, only to freeze again, when looked at.

Mark closed his eyes and shook his head, a gesture he seemed to have picked up from Ally. He dried off his hands with a paper towel and prepared to use it to open the door of the men's room.

If you wanted to get creeped out over anything, the handle of a bathroom door was better fodder than most.

Restaurants always seemed to make you pull on a bathroom door to exit, and push on it to enter, when, of course, it should be the other way around.

People, (in the most liberal sense of the word,) very often used the bathroom and then did not wash their hands before exiting, breaking the oldest and most simple of hygiene rules they should have learned in Kindergarten, if not before.

They would touch the door handle, pulling it open, placing all manner of germs upon the handle, leaving them there for the next, conscientious, but perhaps unthinking person who had retained his humanity and washed his hands before eating. The person would leave the sink, toweling off their wet hands and drop their used paper towel in a trash can, and then place their hand on the door handle, having no other way out of the room, and pick up the germs left behind by an inconsiderate heathen, completely countermanding everything they had just done, to prevent the spread of illness and infection.

Mark was not a germaphobe, but he had long ago learned

the value of simple germ prevention measures when he had been forced to stay after school one day for detention and been forced to help the janitor clean the restrooms. OSHA would have been appalled.

Suffice to say very little actual "cleaning" was done, and the germs were mostly just pushed around the bathroom.

After that, Mark had become very aware of his surroundings, and followed much of the advice of a famous TV celebrity who truly was germaphobic.

Section A, Article One had been, "When you leave a bathroom, especially to eat, be sure not to make direct contact with the handle of the door."

But before Mark took hold of the door handle, he looked at it.

It was made of Black Iron and was twisted down the middle, completing the Old fashioned feeling of the place. But there was something wrong with it too.

It seemed...

Lose?

Shiny?

Almost transparent?

Which was, of course, impossible.

As he looked at it, it seemed to grow more... rubbery? Was that the right word?

The twist in the metal seemed to be... flexing, as if it were not metal but something pretending to be metal. Trying, oh so hard to stay as still as possible, but not able to prevent just the slightest undulation of its skin, from breathing.

Then suddenly, it was a door handle again.

Solid as stone.

Mark shook his head, (it was more of a shudder, than a shake)...

Something had just happened.

A cold chill had run down his spine.

But what?

What had just happened?

He didn't want to touch that door handle, something was wrong with it…

But it was the only way out of the room.

No windows, no other doors, just that one piece of metal and the sturdy Oak door between him and the dining hall.

"Use the paper towel. Just do it quickly." He thought to himself, moving his hand toward the seemingly solid iron.

The handle jumped forward toward him, it slammed into his hand as it involuntarily wrapped around the handle, breaking a blood vein or two with the force of the impact.

"Oh." Said a huge, deep-voiced man, entering the restroom, "Didn't see you there."

Mark shook his hand, to work the sting out of it, "It's alright." He said, not meaning it.

"Don't stand so close to the door next time, little man." The man's voice was as deep as he was tall. Mark hadn't noticed it at first, due to the pain in his hand, which made him look toward the ground, but the man standing in the doorway was a mountain.

Mark was not a short person by any definition, but this man towered over him. He had to be nearly eight feet tall and built broader than a linebacker, but all of it muscle.

His voice, in addition to being deep, was "mushy" as if the man seemed to have no teeth, or he was speaking around a mouthful of food.

Ally's reference to "Andre the Giant" that morning came to his mind, and indeed this man could have been his brother. (His *bigger* brother.) But he was not nearly as affable as Andre had seemed in *"The Princess Bride,"* (one of Ally's favorite movies.) This man was more like Andre in his WWF wrestling days, when he would look into the camera and say, *"Ultimate Warrior! The Giant is coming… FOR YOU!!"*

The man was a positive Ogre.

Mark wasn't one to back down to a challenge, but the

man was so huge and strange, and Mark was still out of sorts from what he had seen, (thought he'd seen) happen to the door handle, that he simply wanted out of that little space.

When the mountain moved toward the stalls, Mark stepped a little further back, out of its way, and then being careful not to touch the door on his way out, tucked through the aperture and back into the main dining area of the Buffet.

To his surprise, Ally was coming back out of the ladies' room at the same moment, a look of confusion and something like dread on her face; the same look that must have been on his, because at the same moment they simultaneously asked, *"Are you alright?"*

"Yeah, I'm fine." Ally said, tugging at her clothes, and straightening them as if suddenly worried about her appearance, "What happened to you?"

"Hurt my hand on the door handle," Mark admitted, "Another guy was... Are you sure you're okay?"

He broke off, "You look like you've seen a ghost."

"Not a ghost." Ally said, but then would say no more, "Hey you want to get something? I'm starving."

"Yeah," Mark said, taking a step toward the food bar, and Ally followed. The two of them each took a large see-through glass plate and began loading things on to them.

A large piece of plate glass, lined with shiny reflective brass allowed them to look down through to where the food lay. Ally stopped at the first couple of stations, trying to choose between a regular "Garden Salad" Or a Caesar Salad, finally deciding to go with the Caesar, and then shoveling pieces of warmed chicken and a little bit of chopped up bacon on to it.

"Look at this." She said to Mark, "Real bacon, not just bacon flavored soy bits."

"Yeah, yeah." Mark said disinterested, what he was looking at was all the different types of Mayonnaise based "Salads" which were laid out before him, Cole Slaw, Macaroni Salad, Egg salad, Chicken Salad, Seafood Salad, and two or three others that Mark wasn't quite sure what they were.

He looked at the tag on the glass in front of him which told him they were variations of the previously mentioned salads with other ingredients.

Ally then moved on to a few more vegetables that were quickly added to the salad; Cherry Tomatoes, Green Pepper, two large rings of Red Onion.

Mark, however, was on to the meats. Slices of Ham, variations of Fried Chicken, Hamburger patties lay stacked, one on top of the other, in a diagonal line, encouraging the diner to take the topmost, with large rolls nearby, Pork ribs with and without BBQ sauce filled two big sections of the buffet, with large vats of sauce of varying degrees of heat and spice, in Red, Yellow, Brown and Dark Green.

"Now we are talking!" Mark said to himself, loading up.

He took his very full plate and walked back over to his chair and dug in, not waiting for his wife to come back to the table.

And who could blame him? He was truly starving by this point.

Moments later, Ally came back to the table, placing two plates side by side, one with her salad, and the other heaping with Seafood, and precariously balanced on the salad plate was a cup of soup. From what Mark could see it looked like the Spicy Calamari Stew, and the two large pieces of garlic toast beside it seemed to confirm that.

Ally had loaded her second plate with shrimp and mussels, pieces of lobster, and a large piece of batter dipped fried fish, with several large fried potato wedges alongside it.

Dead in the center of the plate was a large number of round fried onion ring looking pieces, but they were definitely not onion rings. The onion rings the buffet offered were all, (almost without exception,) larger and darker due to the type of batter they had been dipped in. This was considerably smaller and lighter, and Mark recognized it immediately as Fried Calamari.

"Hey." Mark said around a piece of BBQ slathered rib, "Didn't Hap tell us not to eat the Calamari?"

"Mind your own plate." Ally said, picking up a rolled-up napkin, in which were wrapped a knife and fork, "Hap can eat what he likes, I'll eat what I like, and you know I love Calamari."

"Yeah." Mark said, slurping a bit, "But he seemed pretty emphatic about it. That wasn't an *"I don't like it, don't eat it,"* That was an emphatic, *"It's rancid, you could die."*

"Does that look rancid to you?" Ally asked stabbing, a piece of the Calimari with her fork and putting it in Mark's face. It looked golden brown, crisp and delicious. Mark made a little half-hearted bite at the food, getting nowhere near it, and making a little growling *"chomp"* sound.

"Oh no you don't." Ally said, turning the fork around and plopping the crisp bit of chewy goodness in her own mouth.

"Okaaay." Mark said, in a sing-song voice, "But when you end up in the Hospital with Ptomaine tomorrow evening don't say I didn't warn you."

"Who says Ptomaine?!" Piped up a tiny voice, behind Mark.

Maru was approaching their table, with Mark's sirloin in his tiny hands, the look on his face was that of unmistakable anger, "Has that Old Man at the Grocery Store been lying to you about my food again?"

He walked up to the table and placed the steak on the table, with an audible clink.

Mark swallowed the food in his mouth and used the time to think of a cover-up, "No one." Mark started, "No one said Ptomaine."

"I heard Ptomaine!" Maru said insistently, "Who has been telling you lies about my food?"

"Lo-mein!" Mark explained, "I was just saying these ribs would go great with some Lo-mein noodles. You know like you get at a Chinese take out place? I order that all the time, don't I Ally? We go to the Chinese place, *"The Great Wall"* and I order Short Ribs and Lo-Mein Noodles."

"That's right." Ally lied, "All the time. It's one of his favorites."

Maru Towen seemed to buy it, "Oh." He said taken aback slightly, "Well, this is good. I am so sorry I misunderstood you. But that old man, Happy Howard, he is always telling lies about me. Saying my food is no good! He thinks I am cutting into his business. But I told him, No! No one is coming out here for his Grocery, because he is lousy Grocer! Has no selection, no choices, nothing prepared. People come here from miles around to see me. They go out to Giger's Rest, have much nicer Grocery there."

Maru finished as if he expected them to say something in agreement.

"The food here is excellent." Mark said truthfully, "Best ribs I've had in months."

"Yes," said Ally, "The Calamari is fantastic."

Maru brightened up considerably at this, "Oh you have eaten the Calamari? And you have the soup! Is good, yes?"

"The fried is very good," Ally said. "I'm waiting for the soup to cool a bit but it looks wonderful."

"Best Calamari in the whole state!" Maru said delighted, "Best in the whole country! But we can't say that for certain. Old family recipes for Calamari, very secret, we tell no one."

"Well whatever you are doing, you are doing it right!" Ally said.

"Oh good." Maru said with a big toothy smile full of tiny teeth, "So good. I get refills!" And he stumped off toward the soda fountain.

"Well..." said Mark when he was sure Maru was out of earshot, "That was close, thanks for helping me cover that up."

Ally snorted, "I wasn't about to let you get us kicked out of here. The food is far too good, and besides we wanted to stay the night here. But from now on keep your voice down and keep the T-word out of your vocabulary."

"P," Mark said, casually, tucking into his macaroni salad.

"What?"

"Pto- That word.." he corrected, "Starts with a P, not a T, the P is silent."

"So should you be." Ally said, dunking a shrimp in cocktail sauce.

For a while, the two of them sat there in silence, enjoying the food, which was very delicious, and satisfying. Then Ally started to notice something odd. It might have just been the fact that she was so focused on her plate and devouring the scrumptious food, (It had been a very exhausting day, and though she was used to walking at least five miles a day in the gym on the treadmill, walking out in the hot sun, over uneven pavement, in shoes that were nearly five times the size of her dainty feet, with socks stuffed into them was hardly her idea of a good time.) But as she looked up from her plate she began to realize that there were other people in the room.

Up until now, she hadn't realized their presence.

When the two of them had walked into the large open chamber, she'd had the feeling like the room was empty. But now it seemed to be at least half full of people.

She hadn't been aware of anyone entering the diner, but at the same time, she was sure she would have noticed a sudden mass ingress of people.

She was about to ask Mark if he had noticed anyone coming in when Mark spoke instead.

"Have you noticed all these symbols around this place? It looks very Celtic... I wonder if that's something Maru did or if it's leftover from when Carter built the place. I mean, clearly, the big ones on the bathroom doors were added later, but the ones on the eleven pillars; the ones actually carved in the wood, not just painted on the walls."

"Twelve." Ally corrected.

"Twelve what?"

"Twelve Pillars. There are twelve of them... It wouldn't make much sense to have only Eleven, architecture is usually balanced."

Mark looked around the room again. "I'm sorry to disagree honey but count it for yourself there's eleven."

Ally looked around the room and counted... "Nine... ten.. eleven... twelve."

"No, you must be counting the first one twice." Mark explained, "See how it's a circle? The whole interior of the room is a circle, and each of the wooden pillars is supporting a beam that meets in the center."

"Yes." Said Ally, eating some more of the calamari Stew which had finally cooled enough to take more than just a few sips from her spoon, "And if you count them you'll see there are twelve."

Mark stared up at the ceiling. "Ten, Eleven... Twelve. That's strange... When I look at the ceiling, I see twelve... But when I try to count the Pillars, I only get eleven. It is like I see the twelfth when I'm looking at the ceiling, but when I look away it disappears. Weird."

"Hap said this place had some strange architecture." Ally said, with a slurp.

"Geometry," Mark said still looking up. "Strange Geometry."

"Right. Geometry is a part of architecture. Or do we need to take you back to 5th grade?"

"No." Mark said, "I remember Donald in Mathmagic-Land... What do you suppose that is in the center?"

"What?"

"That big black blob in the center of the room, on the ceiling? Carved into the wood. It looks like it has ropes or tentacles coming out of it."

"Yggdrasil." Ally said, scraping her Garlic toast along the inside of the nearly empty soup cup and sopping up the broth.

"*Gesundheit*," Mark said. Ally rolled her eyes, "The Tree of the World in Norse and Celtic Mythology."

Mark looked at her blankly.

"The Nine Realms?" Nifelheim, Jotunheim, Musphelheim?..." She trailed off.

Mark's expression still didn't change, "Still not getting it."

Ally sighed and let out her final card, "Asgard?"

"Oh! You mean the Thor movies!" Ally pursed her lips, "Figured you'd get that one. In Norse Myth it was Yggdrasil, in Celtic mythology it's the tree of life."

"Doesn't look like a tree to me. I don't see any leaves on it… It just looks like a mass of blackness with lines coming out of it. Looks more like something you'd get a side quest from in The Elder Scrolls Games, than a tree to me."

"Those "lines" are branches and roots, see how they are coming out of the top and the bottom of the "mass" and the circle around it? It shows that all life is connected, sky and Sea, Land and air."

"Everything the light touches…" Mark started, putting on a deep sonorous voice.

"Belongs to somebody else." Ally interrupted, in a nasal, almost Bronxy tone, sounding a bit like Marge Simpson.

The bit complete, Mark asked, "Why would that symbol be in both Celtic and Norse Mythology?"

Ally blinked, "Wow, you really do know nothing, don't you?"

"What?"

"The Norse invaded Ireland and Scotland, and just about everything else." Ally explained, "It's the primary reason so many of the Irish have red hair. It's natural that some of their culture and mythology seeped in. If you look close enough, most cultures, even ones that were never touched by European influence, like the Aztecs, there are a lot of symbols and ideas that crossover. Almost like it all came from one big Mythos that got corrupted over thousands of years."

"*Aliens!*" Mark said, with a smug tone, putting his hands out in front of him, thumbs pointing toward each other and fingers splayed.

"More like *The Tower of Babel*." Ally countered, crunching

into the last of her seafood, "That was really good. I'm going to get some more of that Calamari, and maybe the Stew."

"Wow." Mark said, "What's this?"

"What?" Ally asked. "You... going for seconds... you've always refused seconds. Worried about your figure."

"A little extra seafood and toast aren't going to turn me into a beluga overnight." Ally said, rising from the table.

"Of course not." Mark said, "I'm just impressed."

"Besides," She said, "We are probably going to have to walk back to the car in the morning. I'll burn off the extra calories then."

Ally took her empty plates and soup cup and walked to a small black bin that sat on top of a trash can, placing them inside she turned back toward the Bar grabbed a new plate and proceeded to load up her plate with even more of the scrumptious Seafood.

She wondered how Mark could go through life absorbing so much from pop culture, and still not have put so many of the pieces together. He could quote practically every movie and television show ever made and knew actors, and characters, and storylines, and famous quotations from those shows like the back of his hand, but he never seemed to be able to figure out the "meta-narratives" the underlying connections of history and culture that so enthralled her.

People often said, *"You can't learn anything from watching Television."* But to her that simply wasn't true, if you watched the right things, (not even necessarily documentaries, and History programs, though those would certainly help,) you could learn a lot.

Mark's vast knowledge of Pop culture had been one of the things that had drawn her to him in the first place. It was only later that she realized his brain didn't quite work the way hers did, and for him, it was mostly all about having fun, while for her it was all about learning and *"Building a Toolbox."* She wasn't quite sure what that mental toolbox was for yet but she was sure one day, when the time was right, she would find the thing it was all meant for, and creativity would spill from her like an Oil Gusher.

Her plate full, and a cup of Calamari stew exchanged for a larger bowl, she started back toward the table where Mark sat. She hesitated a moment when she saw the look on his face.

As Ally got up from the table, Mark had finished off a piece of Lasagna, chasing the sauce around the plate with a piece of the Garlic "Texas Toast".

When he looked up, toward Ally, he noticed for the first time the crowd of diners in the restaurant.

Where had they come from? He would have sworn they weren't there a few moments ago...

Okay maybe a few people here or there could have escaped his notice, but not twenty to thirty people.

Then something else caught his attention, none of them were talking.... Or at least if they were, not loud enough that they could be heard as anything more than a faint whisper, now and then.

All around him was the quiet clamor of forks and knives scraping plates, cups being set on tables, and the ice in them tinkling and sloshing as they were picked up and sat down again, but even now the sounds seemed to him to be just fading in, as though they had been muted and silent before, and now someone was turning up the volume on the television set, until it reached what should have been its full "normal volume."

But it was the last thing he realized about the other people in the restaurant that concerned him most of all.

Ally sat down at the table and immediately grabbed a piece of Fried Calamari and popped it in her mouth, "What's the matter?" she asked around it, and even the sound of her asking the question with food in her mouth startled him. It sent a thrill up his back and caused him to gasp slightly.

"When did all these people get here?" He asked.

"So you were wondering too." She said, quizzically, "I

noticed them about ten minutes ago... They must be regulars who used a different entrance or something, I never saw anyone come in and I'm facing the doors we used." She popped another piece of seafood in her mouth, "I'm going to take off these shoes. They are hurting my feet, the socks are really starting to bunch around my toes."

She bent down slightly toward the table to unloose the straps, and zipper that held the boots tight to her ankles and felt the blessed relief as she wiggled her toes in the free, cooling air.

She stretched her legs out under the table and pointed her toes, making them just long enough to brush the edge of Mark's chair opposite her.

She arched her back a bit and sat up, taller.

Mark looked at her like a cow looks at an oncoming train. "What?" she asked as she picked up a piece of shrimp and dunked it in the cocktail sauce. She bit into it...

Oops, it wasn't shrimp, it was the Calamari again, not that she minded, it was sooo good, and with the cocktail sauce, it was different, still good, but different.

"Don't you see them?" Mark asked.

Ally looked over her shoulders left and right, "Yeah I see the other people in the room Mark... What's your problem?"

"You don't see anything strange about them?"

Ally turned around in her chair and looked around at the other patrons, "Well, they all seem to be wearing the same kind of clothes..." She observed, "Looks like they might be members of some kind of club, like maybe a biker gang?"

"What else?" Mark asked, seemingly desperate for her to draw the same conclusion, notice the same small detail he had.

"Well, they're all..." Ally started, but then the words left her mouth as the realization struck home, and then she looked back at Mark and said quietly, "They are all very big."

"That's what I am talking about!" Mark said, "They are all like Gigantor or The Thing!"

"Quiet!" Ally snapped quietly, "They'll hear you."

"Look at them!" Mark said, there's not one of them that's under six feet tall... I can't tell for sure, but if they were to stand up I bet most of them wouldn't be under seven feet! Even the women!"

It was true.

Most of the people in the restaurant seemed to be keeping toward the back of the room, so it was hard to say for certain, but all of the women seemed to be just as tall and broad as the men.

Some looked fat, and some looked thin, and the majority looked like bodybuilders or had the stocky look of powerlifters, but they were all of them positively huge people.

None of them looked like the tall basketball players or some of the tallest people in the *Guinness World Record* books, thin and spindly despite there size, like Stretch Armstrong pulled to his maximum length.

They were all perfectly proportionate.

Their size was accented, even more, as Maru reentered the hall, and made his way between tables, removing old cups and used dishes and replacing a few of the cups with freshly filled ones. His diminutive stature was in stark contrast to their hugeness. Mark felt sure that if even one of them was to stand, they could crush the little man as Mark might a soda can.

"I saw one of them earlier." Mark said in a low whisper, "He was going into the bathroom. I thought he must be one of the workers or something... I never saw him come out again but I wasn't exactly looking.... Ally, where did they come from? They couldn't have gotten past us without our noticing them."

"I don't know." Ally said taking a large soup spoon full of the stew, "And don't you ask, its rude to even..."

But already Mark had his hand up, waving Maru toward them, and the little person had put up a single finger to acknowledge, and ask for "just a moment."

"Mark don't." Ally said, "Just tell him you wanted a refill and don't-"

"Hello, dear ones!" Maru said, approaching, "I am sorry to have neglected you for so long, we are very backed up in the kitchen, I hope you will forgive me."

"It's alright," said Mark, "No problem. I just wanted to ask you-"

"Mark don't-" Ally started.

"I think I am seeing the problem." Maru interjected, "You are wondering about the Big People."

"Well," said Mark, "Not exactly, but now that you mention it…"

"Mark," Ally started again, "It's none of our-"

"Is okay!" Maru interrupted again, "They are having a convention here. We see them every year about this time. Has been a big week for us! Pun intended."

Maru drew closer as if to tell them something confidential. "They pay three times our normal rate! For rooms and food! They call themselves, The Gathering of International Amazons N' Tall-People. G.I.A.N.T." He spelled out, "See they have a very good sense of humor about it all… They are a group that gets together on the internet. And they love me! Wait please!"

The little man ran over to a mostly barren maroon-colored wall and pulled one of the pictures down, and brought it back over.

"We take a picture like this together every year!" He held it up and showed them a group of the large people holding Maru up in front of them, he looked like a baby in the arms of one of the large women, and he held his arms out in space, and his legs splayed in mid-air as if to say *"Ta-dah!"*

"Is always a good time and we love to have them here!" Maru explained. "I see," said Mark, "But if they are having a convention, where did they all come from? I mean, I didn't see any vehicles outside and I'm sure we would have heard a few of them moving around upstairs if they had been up there."

Maru put up a finger as if to say *"Well observed!"*

"That is because most of them were down in the basement. That is our convention space. We also have very good insulation, only the best! Very little sound moves between rooms upstairs and downstairs. You could scream at the top of your voice in one room and the person next door would hear barely more than a muffled whisper, if anything at all."

"Oh." Mark said, almost disappointed, "I guess... I guess that explains everything."

"Very good!" Maru said with it big smile that made his tiny teeth seem too numerous, "Can I be getting you, fine friends, some refills?"

"No," Mark started, "I think we-"

"More for me please." Ally said holding her cup out to the little person, with rapidity, "I think I'm going to go one more round." Mark looked at the table.

As they had been talking Ally had cleaned her plate, faster than Mark would have imagined possible, and the stew was gone again.

"Very good." Maru said, excitedly, "Very, very good!"

He took the glass and moved away toward the fountain quickly.

"There, you see." Ally chided, "Aren't you ashamed of yourself?"

"I guess so." Mark said, "Maybe just a little."

Ally stood up taking her plate to walk past him.

"Ally," Mark asked, "What are you doing? You never have thirds."

"I'm hungry," she said, "I want some more of that Calamari."

"I think you've had enough," Mark said gently grabbing hold of her wrist as she passed.

Several things happened at the same moment, and Mark

didn't have time to process them all until later.

The first was that Ally's skin seemed very hot to the touch.

Like many women, Ally always seemed to be cold, and if you held her hand, you could feel it. In the middle of an August day, Ally sometimes felt the need to wear winter gloves around the house and she would often wear two pairs of socks to keep her feet from freezing.

But now, at this moment, her skin was warm and slick with sweat, in a way that Mark had only felt once before when nearly six months into their time dating Ally had come down with a severe cold and a fever of nearly 101 degrees.

The second was that at his touch Ally looked at him as she might, had he just called her father the vilest name imaginable. It was a rage, a fury that Mark had never thought to see in his wife's eyes.

The third was that almost faster than he could register his wife had extricated her hand, grabbed him by the shirt and forcibly pulled his face nose to nose with hers, and for just the briefest of moments, his posterior was removed from the chair beneath him.

Had she actually picked him up, single-handedly, or had he just been jolted out of his chair?

"I. Said." She repeated speaking through clenched teeth, "I'm. Hungry... Leave. Me. Alone."

The next moment she had let go of him, and marched back over to the Buffet, using the same plate again, and loading it for a second time.

Mark, more confused now than he had been all day, sat in worried silence, as Maru walked by, and placed a freshly filled cup on the table.

"Sure you don't want a refill?" he asked, and when no answer was forthcoming, he shrugged and moved on, while Mark stared down at the table wondering, *"What just happened?... What the heck, just happened?"*

Within moments Ally was back at the table, her plate

piled high with the Golden battered Calamari.

It looked as if, rather than using the tongs this time, Ally had used her plate as a shovel and scooped up what would have been almost half a tray of the crunchy seafood. This time she didn't even seem to be bothering with the cocktail sauce or anything else for that matter. She ravenously devoured piece after piece, by hand, sometimes two or three pieces at a time.

Mark could hardly believe what he was seeing. He had never seen her like this over anything. She adored chocolate and (while she didn't eat much of it,) Cheesecake. He'd seen her dive, spoon first, into a half-gallon of Ice Cream, on occasional evenings when the workday had been too difficult, or when she'd been particularly depressed, or even angry at him.

She had often said if she didn't keep her self-control, she could eat all three of those, nonstop, all day long. It had been a joke, of course. But this was not. She was scarfing down the little nuggets with amazing rapidity.

On top of what she had already eaten in the last hour, it was the most he'd ever seen her eat... Short of a hot dog eating contest, it might be the most he'd ever seen anyone eat.

He might have tried to stop her, but given his previous attempt, he feared what her reaction might be. And at this speed, he just might lose a finger, if he got within a foot of that plate.

Nearly half of the plate was gone when all of a sudden Ally stopped.

She didn't slow down.

She didn't show any signs of stopping.

All of a sudden she pushed the plate aside and the *"feeding frenzy"* look, seemed to have left her eyes.

She picked up a napkin and wiped the corners of her mouth and then her fingers individually. She balled up the napkin and picked up her drink, taking a long pull on her straw, emptying half her glass, (not a particularly astounding feat, considering both what had gone before, and that the cup was loaded with ice.)

"Are you… done?" Mark asked carefully.

"Yup think so." Ally said, as though nothing had happened. "O…kaaay." Mark said, handling her with kid gloves.

Suddenly, Ally let out another of her loud involuntary burps, the twin of the one she had given in Aaron's truck. Loud and long.

From across the room came a loud round of applause, which sounded like three dozen Christmas Hams being smacked together, followed by a round of deep unsettling laughter.

The Members of GIANT were all clapping and laughing at Ally's eructation.

Had they been watching her eat?

Or was it just the loud sound she'd made that drew their attention?

Either way, Ally stood to her feet, faced the herd of Big People and placed both her arms out in space, hands bent at the wrist, crossed her legs one over the other, and gave a splendidly gracious and graceful, *"Ballerina Curtsy."*

This only prompted more laughter and greater applause.

She sat back down and bent over to get her husband's oversized shoes, and stuck her feet in them. There was a bit of struggle, and finally, she gave up, "I think the socks are all wet and swelled, I can't get my feet in them right now. And I don't want to pull out a bunch of wet stinky socks in the middle of the dining hall. I'll just carry them."

Mark was silent, and she looked up at him.

"Did you hear me?" She asked. "Yes… I heard you." Mark said, "What was all that?"

"What do you mean?" Ally asked, without any trace of guile.

Mark was astonished, "The Feeding frenzy you were in just now. Grabbing me by my shirt like that… That look in your eye… I thought you were going to kill me."

Ally's face screwed into a mask of confusion, "I don't

know what you are talking about. I was just hungry, that's all."

Mark wanted to say more, but he just got up, and walked over to the doorway, where a large sign read "PAY HERE."

He figured if she didn't want to talk about it, he wasn't going to press the issue, not at the moment anyway.

Ally rose and followed him, her bare feet, padding along the red carpeting.

Through the doorway was a little counter space. This had been something installed before Maru Towen took up ownership because it was nearly four feet high and Ally's head would have only just been visible to the person behind it.

Here the décor of the Tutor style Chalet reasserted itself. The Walls were white with oaken wood beams, and it felt like stepping back through time into a simpler age. Like a cottage in a storybook.

Mark rang the little old fashioned bell on the counter, and from behind them, Mark heard Maru's little voice cry out *"III'mmm Commmming!"*

Mark looked back at his wife to make a comment and saw that he had been mistaken in his estimation of where the counter space would approximate on Ally. He had thought that the counter would be at about her shoulder height, but he saw now that she could easily put her elbow up on the counter and lean against it.

He also noticed that Ally's skirt was not as long as he had thought. He had thought that, as with most of her other dress skirts, the hem landed somewhere around her mid-calf muscle, but this one was clear up to her above her knees.

Mark wondered why he hadn't noticed this before. He loved to look at his wife's legs, they were the prettiest-

"I'm coming!" The cry was repeated and Maru scampered around them and back behind the counter. He climbed up a small step ladder and soon his head was eye level with Mark's.

"I am sorry for the wait, my dear friends, oh so sorry!"

"Not a problem." Mark said, "We wanted to pay for our food, and I wanted to know if you had any rooms available.

"Oh yes, no problem!" Maru said, "But only one room tonight because of the convention. It's the honeymoon sweet. But I'll give it to you for the regular price."

"Well, that's awfully nice of you." Said Mark starting, "But I can't ask you to-"

"Maaark." Ally said, quietly, "Shut up. This nice man has offered us a very nice room at a low price. Don't argue with him."

Maru laughed, "Your wife is a very wise lady! And has a healthy appetite! You should feel very lucky, Mr. Mark."

"Thurston," Mark said, putting out his hand.

"Mr. Thurston." Said Maru, grabbing the first two fingers of Mark's considerably larger hand with his tiny one. "That will be, 20 dollars for the food, and 40 dollars for the room. So $65 with tax, please."

"Is Credit ok?" Mark said fishing out his wallet.

"Yes, Very okay," Maru said, pointing to a very old, but reasonably clean card reader.

Mark slid his card. Maru punched a few buttons. "Wow, $40 for the Honeymoon Suite." Mark said, "Can't beat that!"

"No sir." Said Maru, "All of our rooms are nice, but people charge too much for one night stay in hotels today, the honeymoon suite is only $80 normally. You tell all your friends, and maybe they come here to spend the night? I can always use the business."

"If the room is as good as the food, you can count on it," Mark said, taking the receipt from Maru after it printed out.

"Thank you," Maru said, "Is up the stairs, and the second door on the left. Enjoy your stay, and don't hesitate to let me know if you are needing anything... Anything at all!"

So, together Mark and Ally trouped up the long wooden stairs, which were covered in the same soft plushie red carpet as the dining area, Ally carrying Mark's Combat boots in her hand.

6

When Mark entered the room he was hoping for something a little more impressive, but the "Honeymoon Suite" was more or less like any other hotel room in a quaint little establishment.

Nothing too big or showy, adorned the walls, the bed was probably a little larger, a single King instead of a queen, (or two smaller beds).

Ally dropped the boots in the corner and made a beeline for the bed.

She flopped on to it, face first and made a muffled comedic snoring sound, into her pillow.

"Don't do that." Mark said, "you've still got dust all over your clothes from the road."

"I don't care!" Ally said, not lifting her face from the pillow. She turned her head to the side. "Actually I'm feeling better than I have in a long time… Feels like years."

"Really?" Mark asked, "Because if I'd have had to guess, I would have thought you would feel like you wanted to die, after the day we've had."

"Oh, I did." Ally said flipping over, and out of the bed, on to her feet in front of Mark, "I wanted to curl up in bed and sleep for days when we were down at Hap's store. But now that I've been off my feet for a while and I've had a good meal, I feel like I could go a few rounds in the ring!"

"You don't box," Mark said with a laugh. "I bet I could take you on." She said putting up her fists in a perfectly awful imitation of a fighter.

"Take it easy, Chun-Li." Mark said, "I don't want to fight,

all I want to do is get out of these dirty clothes and into my sweats and go to sleep."

"What? Are you afraid? Huh?" Ally taunted, "Are you scared, you little diaper baby?" Out of nowhere, Mark felt a massive thump in his gut. It knocked the wind out of him for a moment, sending him into a coughing fit.

"What.. the…" he tried to speak but he could barely catch his breath, "How…" The next moment he had slumped on to the bed, Ally by his side.

"I didn't hit you that hard." Ally said, "Are you okay?"

Mark gasped, "I will be… You hit harder than you think." Mark said, finally breathing normally again.

Ally snorted, "Hardly. I guess I just took you by surprise."

"Something like that," Mark replied.

"Are you okay? I want to go change. This dress is bunching on me… I haven't felt comfortable for a while now."

Before she had punched him in the gut, Mark had noticed that Ally was picking at her clothes quite a bit. And it seemed to be tight across her shoulders and back from the way she had been moving. She was constantly tugging at the hem of her blouse as if she feared it was riding up her midriff.

"Yeah." Mark said, waving her away, "You go use the bathroom first. I'll be waiting. I'll put on the TV or something."

"I don't think there *is* a TV." Ally said rising to her feet once more and picking up both their suitcases.

"I'll put on some music on my phone then," Mark said, "Will you just go?"

"Afraid I'll punch your lights out again?"

"Yes, actually." Mark said.

"Dang Straight." Ally said closing the bathroom door behind her.

Mark reached into his pockets and pulled out his wallet and his cell phone. He had turned it off not long after leaving Hap's store because it had been completely useless out here in the middle of nowhere, no cell towers, and no GPS. Now he turned it back on and while it booted, he stripped away his dress shirt, and his shoes, leaving him in his white sleeveless undershirt and pants.

He stripped his socks away, curled his toes and stood up to walk around the room like that. It was a trick he had heard once on some old action movie, that had ultimately landed the hero in a lot of trouble, as he had to fight the bad guys while walking around on a ludicrous amount of broken glass, but surprisingly the trick really did work as a stress reliever after a long day or a long flight. As he did this he heard the shower turn on in the bathroom. He stretched and heard his phone drop a text alert.

Could it be there was some signal here in the Hotel? Even Wi-Fi, perhaps? His phone could make calls using Wi-Fi.

He picked up his phone and saw the no signal symbol at the top of the screen. He sighed in disappointment.

Unlocking the screen of the smartphone, he went to the Wi-Fi settings and turned on the option so the phone could search for a signal, but all it showed was a list of previous connections he had made to different routers.

Still, at some point, he had gotten just enough signal for a lone text to make it through and it must have been just as he was turning his phone off because the time stamp was marked for almost 2 hours before.

"We have received your request for assistance. We anticipate arriving at your location at approximately 2 am, if you are not with your vehicle; please make sure the keys..."

He closed the text and opened up the music program. He started it playing and set it to random because he wasn't quite sure what he had on his phone at the moment as he was used to letting most of the music stream through the app. It started playing a song he hadn't heard in nearly a year but remembered liking.

He stood up and sashayed over to the small mirrored bureau, moving in time to the music. He opened the drawers and was surprised to see that none of them had a Gideon Bible in them. Was it possible he had found the one hotel in America that hadn't been visited by the religious organization?

The drawers were completely empty, and Mark turned to get his suitcase, only to remember that Ally had taken both of their bags into the bathroom with her.

It was only then that it struck him as odd that she should do that. Did she have something that she wanted in his suitcase? He didn't remember her packing any of her things into it, but then who knows what she might have brought along when he wasn't looking.

She was always more worried about her looks than she should have been, in his opinion... until tonight at the dinner table, that is, when she had let off another of those tremendous burps.

He had heard her do it before on occasion, but when it happened she'd always been dreadfully embarrassed, as she had been when it happened in Aaron's truck earlier that day, and while she may not have said it, he could see that she was humiliated and was thinking about her chagrin for sometime after it happened...

But then, just now, she had taken a bow and made a joke of it.

This was more or less how *Mark* might have reacted, had he done it, but it was highly suspect coming from her. Mark stood and stretched, and out of habit, he put his fist on his hips, 'arms akimbo' like Peter Pan.

He felt something crunch in his pocket.

He pulled out the slip of paper and saw it was the receipt for the money they had spent on the food and the cost of the room. He glanced over it, but then realized something was missing.

While the prices were marked, there was no attribution as to what was being paid for. Just the numbers...

This was odd but not altogether unexpected, Maru's cash register and equipment being as out of date as it was, but what *was* strange, was the total lack of Mark's credit card information and name.

It was almost always at the bottom of any receipt paid for with a card, and if it wasn't on this slip it was almost always printed on an accompanying paper from the little unit that the card had been run through.

It was practically the law, and certainly a universal constant; it protected both the buyer and the seller. Mark was concerned that the credit card may not have registered, which would mean Maru was not getting paid. He would check with the man in the morning.

Maru couldn't be making a whole lot of money out here in the middle of nowhere, and Mark had no intention of letting him be deprived of what he was owed by a glitch, especially after he'd been so kind to them, and provided such quality food.

Mark put the receipt back in his pocket and let these thoughts drift to the back of his mind as he listened to the music from his phone. It had changed to something a little slower and he found himself singing along, when he suddenly felt a hand on his shoulder.

He turned around and there was Ally, looking beautiful as always, dressed in his baggy formless sweat clothes.

Her face free of makeup, and her hair hanging down, over her back, still wet from the shower.

This was how she looked at her "worst" and to him, it was how he liked her best.

Her.

Just her.

No makeup, no façade or pretense.

Together they started dancing to the music quietly. Their bodies swaying gently to the music, nothing special or flashy, no spins or twists, just the two of them moving together and as one, her head on his should-

Shoulder...

That wasn't right...

Her head was usually on his chest when they danced. The only time she could put her head near his shoulder was when she was wearing heels… and he could feel she wasn't wearing any shoes at all, her bare toes had brushed his several times already.

He pulled away from her, to look her in the face. "Ally…" He asked confused and growing scared, "What happened?"

"What do you mean?" she asked confused.

"You're taller."

"What?… Don't be ridiculous." She said, laying her head back in the crook of his neck.

He pushed her away this time, gently but firmly, "This morning I could pick you up, hold you to my chest and your feet wouldn't even touch the floor. You're almost as tall as I am now… You must have grown nearly five inches.

"That's… That's nonsense." She said, backing away from him, "I'm more than twenty-five… Twenty-year-olds don't have growth spurts… You're imagining things."

But Mark could see in her eyes something was wrong, and she knew it. He knew her face, her expressions and she had just put something together.

"What?" He asked, "What did you just figure out?"

"Nothing." She lied, tugging at her shirt… But it wasn't her shirt, it was his.

"Why are you wearing my sweats?" he asked.

Ally tried to act offended but failed, "I… I wear your sweat clothes all the time, you know that."

"Maybe on a cold winter's night, but never at the end of summer and your skin is very hot right now."

Mark pointed out correctly, "Ally don't lie to me. What's going on?"

"None of my clothes would fit." She finally admitted, "I had two other dresses and my slip for sleeping in and they were all too small. Even the slip was too tight. I thought I might just be bloated but…"

She ran her hands over her arms and chest and face as if she could feel out if there had been any other changes.

Her hands settled on her jaw, and it might have been the way she was running her hands over it, but Mark thought it did seem a little more square, more solid and pronounced than it had been before. It was as if she had lost a good bit of weight, and her face had lost some of its fullness, but he could see quite plainly that she had not lost an ounce and might have actually put on some lean muscle mass, as well as height. In his shapeless sweat clothes it was difficult to say.

"Mark! Mark!" She cried, "What is happening?! What's happening to me?"

Mark walked to her and held her, she was not only taller but thicker than before. He could feel through the shirt the strong cords of muscle in her back.

"It's okay babe," he said stroking her wet hair, "You're alright... You are going to be alright. Calm down."

"Don't tell me to calm down!" She said, hitting him in the back but still clinging tightly... far tighter than she should have been capable of, to his torso, "You aren't the one going through this."

"Yes, I am." He said, "Whatever this is we are going to go through it together. Do you hear me?"

"Mmmhmm." She hummed into his shoulder, tears falling to wet his skin.

"Now think, baby, think... How do you feel?"

"Scared." She said pulling back and sitting down on the bed.

"Besides that." He said, sitting next to her, "Physically. How do you feel?"

"Good." She said, clearly surprised to hear the words coming from her mouth, "Really... Really good... Like... Like I did in High School, right after I finished a race, or when I was on the cheerleading squad and we'd just finished a stressful routine and executed it perfectly... and like I'm ready to do it again right now! I haven't felt like this in... years... maybe ever.

"Uh-huh..." Mark said, understanding, "That's endorphins. They make you feel happy... Like you said. After a stressful workout or a successful day of hard work at the office, your body produces them to make you want to do it again, its like a reward."

"No," said Ally, you don't understand... I've never done drugs, but I think... I think this must be what it feels like to be on Speed.... Or having adrenaline shot straight into your heart. Everything seems more... More! The colors seem more vibrant, I can see everything so clearly. I can see the individual fibers in the carpet, I can see the microscopic places where the wallpaper glue is failing. It is amazing... But I... I can't turn it off."

"When did you start feeling this way?" Mark asked, putting a hand on the side of her face, and urging her to focus on him.

"I don't know... Its kind of been creeping up on me all evening... I guess it was slightly after I came back out of the bathroom downstairs. I went to the bar and I got my food. I sat down and started eating. Before long I started feeling different."

Her voice trailed off and she looked into the distance, remembering. "Oh, God." She said, "I hurt you. In the dining room, I practically pulled you off your chair and got in your face."

"You didn't hurt me," Mark said dismissively. "I'm alright. You are going to be alright too. Now think. Did you touch anything in the bathroom? Did you wash your hands."

"Of course I washed my hands, Mark, I always wash my hands. I know how neurotic you are about that."

Mark let the mild insult pass, there were far more important things at stake here. "I didn't touch anything." She said, "Except the sink, and the paper towel... I used it the way you taught me. I used the paper towel to open the door."

"You must have contracted it somewhere... I wonder if it's airborne." Mark said thinking.

"Wait." Ally said, trying to process, "You think this

might be a virus?"

"It's the only thing that makes any sense." Mark explained, "Unless you want to believe that we were both drugged and are experiencing the exact same hallucinations... Which is impossible. Like you said, twenty-something women don't just suddenly have growth spurts, and we are in a hotel filled with Big People at the moment. What if... What if the virus came from *them* somehow? What if one of them contracted something. What if the virus adapted... As I understand it some viruses work that way. They infect the host cells, hijack the system, force it to reproduce more virus and then explode when the cells are full of virus and then they go out into the rest of the system to do it again... What if one of the "GIANTS" is a carrier and doesn't even know it? Some viruses incorporate the DNA of the host and it makes the virus stronger, it mutates."

"That sounds more like a "retro-virus" to me. But... That's ridiculous. Its stupid. Viruses don't change people's physicality, not in less than two hours! Not normally." Ally said.

"What about this situation seems normal to you?" Mark asked, "We are way past rational explanations here. Some scientists believe that viruses, retroviruses, are part of what made humans what they are today, adding things to us, becoming one with us. I can't think of a better explanation for this amount of change in a matter of hours. Something is rewriting your DNA, causing your pituitary gland to flood your body with testosterone and Human Growth Hormone and endorphins, oxytocin and Dopamine, to make you feel better about it."

"When did you become a neurobiologist?" Ally almost laughed and smiled as she said it.

"You didn't think I was just looking at my phone all the time when you had the History Channel on did you?"

"That sounds more like Discovery or Science Channel."

"No, it was History." Mark was purposely deflecting to

try and take the seriousness out of the situation, and maybe Ally was too, but she was drawn right back to the subject at hand. "I think... Maybe... Maybe it was the Calamari." Ally said.

"That doesn't make any sense," Mark said. "Don't you roll your eyes at me!" Ally said, with some real anger, and Mark saw a flash of the same expression that he had seen in the dining room. An expression he had hoped never to see again.

"None of this happened until I ate that." Ally said.

"And you think my theory of a retrovirus is ridiculous?" Mark said incredulously, "I think the Calamari was just another symptom, of this... thing... gearing up. Your body needed energy to facilitate these changes and for whatever reason, you locked on to the squid. I know for a fact it has a lot of protein and iron, all things your body would need for this sort of thing."

"Howard warned us not to eat the Calamari." Ally said, "He knew there was something wrong with it."

"Who is Howard?" Mark asked confused. "Howard... Happy... Hap at the convenience store. He told us there was something weird going on up here. He warned us not to eat the Calamari! Why didn't I listen to him?"

Ally began to cry again, and for the briefest of moments, Mark had a picture in his head of Alice crying because she had eaten too much of the cake, and now had grown too large to fit through the door into Wonderland.

Mark hugged her again, and it felt so strange now.

It was very different to hold her than it had been only this morning when he had called her is *"Little Baby Wifey"*.

"I hardly think this is what he was talking about." Mark said, "I think he was just worried about food poisoning... Do you honestly think he would have let us come up here if he knew this was going on? And besides, the only way the Calamari could be the cause is if Maru is some kind of mad scientist, experimenting with growth hormones."

Ally sniffed, "It could be the squid itself that carried the retro-virus, some giant squids grow to be the biggest... *the big-*

gest creatures on earth!"

She burst into tears again.

"Oh, Mark… I don't want to be eight feet tall!"

Mark shushed her gently, "It's alright, you won't be. You're hardly even as tall as I am… and at least now you'll be able to reach the top shelf by yourself."

Mark meant it to be a sort of joke or *"look on the bright side"* comment.

It was the wrong thing to say.

Suddenly Mark found himself flying across the bed and into the wall across from it, as Ally pushed him away, hard.

"Do you think this is funny?!" Ally bellowed, standing to her feet and walking toward him, where he now lay on the floor, her voice having dropped from its high crying tone to a deeper register of rage, possibly deeper than any sound he'd ever heard come out of her before.

Mark scrabbled to his feet, now she was nose to nose with him and just as tall, "Baby please, your hormones are all over the place right now. Think about what you're doing."

"I don't have to think!" She said her voice rising to a high insane shriek, "You're only thinking about yourself! Maybe that's why you married me in the first place; you wanted someone to need you! Someone you had to take care of, and now you're threatened because I don't need you anymore. That's it isn't it? ISN'T IT!?"

"Baby no!" Mark exclaimed, "I never thought of you that-"

"Stop lying to me!" Ally shouted, "Stop. Calling. Me. BABY!"

Mark found himself flying through the air again, this time in the direction of the bed… …Which he missed and landed squarely against one of the small nightstands, which collapsed, breaking beneath him.

Ally bellowed with rage.

"Ally please!" Mark begged, "Please stop! You are hurting

me!"

And that seemed to break through, Ally's rage subsided, and he could see she wanted to run toward him, to help him, but she was also afraid of what she might do.

She put both her arms up and grabbed at her hair in the horror of what she had just done, "Mark!" she wailed, "Mark I'm sorry! I just... *I just... I just...*"

She crumpled against the wall and landed on her backside. She folded into an almost fetal position, her elbows on her knees, and her hands in her hair.

She cried.

She wailed.

She raged, pounding the wall and then did all three again.

Mark meanwhile had pulled himself up on to the bed. His back was hurting from the force of the second impact in less than a few minutes, but he seemed to be alright. He wanted to go to her, to hold her, but he was in considerable pain, and if he was totally honest, he was afraid of her, and what she might do, in this state.

"We've..." He started, "We've got to... get out of here!" Mark gasped, lying on his side, panting, "We've got... to get you... to a hospital!" Ally just sat there on the floor, making little quivering sobs, the same sound over and over again, but then it changed.

The sobs became barely whispered words that Mark couldn't make out, the same three or for words over and over again.

Her pitch lowered once more and back into a deeper register and the words became a chant, over and over again.

Mark couldn't be sure but it sounded like *"Die On Day Gah."* She said it again and again, the words growing in clarity and boldness, and merging, *"Dyon-Day-Gah. Dyon-Day-Gah. Dyondaygah! Dyondaygah!!"*

Soon she was saying it over and over again, as one word,

a call, a name. *"Dyondaygah!!"*

"Ally." Mark said, carefully, "What are you saying?"

Ally didn't react to his words, but her hands came away from her hair, which Mark now noticed had grown considerably longer, (which was to be expected with what happened to her so far, if anything could be considered "expected". Where once it had been just barely touching her shoulders, it was now nearly to her waist.) Her hair was still wet, but now it was drying out and becoming bushier and bushier, lending her an even wilder, more feral look. But it was her eyes which were the most disturbing to Mark.

They were not his wife's eyes at all.

They had not undergone any physical change and it might even have gone unnoticed by many others who did not know her before that day, but there was nothing of Ally in her eyes.

Later Mark would describe it as looking through a window of a familiar house with a new dweller. The walls might be the same, but the furniture and the spirit were nothing like they had been before.

If the eyes were the window to the soul, the thing inhabiting the body of his wife was nothing like hers.

From below him, Mark felt a low rumble; a rumble in time with Ally's chant.

But as it continued he realized it was not something he felt, it was something he was hearing.

A dark chorus of deep voices had joined Ally's chant.

"Dy-on-day-gah!" the voices repeated with Ally, *"Dy-on-day-gah! Dy-on-day-gah!"* From below, Mark heard the tromp of heavy, booted feet, marching in rhythm toward them. Yet the sound did not come from the hallway or the stairs, it seemed to be coming from within the very walls and floor.

"Ally." Mark said, "Ally baby... We've got to get out of here... We have to go right now."

Mark reached down for his shoes and slid them back on to his feet. "You should have come too, Mark." Ally almost whispered in a deep sonorous voice she should not have been capable of.

The other voices continued chanting around them.

Ally now actually looked at him, rather than through him, "You should have partaken. Now you know. Now it is too late for you to make the choice."

"Choice?" Mark asked, confused, "What choice?"

Ally didn't answer but resumed the chant of, *"Dy-on-day-gah!"*

The door of the room opened. And the big people began to file in. There had been no turn of a lock or inserting of a key. The lock was not broken by the force on the opposite side of the door, nor did the doorknob turn, the door was simply closed one moment, and open the next.

The GIANTS were all filing into the room, creating an impenetrable wall of flesh.

If asked, Mark would have been surprised if the room could hold ten of these massive people, but it seemed to have no problem containing all thirty of the people who had previously taken up so much space in the dining area below.

They were all still chanting the name, that single word over and over again.

The name was so strange and yet it seemed to Mark as though he had heard it before this night, like a tune playing just at the edge of memory.

As one, Ally and the Giants stopped the chant, with no signal or reason that Mark could see, the Giants became silent. One of them stepped forward. It was the same Ogre whom Mark had bumped into in the bathroom, he stepped forward and looked at Ally, who in turn faced him.

"Welcome Sister." He said in that same deep burbling voice that had so chilled Mark when he'd heard it before, as though he were speaking around a bag of marbles or (Mark shuddered at the thought,) a mouth stuffed with seaweed, "You have partaken of the sacred body of Dyondaygah. You were wise not to heed the warnings that were given to you.

You are small now but you shall grow in size and power. Dyondaygah will be your food. You shall be like us, and you shall, in turn, be sustenance for the great one, and you will widen the door. It is an honor that has been bestowed on you."

"I am honored." Ally said, "May Dyondaygah's coming be made manifest in me."

"May Dyondaygah's coming be made manifest in me." The GIANTS repeated as if this were some sort of catechism.

Mark still sat on the bed, not able to move. He had been frozen from the moment the door opened and the GIANTs filed in.

"Ally" Mark finally worked up the courage to speak, "What are you doing? We have to get away from these… things!"

"This one has not partaken." Said the Ogre, "This one is still a weak mortal."

"Weak mortal. Weak mortal." The GIANTs repeated while Ally remained silent.

"He will be taken to the altar of Dyondaygah, and made a sacrifice."

"Sacrifice! Sacrifice!"

"Sacrifice." Ally said, a moment after the rest.

"He shall look upon Dyondaygah, and be divided."
"He shall be divided." Ally said, alone.

Mark stared back at Ally in shock.
What was she saying?
Was she capable of understanding what this all meant?
Did she comprehend what the GIANTs meant to do to him?

He didn't quite know what all their talk was about, but it was pretty clear it wasn't going to turn out well for him.

"The time is not yet right." The Ogre said, "there are many hours before the Waxing Gibbous Moon will be in position as the Stars grow right for the coming of Dyondaygah.

The sacrifice must face him while still a living being, to please Dyondaygah. He can only be a proper sacrifice if he is still sane, that Dyondaygah might break him."

"*Break him. Break him.*"

"Take him to the kitchen." Said a tiny piping voice, and while it had not before, the coming of this new voice sent chills down Mark's spine. Not because of the words it spoke or its shrillness, but because with its coming Mark's last hope of rescue seemed to be lost.

Maru pushed into the room between the legs of the big people who blocked his path.

"Make way. Make way." He said making all kinds of little shooing noises that almost sounded like an engine failing to engage, "*Oh-ja-ja-ja-jah!*"

The Ogre spoke again, "Make way for the High Priest of Dyondaygah!"

"Yes yes." Said Maru, dismissively, "All praise and power to the Great Old One Dyondaygah, may his tentacles embrace us all."

"*May his tentacles embrace us all!*" Repeated Ally with the GIANTs.

"Well, Mr. Thurston," Said Maru, "It would seem you didn't have any of my delicious stew or the Fried Calamari. What a shame. You have missed out on a true culinary delight! I am told it is quite delicious."

"Why you little Son of a-" Mark rose and rushed toward the minikin, and was within arm's length of him when the Ogre reached out and grabbed hold of Mark's head. Not just his hair or his throat, but Mark's entire head.

The heel, and palm of the massive mitt covered Mark's face, from his chin, and up into his hairline, while the fingers curled around Mark's skull, down to the top of the occipital bone.

"You will not touch the High Priest of Dyondaygah!" The Ogre said, and did not relinquish his grip until Mark stopped resisting. Only then was the suffocating hand removed and

Mark fell backward, on to the bed.

"Now, let us have no more of that!" Said Maru, walking up to the foot of the bed, "Just because you are going to be a sacrifice, doesn't mean we can't be civil until the time comes."

Mark breathed heavily, "What did you do to my wife?"

"Answered her dearest wish, I should think." Maru said, "Though I've had very little to do with it. I merely served you food and drinks, and gave you a room to stay in."

"Her dearest wish?" Mark spat, "Look at her! She's... She's gone... That's not her in there, you've made her a slave... A prisoner in her own head."

"Not so Mr. Thurston," said Maru, "Not so. We did not bring her here. We did not make her wish. We did not force her to partake. It has all been of her own volition as it must be. The Fellowship of Dyondaygah must be taken in ignorant heed of the call. Those whom Dyondaygah has not called will not partake and those whom he has called will eat... But now that you know of the choice, you can not make it."

"There was no choice!" Mark raged, "Tricking someone into being poisoned is not the same as choosing to drink the poison!"

Maru smiled and laughed, "That is where you are wrong my friend. You and your wife were warned by that meddling old fool, Howard, and yet you still chose to come here. Howard shall be dealt with, but all proceeds according to the will of Dyondaygah. Had you both not eaten of the sacred body, you would have left here in the morning, free as.... Free as... Oh, what is that American expression?"

"Free as a bird." Burbled the Ogre.

"Yes! Free as a bird." Maru continued, "There have been several state Police Officers who have dined here many times, and they have never partaken of the sacred food. It does not call to them. It is almost as if they do not see it. They certainly have no desire for it, for Dyondaygah has no desire for them. Had you both partaken you would be among them now."

He pointed to the Big People, among whom his wife was

now numbered, "But because your wife has partaken and you have not... I'm afraid we can't have you going off to tell others about us. But do not worry, all will know soon, with the complete coming of Dyondaygah."

"*Dyondaygah!*" The GIANTs all repeated. Maru looked disgusted over his shoulder, "Do you really have to do that?"

Maru looked back at Mark, "Your wife has wished for many years to be taller and stronger." He explained, "I know this because it is the same with all who come to be the sustenance. They have felt small and used all their life and wished for the strength and size to make their wishes come true. Man's heart sends out signals into the universe Mr. Thurston, as surely as one of Mr. Marconi's little telegraph machines used to send signals across the sea. Dyondaygah and others of his kind wait and listen for such signals. Wishes and longings draw them as surely as Mr. Pavelov's bell draws the dog, Mr. Thurston. If one is worthy, Dyondaygah brings them to me, and the Towen. If he has chosen them, and they wish it, they will consume the sacred food of Dyondaygah, and he shall give to them a new strength and a new life in his service."

"Strength and Life in his Service!"

Maru rolled his eyes, and tisked several times at their mindless repetition, "You see what I have to deal with?"

"Granting their wishes, while taking away everything that made life worth living?" Mark asked, "Taking away their minds and free will?"

"Of course." Said Maru, "such has been the way of "Evil", since before the long eons of anything like what you consider to be "time" began. Of course, Dyondaygah is beyond all concepts of "Good and Evil" as any true god must be."

"But why..." Mark asked, "Why are you doing this? If this food is so powerful, why are *you* still so small? What is Dyon-"

Mark felt as though someone had taken a baseball bat to the side of his head, as the Ogre backhanded him, flinging him backward, laying him out on the bed.

"Do not *ever* dane to speak his name with your unclean

lips!" Said the Ogre, "Only the High Priest and the Partakers may speak his name!"

Mark heard very little of this as he was already passing out from a combination of the impact and sheer panic.

"I think that is enough answers, for now, Mr. Thurston," Maru said, standing up on the bed and looking down at him. "All of your questions will not matter anymore once you come before the presence of Dyondaygah. And you will not be sane or alive enough, in the way you understand it, for those questions to matter after that."

Maru looked back at the Ogre, "Take him to the Kitchen and bind him until the hour of Sacrifice has come." And with that, the last ounce of Marks consciousness left him and he was engulfed in blackness.

7

When Mark began to come to consciousness, the first thing to breach the darkness was the sound of a waterfall.

A long cascading watery rumble filled the air around him.

He felt certain he must be in some dark cave underground where a river ran nearby.

But suddenly the rush of the water stopped.

Confused Mark opened his eyes, but closed them again quickly when they were overwhelmed with a bright burst of light.

In his quick, but foggy glimpse he perceived that he was in a kitchen and that the waterfall must have been water being put in a pan or bucket.

Both, from the pain of his head injury, he'd been dealt by the Ogre, and the brightness of the light, he groaned.

"Oi, whatcht!" said a voice that sounded British, deep and froglike, but not nearly as disturbing as the inhuman voice of the Ogre, and the other GIANTS.

"Yeah!" said another voice, higher pitched and more nasal, "Look-at! The sacrifice is coming awake!"

There was a sickly wet plop and Mark felt warm water being splashed on his legs, but it wasn't a deliberate pouring, more like something else was being done with the water and the backsplash had brushed his legs in the process.

"Where am I?" Mark asked, not opening his eyes, as the slopping sound began to move about the room some.

Mark realized it was the sound of a mop, scrubbing a tile

floor.

"Yah hear that?" Said a third voice that was distinctly Irish, "He wants to know where he is?" And the projector of the voice turned toward him, "Did you think it was all a nightmare, mate?"

"Aye, that he must." Said the second voice, "Know I thought it was an 'orrible nightmare when I first woke up in dis place."

"Oi, whatcht!" Repeated the first voice, "Don't let Maru hear you talkin' like that, or he'll have one of the GIANTs string yah gizzards and have you on the menu afore weeks end."

Mark could feel that he was sitting in a sturdy wooden chair, his arms and legs tied down tightly to the arms and legs of the chair with cords of rope. Not plastic zip ties or metal cuffs of some kind, but actual rope, and for a moment he felt like he was stuck in an old melodrama or a Jay Ward cartoon.

Carefully Mark opened his eyes.

Because he was ready for it, the sting of the white light around him was considerably more bearable.

"Kaw!" Said the Second voice, "He's op'ed his eyes. I had eyes like that before I came here. Pretty blue ones, dey was."

The first voice laughed, "You ain't never had nothing but the eyes you have now, you old toad."

"No honest, I did," replied the second again, "Just as small and clear, though of course, we see better now."

"Great," Mark thought out aloud, "I've woken up in the middle of a British Three Stooges routine."

"More Like Gilbert and Sullivan I should think." Said the Irish voice.

"Nau!" said the First one, "Monty Python's far more my speed."

Mark's blurred vision began to clear and the white haze began to soften into more recognizable images. There was a figure pushing a mop around, a second was filling a sink with dirty dishes, and the "blub and clank" of pots and pans being immersed in water, while the third seemed to be busy putting away the already cleaned utensils and glass plates until they were needed for their next use.

"Please," Mark begged, "You have to help me! My wife, she's been... She's being held, hostage."

Mark lied because he knew how ridiculous the truth would sound.

"Being held hostage, he says!" Said the first voice which came from the mopper, "Doesn't realize where he is yet, says I."

"And he surely ain't gotten a look at *your* mug yet." Said the second voice, which belonged to the Dish Washer, "Or he'd know it was hopeless."

The one holding the drying towel, put it down, picked up something else and moved toward Mark with it, "Here mate, this will clear your head and wake you up."

A cup was put to Mark's lips and a warm fluid was poured into his mouth, Mark might have drunk it, but just before the first drops could run down his throat, he remembered that he was still in the Buffet, and what the food here could do to you if you ate or drank the wrong thing.

Mark spewed the fluid out of his mouth, recognizing the taste better as it left than he had when it was poured in.

"Oi!" said the Mopper, "I just cleaned over there! Now I gotta do it again!"

"It were only coffee," said the Dryer, "There were no need for that!"

Mark gagged, "It's poisoned! You people are trying to kill me. Turn me into a freak like those Giants."

"Oh no," Said the washer, "That time's long gone by for you. You didn't eat of the sacred food. That opportunity has passed you by. Who knows what it would even do to you at this point. Probably nothing, seeing as you know about it. Then again it might make you like us. Who knows?"

"How could it not be effective just because you know about it?" Mark asked, "A poison doesn't stop working just because you know it's there."

The Dryer answered, "That were a proper question. It don't make much sense, do it? But that's the way things is with Dyondaygah. Once you know, the food is useless, it's only effective if ya eats it not knowing about its capabilities. All part of the Choice."

"It's not a choice, if you don't know you are making it," Mark said.

"You'd have to take that up with Dyondaygah, mate. And as fate would 'ave it, you'll have the opportunity afore long. Though, I don't suppose he'll be much in the mood for talking when you sees him. And you'll not be talking afterwards neither, leastways not so *we'd* know about it."

Mark's eyes were now truly beginning to focus and he looked toward the figures as they spoke. There was something wrong with them but Mark couldn't put his finger on exactly what. They seemed to all be short and squat.

Not short dwarves like Maru, but more like dark waddling figures as if frogs had somehow learned to walk upright on their hind legs, like Braer Frog from the Uncle Remus stories, or Mr. Toad from Wind In The Willows, only considerably less cartoony than any representation he had seen.

As the image resolved, he had to stifle back a scream, the figures indeed seemed to be giant frogs or toads, but more humanoid than any frog had the right to be.

One, the Mopper, was fat, enormously fat, but his legs were thin as twigs, which should not have been able to withstand his tremendous girth.

The Dishwasher, also frog-like, reminded Mark of "Gollum" from the 1970s animated version of The Hobbit. Grey-skinned with long trains of wet fur-like hair hanging out of his yellow gloves. His eyes were huge and grey and seemed to be more on the sides of his head rather than to the front as a man's might be.

All three of them had similarly large, oversized eyes, eyes meant for seeing in the dark. But was it the depths of a cave or the depths of the ocean from which they had come?

The Third, The Dryer, seemed like the other two, only his arms were long and spindly, giving him a more ape-like appearance.

He also had the agility of an ape, for as Mark looked at him he put a large pot on to the top shelf, not by reaching up, but by climbing on a series of small pipes which stuck out from the wall and holding the pot with his feet.

All of them had hideously wide mouths, with needle-sharp teeth that reminded Mark of a Piranha, except for the Mopper, who's teeth reminded him more of an angler fish, the way they spiked up above his jaw and lips.

They were wearing white cooks shirts and aprons but not much else. Their skin, where not covered, was shiny and smooth looking like a serpent's but with patches of long hair dangling from the wrists and knees.

"Kaw!" Said the Mopper, "Seems to me as he's finally gotten a good look at us, Mateys!"

The other two laughed in appreciation. The Irish voiced one, (the Monkey like one,) said, "And here I was a-thinking he was just uncommon able to hold in his surprise!"

"You're... you're..."

"The word you are looking for is *Squamous*." Said the dishwasher, "*Scaly and covered with flat thin skin cells, or Frog like.*"

"I think he was looking for the words, *"Hideous monsters!"* Said the Mopper, sloshing more water out of his bucket and on to the floor where the coffee had been spit, once again wetting the legs of Mark's pants.

"Speak for yourself." Said the Irish sounding Dryer of dishes, "I think my profile is out of this world!"

"Yeah," Interjected the Mopper, "But not far enough, we can still see it!"

This brought gales of laughter from all three of the Froggy creatures.

"Don't worry about our appearance mate," Said the higher-pitched voice of the Dishwasher, "We are as clean as you are. Somewhat cleaner I'd say, being as, if I may say so, its quite obvious you haven't had a shower since some time this morning. If I may state the obvious. All the food we serve here is healthy and meets with all the standard requirements for food safety."

"You… you prepare the food?" Mark said, surprised to find himself conversing over something so commonplace with creatures that could barely pass for human.

"Of course we do!" Said the Mopper, "You dinn't think that Maru, High Priest of Dyondaygah, would soil his precious little hands with something as commonplace as cooking the food, or cleaning the pots, did yah?"

"He only takes the food out and places them in the trays because if we was to do it, we might give the game away and scare off the customers."

"What…" Mark started, "*What are you?*"

"Well now that's the proper question ain't it?" Said the dishwasher, "Some say we is the descendants of Father Dagon and Mother Hydra."

"Some says we were among the first patrons of this fine establishment, who ate the sacred food and it didn't take. We became as you see us now." Said the Dryer, placing a stack of clear glass plates on top of a bigger stack.

"And some says, we's Frogs that was exposed to a mutagen ooze in the sewers of New York, makin' us as we are. Then we was trained in the ways of Ninjutsu, by a large anthropomorphic Mole!" Said the Mopper, breaking into a guffaw.

"No no!" Said the Dryer, "It was a large cockroach!" They all laughed.

"Come to think of it, I don't remember much of anything before I was here." Said the Washer, "I think I remember something about a town called Innsmouth, in Massachusetts I think it was, but then I can never be sure. Might have been something I read in a book once."

"I didn't know you could read." Said the Mopper.

"I am a creature of unknown depths." Said the Washer.

"A creature *from* unknown depths, you mean!" The Dryer said, making them all laugh again.

"Please," Mark said, "You have to help me escape, they're going to kill me! And my wife, she's…"

"She's one of the Big People now." The Dryer said, "She was about, what… 117 centimeters, last we saw her?"

The Mopper groaned, "I hate it when you use metric, why can't you say 5 foot, 10 like everyone else?"

"Because everyone else in the world uses it, it's only the American's what uses feet and inches."

"Please!" Mark said, emphatically, "I have to try to save her, I have to get away from here."

"Oh, there's no saving her now, mate." Said The Washer, "You might be able to save yourself if you could get away, but her, she's eaten the sacred food, ain't no one ever come back from that."

Mark felt something inside of his heart twist and break, was there truly no hope?

Was Ally destined to be one of the giants forever, possessed by some sort of Hive mind of the servants of Dyondaygah?

Whatever he… it… was?

No.

No there must be away back.

He would find it.

He would get his wife back.

Somehow.

"Can't you please let me go… Even if you just loosen my bonds and leave the room for a minute." Mark said, "I promise not to tell that you helped if they catch me."

"Aww." Said The Mopper, and it sounded like he was struck with some compassion for the man's plight, "The poor little blighter… Let's us, let 'im go."

"You're a mutton head, Tom as I've said before." Said the Dryer. "My head ain't made of Mutton, William, It's made out of fish!" said Tom.

"I think Tom is right." Said The Washer, "We should at least give our mate here a fighting chance. I hate to see anything die too easily."

"He don't have a chance, Bert." Said William, "Even if he made it past the Big People, he'd still have to contend with the external defenses."

"Which I've never seen deployed," said Bert, "It would be worth it just for that, never mind that we'd have a little sport, an entertainment, you might say, before the Conjunction."

"I'll tell you what, boy-o." Said William The Dryer, "I'll just happen to drop a knife within the reach of you, and then we'll all have something else to do at the same time. If you can get to the knife and free yourself, we won't be here to stop ya."

"Right!" Said Tom The Mopper, "And when you get caught, you be sure to tell them we was watchin' over ya as best we could and you managed to get away only when our backs was turned. Right?"

"Definitely, you have my word. Absolutely. Yes." Mark said, nodding vigorously.

"Right then!" Said William. He climbed up over Mark's head with two big pots, stacked one inside the other, and a large sharp knife in his back paw-like foot.

The Pots were placed in the proper spot and just as he arranged the Pots to his liking, they fell to the floor and made a loud clang, covering up the skittering sound of the knife, which dropped less than a foot from Mark's chair.

"Oh dear," said the Irish voice of William, "Look what I have done! I've damaged the pot! I shall need a hammer to bang it out smooth again!"

"Oh yes," said Bert the Washer, "I shall come with you and make sure you have a helping hand! Tom, watch over him and make sure he doesn't get away, won't you?"

Bert winked one of his large wall-eyes.

"Right!" Said Tom, "He won't be getting away under my watch."

The other two Frog-men left the room, leaving Tom

alone with Mark. Tom stood there, watching Mark, turning his head so that first one eye was watching him, and then another.

Mark waited for a long moment, and then said, "Tom… Don't you have something you are supposed to do?"

"Nope 'verything is done for the night, I was thinking of going to bed and catching a few winks before the Conjunction. But I have to watch you until they get back."

"Weren't you going to do something that would make it so you don't see me for a little while?" Mark utzed along.

"Why would I do that?" Tom said, "I'm supposed to make sure you don't get away."

"But you wanted to see some sport… Right?"

"Yeah." "And if I'm tied up to this chair there won't be any sport, right? The giants will just come and take me away… Riiight?"

"Yeah," Tom said, a bit of light beginning to dawn.

"So… don't you have something else you need to do?" Mark said, craning his neck, implying Tom should leave.

"Oh… yeah… I suppose, I need to clean out the grease trap… That hasn't been done in a while."

"Good." Mark said, "You go do that. I'll be right here."

"Okay." Tom said waddling away, "I always like cleaning out the grease trap. Something about the smell reminds me of home."

As soon as the last frog-man was out of sight, Mark began to inch his way over toward the large knife that had been dropped by the monkey-ish Frog-man.

It was only a few feet away, but Mark didn't know how he was going to get at it. He had been hoping that the Frog-Man would put it in an easily gotten to location, but it lay gleaming on the floor, just out of reach.

The chair was not tied to the floor or bolted down, thankfully, but his legs were tied to the front legs of the chair, and he had to hop, and thrust his backside forward to get the chair to move.

Soon he was just a few inches away, but the knife was still on the floor.

"He's doing awfully well." Said the voice of Bert, from somewhere off to his left.

"Yeah, but he's at the hard bit now, getting the knife into his hands." Said William, in a slightly lowered tone that could barely be called a whisper. "Maybe you should have put the knife on the counter, next to 'im."

"Nah, would have been too easy, counter's on wheels, could have bumped the counter with 'is legs, would have literally fallen in 'is lap."

Mark sighed, "I can do without the Sports Center commentary."

"Oi, you think he was talking about us?" William asked.

"Nau," said Bert, "Leastways if he did, he might keep a civil tongue in his head, lest we take offense and decided to come back in the room and block his escape."

Mark gritted his teeth, to keep another snide comment at bay, and braced himself for what he knew he had to do, which was likely to hurt a lot.

He forced all his weight against one side of the chair and then the other, back and forth, until at last, he had built up some momentum and…

Oh yeah.. that hurt…

It really, REALLY hurt.

The chair slammed into the floor so hard that the arms broke off both sides, as well as the rear left leg.

The chair practically dissolved underneath him and while this set him free, for the most part, (his hands still had bits of the arms tied to them, and while his legs were still bound they were not nearly as tightly held as before,) he could barely move for the pain it had caused.

"Aw, that was disappointing." Said Bert, "He broke free in one move. I was figurin' he'd at least have to inch a little more to get hold of the knife."

Mark, barely conscious of the ongoing dialogue between

the Frog-men, remembered the knife through his pain and reached out for it, but it wasn't there.

Where had it gone?

Where...

Oh... drat.

The knife had been hit by the chair on the way down and while it had not gone skittering away, it had flipped blade up and landed underneath him.

In the initial pain of impact, Mark hadn't felt it, but now as one pain dulled another flared. Pushing up with his hands Mark felt the knife fall out, long ways, from the meat of his thigh.

Fortunately, the blade had not hit him "point up" so the gash was not deep, but it was long, a full eight inches from his thigh to just above his knee.

His thick jeans had deflected the force somewhat, but not enough.

"Oh, he's spilt his own blood." Said William, "That's not good. The defenses will lock on to that like hounds."

"Look at the bright side, there's a mess Tom can look forward to cleaning up... Do it with his tongue most likely. I shouldn't be surprised."

Mark picked up the blade and sawed through what remained of his bonds. Then using the counter, he pulled himself up, doing his best to ignore the searing pain in his leg, hips, and back.

Once his legs were free, he dropped the knife on the ground, pulling himself on to his feet and began to hobble his way toward the kitchen door.

"You know." Said Bert, "I always wonder why the hero does that in the action movies." He sniffed, "He has a weapon in his hand, and he leaves it behind once he thinks he's done with it. Next thing you know, he's attacked and that weapon would have come in mighty handy."

"Tis so the 'ero has more to overcome," Said William, "If he'd used his common sense and taken the weapon with him, the battle might be over to quickly."

Mark groaned inwardly, but knowing they were right, he turned back, retracing the four or five steps he'd taken already, bent down and gritted his teeth against the pain, as he picked up the big knife, stained with his own blood.

"Aww, he took it." Said Bert, "I was hoping to get to lick it clean. One of my best chopping knives, that is."

"You know Bert," William said, as Mark limped out the kitchen door, "I think he might have heard us."

Tom, drawn by the sound of the closing door, squelched his way back toward the sinks. "Oi... He's gone. Did I miss something?"

"Nau." Said William, "Nothing much. The fun is just beginning!"

Tom looked at the floor where the broken chair lay, "Oh look!" He said with delight, "He left us a tasty treat on his way out! How thoughtful of 'im!"

8

Mark limped through the door of the kitchen and found himself in a small ramped hallway, lined with Oak on both sides.

It was not paneling, but solid Oak.

To Mark, it felt more like being in the heart of an old ship, than a house on solid land.

Quietly he crept down the hall, knife poised at the ready.

When he reached the end of the hall, there was an open doorway to his right.

He heard nothing from the other side, but there might be someone out there waiting for him.

He thought to use the knife as a mirror, but while its hazy surface would reflect light, it was no good as a mirrored periscope, and the gleam was more likely to give him away, than aid him in any realistic way.

Giving in to the hunchbacked stature which the pain in his leg was already forcing him into, he kept low and stuck his head around the corner.

He was looking out into the, now empty, dining hall of the buffet. The lights were low, and this gave the Maroon colored floors and walls even more of the appearance of blood.

The bar where the food had once been housed was now vacant, leaving only metal runners and void spaces behind.

The spring-loaded dish holding sockets in the counters were filled to capacity with freshly cleaned plates and bowls ready for the next day's meal service.

It crossed Mark's mind to wonder how such a place, that didn't even seem to take the money they were offered, could manage to run a full meal service every day, such had been prepared when Ally and he had entered the restaurant.

No matter where the "sacred food" was coming from, the regular food, the "real" food had to come from somewhere, and it likely had to be paid for.

But the thought of Ally pulled him back into the moment.

What was he going to do about her?

Should he try to find her?

Hunt her down and try to convince her to leave with him?

No.

Wherever she was, she was likely surrounded by the Big People.

He was pretty sure that they would not leave a Neophyte alone during the first few hours of whatever "*conversion*" was happening to her at the moment, and with the "*conjunction*" at hand.

Whatever that was.

Mark didn't know what a lot of things meant, but Ally had said something about Dyondaygah's coming being made manifest in her, and the Ogre had said something about "*widening the door.*" So it was likely they would keep her nearby.

No, the best thing to do was to go and get help.

But what help was there?

Hap and his son of course.

But if they were even still at the grocery store at this hour of the night, what could the three of them do?

There was a telephone, and they could call for help, but who could you call for help in a time like this?

The police would never believe the truth, and telling them that you and your wife had been held captive at a local motel sounded like a crank call even to Mark who was going through it at the moment.

He could hear them laughing and hanging up already.

"And the Ghostbusters are all the way out in New York."
"Stop it." He told himself. This was no time for jokes.

Even he was amazed at his lack of seriousness in a moment like this.

When they got out of this, he was going to have to work on that.

It was a defense mechanism and he knew it, but he still couldn't get over the fact that he'd allowed such a frivolous thought to cross his mind when his wife's life, nay her very soul, might be on the line.

From somewhere deep below him, he heard a rhythmic pounding begin, and after a moment he knew it for the sound of drums.

It seemed to be a five-count, and every fifth beat was louder than the previous four.

It was a tribal and ancient rhythm, and then the voices, indistinguishable became audible, and while Mark could not hear the words chanted, he knew beyond any doubt what they were meant to invoke.

He had waited long enough. Too long.

Who knew when someone might come along, or the Frog-men decided to up the ante in their *"Sport"* by sounding the alarm, and letting Maru and the Giants know he had escaped?

No time for planning.

No time for thinking about who to call, if he made it to a phone.

There was only the need to act, and to do it now.

Mark kept low and made his way threw the dining hall.
The pain in his leg was excruciating and blood was run-

ning down from his injury.

As he passed a table he grabbed a few napkins from the dispenser and threw them in his pockets, hoping he'd have time to dress the wound later, there was no time for it now.

Idiotically, he heard the lines of an old song by the Guess Who playing through his head:

"No Time left for you! No time Left for you. I've got, got, got no time."

He made his way to the main door, through which he and Ally had entered this Hellhole of madness.

He pushed against the doors.

Of course, they were locked.

He looked for some sort of keyhole, a tumbler switch, a digital keypad, anything. But there was nothing.

He looked above and below for "post locks" going into the floor or the jam above the door.

Nothing.

How was the door being kept closed?

Was there some kind of magical force field surrounding the Buffet?

Something that kept the doors closed and wouldn't allow you to leave without a passphrase or magic charm?

Would he be able to get out even if he broke a window?

Would he meet up with some sort of invisible force field, that would bounce him back, or worse still, damage him in some way?

It seemed silly.

It seemed nonsensical.

But if a five-foot-tall girl could be as tall as him in a matter of hours, just because she ate some seafood…

If a squad of Giants and a midget take him captive and put four Frog-men in charge of watching over him until he could be sacrificed to some sort of Ancient Deity, was a force field too much to be believed?

>The Frog-Men had said the Buffet had *"outer defenses."*
>Maybe this was it.
>Maybe they...

"No." Mark said quietly, but aloud, to himself, "It couldn't be that simple."

He pulled on the door.

And the door gave, the sounds of the steamy night coming from beyond.

"You have got to be kidding," Mark said to himself, as he set foot outside.

He had remembered that when he and Ally had entered the Buffet the doors had opened inwardly and he had been pushing against them from the inside.

"At least they weren't marked "Pull" or "Push," Mark thought to himself, *"Then I really would feel like an idiot."*

"Mister Thurston?" Came a tiny piping voice from his left, "Leaving us so soon?"

Maru stood there just a couple feet from where Mark crouched, "I was just enjoying the night air, it's such a pleasant evening. I would have been so sad to have missed you on your way out."

"Cut the crap." Mark said, with a boldness he was far from feeling, "So are you going to call out your hoard of giants or what?"

"Such impertinence, Mr. Thurston." Maru said, chiding him like an uppity school teacher who thinks herself so far above the students who have broken the rules, "You know you really should be nicer to me. I can make things easier on you when you come before the great one, or I can make them... exceedingly difficult."

"Well," Said Mark, resignedly, "I've never been one for doing things the easy way. Just ask Ally."

Without another word or a moment's hesitation, Mark grabbed the man by the collar, as if he were a suitcase, and threw him headlong into the doorway of the dining hall.

He did not pause to see how far the dwarf flew or where he landed. But he heard the impact and the wailing from behind as he immediately began to run across the parking lot.

Later he would think that describing his loping stride as "running" would be too generous.

Lewis Carol had created the right word: *Galumphing*.

But call it what you will, he made his way across the parking lot, and toward the slope of the hillside.

From behind him, he heard the high screaming shriek of Maru's voice as the little man made his way back to the door of *The Olde Towen Buffet.*

But the voice was not far away and distant as he would have expected. The sound hung in the air and rumbled in the earth. It rang in Mark's ears as though it had been shouted right next to him.

"*You can not leave Mr. Thurston!* YOU DO NOT HAVE MY PERMISSSSSIOOOOOON!!"

It was then, (likely activated by Maru's call,) that the "*defenses*" the Frog-men had inadvertently warned him of, were activated.

As Mark ran across the driveway, he saw something breaking through the pavement in front of him.

At first, it looked as if hundreds of broods of vipers had somehow managed to break through the pavement in a dozen different places all at once.

The things twisted and writhed as they moved forward out of their holes. But they did not end as snakes might have, they kept extending, kept growing longer and larger.

Then they seemed to form curled little green shoots, which quickly turned brown and burst open.

They were not snakes, but plants of some kind.

Later Mark would identify them as being not unlike another plant native to the soil of Kansas, *"Devil's Claw."*

But very quickly it became apparent there was nothing natural about these plants, and they were huge, bigger than any "devil's claw" plant had been since the time of the dinosaurs.

The average Devil's claw plant, full-grown was not much bigger than a man's hand. But these were massive, five or six feet in circumference, and full of twists and spurs.

They reproduced with amazing rapidity before Mark's very eyes, and their "vines" were more like strong branches than easily snapped twigs.

When the pods broke open, the seeds had hardly touched the earth before new plants were spreading over the ground, repeating the process.

And the "claws" did not stop growing once they had released their seed, they kept growing and expanding in curled hooks. The ends of which were razor sharp.

All of this takes time to read, there was barely time to see it in the moonlight and what little light came from the parking lot lamps.

They grew huge, their green and purple talons reaching out and grabbing at Mark as he passed by.

The curled vines grabbed and sliced and dug into his pants legs, more like small swords than thorny plants.

One grew up fast and wrapped around his leg, pulling him to the ground.

Mark fell face-first into a mess of the growing plants, which were now sprouting all over the hillside of the great burial mound.

They cut at his skin as they grew.

They did not seem to be under the direct control of Maru, or have any intent or will of their own; they simply grew at an astonishing rate and ensnared anything that came within their coils.

Mark tried to push himself up and out of the swiftly tangling mass of plants but one or two of the coils had already begun to wrap around his head and neck.

He felt its pressure against the sides of his head, wrapping around it like the two hands of the Ogre within the buffet might have done. Only rather than being soft and fleshy as even the strongest of hands were, these were hard and stick-like, and did not yield in the least.

He felt the strong coils gathering around his legs as well, while other vines began to poke and stab at him from the sides.

But his left hand was still free and in his left hand was the knife.

William the Frog-man's best chopping knife.

As the vines continued to wrap around him, Mark began to hack at the vines, which had already grown hard as a sapling.

He chopped at the ones nearest his head first and felt them give under his blows, first one then another broke away.

A few times he came way too close to his face with the blade before the vines snapped.

But it was working! Where the vine was cut it did not grow back, and soon his head was free.

He screamed as one of the plants found the wound that was still oozing blood and began to push into it.

He looked down and saw that the vine itself was turning red and pulsating slightly as it worked its way in, taking in his blood as nourishment.

These plants were carnivorous!

Quickly he hacked at the stem which had found its way into his leg and it broke off. Then he cut away at the other smaller claws which were biting into his skin.

A few of them had broken the flesh but were only just taking in the small drops of blood from where they had done their work.

With three solid whacks and a twist, he was free again.

He clambered to his feet, pain racking his body.

But now the plants had seemingly stopped growing, at least in his general vicinity and at such speed.

They had started on his path, and so finished first. Around him growing out from the center, the plants were still growing, twisting and writhing, but in front of him, all was still.

He began to hop through the viney monstrosities, which were already turning brown, and grey, looking as dead and lifeless as most of the other plant life in the area did.

Somehow Mark knew exactly why the plants had died so quickly.

They had not been meant to feed on water and soil as the plants of this world do, but on something else.

And while they grew up quickly in the dirt of this world, without an immediate and vast supply of blood to hand, they would quickly die from lack of nourishment.

In death, now the plants had grown hard and nubby, and their sharp points snapped and crunched under his feet.

Some of them felt like they may have punctured his shoes, but this didn't stop Mark, he kept moving through the brambles and though they caught on his clothes Mark had made it to the base of the hill in less than a minute of breaking free.

He was on the edge of the line of plants when suddenly he was jerked back and up into the air, by the back of his undershirt.

Just as he had thrown Maru, the Ogre now held him up in the air.

"You have harmed the High Priest of Dyondaygah!" The mush-mouthed Troll began, turning Mark to face him, "For this, there can be no atonement! You will- *GAAAARRRHH-GHH!!!!*"

Mark found himself thrown back nearly a yard beyond the edge of the line of devil's claw-like plants, and as painful as it was, The Ogre's pain was manifold, for as he had turned Mark around to face him, Mark had plunged the chopping knife deep into the eye socket of the giant, which had practically exploded all over Mark's hand.

He had driven the entire blade through the monster's head and sunk it to the handle.

The giant screamed once more in agony before falling into the tangle of plant claws, the sound of snapping and squishy flesh being stabbed by thorny plants all the way down.

The Ogre thrashed about in the nest of Razor Devil's Claw, causing more holes to be punched into his flesh, but he was in so much excruciating pain from the injury done to his head and eye, that he hardly seemed to notice.

But Mark knew the evil thing, that likely had once been a man was already dead.

Nothing, not even something powered by the "*Sacred Food of Dyondaygah,*" could survive that much damage and live.

Mark knew that he should run.

He should be making for the Grocery store, or better yet the highway. Any moment the rest of the horde of Giants could be on their way. And who knew what other "*external defenses*" the Towen might have in store. Just because he had reached the end of the rapidly growing Razor Devils Claw did not mean he was out of Maru's reach, but he could not help himself.

He watched as the Behemoth thrashed less and less and finally grew still upon his thorny bed.

Mark was just about to run when he heard something, a gurgling, rumbling, which could have only been coming from within the Giant.

The moment was like a nightmare.

It was like that moment in the dream when you think something might happen and because you are dreaming and the thought originated in your brain, it happens in the dream…

But this was no dream; nightmare or otherwise.

Mark thought to himself, "*Alien.*"

And as soon as he did, something exploded up out of the Ogre's stomach cavity, like a coiled Jack in the Box.

What it was, could only be described simply as "*a tentacle.*"

But that description would fall far short of what it was. It was unlike any tentacle Mark had ever seen before.

It was a column of flesh, massive and lithe.

Its alternately wrinkled and smooth skin was speckled with dark greenish grey spots, while in some places dark hairs stuck out from it, like those that cover an elephant's hind legs: thick, course and capable of stripping the flesh from a man's body, if they rubbed against him.

It undulated in midair for what seemed like an eternity but must have been little more than a second.

In his adrenaline-fueled state Mark took it all in... At least as much of it as his mind could handle.

There were aspects to this thing that could never be described in such a paltry and pitiful conveyer of information, such as language is.

Mark was sure there were things about it that the human brain could never understand, let alone conceive.

Where one might have expected to see *"suckers"* on the legs of an octopus or squid, there were indeed round ovoid spaces. But, while some seemed to be like suckers, just as many were filled with multifaceted and bifurcated eyes.

Eyes like men, horses, and goats, eyes like that of a fly, and eyes that were like nothing Mark had ever seen... Yet he understood, that they were meant for seeing, nonetheless.

A third of the orifices were full of tiny mouths and nasty pointed yellowing teeth, while others seemed to have other smaller tentacles coming out of them. While still more had organelles extruding from them, the purpose of which Mark couldn't begin to guess at... Or maybe he just didn't want to.

In the places between the sucker-holes, there were thousands and thousands of little razor-sharp extrusions that Mark thought of as teeth, but were probably more like sharpened fingernails, for they had no meeting place where the act of "chewing" might take place.

As it shimmered in the moonlight the overall impression of its color was still black, but now with shades of opalescence running all through it, like gasoline spilled on living blacktop.

It seemed to dangle in the air before Mark allowing him to take it in. But then it slapped to the ground in the middle of the Razor Devil Claws, smashing them as it fell.

Then, like a large snail, pulling its shell behind it, the tentacle began to drag the fallen body of the Ogre back up the hill through the plants.

The Ogre, dead, did not move at all under its own power and was continually getting wrapped up and snagged on the plants, it was being dragged through the brush like a dead fish on a line.

From High up on the Burial Mound, Mark heard the chant of the Servants of Dyondaygah, begin to fill the night, as the Giants emerged from the building to look upon their fallen comrade.

The strange name echoed over the surrounding flat terrain, spreading out from the ancient burial mound like scum spreading over a pond, and Mark was certain it could be heard for miles around.

But above it all, he heard the voice of Maru screaming, "Stop your blasted chanting! He is getting away! He killed Brisco! *Get him*! Don't let him escape! He's getting away! The Enemy of Dyondaygah is getting away!"

Faster than Mark would have believed possible and with great strides from their massive legs, the Giants began to run down the hill, after him. Many of them were caught up in the Razor Devil's Claw and fell to the ground but within milliseconds, they were back on their feet, their speed renewed, in their anger.

When Mark had stood among them, the plants often came up almost to his chest, but for most of the Servants of Dyondaygah, the plants only came up to their waist or hips.

When Mark had been standing next to The Ogre, Brisco, in the bathroom, he had seemed massive, but now Mark realized Brisco had not been the tallest of Maru's acolytes. Some of them where much taller, ten or even twelve feet tall, and there must have been thirty of them coming down the hill toward him.

Mark stood there frozen, not sure what to do. He couldn't outrun one of these monsters on a good day, with both legs in peak condition. Perhaps he could not even have done it when he had been in High School. He had never been much of a runner, even then. He believed running was the last move; something to do when a plan failed. Worse still, it was admitting failure. He had always been more of a *"Stand your ground, and show no fear"* type.

But now, he couldn't run, and he didn't think he could fight. He would be lucky to be dragged back to Maru in one piece. It was likely whatever dark plan had been made ready for him at "The Conjunction", would be a picnic compared to what they would do to him now that he had killed one of their number.

He had failed.

Ally was lost, a slave to Maru and Dyondaygah, and Mark would soon be dead or worse: Insane; locked in a living nightmare.

It was over.

9

It was over....

Until the blaring of a horn, many times louder than the average, began to sound.

It sounded like the kind of horn you might expect to hear on a large eighteen wheeler or a fire engine.

Mark clapped his hands over his ears as Hap's beat up truck came screaming down the middle of the road, screeching to a halt, as dust flew out behind it.

The horn of the truck never stopped blasting, and as much as the din seemed to hurt his ears it was doing much worse to the Giants. Many of them were grabbing the sides of their heads and falling to the ground in pain.

The rusty passenger door of the truck flew open and "Happy" Howard shouted, "Don't just stand there, you dern fool! Get in!"

Before Mark had a chance to register what he was doing; before the pain in his leg had a chance to scream through every inch of his body, crippling him in unspeakable anguish; Mark was pulling himself up into the cab of the rusted out old hulk of a truck, the door closing behind him, as the force of the truck, rocketing forward, slammed it against the frame. "She'll do Zero to Sixty in Five Point Two! Hold on!" Hap shouted as he stomped the gas.

Mark doubled over in pain from his injuries and rested his head on the dashboard, as the sound of the air raid horn faded and died. Happ flipped a switch, which seemed to control the horn, "It's a good trick, but I can only do it once!"

Happ said, tapping the compressed air tank, which sat between them with his foot, causing it to give off a hollow *"tink tink tink"* sound, "Their size ain't the only thing that gets enhanced by eating the sacred food!" He explained, "All their senses are amplified a hundredfold!"

Mark wanted to respond. He wanted to ask a thousand questions.

He wanted to punch Hap in the face for letting them go to the Towen when he knew something was wrong with the place. But he couldn't bring himself to say a word, he just groaned and lay there with his head on the cold metal panel.

"I know you are hurting sonny, but there's no time for that now! We've got two on the back!" Hap shouted, both hands glued to the steering wheel.

Mark pulled himself out of the fetal position and looked back through the rear window of the cabin.

The Giants were striding close behind them. Many of them were falling behind, but a few still kept pace.

Sixty Miles an Hour, and they were keeping up with them!

Two of the giants had grabbed on to the sides of the vehicle and seemed to be trying to alternately dig their heels into the ground or climb up into the now-empty bed of the truck, but the speed and Hap's occasional swerving prevented them from doing either.

"Do you know how to shoot a shotgun?"

"Point and Click?" Mark asked.

"Kids today!" Hap said with a shake of his head, "Take that gun down off the rack and shoot those sons of bucks!"

Mark took down the single-barreled shotgun, making sure not to hit Hap in the head with the butt, and opened the back window. He pointed the gun out the window, the long tube pointed at a Female Giant on the rear passenger side.

For half a moment, he thought it might be Ally, but no, this woman was a redhead, and Ally was not.

"Fire, son!" Hap said, "It don't matter if you know them!

They ain't human anymore! Shoot 'em!"

Mark took a second to aim again and pulled the trigger. The recoil slammed into his shoulder so hard, he thought it had broken his clavicle, as it bucked him back into the dashboard.

Hap cursed, "Consardit son! Have you never seen a movie!? Hold that thing tight to your shoulder!"

"Now you remind me," Mark said mostly to himself, pain seemingly coming from all stations now.

"Get up there and do it again!" Hap shouted, "Only this time don't miss!"

"Where's the other bullets?" Mark asked aloud.

"Rack the action!" Hap said, "Good Lord, you don't know anything about guns do you?!"

"I lived in Chicago all my life, stricter gun laws!" Mark said.

"And you obeyed them?" Hap said amazed, "God in Heaven, how are you still alive!?"

Mark took hold of the wooden piece underneath the cold metal of the gun, pulled it back and pushed it forward.

He heard that beautiful music known to make the wielder bold and the target pee their pants, as simultaneously the hammer was cocked and the next shell was brought up into the chamber.

He aimed again, just as the Red Head found purchase and pulled herself up into the truck bed.

Mark felt the rear suspension bend down under her considerable girth, but this also gave him a clear target.

Holding the stock tight to his shoulder, he fired again, and this time he blew a hole through the center mass of the Giantess, and apparently whatever had lane inside her as well.

She fell straight back, over the tailgate, on to the road behind them; the two or three remaining Giants trampling over her remains in their pursuit of Mark and Hap.

"Nice shot!" Hap called out, over Mark's still ringing ears, "Hang on!"

Hap spun the wheel hard to the left and the truck left the paved road, turning off into the grassless flatland.

"We still got the other one on the left! He just passed the rear wheel well!" Hap said, "He's hanging on good! Give him what for!"

Mark racked the slide again, was about to fire when the truck went over a considerable bump in the land, slamming Mark against the ceiling.

The Giant, who was hanging onto the side lost his grip and fell off rolling under the tires, causing the truck to buck even higher than before from the rear.

"*Woo Woo*! We did it!" Hap yelled.

Mark slumped back down into his seat. "Gives a whole new meaning to riding shotgun, don't it son?!" Howard said, still excited.

"Where's the safety on this thing?" Mark asked.

"Safety on a shotgun," Hap grumbled. "City Folks."

"We need to go back." Mark said, "We need to call the police or the Military or... Something!"

"We'll go to my place and talk it over," Hap said. "We need to get that leg of yours tended to. That could go gangrenous. You need to get to the hospital."

"My wife is still in that place!" Mark said, "and she... She..." Mark drifted off and silence filled the cab as Hap drove over the unpaved hardpan.

"She ate the Calamari, didn't she?" Hap finally said.

"You know?" Mark asked, "I mean, you really know?"

"Yes. I know son. I tried to warn you, but you didn't listen." Mark was getting angry now, "Didn't listen? Didn't listen! I thought you meant it was expired, I didn't think you meant it was supernatural!"

"No such thing as the supernatural, boy." Hap explained, "If it happens in this world, it's natural, it may just be highly unusual from your Point of View."

Mark felt fury building inside of him, "Why didn't you tell us it could take over your mind, and turn you into a... a..."

"Would you have believed me?" Hap asked, not waiting for an answer, "Besides, I wasn't allowed to say any more than I did. I literally couldn't."

"How hard is it to open your mouth and tell us there's some sort of cult over there and they worship a demonic god, and he'll turn you into his Giant slaves if you eat his "Sacred food?"

The truck bumped over a ridge and back on to paved, if bumpy road, "Don't you understand yet son? The power of that ... thing under the Towen, it's not limited to the building itself. It spreads all around this place, you can even see where its power ends. You must have seen how dead everything is around here. You must have seen the ring of mushy, acidic looking plants."

Mark thought back to the blackness mixed with water that had spilled out of one of the plants he'd picked up and crushed.

"That's the line of his influence." Hap explained, "that's the furthest place his power can reach... or at least it was. Now that your wife is one of them, it will be reaching out a little further. With every person who joins the cult, the line extends a little further, and the door opens a little wider. I don't know how many it will take, but everyone we can turn away is another life saved and another day this world gets to live."

"Towen said-" Mark started, but Hap cut him off.

"The Towen talked to you?"

"Towen is Maru's last name," Mark explained. "Son I don't know what he told you, but that place was called the Towen, long before Maru and his giants showed up. Towen is an old Druidic word. It means a place of Ritual Slaughter."

Mark was taken aback by this, which brought him back to his original question, "So what do you mean you "literally" couldn't tell us?"

Hap sighed, "The thing under the Towen won't let us. It's all part of the choice. That's the way Maru explained it to me anyway. The Travelers are drawn to the Towen, and no one can be allowed to warn them of what lies beneath. They must be allowed to choose the food without warning of what it can do. If someone like me tries to tell, within the circle of influence, the words will simply not be able to be communicated. Its taken different forms. I've tried saying it and found I could not speak. I've spoken it and found the travelers could not hear me. It was either nonsense babbling to them, or I seemed to be moving my lips and they could not hear. Other times I've tried writing it down, but the ink would not flow from the pen, or the piece of paper seemed blank to the reader. Believe me, son, I've tried everything, but until someone knows, they can't be told."

"And I don't suppose Maru has let you go without being warned not to meddle," Mark said putting things together.

"That he hasn't." Howard said, "I've tried telling people not to eat up there at all because the food was no good, or it was unhealthy or poisonous. That everyone who eats there gets sick. For whatever reason, all those things... lies basically, they could be told. I could say whatever I wanted. I could tell about the history of the place, so much as I knew, and what happened before Maru came and turned the old Carter Place into a restaurant, but I can't say a word about anything that's happened up there since the coming of that little Munchkin and his demon god."

"How did you know to come?" Mark asked. "I doubt you could see it from where you were in the Towen, but I could see that A-rab-Boriolus thing I told you about from my house. It hovers over the place whenever the Towen is taking on a new convert, or when they are about to have one of their "Conjunctions". I didn't know if either of you was the convert, or if someone else had come along. But something told me tonight would be different. No one has ever made it off of the Towen alive before today… At least not anyone who lived very long…"

"But what about-"

"No more for now." Hap said, putting an end to the conversation, "We can talk more freely once we get to my house. The Giants can't come there and the circle of influence hasn't reached it yet, at least I don't think so… It hadn't before tonight. Besides, I have some things you should see that will help you to understand better than just talking about it could ever do."

10

A little less than an hour later, Mark sat on the toilet in Hap's bathroom.

His blood-stained pants had been removed and his left boxer shorts leg was hiked up nearly to his pelvis. The wound in his leg had been cleaned, doused with rubbing alcohol and then peroxide.

Fortunately, his jeans had indeed blocked the majority of the impact from the knife, and while the wound did cut deep into the skin, it hardly went much deeper than that.

"Might have nicked the muscle a little bit," said Hap, "But nothing that won't heal on its own. Going to need a lot of stitches though."

"Can you do it?" Mark had asked.

"Of course I can, I was a field medic in the war."

"Which war?"

"Does it matter?" Hap asked, "Problem is I don't have any medical thread in the house. Have to use some of Mother's nylon upholstery thread, I think. Don't have any liquid bandage in the house neither. The best I can do is some crazy glue. But we really should be taking you to a hospital."

"I don't have time to sit in the E.R." Mark said, "I need to get what information you can tell me, and then get back to the Buffet, and get Ally out of there."

"You want me to tell him Pa?" said Aaron, bringing his father the thread and glue.

Hap smiled at his son, "No Boy, your time for such work will come, but I think its best you go outside and keep a watch. With Mrs. Thurston as part of the cult now there's no telling how far the circle of influence may have spread. It could be just a few feet, it could be nearly half a mile. I want you out on the porch with the rifle. If you see one of the Big People coming, you know what to do."

"Yes, Pa," Aaron said, turning to a glass-fronted gun cabinet and taking out a rifle with a scope on it. He and his father exchanged a meaningful look and then Aaron left the room to man his post.

Hap came back with the supplies and a curved needle. He threaded the needle and dumped some rubbing alcohol into the white cap of a deodorant spray bottle and dropped the needle in it, to sterilize.

He walked back out of the bathroom and came back with two short glasses and a bottle of Whiskey.

"You're going to want some of this." Hap said, "I don't have any anesthetic to numb the pain. This will have to serve."

Mark looked at the bottle, "I don't drink."

"Maybe now is a good time to start." Hap said pouring some into the glasses, "Besides, it's going to taste better than the truth."

He handed Mark his glass, clinked his own against it, and tossed it back.

Mark sipped at the golden liquid and had to resist the urge to spit it right back out. It burned and was nasty, like drinking straight Peroxide.

"Don't sip." Hap said, "Take it down quick, that way it only burns your stomach and not your throat."

He took the bottle, and dumped some of the noxious liquid on Mark's leg, causing Mark's vision to blur as his eyes crossed involuntarily, and he had to stifle a scream, into a pained hum.

"Drink it down," Hap said pulling up a chair. Mark obeyed, doing it right this time, and quickly noticed that it really did help. It still burned, but at the very least the burn in his throat took some of the edge of the pain in his leg as Hap began to stitch.

"Your son seems pretty accustomed to all of this," Mark said, through barely clenched teeth.

"Yep." Said Hap, "He's a good boy. Takes after his mother."

"I suppose all this is the reason why she left?" Mark asked.

Hap hesitated, looking at the floor but not seeing it, "Yeah." He said simply, "A few other people know about what's going on around here. Mostly they figure if they keep themselves to themselves, it won't touch them. But they're wrong. Sooner or later this is going to affect everyone unless we find a way to put a stop to it. Vestal, she just couldn't take anymore."

He set back to his work, cutting a suture with a pair of short scissors, and starting in on the next, making Mark wince and take another swig from the glass, "Saw too many people go up into the Towen and never come down again. Then some people would come back out completely untouched. Police officers even eat there from time to time…"

"It's like they don't even see the Calamari." Mark quoted, "Maru said something similar."

"Yeah." Howard said, taking the needle and dunking it in the sterilizer again, "And like I said we can't tell them, no matter how hard we try. Cars come and go up there. We don't know where they come from, or where they go. Mostly I think their leftovers from the people who've been taken. But none of them seem to run. I think the giants push them around to make it look good. Don't know why the cops don't run the plates, I'm sure they'd come up as belonging to missing persons. Must be all part of the magic."

"Magic." Mark said, incredulously, "First you say there's no such thing as the supernatural, and then you say magic? Make up your mind."

"Anything we don't understand and can't explain, we just call magic around here. It's shorthand. It's like, when you don't know what an object is, you call it a thing. You know there's an explanation to it, and its all part of the natural order somehow. But try explaining how a cell phone works to most people and before you are half done their eyes will glaze over. All they care about is, *"I push the button, and speak into the magic talky box."* Heck, most phones don't even have buttons as such anymore."

"Point taken." Mark said, "So you were going to tell me more about the Buffet and what it is."

Hap sighed inwardly, "You aren't going to like it son, so I'll give it to you straight. Your wife is dead, and maybe something worse. Her body is still walking around, bigger and stronger than ever, but her mind, and maybe even her soul, are gone. Leastways they will be soon if they ain't already."

"I can't believe that." Mark said, "Maybe those other things, but not Ally. Not yet."

"Back in 1889," Hap said as though Mark had never interrupted, "A man named Carter came to this area. John Carter, like the Edgar Rice Burroughs character. He wanted to build the biggest, grandest mansion in these parts. He bought up every parcel of land for about 10 miles. Thought he was going to make something out of this place, maybe a new town or a resort or something. I don't know. The Indians that used to be around here had mostly been driven off by then, but the few that remained warned Carter not to build on that hill. They told him it was a burial mound.

'Now as I understand it, Burial mounds are not all that common around here. Mostly the Indians in this part of the country used pits, mass graves to bury their dead. But this mound, the Indians said, was not built by a local tribe. This mound was built by Indians from Ohio and Appalachia, nearly a thousand miles away, possibly the Seneca or Cayuga.

'The Indians told a story about a race of Giants, men they called the "Allegewi." The story goes that these men were the last of a tribe that had been nearly wiped out in the East, by the same Indians who now pursued them. They were originally found in the mountains and valleys near what is now considered Pittsburgh. They were a race of giants."

"Giants," Mark said, not missing the significance.

"Yes." Hap continued, "The bodies of the Allegewi, (some have even translated it as "Tall-agalway",) were found in burial mounds much like the one on which the Towen now sits, all over that region in the 1920s through the 1940s. They were a big people, eight to ten feet in height, maybe taller, long thought to be a legend. But the Indians in these parts knew there was more to the legend than stories to frighten children. They told Carter, that the mound was built to bury, not only the remnants of the last of the Allegewi but a structure they had built for their strange god."

"Dyon-" Mark started, but Hap involuntarily yanked hard on the needle, and put up a hand to stop him.

"Don't say that name!" Hap said emphatically.

"Right," Mark said, once again through clenched teeth. Hap went back to his work, "I'm sorry. I didn't mean to do that. But you must understand by now, he's not only real, but he's close and the last thing I need is for his attention to be drawn this way. I've already put my family in danger by helping you. If you have to reference him, just day the letter "D", and I'll know what you mean."

"Got it. Sorry." Mark said, "Go on."

"The Ohio Indians had chased the Allegewi after they had gone to war with them in Pittsburgh." Hap continued, "I've done some research into it and as near as I can tell The Ohioans originally just wanted to pass through the land of the Allegewi, and they left them alone. But then something happened, no one is quite sure what. It may have been that there were too many of the Ohio Indians, and it spooked them. It may have been that the Ohios witnessed a forbidden Allegewi ritual. But knowing what I do, I suspect their demon god called to some of the Ohioans the way he called to your wife. The Ohios saw what their people were becoming and realized the Allegewi were an abomination before the Great Spirit. They went to war with them and won. The Seneca claimed the area, and named it and the river after the people they had defeated, in memory of the victory. The name was bastardized somewhat over the years. We would know it as "The Alleghany River."

Mark knew very little about Pittsburgh, having never traveled much further east than Columbus Ohio, but he knew that the Alleghany came together with another river and formed the Ohio right in the heart of the city.

He knew this because of an old Disney movie he had once seen about *"Davy Crockett and the River Pirates"* where the legendary outdoorsman had met up with *"Mike Fink: King of the River."* As far as he knew the story was entirely fictional, but it was his only source of knowledge about the city.

"So they weren't satisfied with merely running them off," Mark said as Hap cut another piece of thread, "They wanted to exterminate them."

"Wouldn't you?" asked Hap, "Knowing what you know now? If they built altars to Dy-... to their god there, isn't it likely they'd try to do the same again?"

"And that's what the Towen is." Mark put together.

"And that's what the Towen is." Hap repeated, nodding, "The Allegewi had enough time to build an altar here before the Ohioans could find them. I don't know if the doorway to their god was something that was already here and they built the altar around it, or if they made the door by building the altar. But one way or another, the Allegewi opened it and began performing ceremonies here.

'The Ohioans found them, killed the last of them, and buried the structure they had built, a structure of massive stones. Primarily Sandstone, Quartz and Igneous Rock. Built in a circle."

Hap looked at Mark meaningfully, waiting to see if he could put it together. Mark looked back, pondering, "Stonehenge?"

"Stonehenge." Hap replied in the affirmative, "I don't know if they are exactly related, per se, but I do know that structures like that have been found all over the United States and other places in the world. Structures created by civilizations that shouldn't have had the technology to move massive rocks like that. Let alone the power to do it by hand, and yet there they are, a thousand years or more later, and you can still see them today. Maybe those other places are like the Towen, only they didn't take. The door stayed closed. But here in this place, the door actually opened."

"And Carter knew all this and built on it anyway?" Mark asked.

Hap nodded, he did more than build on it, he used it for the foundation of his house. Have you noticed how the house is mostly oblong and rounded, even though it was built in a Tudor style? Tudor is very boxy most of the time. There are exceptions to every rule, but the Tudors, they are mostly boxes, built on top of and to the sides of other boxes, except for the roofs, but the Towen on Carter's Hill, it follows no rules."

Hap brought out the tube of crazy glue and ran a bead down the length of Mark's cut and then gently spread it with his finger.

Mark felt the slight tingle of heat as the glue fused his skin back together.

"Reckon that will hold," Hap said, running hot water from the sink over his fingers and wiping them on a cloth towel. He stepped outside the room for a moment and then came back with a pair of old, worn Overalls.

"Here you go, these ought to fit you." He said handing Mark the overalls, "You and Aaron are about the same size. Put them on and bring the bottle out to the table. I have something I want to show you. Aaron said you can have them, by the way. He just got a new pair last week. I doubt you could fit into the clothes of a fat old man like me... They'd be falling off of you."

"They wouldn't be falling off of Ally," Mark thought darkly, "Not anymore."

What was happening to her while he sat here talking to this old man, and drinking Whiskey? Every moment that passed by was another moment on the ticking clock. Another moment less to save his wife. Another moment for that tentacle thing he'd seen sprout out of Brisco The Ogre to form and attach itself to her, bonding with her, perhaps growing as she grew.

The longer it was in her, the more attached it might become, a symbiotic parasite feeding off her even as it made her stronger, robbing her of her free will making her less and less human.

God, what if she was already…

No! NO!

He would not allow himself to think that way. There must be away.

Please! Please let there be away!

Mark put on the overalls which were a little snug in the seat, but not uncomfortably so, picked up his glass and the bottle and walked over to the table.

"Here," said Hap, "Take two of these, they'll help with the pain."

"Drugs with Alcohol?" Mark asked, "Is that such a good idea."

"Under normal circumstances, I'd say no, but there's nothing normal about tonight. And since you won't go to the hospital, I want to do what I can for you before I send you back in among the wolves to die."

Mark blinked, taken aback by what Hap had said.

"I could take you up the road back to the Highway, put you at your car." Hap explained, "You could drive on home to Chicago, and move out to your new job in LA and hardly have to tell a soul about your wife. If her mother and father call, you could tell them you had a fight and she ran away. Who knows what happened to her after that? She might have run off and changed her name. She might have gotten drunk and died in a ditch somewhere. People go missing all the time in this country, most are never found. There might be an investigation, but pick a good story, not involving this place, mind. Stick to it, and they wouldn't be able to pin anything on you. You could go on with your life, maybe remarry and have those kids you've been wanting but that she was always too selfish to give you. You could do all that… But I know you won't. It's not in your nature. Knew that from the moment the two of you walked into my grocery store. Somehow you two really are still in love of one another, after being married… what? Five years?"

"Seven," Mark said, taking a deep breath, "Seven next March."

Hap nodded, "Even if I drove through town at 90 miles an hour, determined not to let you go back to the Towen, you'd jump out of the truck, bad leg and all, and go charging up through the Devil's Claw to break into that place and try to save Ally. No holds barred. Balls to the wall."

Mark fell into the chair next to the table, where Hap sat and wept.

He wept like a child.

Sobs racked his body and he put his head in his hands, rocking back and forth.

It's been said that *"Weakness is hard, but strength is exhausting."*

From the moment the car had broken down, the tire, ripped to shreds, Mark had been holding in his emotions as best he could. He couldn't curse and swear at the tire like he wanted to because he knew that would only escalate things between him and Ally, even if his frustration was not directed at her.

When the changes had begun and Ally was frightened out of her wits, Mark, just as scared, had hidden it as best he could; trying to be the rock she needed in the turbulence.

Even when she'd thrown him across the room, twice, he knew this was not her, so even if he had been capable, he could not have defended himself at the risk of hurting her. His escape and everything that had followed was all about being there for Ally, holding in his terror at the inexplicable nightmares he had seen.

He knew he had to be strong. He had to make it through, for her.

And now, with the prospect of leaving her behind set before him, he saw in his mind, the black void his life would be without her.

Even if every word Hap had said came true, exactly as he said it, and Mark could go on to live a successful and fulfilling life, it would still be a life without her.

And that was no life at all.

And with that realization, he'd had no strength left.

It would have been better to have stayed in that chair in the kitchen of the Buffet. Let Maru and his horde take him down below the house, and have their way.

Sacrifice him. Bleed him dry. Burn him at the stake. Cut the living heart from his chest.

Anything would be better than living the rest of his life knowing he had left Ally behind to this strange living death; a meat puppet on the strings of a loveless demonic god.

Mark felt an arm reach across his back, and Hap's voice came from less than an inch away, "That's it, son. Let it out. Just let it go, there's no shame in it."

After a while, Mark was able to regain some of his composure and Hap returned to his seat, "You are going to go back," Hap said matter-of-factly, "But you need to have a plan before you do, and in order to do that, you need to be informed about what you are up against."

Hap pulled a small leather-bound book to the center of the table.

"This," Said Hap, "is the Arcane Diary of John Carter, of The Towen."

11

Hap flipped through the book, "There isn't time for you to read the whole thing right now, but in this, Carter tells of how he came to this place and chose the location of the Towen. He was warned by a few of the locals that even the Indians had avoided that knoll and believed it to be cursed. But when he uncovered the tops of the loadstones, *Sarsens* he calls them, he was determined to use them as the foundation of the house."

Hap showed him a couple of designs that had been sketched into the book, outlining the pattern of the Sarsens and the best ones to use for a foundation, "Carter noted the similarities between Stonehenge and the circle the Allegewi had left behind, so he started looking into Celtic myth, as well as what little lore there was left of the Allegewi. They lined up on several points, including the fact that the Druids, like the Allegewi, used their circles for ritual slaughter of both men and beasts. So he called the house the Towen very early on, not knowing how true his naming of the place would be."

Hap landed on a page traced with a myriad of symbols that looked somewhat familiar to Mark, "Some of these symbols he got from Celtic Lore and others he took from markings on trees that were found nearby, and the exposed tops of the Sarsens. From what I can tell this area was well populated with trees, more so than much of Kansas. It was very fertile, which is part of what drew Carter to it. He felt certain that within a few years of tilling the soil, he would have this land made into one of the great farms of the West. He planned to carve-"

"Those symbols are all over the Buffet." Mark interrupted. "In the main dining area, the bathrooms, the hallways; practically every place there is a joint in the wood, there's one of these."

Hap nodded solemnly, "That's what it says here... To him it as all a sort of joke or, at best, a tribute. He didn't believe in the power of the things he played with. It was the mystical equivalent of a child playing with his father's gun. Still, all might have been alright, except for something that happened while the house was being built."

Hap began to read:

July 27, 1889.

The life of a young man was lost today. Eric McConnell, an Irish Roman Catholic. He was murdered by William McGinty, a Mormon. There seems to have been some antagonism between the two men for some time, both on count of their opposing religions, and some matter of a card game the night before.

By all accounts, McGinty, (a fastidious craftsman, specializing in decorative wood carving, and a very large brutish man,) attacked Eric as he crossed the construction site, approximately where the main concourse will be, when the house is completed.

McGinty struck Eric with a large beam of wood. He then proceeded to stab him repeatedly with a large wood engraving tool. Witnesses said the attack was entirely unprovoked.

McGinty had been working on one of the main beams, already placed. He was carving one of the many decorations I have instructed to be placed around the building, when he stood up, turned and walked across the twelve support beams, to the center of the Sarsens, which will eventually form the hub of the main concourse, and there McGinty proceeded to bleed the very life from Eric.

Eric was dead before anyone could reach them.

His blood fell to the ground below and was soaked up by the earth so quickly that there was not a trace of it left by the time Eric was picked up and placed on a board to take him to the coroner, in Dubuque.

McGinty had to be dragged away from the corpse by five strong men. When the man came to his senses, he claimed to have no memory of attacking Eric.

He remembers being angry at him the night before, but claims to have "put all such trivial things aside."

McGinty claims the last thing he remembers was going about his work, carving the symbols, and the next thing he knew he was in handcuffs, tied to a post in the police wagon."

Hap withdrew an old scrap of paper from the book, "Clipping from the newspaper on the next day. Says McConnell had no family to speak of, no wife, and no children, having come from Ireland after the death of his Sainted Mother."

Hap passed the piece of paper over carefully so Mark could look at it.

"So?" Mark asked after a moment's examination.

"So?" Hap returned the word as if the answers were obvious, "A young man is murdered on a place of ancient slaughter, by a man who moments before was carving ancient symbols on wood, wood that had been growing on that land, and that boy's blood stains the ground and just *disappears*?"

"Maybe the ground was just dry, and the blood…" Mark started, and then the gears kicked into place, "There would still have been red on the ground, even if it was dried up, the blood would have been there, and visible."

"Right." Said Hap, "But he says there was not even a trace. What's more, Eric was an Irish Roman Catholic and unmarried, a true follower of his faith, with no wife or children."

Mark waited for the punch line.

Hap shook his head, "I know in this modern era, especially since the 1960s such things aren't thought of much, but we are dealing with powers far older than you can imagine. It used to be that such things as the consummation of marriage were a very important thing, taken very seriously. And few good Irish Roman Catholic boys dared violate that sacred rite."

"*Consummation*," Mark said, mulling over the word,

looking for meaning in it.

"Dad-rat-it, son! He was a Virgin. A virgin sacrifice on a Pagan altar. Murdered by a man who had been carving ancient symbols."

"So you're saying the symbols made him do it? That somehow, carving those symbols gave Dy-... The demon god power over him, and made him sacrifice McConnel?"

Hap looked at him seriously, "Son, if it's going to take you this long to piece things together in your head, we are in a heap of trouble. Don't you ever challenge your mind at all?"

"I'm a child of the Movies," Mark said, seriously, "I'm used to having everything explained to me, Pointe Blank, in an hour and a half. Puzzle-solving is not exactly my forte."

"Well if you've gone through all your life with ears closed and mind asleep, wake up now. Your wife's life and a good deal many more may just depend on it."

Mark rubbed his forehead in deep thought, "So you are saying that this guy's death may have opened the doorway to this... *Thing.*"

"I'm saying it got his attention." Hap explained, "Most likely whatever is there has always been there. There are thin spots between this world and others, as well as between this space and other places in our universe. According to some theories of Quantum entanglement, all spaces are the same space."

"Wait." Asked Mark putting up a hand, "How do you know about Quantum Physics?"

"I'm an old man," Said Hap, "When I'm not warning people off that place, I spend a lot of time watching PBS and the History Channel. The point is, that this boy, being killed in a thin spot, got the attention of something and probably wore the thin spot thinner. The Indians buried that circle for a reason. Placing a house on top of it was asking for trouble, spilling the blood of an innocent on it was like going up to a man's back porch and ringing his doorbell."

"So, what else is in that Journal?"

"Not much else, until after the house was finished." Hap said, taking up the book again and flipping pages, "He moved in with his wife in October of 1889, just after the harvest."

"Halloween," Mark said, looking off to one side.

"The very day. But nothing happened that night. These things don't move by our calendar, son. They do their own thing. They have more to do with the deep stars and perhaps the moon than they do with our petty rotation around the sun. Our star is but one of millions."

"The time is not yet right. There are many hours before the Waxing Gibbous Moon will be in position, as the Stars grow right for the coming of Dyondaygah."

Mark shuddered, remembering those words from the mouth of Brisco the Ogre. Now there was very little time.

Night had only just fallen when The Ogre had spoken those words at about 7 o'clock, and now it was almost midnight.

Who knew how much time was left?

Only that the moon would still be in the sky when the time was right, and all the while, "the sacred food" was changing Ally.

"John Carter lived in that house for nearly two years before something of real significance happened." Hap continued, aware Mark was in deep thought, but seeking to pull him back to the history at hand, "One thing significant was that the land almost immediately began to fail. What had been lush, verdant grassland quickly became fallow. The Stream that used to flow through here, just a little ways behind where my shop is now, dried up, and all the pretty flowers Mrs. Carter tried to plant around the Towen began to shrivel up and die. But that's not altogether strange even in the most natural of places. Weather patterns change, water finds a new path. While it was certainly upsetting to John, I'm sure he didn't see anything unnatural in it."

Hap read from the book once more:

"May 2, 1891:

Bad Luck continues. We lost three servants today as they continue to claim that some strange force has invaded the house. Anna has claimed that she hears rats in the walls, and something scrabbling at the foot of her bed nearly every night.

Yet we've seen no evidence of rats or any other vermin.

She has taken her leave saying that she can not sleep nor take any comfort at all when there are rats about.

Meanwhile, another servant, Maggie, has claimed that she found herself in a room of the house she didn't recognize. She has been with us almost since the day we opened the house, and yet she claims this room was located between the third and fourth guest bedroom.

Naturally, there is no room, nor even a closet there.

But the truly strange thing was what she claimed to see inside it: A large dark stone room, fully as big as the main hall, with torches of flame around the walls; flames that gave no heat, nor did they seem to need fuel.

Her description put me in mind of the Electrical lights I saw a demonstration of in New York a few years back, but according to her they burned very bright, and of course, we have no source of electrical power within the house.

Maggie said within the room was a man, tied to a metal stake, as he would be burned, and he pleaded with her to cut him loose before someone came.

The poor child was terrified and slammed the door of the mercurial room shut and ran out of the house.

One of the servants was able to coax the story out of her, but she has sworn an oath to ever reenter this house.

A Third servant, Marshall, was on his way to the house this evening when he claims he saw strange lights above the Towen; much like what explorers have claimed to see when they travel to the far reaches of the Arctic, but primarily of a deep scarlet, green and purple hue.

He also has refused to reenter the house.

If this continues I shall have no one working for me before long, and this house will be in shambles."

Hap skipped forward to a previously marked place in the book. "Things just got weirder and weirder there but I've already told most of that to you when we spoke this afternoon. Ultimately, John was driven nearly mad by the strange goings-on around the Towen. But it was the symbol in the middle of the Main Hall that finally drove him to do what he ought never to have done. Dig up the Sarsens beneath the house."

"I thought you said the house was built on the Sarsens. Wouldn't he be undermining the foundation?"

"Not unless he removed the stones themselves, but he didn't, he couldn't. Not only was the house now sitting on them, but they go down very deep into the earth. He only exposed the top fifteen feet or so."

"Maru mentioned that there was a basement, said it was where the meeting hall or convention space was."

"It's a convention alright." Said Hap, all year long, twenty-four-seven, those… They never stop chanting the name of their god. But I'm getting ahead of myself. The symbol on the ceiling, did you see this?"

Hap held out the book toward him and showed the symbol that Ally had identified as Yggdrasil.

"The world tree from Norse myth." Mark explained, "Ally saw it and told me about it, something to do with *"The Tree of the Universe connecting the Nine Realms and Thor, the god of Thunder."*

"That ain't no tree son. That's him. His symbol anyway. That wasn't carved into the wood by any craftsman. It was burned there."

"Burned?" Mark asked.

In lieu of an answer, Hap turned to the book again:

"The spot on the ceiling of the main hall has grown larger. We have tried painting over it, but no paint will stick to it. It has also begun to create a starburst pattern. The marking has

appeared in the direct center of the hub, where the twelve pillars meet. I know it was twelve pillars I had designed, but now and then I see eleven, and I know I am not mad, for others have noted it as well."

"The next day:" Hap said, continuing to read, but turning the page,

"The mark is forming a design. Some unseen hand is doing this, and it is happening even as we look on.

The wood smolders and is hot to the touch, and now more markings begin to form around it. It seems to me to be the symbol of some great beast. The Name I hear in my dreams at night?

I've seen what the symbol will be when it is completed: The many arms of that great being, reaching out to join the earth and sky under his dominion."

"Then he's written this word over and over again. Which I won't even try to pronounce."

Hap said, pointing to the word in the book, written repeatedly, down to the very bottom of the page,

"*Fhatgn, Fhatgn, Fhatgn.*"

"I've looked that word up on the internet and as near as I can figure, its some ancient dialect, possibly Babylonian or Druidic, that means *waiting*, or *to wait while dreaming*."

Then Hap took the book back and flipped forward a page or two,

"*He calls to me now even in my waking mind.*"

Hap read: "*His symbol is complete, claiming the house which I have built with my own two hands as his own!*

I would give it over to him freely if only I could leave it. But I cannot.

He beckons me.

He orders me.

He commands me.

I beg only that once I have done what he asks I will be allowed to leave. Leave and never return.

The Stones.

The Stones must be uncovered.
The Doorway unearthed.
The Nexus reborn.
The Confluence!
The Confluence!
It shall be done as you command!
Please!
Let me rest!
Let me sleep and on the morrow, the work shall begin. This I swear! This I-"

Hap stopped reading, "Then it dissolves into that word over and over again, but this time a second was added."

He turned the book around so that Mark could see:

Fhatgn Dyondaygah! Fhatgn Dyondaygah!

The words were scrawled over the page repeatedly, becoming more and more of a mess, until it reached the bottom of the page.

Mark put the book down on the table. "How do you have this?" he asked.

"Twenty years ago, they were emptying out the building." Hap explained, "They were selling everything that they could at the time. There were all kinds of rare antiques; it was quite the to-do. The house had been empty for some years at that time, but the Carter estate had kept the house and everything in it in good order until about the year 1985 when the money finally ran out, and the place was sold. It had passed through a few hands, but no one ever really lived in it... at least not for long. The longest I ever heard of anyone staying in the Towen, before Maru, was a year and a half.

Hap got up from his chair and began to make himself a fresh cup of tea, "Twenty years ago, the current owner wanted to unload the building but couldn't, and somehow a whole load of taxes had come due when he purchased it. Taxes cost almost as much as the property if not more, from the way I understand it. So the owner was selling off everything from inside that he could, including the books. While there were a few first editions that Carter and others had collected through the years, and left behind, there wasn't all that much of value. The owner fished out all the really good ones; hired a man who knows about that sort of thing, I'm sure. Then they put everything else in five boxes and put the lot up for sale."

Hap walked over to a closed-door across from the table and opened it so that Mark could see inside.

When Hap turned on the light Mark could see that the next room was positively filled with books, of all sizes and colors.

"My father was still alive at the time and he bought the whole lot, for $500. He was quite the bibliophile, my father. Treasured nearly every book he ever got, I dare say. Never got rid of one, unless he already had a better copy, and even those he'd take to a used book store, more often than not, unless a book was severely damaged. Found this and a few others like it among them. Journals and ledgers mostly, still wouldn't throw them away. Always said they might come in useful somehow."

"So John Carter dug up the basement," Mark said, getting back to the history.

Hap walked back to the table, "Yeah, the very next day he sent a servant out with a telegram asking for workers. Within a week they had begun to excavate. They dug out a path into the space beneath the house from the back yard and dug out the dirt from around the stones, under the main hall. Built a staircase down into it and enclosed it, made it a new part of the house. They fortified the spaces between the stones with cement, so the dirt wasn't coming loose and pouring inside. They made sure not to damage the actual monument itself."

Hap found the correct page:

"The walls beneath the hall must be made secure, but all he requires is that the inward parts of the stones, facing the altar, must be exposed.

I would tear down the whole house if I thought it would bring an end to my misery, but he has told me that even if I were to end my life before his work is done, I should have no rest in the next world.

I must uncover the altar, I must make his ingress clear."

"Then he drew these symbols on the next page. Some of them were not known to any language and mostly they seem to represent things, rather than words. Most of them look like creatures of Native American lore, the Weindego, the Apotamkin, The Horned Serpent, The Rainbow Crow, Skin-Walkers, a gryphon like creature called the Piasa, the Miniwashitu. But then there were others, things that seem to have no basis in Indian lore, far older and far stranger: A man-shaped creature with massive batwings and long ropey hair dangling down from its face, a multi-eyed goat, with hundreds of smaller goats, below her, but all connected to it as well. Large blobs covered with eyes, with feelers spreading out from them. They are Great Old Ones, elder gods from before the dawn of time, cast out and weakened by the creation of our world, and time, but always waiting on the edge of eternity, looking for a way back in. But in the midst of all this lay the great emblem of the demon god. The exact match of the mark that now lay on the ceiling of the great hall."

"It's still there," Mark said thinking back. "They painted the room maroon, and the beams black. They put down maroon carpet as well, but the mark is still there on the ceiling, plain as day."

"I had no doubt it would be." Hap said, "The link has only grown stronger in the years since. Maru has shaved the thin spot down to a little more than a hair's width. Soon, the Nexus will open completely. The Confluence of dimensions will be complete."

"And what happens then?" Mark asked.

Hap looked at him, "What always happens when an apex predator enters a new feeding ground?"

"No." Mark said simply, "That isn't his game."

"What do you mean son?" Hap asked confused. "The Big People... The Giants up there at the Towen. They were going to sacrifice me to him... to It. They didn't talk about it eating me. They said It would want me alive, that it wanted to break me."

"Some animals prefer their pray alive." Hap explained, "Raw and wriggling. They say lobsters don't taste the same if you kill them before you throw them in the pot. Even if you kill them just a few seconds before they are cooked. Their fear and pain flavors the meat."

"Still." Mark said, "I don't think this is how he works. Maybe he wants all those who are not under his thrall to be insane, but he wants servants, more than he wants food."

"Son," said Hap, "I wasn't going to tell you this until later, but the truth of the matter is these things have no interest in mankind at all. We are too insignificant to them. These beings, they are cosmic. We are like ants to them. Or at the very most beasts of burden or for food."

"And yet we keep ants in farms in our houses," Mark said distantly, "and use certain types of ants for a number of projects. Ants are not without their uses, even to gods." Mark said looking at the floor and then the ceiling, "What if this one has noticed us. What if he has a use for us? He must otherwise he wouldn't be creating the Giants and drawing the Frog-men to him if he didn't have a use for them. Brisco said that Ally would eat of... of Him... and in turn, she would be his sustenance."

A strange look came over Hap's face.

"You've thought of something haven't you?" Mark asked.

"Not thought of it, but understood it better. You might say."

Hap stood up and walked into the library. Moments later he emerged with a book. He flipped pages until he found the one he wanted, then pointed to a passage:

"His flakes poison the water. His coming fallows the land. His soldiers grow tall and strong on the food from his hand. He is the food of his people and his people are his Nourishment."

"This is talking about our adversary." Hap said, "It's believed to be one of only a few bits of writing from the time of the Allegewi. Not written by them, but about them."

"Its bunk." Said Mark, looking it over. "Look at this. It rhymes. What are the odds something from 10,000-year-old Native American tablets would rhyme in modern English? And correct me if I'm wrong, but Native Americans didn't have a written language, they used pictograms mostly. I highly doubt they were worried about pentameter."

"Yes." Hap said, "The same thing I thought, but what if the person who translated it took some liberties, what if they changed words to suit their rhyming scheme, and mistranslated it? What if that line should read *"The Food 'of' his hand,* not *"from"* his hand."

"You have partaken of the body of Dyondaygah. The Sacred food." Mark quoted. "I thought it was hyperbole. Like saying *"you ate my food, from my table."* But what if…"

"Where does he get it?" Asked Hap, "Where does Maru get the Calamari? The Calamari he has fresh every day. We are landlocked, more than 500 miles to the ocean, in any direction. And yet Maru has fresh Calamari every day."

"It's actually *him*." Mark said, "The Calamari is the actual body of the demon god. His symbol. Many of the symbols, they look like things with tentacles, and the thing I saw come out of Brisco… He was dead, but it was still alive. Could they be eating part of this demon? Wouldn't that hurt it?"

"Does cutting off a toenail or your hair, hurt you? Especially if it's done right?" Hap asked, knowing the answer, "At least part of this Monster is an Octopus, or Squid like creature, at least that's how he's manifesting in our world."

"What do you mean?" asked Mark, "A thing is what it is."

"You are thinking in human terms; in terms of the physical world, things we think we understand." Hap explained, "These creatures… Some of them at least… They are more spiritual than physical. They can manifest in whatever physical form they choose. Sometimes they pick something close to their nature, other times they choose forms for the purpose of deception."

"Or so they can feed," Mark added pointedly, recalling Hap's earlier comment.

"Yes," Hap said, a trace of fear in his eyes, "They are something much more than a body, and even if you somehow hurt that body, you wouldn't really be hurting *it*. So by cutting off a piece of it, and feeding it to an unknowing human, it is still somehow part of the whole. It may be acting independently, but still slaved to the mind and will of the real monster."

"But how... The Calamari was cooked... It was deep-fried. How could there still be any life in it?"

"There's still life and energy in any food you eat, especially anything that comes from the earth; wheat, grains, oats, pigs, cows. If there wasn't still some energy in them they wouldn't be of any use to you. You can bake the bread, but that doesn't mean the flour doesn't have nutritional value, that's life of a sort. Your body processes that energy, and uses it to fuel itself."

Hap continued, "What if, in some way, the body of the monster, never really dies. What if even when it's cooked and made into food, there is still life, still consciousness in it? If the food is eaten by an unknowing person, it can begin to grow, begin to become part of that person. It changes them, accelerates their metabolism; makes them strong. It turns them into a red hot engine of vitality and power, and they do not die."

"Ally's skin was burning hot." Mark said remembering, "She's always been so cold-blooded, but she felt terribly fevered. All of them were, come to think of it. When they came into the room the temperature went up considerably. I thought it was just my terror, but now that I think about it, it did get warm in there. But... But how would the Monster be able to take sustenance from them without eating them?"

"Tesla had a theory that energy, electricity, could be transmitted over great distances, through the air, without wires. He almost made it happen too. He might have done it, if J.P. Morgan hadn't pulled his funding after Westinghouse sold out. The energy would have been accessible to anyone, for free. All you would have to do is add a special wire to receive the energy, to pull it out of the air. And if Quantum Physics teaches us anything, its that energy and matter can travel from one place to another by what seems to us to be an indirect route. If energy can travel through space, why not dimensions?"

"Wouldn't modifying a human like that eventually kill it?" Mark said thinking aloud, "When a person takes growth hormones and steroids and testosterone supplements it causes all manner of problems, it can lead to cancer or brain aneurisms, heart defects, major deformities."

His heart sank when he thought about what he had just said in connection with Ally. Even if he was able to save her somehow, to get that thing out of her, how long would she live?

Would it be worth the risk, especially if she was going to die anyway?

Would it be a life worth living as a hideous ten-foot-tall monstrosity?

"Did any of the Big People seem deformed to you?" Hap asked, "Other than their size and power, their Gigantism, did they seem malformed in any way?"

Mark thought about it. He thought about the Ogre, Brisco in particular. While he had been massive with a particularly ugly face, he might have always been ugly. Some of the Males had looked quite handsome, the females quite beautiful.

"No." Mark said, "Not now that I think of it."

"We are dealing with something from beyond our world. A Creature of Superhuman ability that must be over 10,000 years old at the least, but is almost definitely far older than we can even express in Eons. The problems you described are what happens when humans dump foreign chemicals into their bodies to force change; or when something goes wrong in a person's body; signals getting crossed. This creature is working from within. Rewriting signals and causing the body to do exactly what the Creature wants, using the body's natural chemicals and hormones; rewriting DNA for all we know, with all the precision of a master computer programmer. To him the human body might be as simple as a child's chemistry set would be to a Chemist with fourteen PHDs."

Mark thought about what they had just put together, "But if Maru is..." Mark swallowed hard, thinking about how close he had come to ingesting part of an Alien being, when Ally had snatched the Calamari away from him, only to plop it into her own mouth, "If Maru is serving parts of this thing, it must have a physical body, and parts of that physical body must be making its way here... Into our world... Is it possible, its not some sort of trans-dimensional creature, but something that is here, now, living underneath that building?"

"No son, he's not there, leastways, not in the way you are thinking. Not trapped in a chamber under the earth. He's somewhere else. Somewhere linked to this world by the Sarsens."

"Then how is Maru getting the sacred food... The Body of this monster. If it was able to get an arm... A tentacle- through, why wouldn't he be able to draw the rest of himself into this world?"

"To answer that," said Hap, "We'll need to go back to the journal."

"The chamber is opened. The Path made clear." Hap read from the journal.

"*The Night of the Waxing Gibbous Moon approaches. I feel it more powerfully than ever before. The draw of D-----. This house is now his in full. It is a magnet, a beacon. His servants are already in this world, and they will find their way here. It is not for me to open the door, I have merely cleared the path.' True to his word, the moment the last spade full of dirt was removed from the basement, I finally found rest. While I still feel the tug on my skin, and in my bones, the voices were gone from my brain. I crawled up the stairs to my bed, where at last I slept peacefully for the first night in weeks. I slept all that night and most of the following day.*

I alone remain in the house. My wife left weeks ago, and all of the servants went with her, and for this I am glad. I don't want anyone here when the Confluence arrives.

It may be the end of me.

It may be the end of the world.

Tomorrow night, I alone shall be in the chamber.

I was foolish enough to build my house on his land, warned as I had been so many times, and I, alone must greet the new Master.

I believe I will never again leave this house.

I shall wait upstairs tonight.

If I am correct the door will appear.

I will free him, and if I fail the task will fall to him.

And then tomorrow I shall greet the new Master.

If I die, I pray it will be of some good to the world."

"That made no sense at all," Mark said. "First he's down in the chamber, then he's upstairs in the hallway, waiting for the door. He's the only one in the house but if he fails the task will fall to someone else… It's madness."

"Wait until you hear the next part." Hap said, "This is the part that has vexed me for years."

"The Ocean. The sea. The spires. D------ is the Ocean. I could not do it. You can not destroy the ocean!

The sky and the land shall be one under his Ocean! His arms have passed through and still lay below!

The door is shut closed, but his body lies within! The Ocean Made Flesh! The secret rests with him now, for he is the secret!

Not now but soon!

Soon!

Turn back the tide!

Bury the Ocean once more! Not through this door! Not through this door! "Yet some there be that, by due steps, aspire to lay their unjust hands on that golden key, that opes the palace of Eternity."

Forever!

I have seen!

Eternity!
Forever!
I have seen!
Eternity!"

"Then he just wrote *Eternity, Forever, I have seen*, and the name of the Demon god over and over again." Hap explained, "And that's it. That's the end of the journal. Three days later, John Carter showed up in Dubuque, foaming at the mouth, and babbling like an idiot. Eventually, they locked him away in an Asylum in Wichita, where he eventually died, on the night of the Waxing Gibbous Moon, in October of 1905."

"So whatever he saw down there, it finished the job," Mark said.

"Job?"

"Driving him insane."

"Oh," Hap said, understanding, "Yes I suppose so. But there is something that this tells us."

"Like what? That Carter had studied Milton? Or That whoever looks at what goes on in that room, and hasn't eaten of the "sacred food" will end up Koo-Koo for CoCo Puffs?" Mark was amazed at his ability to crack wise even at this direst of moments.

"Possibly." Hap said not acknowledging the joke, "But it also tells us that when "The Confluence" happens, and the Nexus between spaces or dimensions opens part of D seeps through. It seems to take on a physical form, if he didn't have it already, and enters our world."

"And that he leaves part of it behind." Mark observed, "That's where the sacred food comes from."

"Correct."

"But then where are they getting it from every day. Maru said the Calamari was fresh every day, and if this "body" does react anything like Octopus or Squid, then it would start rotting pretty fast."

"Things that are alive usually do not rot." Hap observed,

"It may be that its body lasts longer because there is still a form of life in it, even if it's disconnected from the whole. Then again Maru may have worn the thin space away to the point that a new tentacle or two can come through every morning. Who knows... and does it really matter? We are dealing with something beyond the human mind."

"But that's just it." Mark said, "Maru hasn't eaten of the Sacred Food. I mean look at him. If he had eaten that, wouldn't he be as big as they are? And his eyes. Even in Ally's eyes, mere hours after eating the food, there was something different about them. Less of her."

"Almost none of her, if any." Mark pushed away that nagging voice at the back of his mind that kept rearing upon him, "*Its too late. You can't save her. You are going to die if you try.*"

"Maru is their High Priest." Hap explained, "He needs to keep his mind so he can work for the Demon god. He must have some kind of protection we don't know about. Whether its something bestowed on him by the Demon or if its some talisman he keeps. I don't know. But I doubt its anything you could get your hands on."

"What about him?" Mark asked. "When did Maru show up?"

"When I said," Hap explained, even though he hadn't, "When they were selling all the books, my father collected about twenty years ago. We were there at the auction, and the books were one of the first things off the table. There were only two or so lots sold when a car pulled up and a man got out of the car. He walked up to the auctioneer who was just about to open up bidding on a set of hand-carved chairs. He said something to the auctioneer and there was a bit of an argument. The next thing we knew the auctioneer was closing the auction saying that everything remaining, including the Towen itself, had been sold. Pa practically had to fight with them for the books he'd purchased. The man came and said that he'd gladly pay Pa back and double his money if he would leave the books behind. Pa refused and the man was up to almost $2000 if Pa would just let them go. Pa was always a stubborn old cuss, especially when it came to books. And he figured if they were willing to pay $2000 they must be worth at least four or five-thousand. He was wrong of course. Turns out he may have overpaid for the books, at least as far as collectors were concerned. But not long after Maru showed up we realized the books, that one, in particular, was absolutely priceless. Carter had a lot of books with unpronounceable names, no one had ever heard of, which we think he started collecting after the strangeness began up there. Books about the Native Americans around here and Pittsburgh, and some far older and stranger-, The Chronicles of Abdul Alhazred, The Outsiders, The Ulthar, The Walls of Sleep, The Necro-com, things like that. And those are just the ones I can pronounce."

"We're getting off track," Mark said, "Maru, when did you first see him?"

"Not long after the auction, might have been about two or three days later. Pa was at the shop, sitting on the porch. He wasn't doing too much by that time, but he would come out to the shop every day, sit on the porch and talk to anyone who would stop by until their ears were ready to drop off if they'd let him. He was sitting there, and he called me and Vestal outside. We came and there was that little monster, all smiles, and teeth. He seemed amicable enough. He said that he was our new neighbor and was going to open up a restaurant on the Towen. Pa started into warning him about the place, but he said he already knew all about it and was very excited to see what would happen there. About a year later he had the place fixed up and open. People started disappearing not long after that, and the lights above the place became more frequent.'

'We didn't know exactly what was causing the people to disappear, but for many that did, we later noticed a new Big Person. Men, and women, and while at first taken aback by their size and power, if you looked and remembered, they were the same person as had disappeared, however long ago, only much bigger and more muscled. It was almost like the difference between seeing an actor in person and seeing them on a big movie screen. Only this was far worse of course because while they might look the same in the face, they were nothing like they had been, behind the eyes."

Mark thought of how he had seen the same thing in Ally's eyes and mourned within, fearing he might never see her divine spark again.

"Then about three years after the big people first appeared, one woman escaped the Towen." Hap continued, "She ran down the main path, but there were no giant Devil's Claw plants coming out of the ground to slow her down. I don't know if that was a recent addition because of her escape, or if Maru didn't activate it because he knew she wouldn't live long enough to tell the tale."

The crevasses in Hap's face grew deeper as he recalled the woman he could not save. "Pa was on the porch early that morning." Hap recalled, "And we'd just opened up the store when he saw her coming down the Hill. Her body was a bloody mess, and her eyes were half-closed from the bruises. She looked like a fighter who's gone 10 rounds in the ring with a man twice his size. But she was quite mad. She kept talking nonsense as far as we could tell. Toward the end when we had called the Ambulance, though we knew it wouldn't make it here in time, she seemed to come back if only a little to herself. She said three things that I've never forgotten. The Name of the Demon god. Her husband's name. And then the words *"Sacred Food. Calamari. Don't eat the Calamari."* And then she repeated that blasphemous name, again and again, until she died."

"Surely the police looked into it," Mark said, flexing his hurt leg.

"Oh they did, but when her husband came down from the Towen and said that his wife had suffered from fits of dementia, and this was only the latest, there wasn't too much more investigation into the matter. Leastways not so I heard anything about it."

Mark thought for a moment, "But her husband came down from the Towen... Was he one of the Giants now?"

"He was, but not so you'd know it." Hap answered, "Especially if you hadn't seen him before. He was a short, rather ugly little man when he left us, but when he came back he was about 6'2, and he had that hollow look they get. He went back to Dubuque with the officers and must have taken care of some business with them. But he came back. He was still 6'2 or so at the time... He's gotten bigger and uglier since. Whether it was his first name or his last name I don't recall, but his wife, she called him Brisco."

If Hap saw recognition in Mark's eyes, he didn't say anything about it, he merely continued, as if he hadn't been interrupted. "We tried to warn people... But I've already told you about that, and how we can't. We must have gotten close a few times, because there have been occasions when Maru has come down and threatened us, with at least two of his "Big People" by his side. It was like something out of a bad gangster movie. Told us if we didn't back off, he'd have his Giants rough up our shop, or worse. Hasn't stopped us from trying though. We found for whatever reason we can say what she said, *Don't eat the Calamari*. Likely because it's not the sort of thing that serves as a direct warning, or tells the travelers why. All we can do is our best. We have to try. And speaking of trying, its time for us to use what we know against him."

"What do we know?" Mark said, despairing, "That Maru has access to the powers of an ancient being who, merely looking at it will cause most men to go insane? That my wife will likely be one of those things forever, and if I go back to the Towen, I'm as good as dead!"

"Calm yourself boy." Hap said, pouring more tea into Mark's cup, "There, drink that. Maru has some advantages, I won't lie. But we have some too."

"What advantage do we have?" Mark said, half-heartedly

stirring sugar into his tea, not interested, but doing it anyway.

"Being on the side of right for one." Hap said, smiling, "Darkness is great. It's true. But one candle can banish the darkness. As Dark as the night gets, one small light will always be more powerful."

"Thank you George H.W. Bush," Mark said with a disgusted snort.

"Something akin to that." Hap said, "It wouldn't have become such a popular slogan if there hadn't been some truth in it. But if the will and powers of those who walk in darkness are so great, then there must be an equal, if not greater, source of light in the universe. Shadows can only exist in the presence of light, and the deeper the darkness of a shadow, the brighter the light must be."

"Platitudes." Mark said, sipping the tea, "My wife is a slave to a demon god, and the world could be ending, and all you're giving me are platitudes."

"An often repeated truth is repeated primarily because it is true. Mark, people who study these things often get so wrapped up in thinking about the evil beyond the world, that they don't stop to think about the opposition."

"You're talking about God." Mark said, "The Judeo-Christian God. I gave up on believing in him about the same time I gave up believing in Santa Claus."

Then with sudden anger, he pointed at Hap, "And if you say *"It doesn't matter if you believe in him, he believes in you."* I'm walking out of here because that's just hogwash, plain and simple. It's what foolish old men say when they don't have any other argument."

"Well." Hap said, "*There's* a reaction a psychotherapist could spend a week analyzing. But I'll say no more on that." Hap said putting up his hands, "Whether you believe in them or not, we are on the same side as them, especially when it comes to any move we make against the Demon god. I don't care what you believe in son, because I'm willing to bet twenty-four hours ago you didn't believe in *"Sacred Food"* that could make you and your wife into the Giant Servants of an ancient power, but here we are. I'm just saying, there may come a time when you need help, when no one else can help you. And when that time comes, don't overlook what might be your last hope. Personally, if I was going in against an ancient evil, I'd want a stronger, and older good on my side, if it existed... But I'll say no more."

"I'm sorry." Mark said, "It's a touchy subject with me. Not worth going into."

"Its time now we focus on what we know." Said Hap. "We know that on the night of the Waxing Gibbous Moon, (which is tonight,) the door to the other realm opens wider than it does at other times."

"So when does that happen exactly?" Mark asked, fearing he might already be too late.

"The hour just before dawn." Hap said, "Which tonight is about 5:30 am."

"*The darkest hour is just before dawn,*" Mark said meaningfully. "What? No. That's just something people say, it doesn't mean anything. The darkest hour is Mid-night. Not Midnight, 12 am, you understand, but Mid-night, when the light is furthest from this side of the earth. That's the darkest hour. Midnight is probably happening right now, in which case we would be far too late, especially by the time we got you back to the Towen. But the hour just before dawn, that's the time when darkness is falling, when it puts forth its last effort to hold its ground against the light."

Hap seemed to think for a moment, "Then again it may have nothing to do with that, and it's when this side of the earth is closest in Quantum space, who knows. The point is that the A-rab-Boroliolus is always strongest at that time of night, on this day of the lunar month. You can stand out on the porch and watch it from here."

"If that's the case why hasn't someone noticed this "*Aurora Borealis,*" Mark corrected, "and filmed it. It should have been on the news by now, or at least one of those shows that are on constantly on the crack-pot channels."

"Doesn't show up on film." Hap explained, "Believe me I've tried, and it has shown up in the newspapers down through the years. But son, there's hardly anyone out here most of the time, and since 1980-something if it's not on video or at least pictures, no one cares about it anymore."

"Pics or it didn't happen," Mark said shaking his head.

"Precisely." Hap said, "And in the middle to the end of August the official sunrise is about 7 am, but it starts getting light about a half-hour before that. So that means about 5:30 is one hour before dawn, so whatever you are going to do, you better have it done before then."

"So what are we going to do?" Mark asked, all but in despair, "What can we possibly do?"

"I'm glad you asked son." Hap said with a grin, "I'm glad you asked."

12

Maru sat on his golden throne in the heart of the Towen, his long scepter in his hand. Before him, the acolytes of Dyondaygah danced in the firelight.

A ring of flames encircled the outline of the Sarsen stones. The trough filled with petrol was one of the few things he had added after he'd acquired the building and the ancient ground beneath it.

He thought about the places he had tried before.

England, Ireland, Germany, Egypt, Iran, and Al-Quds. (Which he refused to think of by its Hebrew name. It was a place he certainly never really expected to find a path to the true gods, but after all, Alhazred had mentioned it several times in some of his more obscure writings, and "Holy Places" rarely acquired that reputation without proof of some manner.)

And when those places had failed, he had moved to the "new world"; Arkham Massachusetts, where he had helped to found the now prestigious Miskatonic University, Roanoke, where he had acquired little of note, and finally Pittsburgh.

Yes, that was where the trail truly began. After nearly two hundred years, the path to Dyondaygah began in the muddy banks of the Three Rivers. He should have known...

He really should have.

The ancient writings told of how Dyondaygah tended to favor the places where roads came together. He was the Confluence after all; the place where earth and sky would meet and be consumed; become one, as part of the great Ocean that was Dyondaygah.

Maru had always thought that it would be at some great crossroads that he would find the door. But never had he thought about the rivers.

It was the discovery of the bodies of the Giants that had tipped him off.

In 1932 the bodies of several Giants, both men and women, had been found just north of where the rivers came together at what the locals vulgarly called *"The Point"*.

A great burial mound had been dug into and a seven-and-a-half-foot tall woman, and several eight and ten-foot-tall men had been excavated.

Now, virtually every place in the world has had its legends, and a good deal of them involved giants, some thirty or even fifty feet tall.

From Homer's Odyssey to Paul Bunyan, tales of giants were common.

A few years later, the atomic age would herald in a few new ones in the films, *The Amazing Colossal Man* and *The Attack of the 50 Foot Woman* and so on.

Pittsburgh itself even had a legend of a "Man of Steel" long before a comparatively diminutive comic book character would take on that moniker; Joe Magarac, whose height seemed to vary by who was telling the tale.

But this was no folk story, or (pardon the pun) Tall-tale, these had been real bones, of real giants.

The story had made headlines all across the nation.

Even if he hadn't had his connections in the American Smithsonian Institution via his students and financial donations to MU, Maru still would have heard about this discovery.

He immediately pulled the strings he had readily at his command and had the Smithsonian arrange an opportunity for him to examine the bones himself. And when they were finally before him, he saw the markings he alone could recognize.

These Indians, (they were not yet called the politically correct name of "Native Americans" or, Cthulhu devour us, the

"*Indigenous Peoples*")... These people's bones had the markings of the followers of Dyondaygah.

From there it was a simple matter of looking into the local legends and archeological discoveries.

He learned the stories of the Allegewi, and how they had been driven out by the local tribes.

It was even less trouble finding the spot where the Allegewi temple had once been. But alas, it was destroyed long ago.

The fools. The empty-headed fools. They had built a fort over it.

At the confluence of the rivers, *Fort Pitt* had long ago desecrated the path to Dyondaygah.

But if the legends were to be believed, it was highly unlikely that the men who built that fort had any idea of what had once lain there. It was likely the local tribes had destroyed that most Holy of sites not long after running off the Allegewi ...

In fact, it made sense.

It was the very destruction, the forsaken nature of the place which had made it possible for the followers of Dyondaygah to escape.

Once you had partaken of the Sacred Food: The Body of Dyondaygah, you could never be very far from his presence. New converts could stay away a little longer, it was how Brisco had been able to return home after the death of his wife, in order to clean up that messy little affair, and even he had returned just in the nick of time. But it had been nearly a year since the last conversion and now all of the Devoured were bound to the Towen, to leave the circle of influence would mean death.

It was the whole reason he had not been able to send the Devoured after Mark Thurston, to the house of that meddling fool Howard.

Yes, he knew exactly where they had gone, and for the moment, they lay beyond Maru's reach. Perhaps when once the Conjunction had occurred, and Alley was truly part of the circle, his territory would widen, and then both Howard and his son would pay...

Or Dyondaygah would finally emerge and then such petty concerns would no longer be of consequence.

The more servants Dyondaygah had, the wider his circle of influence, and he must have indeed had many in the place that was now called Pittsburgh.

But once he left a place, his temples desecrated and abandoned, his progeny were... well, not free, they could never be that, but they were set loose; loosed upon the world, so that Dyondaygah might establish a new place of worship, and a new door.

If the followers had survived, it would have become their duty to seek out a new place of refuge and begin the creation of his cult once again.

The Allegewi would have been led to this sacred place where the barrier was thin, where they could once again be whole, and connected to the power of their god.

They would have once again set up the sacred stones, said the blessings, and begun the thinning.

Maru now had a lead.

It had been difficult many years of false starts, and rabbit trails. Using his connections he had convinced the Smithsonian it was to their advantage to collect and catalog all such discoveries.

When possible the finds were to be collected and buried deep within the vaults of the Smithsonian collection, only to be seen by himself and a few others of his choosing.

Different directors over time had required different reasons to keep such things quiet and out of the press.

The favorite seemed to be military applications.

"We could use them to our advantage, we might be able to grind up the bones and make a formula that would produce "Supersoldiers".

(Later this had been amended to *"We could study their*

DNA and replicate it.")

For others, a little monetary consideration had been enough.

But after all, it didn't take much to convince people to continue keeping a secret that had already been kept for decades. And humans had a wonderfully short memory.

Maru knew that no matter how technologically advanced, no matter how sophisticated the *"gene splicers"* became, they would not be able to reproduce the changes wrought in the human body by consuming the body of Dyondaygah for they were of his power and his alone.

It was just twenty short years ago now, that Maru had almost lost the second temple of Dyondaygah on the American continent forever. After years of searching, digging in the dirt, following every trace, the story of John Carter and the Towen, at last, reached his ears.

He had kept his ear to the ground, listening for stories of weird occurrences in the woods, stone formations of surpassing strangeness, and of course the presence of Giants. Looking for stories from the Indian tribes was more often than not fruitless.

The legends of the Allegewi had spread far and wide and while some of the details changed, there was rarely any evidence to back them up.

Then he heard the tale of a large splendid house that was for sale. He heard how, despite its surpassing beauty as a home and as a historic, and well-kept landmark, no one was interested in purchasing the place because of its strange history, and the fact that it had been built directly upon an ancient Indian Burial mound.

Only a few years before a movie based on a similar premise, (*a haunted house on an Indian Graveyard,*) had permeated the culture of America to a level that most of the housing market in a number of places across the country had almost totally collapsed, Pittsburgh among them.

It was a place deeply steeped in the lore and history

of the Native American cultures, and hardly a stone could be moved without disturbing some ancient place sacred to one tribe or another.

With just a small bit of digging, Maru had discovered a number of the strange facts connected with the place, and he was certain that Dyondaygah was near.

His fears had deepened considerably when he found out that the current owner was in the middle of planning an auction to clear out the building and eventually have the land redeveloped as a strip mall, or some other American abomination.

Immediately, he had called upon his team of lawyers and agents. He had to intercept this as soon as possible.

That very day the auction was shut down, with all the assets that had been sold that day reacquired except the grievous loss of the Library.

Most of the books that had been sold before the auction were not worth the trouble of reacquiring, they had merely been a lot of First editions of works of Fiction, Mark Twain, Charles Dickens, Shelly, Keats, Yeats, and so on; nothing of any intrinsic value. But the rest of it; the books that Howard's father had bought for a piddling $500, they had been the true treasures.

John Dee's translation of the *Necronomicon*, *The Book of Lost Stars*, *The Machinations of Wilber Whateley*, and many others, they had all just eluded his grasp…

But not for much longer, if Dyondaygah's will permitted.

With those books in hand who knew what power he might wield?

But such things were not to be wondered after, at least not until after the Conjunction, Then we shall see, what we shall see.

Now the Towen was his, and he hadn't even needed to uncover the Sarsens below it. Carter had done all. Perhaps even at the behest of Dyondaygah himself, who knew?

The path that led to the basement was a later addition,

and the dirt walls were paved over, in such a way that made Maru believe that whoever had done it, had known that the Sarsens must be exposed to make the path clear.

Yes, Maru owed quite a bit to John Carter.

Oh, that glorious moment when he had first knelt at the feet of Dyondaygah. There had been nothing like it in his more than two hundred years of life.

The Chanting of the Great Old One's name could not be done by one alone, when his father had taught him the ancient rites long ago. But now in the twenty-first century, and even the latter part of the twentieth, it had been as simple as recording your voice on a loop and playing it through one manner of recording device or another.

Maru had wondered why such a thing as a Tape or CD player would be enough to summon a great Lord of the High Past. Didn't it require a soul behind it; channeling its energy and vitality toward its devotion for the Masters?

Apparently not.

The doorway seemed to be opened by a mere "sonic trigger", in concert with the Sarsen Stones of course. But when he thought about it, even that made sense and gave credence to the ancient belief that merely saying something's true name could summon it, or (with the proper ceremonies,) give you a level of control over it.

He had read many times of people, (fools,) simply reading aloud the words of some accursed tome on to a tape.

Later when that tape was played again, it was just as effective in summoning the spirits of the Malicious Deceased to inhabit the bodies of the living.

Once such tape had been played over a local television station, as part of a Halloween Celebration and the Kandarians had quite the field day.

Maru was not such a fool and had known exactly what he was doing when he began the looped recording of his voice calling out the incantations that would draw down the attentions of the mighty Dyondaygah.

He had made the blood sacrifices as the rites prescribed and then he had begun the actual call that would open the doors that the great one might appear.

He had brought his tiny hands, coated in that blood, together and made the sacred signs, under the unseen light of the Waxing Gibbous Moon.

And the Gate Opened.

Had he not been steeled for it, the mere sight of a hole in reality opening before him might have driven him mad.

The floor had seemed to be sucked away beneath the blood offering as it was absorbed into the nothing between stars, while grains of sand seemed to hover above the doorway as if suspended by magnetic fields.

Maru knew better than to look down into that doorway. The sights that could be looked upon through that door, as the path opened were not for mortal eyes, and despite his considerable age, he knew himself to still be mortal, for now.

Neither was Maru to approach the pit.

If Dyondaygah was to speak to him, Dyondaygah must make that decision, and come forth in whatever form seemed good to him.

First, no light had been visible from the socket in reality, then slowly a dim eldritch light began to glow up threw it.

Soon it was an overwhelming sickly golden glow, tinged with a rotten green, as though the light of a dying sun were reflected in an overly tarnished brass mirror.

Then the first tendril had snaked its way up and out of the pit. Followed by another, and another, and another; five in total.

They formed a five-pointed star of writhing, undulating, curling, muscularity.

They gave the impression of tentacles, such as one might see on the bodies of octopuses and squid, and yet they were nothing like them at the same time.

The feeble human brain, even Maru's was apt to look for metaphors, touchstones of reality to grab on to, it was never prepared for something with which there could be no comparison.

It made Maru wonder how cognitive abilities could ever have formed in the first place because somewhere in infancy the mind had to start making connections and comparisons.

But what did you compare things to when, up until now, you knew absolutely nothing of anything?

What happened before you had "First impressions?"

It must have been so horrible that the human mind had adapted over time, making mankind forget that first moment of understanding, less it be caught in a state of everlasting awe.

Up from the midst of the five-pointed star rose a greater tendril, larger, rounder and fatter than the others.

It was covered over with all those strange protrusions, that Maru would later be accustomed to seeing on the rare occasion, like tonight, when the glory within one of The Devoured was exposed.

Then the form seemed to change, shrink and become less defined. The skin became as cloth and one large "sucker" seemed to open wide and deep until the semblance of a face began to emerge.

No one could have looked at that face and come away able to describe it outside of the fact that it had two eyes, which could not be seen, except as glints of shadow, a nose and a dark mouth, the interior of which was just as black as the rest of the face.

It was if the faintest stroke of a pencil had drawn a slightly lighter black face, on black paper. Before Maru stood a figure clothed in a hood, who's head nearly touched the ceiling, and who's feet could not be seen, as they were either non-existent or floated far below what would have been the ground.

Maru had fallen to his knees, in abject, horror, humiliation, joy and subjugation.

But how much greater were all these emotions magnified, when he first heard his Lord and Master, whom he had sought for so long, began to speak.

"Maru. Stand. Stand before your Lord. I am the great Dyondaygah, whom you have long sought. Rise and look to me, oh diminutive slave."

The voice was high and reedy, yet with a base that somehow shook the ground at the same time.

Where it not for the vibrations beneath his bare feet, he might have wondered whether the voice was in his mind or actually disturbing the air enough to breach his auditory canals and create the sounds he heard.

Dyondaygah had not spoken to him in English, but in the ancient tongue that even his father did not know the proper name of. Its sounds were alternately thick and guttural, and high and lilting.

It might have been an ancient Sumerian dialect, or something far older.

Maru could not be sure if Dyondaygah, (who could speak all languages that ever had been or could be,) had chosen it because it was his "native" tongue, or if because it was what Maru had almost expected. The Language of the Old Ones.

Maru raised his eyes to look at the mostly hidden figure, robed in thin cloth-like flesh, then raising himself to his full height he splayed his hands and opened his arms wide.

"Welcome, oh truly tremendous one!" Maru had proclaimed, astonished at his boldness, "This world has long awaited your coming and it is prepared for your arrival. It is yours to command!"

"It. Is. Not." Replied the figure, sneering, "This world is not prepared for the gift I bring, Sameness. Oneness. Wholeness. It can have these things only in me, when I have devoured all. Then and only then when all that once crawled over this insignificant globe has found its purpose in me, then we shall stretch our arms toward Mars and beyond! You will be the catalyst of this great becoming and for it, you shall be greatly rewarded, you shall reign with me and your size shall increase as mine does. For lo, I have looked into your heart Maru Son of Gram and Katya, and I know what you have always desired;

to be as I am, a master of men, and an eater of worlds. All this shall be if you do as I command."

"Command me, Lord!" Maru shouted, falling to his knees.

"Behold my body." Said the figure gesturing to the five tentacles, "Though I speak to you and stand before you, I may not yet pass beyond the circle of this Alter; this Towen. I may not come full and alive as I am into the realm in which you dwell. Only by inhabiting the bodies of mortal men, may I enter this world, so that I may gain a foothold in it. You will take these, my glory made manifest, and feed it to those who I will send unto you. Their hearts will be prepared and their wishes shall be granted as they are made strong in me, that I may grow stronger through them. You shall make this into a place where the adept may come to feed."

At that moment, the tentacles which had until now slowly writhed and flopped upon the floor, chopped off at the mouth of the yawning abyss.

Still, they undulated for a few moments more until at last, they were still. "My body does not die, in this world, nor my own," said the shade, "But here in the world of matter, it must obey the laws of matter, and in order for my flesh to have strength in it, I must be connected to a living host, until the time of my emergence is fully come round. Feed my children. Feed them my body. *You* shall not eat of my body, for you are my disciple, servant, and slave, and while you must use it, and distribute it, it is not for you to consume. But soon you shall consume much more than this. Soon you shall fulfill the purpose for which you were brought into the world under certain ceremonies. Your parents have told you of the great work you would do, and though it may have cost you stature in this dimension of matter, you shall have stature beyond the understanding of man when I rule earth and sky and sea. Your great work begins. Do not fail me."

"I shall not fail you." Maru said, as the form sank beneath the ground and the stones which had fallen away swirled up from below to reclaim their place in the world of Man, as though the rift had never been.

Maru had collected the tentacles and made them into the first batch of the sacred food, he had prepared it with his own hands, a task he now left entirely to the Frog-men, and before he had even had a chance to make a sign for the restaurant, or buy the tables and chairs he would need, the first "customers" had arrived at his door.

They had practically made a beeline for the Calamari, as though it was what they had come there for. All five of them in one night had consumed the Sacred food.

The "anchoring" of Dyondaygah to the world of flesh had begun.

Now, the acolytes of Dyondaygah moved in toward the center of the ring, their strange dance continuing toward its climax. Standing on the verge of the ring was Ally.

While she chanted the words and called out the name, she did not dance. She was not yet whole.

Though she had increased in size and strength, the conversion would not be complete yet for many days. And there was still a chance her body might reject the Sacred Food...

Or it would reject her, Maru was never quite sure how that worked even now.

Thus far it had only happened once, and the rejected had not survived.

Maru was certain that this would not be the case with her. Especially after the night's Conjunction, when the two, Dyondaygah and Ally, would become inextricably linked.

While Maru had examined the body of the man who had rejected the Sacred Food, the part of Dyondaygah which had tried to attach to him, was already gone from his system, so Maru could learn little of how the connection worked on a physiological level.

Certain markings on his spine and the way it had been cracked led Maru to believe that until the new Giant had confronted Dyondaygah the Sacred food had only taken up residence in the body, exuding whatever signals and chemicals it needed to induce the growth and control it required, but it had not yet tapped into the central nervous system.

How it could do this might well be asked, as Maru had asked, but as a faithful servant he understood that Dyondaygah was beyond such petty concerns.

When the time of the Conjunction had come, the body of Dyondaygah had tried to make its solitary and everlasting connection to the Man's body, and something had gone wrong.

From what Maru could tell by observing, the man had put up some resistance to the final becoming. Normally by that point in the process, the initiate was huddled in a ball on the floor, if he was heard to say anything at all, the words were usually:

"Yes. Yes."

Not in some paroxysm of ecstasy, or terror, but almost in a solemn legalistic way. Maru thought it sounded as if they were listening to a lawyer reading a contract over the phone to which they needed verbal consent in order to proceed.

After a time, before the Conjunction would end, they would rise to their feet, under their own power, and praise the name.

Then they would turn to Maru, and receive the blessing of the High Priest. Then their power would be joined to the Master's and Dyondaygah would attempt the emergence.

But this time, the man had been saying:

"No. No. You will not. I refuse. All the same, I refuse."

Maru could not believe that the man's will had been strong enough to resist that of Dyondaygah. Nor, could he believe that any man, or woman, called to this sacred place, having eaten of the Sacred Food, could be so arrogant and self-centered as to refuse the communion of Dyondaygah, to become part of the one, the whole.

It was beyond imagining.

Something must have been wrong with the man on a

biological level, and the conjoining did not take.

The man, now nearly seven feet tall, when he had barely been Five, upon his arrival, had bellowed in a deep banshee scream. He had shot to his feet, in a manner unlike Maru had ever seen.

He writhed, his head wrenching violently from one side to the other. Then his whole body had spasmed until there was a sickening snap, and the top half of the man's body had sagged to one side, his spine broken.

While the man's legs still stood on the ground, somehow supporting this odd off-balance weight shift, the Sacred Body, the tentacle of Dyondaygah, had slimed its way up and out of the man's mouth.

Only when the last of it had exited the man's body, did it fall to the ground; dead.

The tentacle meanwhile, slithering like a serpent, had returned through the vortex, which was still open between the place where its master lay and this world.

What became of it Maru would never know.

Later Maru had asked the demon god what had happened on that strange night, but no answer was forthcoming.

Maru gazed across the room at Ally. She was beautiful. She had been before coming to the Towen, and she would be more beautiful still once her becoming was complete. Perhaps he would even ask Dyondaygah if she could be his.

Maru had never made such a petition before, and the Master was very generous to his servants. Once a person was joined to Dyondaygah, all familial ties were, of necessity, broken forever.

After all, while the person did seem to retain some semblance of whom they had been and memories of those they had known after the becoming, they didn't seem to care about such things very much anymore.

Never mind that it would be pretty strange if they did make contact with a family member again, and they saw the massive changes in their loved one.

When they came to the Towen together, as husband and wife, it was usually the case that both would partake of the sacred food.

Afterward, they would not have the same feelings for each other they once had. All such silly ideas of *"love"* and *"mutual attraction"* were simply facades to make capital out of each other somehow, (Maru was never quite sure what that "capital" was exactly, but it didn't bother him either way,) and when they were part of the One, such facades fell away.

When it was the case that they did not both partake of the Sacred Food, the other one was never much of a problem for long.

They were disposable.

If they died when their mate had begun the transition, slain in the fit of rage, which often accompanied the first hours of transformation, (a thing that had happened several times,) that was fine.

If not, such as tonight, then they would be sacrificed to the Great Old Ones.   Even Mark Thurston would not be much of a problem, if he went to the police, no one would believe him.

If the police did come they would find nothing amiss.

Even if they saw Ally, they would never believe the powerful Amazon they would look upon could have once been that petite little thing Mark would have pictures of in his wallet.

But Maru doubted even that would come to pass. Mark had been a weak man. Weak in his mind, weak in his soul. He would never have the courage and audacity to-

Through the noise and rhythmic pounding of the ceremonial drums a new sound pierced the night. It must have indeed been very loud in order to penetrate the walls and dirt below the Towen.

A new rhythm thudded into the chamber. Maru raised a hand in the sign which called for silence and the drumming

and chanting ceased, but for two of the Children, who had been tasked with ensuring the chant never fully stopped.

The music continued to pound through the cement and vibrated the walls of the Towne with every base note.

"What in the name of Nyarlathotep is that!?" Maru asked the room full of Giant Worshipers.

Not sure if their High Priest expected an answer or not, they looked at each other in questioning silence.

"Well!?" The little man screeched, striking his scepter on the ground before him, "Don't just stand there! Half of you come upstairs with me, and the other half, continue chanting! You know how this works! The ceremony must not be postponed! The conjunction occurs in less than two hours, and we must clear the way for the coming of the Confluence!"

Still, the giants waited, not sure which of them should do what job.

Maru groaned and said pointing, "Everyone on that side of the drawing of the Night Gaunts, continue chanting. Everyone on my side of the Night Gaunts come with me. Ernest! Pick me up and place me on your shoulder."

"What of the new one?" Asked one of the female giants, "What is to be done with her?"

"Keep her down here at all costs. This is Mr. Thurston's doing I have no doubt. Ally, you are to stay here and not leave with anyone. You belong to Dyondaygah, you will listen to the will of his Priest, do you understand?"

"I hear the will of the Great one and his Priest." Ally said in a low sanctified tone, "All will be done as you have commanded."

"Good." Said Maru, "At least someone around here knows how to give me my due respect! Even if it is the new girl! You will go far in his service."

"Thank you, my Lord." Ally said, crossing her hands over her chest and then uncrossing them, keeping her elbows at a ninety-degree angle and putting her hands out as if holding a tray. It was a sign of devotion all the Children of Dyondaygah knew inherently.

"Well... What are you waiting for? Hop to it!" Maru shouted, causing the drums to begin their rhythm again, and the chants restarted, as Maru was picked up and placed on the shoulder of the one called Ernest.

"Dash it all, you fool!" Maru shouted as they began to ascend the stairs. "How many times have I told you to watch my head, when we walk through the stairwell!"

Ernest made a noise that was half contrition, half disinterest, as they climbed to the first level, and walked down the short hallway which led into the dining hall.

The music from outside was clearer now and while Maru did not recognize the tune, (if there was anything that could be called a tune about it,) he could hear it was what the people in the outside world would have called *"Rock and Roll."*

"I don't like it." Snarled Maru, in his high piping tone. "If that old fool, Howard has anything to do with this, I'll have his broken body stuck on a pitchfork!"

13

Hap stood at the bottom of the hill.

He had daisy-chained several large, powerful speakers together so the music would be certain to draw out Maru and as many of the Children of Dyondaygah as possible.

The speakers were not just home entertainment stereo systems. They had been designed for special outdoor events; car shows and the like. They broadcasted sound at a volume that belied their size.

Before leaving his home he had connected all the wires he would need and stacked them in such a way that placing them at the base of the Towen mound would be the work of only a few minutes. Then he had deliberately chosen some of the worst music ever made to blast at full volume.

He climbed up into the cab of his truck and strapped on a wireless microphone that was connected to the speakers. The device was designed to automatically lower the volume of the music when the microphone was switched on, to a point where the speaker could be heard clearly.

Within moments of when the music started playing Hap saw the doors of the Carter Place open and nearly fifteen of the Giants had filed out on to the parking lot.

Hap could see them quite clearly in the light from the lamp posts.

"Dear God," he prayed, "*please let this work. Let us be able to save Ally. Let us defeat this evil, if only for a little while. And hasten the day in which you throw the likes of Maru and all those who do the will of evil into the pit. Amen.*"

He switched on the Microphone.

"Maru!" He called over the microphone. "Maru! Where are you, you sawed-off little Hobgoblin!? I'm calling you out!" He regretted it the moment he said it, and shook his head. He sounded like a bad spaghetti western.

At the top of the hill, a sixteenth Giant emerged, stooping low, both to avoid knocking his head and the head of the little man on his shoulders. Maru held in his hand some sort of long walking stick or cane, the head of which was topped with a small golden ball, that looked as if it were highly decorated, like a King's Scepter.

"Mr. Howard," said Maru, his voice inexplicably carrying to Hap, as though he were mere feet away, rather than nearly 100 yards away. "I am very unhappy with you. You hurt at least three of my people and blew a large hole in one of them. You should no better than to be here tonight. I see you are alone. Where is that fine young gentleman, Mr. Thurston? Why is he not with you?"

"He ran away!" Hap said over the microphone, "As you should do."

"Oh Mr. Howard, I think you should know, I believe you are lying to me." Maru answered, waggling a tiny finger, "If you are not here to rescue Mrs. Thurston, then tell me why have you come here at nearly three in the morning and disrupted our rest?"

"You weren't resting anymore than I was." Hap said, "This is your last warning. You and all your Giants are going to leave this place or I am going to drive you out! This is our place, we were here first!"

"Mr. Howard, we both know that isn't true." Maru said in an almost sing-song tone, "The Temple of Dyondaygah was here long before you or even I, and I am much, much older than you could ever have been, and if you continue to interfere I will not be merciful."

Howard knew that the die was already cast, there was no turning back, and there was no point in bandying words with

Maru.

In answer to Maru's last taunt, he turned off the microphone returning the music to full blast, just as the singer wailed, *"Ooooohhh yeah!!"* and the pounding rhythm hit its full tempo.

"And the man in the back said everyone attack!..." The lead singer belted as Howard pushed the gas peddle all the way to the floor, and began the long charge up the hill.

The Giants stood their ground, as the truck, its tires wrapped and reinforced by snow chains began crunching over the now-dead remnants of the giant Devil's Claw plants. Behind him, falling out of the back of the truck was a measure of chain link fence.

As the truck rampaged up the ancient Indian Burial mound, the chain-link pulled up more of the Devil's Claw, leaving behind a semblance of a path.

The hooked, razor-sharp pods and branches adhered to the fence and while much of the roots were left behind, a path was being made.

But this was only secondary to Hap, a path through the weeds was not the goal, but merely an afterthought.

The truck barreled up the hill toward the Giants, and as he approached, Hap showed no signs of slowing down.

"Inside!" Maru shouted to Ernest, *"Take me inside! Protect your priest!"*

As the Truck hit the, now grown-over parking lot, not stopping for a moment, Ernest pulled Maru off of his shoulders and hugged him to his chest. Protecting him as a father might defend his baby, the doors closing behind him.

As Hap reached the doors of the Carter house, he made a sharp, hard turn to the right, an rather than charging into the doors, he began to run down the giants.

One after another his truck smacked into the seven and eight-foot-tall monstrosities, the stainless steel grille on the front of the vehicle preventing most of the damage to the body.

But damage there was.

Each body was like plowing headlong into a horse.

And not one of them ran away.

A couple of the giants fell to the side, and at least one of them went directly under the wheels of the truck, but not one of them retreated.

Seven times he targeted a giant and seven times they made contact with the protective grille.

The music at the base of the hill blasted even louder as Hap spun the wheel and stomped the brake, swinging the rear end of the truck around, so that the front of it was once again facing the Towen.

All seven of the giants it had plowed through were back on their feet. The skin was visibly bruised and broken, as Hap saw the red of their blood staining the ground beneath them, where they had made contact with the pavement.

The Parking lot of The Olde Towen Buffet was well lit, and in the light of those lamps, Hap could see that the other eight giants were now huddling up with the seven injured ones, into a solid mass.

This was exactly what Hap wanted. Of course, he had hoped one or two of them might fall by the wayside, but so far they had played perfectly into his hands.

If Maru had been smart, he would have brought Ally along with him as a shield, but he had not. He had chosen to keep her as far away from Mark and Hap as possible, assuming that she was the goal.

"I'm sorry, but the Princess is in Another Castle." Hap thought to himself wryly. In this case, that was exactly where he wanted her, far away from this fracas, and safe.

"Come on boys and girls!" He said, switching on the microphone briefly, so they could hear him, "Let's go for a ride!"

Hap stomped the gas while holding the brake, preparing for a burnout.

The metal chains on his tires, struck the ground in rapid

succession, causing sparks to fly out around and behind the Truck.

It was pure intimidation, and unless he was very much mistaken, it was working.

The seven injured Trolls and some of the uninjured ones as well had looks of rage and terror in their eyes, as they gazed upon what must have seemed like *"The Pick'em-Up Truck From Hell,"* as Hap released the brake and barreled toward them. He hit the center of the pack dead on, knocking three or four of them off into the distance.

But others grabbed onto the truck and began to attempt to climb into the bed.

"Come on you sorry sons." He said as two or three of them were dragged along behind, climbing up the chain link that hung out of the back.

Once again executing the same maneuver, he stomped the brake and spun the truck around.

This caused two of the giants to lose their balance and fall, flying off of the truck, but at the same time it gave three of them a moment to improve their grip and climb up into the bed of the truck, stomping into the large crates that lined it, spilling out some of the black powder from within.

Once more Hap stomped the gas, and tore out into the parking lot, ripping up more of the oversized, razor-sharp Devils claw that had sprouted from the blacktop.

Bits of plants flew everywhere, as four of the giants began to pound on the roof of the cab, denting it in above Haps head.

"Hold in there girl, just a few more minutes!" Hap said to the old faithful truck, as the glass of the rear cab exploded.

Arms, two and three times the size of a normal human arm, reached into the cab, as Hap wrenched the wheel to one side and then the other, trying to prevent them from getting hold of him.

He squished down into the seat, just enough that he could still see, but also deny the giants a grip on his shoulders.

The giants swung back and forth trying to hold on to the vehicle, when Hap wrenched the wheel as hard as he could, back toward the main doors of the Buffet, where the remaining Giants had formed a barricade of bodies, to prevent exactly what he was about to do.

Hap pushed the gas pedal so hard, he was sure it had come out through the bottom of the truck, then he kicked over a cinderblock he had kept under his left foot, to make sure it wouldn't fall on to the pedal until the last possible moment.

Then he flipped the five-second timer, which had been sitting beside him all along.

"Goodbye Old Girl," Hap said as the truck barreled into the line of Giants and the doors of the Olde Towen buffet.

Bodies smashed under the force of the impact, and were crushed between the wood of the building the metal frame of the truck and its grille, but only for a second, because the next moment, the truck and the Giants and entrance of the Buffet were all consumed in a giant fireball.

Bag after bag of black powder meant for tree stump removal, exploded, triggered by a small spark given off by small series of remote detonators Hap had planted in the small bags.

The entire building rocked on its foundation from the force of the impact and within moments the main dining hall was in flames.

The truck didn't stop and carried the flames and burning bodies deep into the dining room. It smashed tables and chairs and rode up over the beautiful glass and metal buffet bar, which shattered, again and again, pane by pane into a hundred thousand pieces.

The Truck at last stopped, its wheels still spinning, as it was rucked upon the remnants of the buffet line, but the damage it caused did not stop there.

Still quivering from the rear of the truck, the flames began to singe the wood, and melt the paint off of the ceiling.

It might have gone on burning, and taken down the entire building, but for the fact that according to Kansas state law, all eating establishments, no matter how old, were required to have a sprinkler system. It had angered Maru when the law had come down on him. The system had been installed, at great cost of equipment and labor in order for the Buffet to remain open.

But as a result, the accursed building was saved from Hap's assult, as the dining room was quickly doused with a thick spray of water, that choked out the flames coming from the remnant of Hap's truck, the back wheels still spinning at full speed.

Giants, their clothes and hair ablaze, were running in all directions. Some were put out by the sprinklers, while others rolled on the pavement to extinguish the flames. Had they still been weak humans, more than a few of them might have died of their injuries, and third degree burns, but such was the healing power of Dyondaygah, that not one of them was lost.

Maru knew that to the power of Dyondaygah, skin was one of the easiest parts of the body to repair, and while deep tissue would take a little longer, even the most damaged of the Giants would likely be on their feet again, within the hour.

Maru, meanwhile, had not been idle.

He, carried by Ernest, had made his way to the back of the dining room.

When the truck had burst into the room, it had stopped mere inches from where he and Ernest stood.

Immediately, he had sprung into action…

Or rather he ordered the Giants who were still standing to come to his aid into action.

"Put out the flame at the front door!" He ordered, "It's still burning!"

Three or four of the giants who had survived the impact and explosion, wandered in from outside, bewildered and disorientated, none of them were completely unharmed.

From the Kitchen, one of the Frog-men waddled into the room, "Oi, Boss" Said William, "Someone has drove a great dirty truck into the middle of my nice clean dining room. I just finished vacuuming in here! Though I must admit the water spray is rather nice."

"Turn off that truck, you overgrown hop-toad!" Maru screamed at the top of his voice, both in anger and to be heard over the roar of the engine and the susurrant roar of the water pouring down from above."

"I'm not a valet service." William grumbled to himself, as he hefted his lumpy body up and on to the broken buffet bar and into the cab of the truck, through the broken back window. Soon the engine was turned off and the keys for the truck flew out of the window.

The gushing woosh of fire extinguishers were soon heard, as a few of the least hurt giants began to spray down the still-burning wood of the entrance with flame retardant powder.

"You three continue spraying the wood with water, I don't want the fire flaring up again. You six! Get this truck out of my restaurant! We will deal with the furniture in the morning! I want this rotting rusted monstrosity out of my building now!" Maru bellowed.

"That's the end of Mr. Howard." Said Ernest in his deep gurgle, looking at the burned-out remnants of Hap's truck, as William climbed back out of the window, the cab door refusing to open for his webbed fingers, "Hardly seemed worth the effort." Ernest added.

Maru clenched both fists and held his elbows tight against his sides, "Don't you understand, you mindless fool?" He shrieked, "This was not the main attack. This was a distraction!"

"A distraction from what?" Ernest asked his master.

"Thurston!" Maru snarled through clenched teeth, "I don't know what they are planning but odds are he's already here! Ernest, bring all but two of our remaining Children up from the Sarsen Pit. I want the remaining two to continue the chanting but also to keep an eye on Ally. I do not want her to escape. I want the rest of you to scour the building! Thurston is here! I can feel it!"

"Escape?" Ernest asked, "Isn't she one of us now?"

"There is something else at work here... Something I have not felt in many long years. It seeks to defeat us at the moment of our triumph! This goes much deeper than Mr. Howard or Mr. Thurston. With this power by their side, who knows what they might accomplish."

"Something more powerful than Dyondaygah?" Ernest asked stupidly as if the concept were something he couldn't quite grasp.

"Pick me up!" Said Maru, and Ernest obeyed, only to feel Maru's walking stick/ scepter strike him hard across the face.

"That was for your blasphemy! Nothing is more powerful than Dyondaygah! Now put me down. And gather The Children as I instructed you. We must find Thurston!"

Unseen by Maru and the Big people, William waddled back into the kitchen to report what had happened to the other Frog-men, but only Burt was there to hear it.

"So what happened to the body?" Asked Burt, when the tale had been told.

"Waddn't in the cabin, of the truck. Must have jumped out before 'e 'it the build'n. And 'ere I was hoping for a bit of already cooked man-flesh for supper!" William explained.

"You didn't tell the master that?" Asked Burt.

"No." William answered. "Won't he be mad when he finds out?"

"Oh, won't he?" William said with a toothy grin, "Won't he just?"

14

Soot and ash filled Mark's lungs. Dirt clung to his clothes. He hadn't expected the old coal cellar to be clean as a whistle, but he certainly hadn't expected it to still be full of coal, much less to have to push his way up through it.

Hap had shown him the place where the entrance was, in Carter's book. Carter had made a record in his diary of every major design change to the house in his diary and the adding of a coal shoot and furnace had been one of them.

Up until its instillation the place had been heated by a series of Pot Bellied stoves, usually only prepared during winter nights, when it was known in advance someone would be occupying the room.

But at some point, before he had been taken by the madness of Dyondaygah, Carter had decided that he wanted central heating, something that was only just coming into vogue at the time, and could only be afforded by the super-rich.

The main dining area, where the Sarsen Stone ring lay, was not the only area of the house, with a basement.

Mark had waited for the music to start playing before he had even approached the house. He didn't know if the coal shoot would be accessible or not.

In later years when such things became obsolete, (if they weren't replaced and filled in entirely,) coal shoots were usually locked down and painted over. Screws might be drilled in and the gate sealed, or even welded shut.

However, in this case, the coal shoot seemed to be something Maru had given no thought to or had completely overlooked.

There was indeed a layer of thick wood lacquer over the porthole, which had been done as the exterior wood was being resealed, but the door itself was held closed by nothing more than a small, nearly rusted through padlock, that looked like it could have been placed there by Carter himself.

Mark had brought a hammer and chisel, as well as several other things in a gym bag. Covered by the music and Hap's taunts, Mark had made quick work of it.

The lock's mechanism had given with just a few quick strikes, though the metal, still strong after all those years of exposure, held firm.

It was just a few taps with the head of the chisel around the thick varnish, which had already begun to show cracks from the force traveling through the lock, and Mark could open it.

The metal hinges creaked and the glaze over them cracked quite loudly, and had it not been for Hap's distraction and cover up, Mark might have been found out, but as it was, his noises were lost in the din.

Replacing the tools in the bag, and zipping it up, Mark tied the bag to his leg and moved toward the hatch.

The entrance to the Coal shoot had been little more than that, a shoot. Not a tunnel, not a shaft; only a small square metal hatch. Barely 2 feet wide and 3 feet in length, and the hole underneath the hatch was smaller than that.

A few inches shorter and the plan would have failed completely.

Had he been slightly huskier, or even more athletic, he wouldn't have made it halfway down.

As it was, Mark had to go into the shoot headlong, his arms painfully squeezed together, but he was able to make it through—

Until his arms made contact with the coal at the bottom of the shoot, that was.

It had been completely covered by small lumpy rocks

of anthracite. Whenever the last shipment of coal had been dumped into the bin that awaited at the bottom, it must have been filled up to the top, and never a shovel was removed.

Summer preparation for the winter to come. Mark thought.

Or rather that's what he might have thought had he not been panicking.

He was too far in to get back out on his own. His legs and hips were past the entrance, and with the tool bag, now under his feet, his shoes could gain no purchase on the metal slide beneath them.

He couldn't call for help, there was no one to help.

Hap was busy and might not survive the suicide mission that Mark had tried to talk him out of.

Ally was likely somewhere in the house beyond, her mind enslaved to something Mark couldn't even understand, let alone think about.

It was likely even if she was to come across him in this state she would only laugh at him, (if she was still capable of laughing.)

She might even turn him over to Maru.

He had a terrible picture in his head of one of the Giants, sweeping the perimeter, walking around the side of the house and seeing the hatch sitting open and reaching down with one thickly muscled arm, pulling him out of the hole, by one leg, like a man removing a dead fish from the cooler.

In his mind, he heard the voice of dead Brisco: The Ogre, *"Well look what we have here. Hehehe. Welcome Back, Little man."* And a shudder passed through him.

He had to think.

Had to get out.

Had to push.

Mark drew himself further down into the slide, kicking and pulling as he went until he was up against the pile of rocks. He began to push at them, nudging them aside. One by one, they gave.

Mark dug at the top of the shaft, pushing the blackness

away, and slowly he felt his fingers move up into space, space unimpeded by rocks.

He redoubled his efforts and slowly his path was cleared, not into light, but a void.

He pushed against the coal and pulled himself closer to the gap, which slowly grew wider and wider.

Finally after what had seemed like an eternity to him, but had actually only been a matter of minutes, he was able to push his arm, and then his head, and chest into the room.

Rocks fell to the ground below and made considerable noise but Mark didn't care, he was free.

He could breathe; he was no longer standing on his head.

But his relief was short-lived, because just as he had gotten his rear clear of the hole, the entire house, and the mound beneath it shook, first with the impact of the truck, and then with the force of exploding gun powder.

The surprise of that moment, sent Mark spilling down to the floor below, landing on top of the lumpy coal, and crushing some of the weaker chunks, but not enough to lessen the pain of the impact.

His pain was secondary.

Ally was all that mattered. He began to try to move...
Nope.
Pain!
The pain was all that mattered.

He swept the rocks out from under his side with his arms as best he could and struggled to find purchase.

Finally, he was up. Hap had bought him time, he couldn't afford to waste it. If there was fire, as he had hoped there would be, beyond the explosion of the gunpowder/ tree stump remover, the Giants and Maru would be busy with that.

If they were lucky, the whole place would be in flames in a matter of moments, but Mark knew that was too much to ask for.

The flames would be put out, either by sprinklers and fire extinguishers or by other means. But if Maru had to call out all his giants to focus on the flames Mark might stand a chance of getting to Ally. Once there, he planned to try and gain the upper hand on her.

This wasn't her fault and even if he had to fight her, he planned to get her out of this place, dragging her out unconscious if he had to.

He had not forgotten the amazing strength she had already acquired in the mere hour or so between the time they had left the dining hall and when she had thrown him across the room.

But Hap had helped him prepare for that too.

He had two options, and the plan was to use both of them.

One was a bottle of chloroform, the second was a syringe.

"When you get near enough to her," Hap had instructed, "Throw the liquid in her face. Don't waste time putting it on the rag first. If you throw it in her face, in her eyes might even be better, it will make her gasp, she won't be able to help it, it's an involuntary reaction. That will make her breathe the poison in immediately, then dump it on the rag, and try to get it over her mouth and nose. That should knock her out."

"What do you mean should?" Mark had asked.

"She's still undergoing the change," Hap had explained, "You told me she was a raging volcano of heat when you touched her. That means the thing inside her is making her metabolism go full tilt, to produce the growth and change it wants. You are only going to have a few moments. The chloroform will definitely make her woozy, but it won't put her down for long. That's what the needle is for. Basically, it's a Mickey in a syringe."

"A Mickey?"

"A Roofie?" Hap asked, hoping Mark would understand

that term.

"Got it."

"Good." Hap continued, "Half the syringe should make her more pliable, she won't know what's going on for a while, but she'll be able to move as you guide her. But again with her metabolism, she might burn it off quickly. If she does, give her the other half. If you do that, she's likely going to pass out, and you'll have to drag her. I'll try to help you if I'm able, but that's assuming I'm still alive at that point."

"Why do you know, let alone have all this stuff?" Mark had asked.

"Some things you don't want to know the answer to, boy, but suffice to say I haven't lived in Kansas all my days, and I've seen enough to know that in this world what I'm showing you is the minimum of what you need to survive. And like the boy scouts used to say before the Commies got to them, "*Always be Prepared.*"

Now Mark was on his feet and brought out the small pen flashlight he had kept in his pocket. Its LED beam lit up the entire room and he could see he was in a small storage space, maybe fifteen, by twenty feet, the majority of which was taken up by a large coal furnace. He looked around for a more modern one, but apparently that was located somewhere else in the building, likely for better access to a natural gas line or electricity.

This space was abandoned and hadn't been thought of at least since Maru bought the place. It was possible Maru didn't even know it existed.

Along the walls of the room were several tools meant for the maintenance and feeding of the furnace, including several large shovels.

In the middle of the room, was a large wooden ladder that looked sound enough, more importantly, it seemed to be the only way out of the room.

Limping a bit, Mark made his way too and then up the

ladder. But of course, the door above him would not budge.

Stepping up against it, he pushed harder putting his back to the problem. The hatch suddenly lifted some, enough that he could see light coming from under a nearby door, but not enough to open.

Shining his light around he could see there was another padlock that had been added to the door, presumably to keep people out, not in. This was a more modern piece of metal. Not the sturdy iron lock and hinge that had held together for more than a hundred years completely exposed to weather, but something from the last twenty years, barely much better than tin.

Mark climbed back down the ladder and retrieved one of the spaded shovels.

He climbed back up, pressed his back against the overhead door, and placed the shovel into the crack and pulled down on the handle. It budged a little bit but still didn't go far. Mark released the tension, and then pulled down hard and fast, trying to jolt the metal screws out of the wood.

What he did was to jolt the wooden ladder out from underneath himself.

The next thing he knew he was dangling from a shovel handle, 5 feet off the ground, both hands struggling to hold on to the shovel as if it were a monkey bar.

Fortunately, he had reasonably good upper body strength and was still able to hold onto the shovel without much difficulty…

Unfortunately, he was now trapped between the ceiling and the floor… But his weight soon solved that problem for him as well. He heard a slight creek, and that creek became a groan, and before he knew it there was a tremendous crash, (much louder than a simple lock breaking should have been,) as what was above the door fell over, releasing the pressure against the hatchway, breaking the lock, sending him to the ground below.

"*Oh, now that's done it!*" Mark thought after the pain subsided enough for him to think anything at all, (besides expletives,) *"Everything Hap just did is for naught and they are going to find me and I am going to die!"*

He waited.

He listened.

Nothing.

Perhaps.

Perhaps, no one had heard it...

Maybe it was missed because the Giants were all still busy fighting the fire.

Perhaps...

There was a creek on the floorboards above him, a stomping wobbling creak.

Then another.

And another.

It moved across the floor in a wide awkward gate.

"One of the giants." Mark thought.

As quietly as he could, he made his way toward the cold black iron furnace and hid in the space between it and the wall.

Maybe, just maybe, if he hid here, and they did look down into the furnace room below, they wouldn't see him.

They would think that the noise and whatever had fallen had been caused by the vibrations from the Truck's impact and the subsequent explosion.

Above him, he heard a door open.

A deep voice grumbled and threw something big, heavy and metal, out of the way. It came over to the broken hatch and pulled it open with a loud metallic creek, letting the light, (which the investigator must have turned on,) shine down into the dank space below.

The Investigator grumbled low in his throat and then hopped down into the chamber below.

The wooden ladder clattered beneath its feet.

"Please don't have night vision." Mark prayed silently, " Please don't have night vision!"

The figure moved in the blackness, scanning the room. He didn't seem to detect Mark or anything out of place. Mark could see nothing but a slight shadow moving about in the room, cast by the light above, and he didn't dare look out to see who it was, he barely breathed, let alone moved.

Strange it was then that as the Investigator turned and set the ladder up against the ceiling, the pipe from the furnace, directly above Mark's head suddenly chose that moment, in all its long years of being in place, to suddenly and inexplicably let go; dumping a ton of black ash and soot down on to Mark's head.

Unable to stop himself, Mark coughed and gasped as a plume of black smoke filled the basement.

The figure ran toward him as he rasped and gurgled, stepping out from behind the furnace.

"Gah!" Screamed the investigator, seeing Mark coming out, his arms raised above his head, "A Night Gaunt!! It's A Night Gaunt! I knew they'd come for me one day!"

"No!" Mark rasped, and tried to shush Tom, "It's me! It's Mark Thurston! I'm not a Night... whatever."

"Oh... You... I didn't reckon we'd ever see you here again. Did you come back here for the Calamari? I thought we told you it wouldn't work for you now, seeing as you know about it."

"No. No," Mark said, still spiting and brushing away soot, "I've come back to get Ally. To get my wife."

"Oh there's no point in that, cause she ain't your wife no more. Leastways she won't be after the Conjunction and if she rejects it, what's left of her, to be getting at, won't be worth getting gotten, when you get it."

"Well, I'm trying to get her out of here before that happens," Mark said, not quite sure what all that nonsense added up to.

"I should probably tell Maru that you're here." Said Tom,

making for the Ladder, "I'm always supposed to tell him when we 'ave guests."

"Tom, I'd appreciate it if you didn't." Mark said, knowing he had been able to make appeals to the Frog-men before, "I'd rather Maru not know I'm here until absolutely necessary."

"Oh nau, I have to be telling him, you see, he was quite angry with me and the boys when we let you get away earlier tonight, and it would make him very happy with me, in particular, if I was to get you back to him, so Dyondaygah can break your mind."

"I'll make it worth your while." Mark blurted out, not having the slightest idea what he could offer this thing.

"Right then." Said Tom, expectantly, "What have you got for me?"

"I don't suppose money is worth much to you," Mark said, uselessly.

"Nau, nothing to spend it on here." Tom said, "That's one, you got two more."

"Two more?" Mark asked, "Two more chances to offer me something that I wants so's I won't rat you out. What else you got?"

"I don't suppose freedom would mean much to you either. If I can beat Maru, and save my wife, you might be free."

"Nau. Freedom's not worth much to us Frog-men, serving is in our nature. We serve the ones what's got the most power when they got it, and when they don't anymore, we eats them if we can, and if we can't we move on to the next Dark Master... That's two. One more."

Mark pushed the never-ending cloud of soot off of himself, as much as he could, there had to be something he could offer Tom, but what?

"3... 2... 1..." Tom suddenly counted, "Times up."

He started to climb the ladder.

"Mischief." Mark heard the words coming out of his mouth before he even knew the thought was in his head.

The Frog-man stopped and turned toward him, "What's

that now, eh?"

"Mischief." Mark repeated, "That's all you want, isn't it? That's why you let me go the first time, isn't it? You wanted to see what would happen... What problems I could cause. The chance to do Mischief."

"I'm. Listen-ing." The Frog-man annunciated, resting one arm across its distended belly, and then placing the opposite elbow in that hand, with his other supporting his chin.

"If you don't sound the alarm, don't tell Maru that you saw me, I'll have the chance to cause more problems... You think the truck through the front door and the fire was mischief? That was just the opening round! That was the appetizer. Let me go, and I'll give you boys a show like nothing you've ever seen before."

"That'll do it." The Frog-man started up the ladder again, seemingly satisfied, "But mind." He said stopping, "If you fail, once Dyondaygah has broken your mind, if you stay in this dimension, and the Master doesn't take your living corpse for his own... If me and my mates are not pleased by your performance, we will strip you to the bones, and gnaw on the marrow for days to come, my lad."

"If I fail," Mark said, almost more to himself, than Tom, "I'll consider that a mercy."

"Nau," said Tom thoughtfully, "You won't."

15

The Frog-man had gone scampering off into other parts of the house. At the moment, he really was more interested in letting Mark cause problems than he was in being rewarded for catching him.

That suited Mark just fine.

It was hard enough to look at that monstrous "*squamous*" thing and his "mates" let alone trying to look them in their wall-eyes and speak to them as if they were human.

Closing the hatch, and setting the metal shelf, which had previously been placed over the hatchway, back into position, Mark hoped that the quick clean up would be enough to hide his point of ingress.

If he really could count on Tom not to tell, the last thing he needed was one of the giants to stumble across a mess next to a door in the floor, leading to an unused basement, and then putting two and two together.

Opening up his tool bag, Mark removed a shotgun and box of cartridges.

Despite Hap's protests, Mark didn't like the idea of tying a loaded shotgun to his leg, and dragging it around, even just to get it through the coal shoot, and into the house.

"There's nothing more useless than an unloaded gun, going into combat." Hap had beefed.

"I can think of something "more useless." Mark had quipped, "A dead man who thought tying a loaded shotgun to his leg and sliding down a coal shoot was a good idea."

Now Mark loaded four rounds into the gun, (three in the tube, one in the chamber,) and placed another four in his back pockets, two on each side. He had another four still in the box, but if he started firing, it would likely be better to run than try to go for them. Still, better to have it and not need it, etc, etc.

With the gym bag's strap tightened to his shoulder, and the shotgun at the ready, Mark began to creep down the hall.

Because the house was more than a hundred years old, nearly every step Mark took made a sound.

Floorboards creaked under his weight, no matter how gently he stepped.

Under other circumstances it might have been almost comical; sneaking like Scooby-Doo, complete with over the top sound effects, lacking nothing but a groovy 60s music track.

But for him, there wasn't anything the least bit funny about it.

He couldn't remember if the dining hall's floor had squeaked so loudly, if at all, but he certainly hoped not.

He would have to walk directly over the heads of the Acolytes. While their attentions might be focused on the worship of their god, a sound from above, where there shouldn't be one, would undoubtedly draw attention.

Mark had hoped that the fire and explosion of Hap's truck might draw all of the Giants and Maru up out of the cellar. If that had happened, they might have either taken Ally with them or left her below.

If she was with them he might have tried to draw her away from them somehow. There was a possibility that as a new acolyte, not fully initiated and trusted, she might be left behind in the chamber while the others left to assist if that was the case, he had hoped to somehow get the drop on her, and any guards who might have been left behind.

But now that he was in the building, none of those options seemed likely.

Just what was he going to do?

He and Hap had discussed several contingencies, but there was no way of knowing what was going to happen or how Maru's minions would react. Improvise. That's all there was to do.

"*Distract. Get in. Avoid the Giants. Get Ally. Get out alive.*" That was the plan. Try your best to stick to the main plan, and make up the rest as you went.

As he reached the end of the hallway, it opened up into the reception area of the hotel.

Mark had come out next to the stairs that led up to the second floor.

The sprinklers had been set off in this section as well.

As Mark entered the lobby, he saw the crimson carpet, turned dark as blood, and felt it squish beneath his boots.

While the weight of the water helped prevent sound from the creaking boards, he now ran the risk of any quick movement being given away by sloshing sounds.

He came to a cross-section, where the hallway he had been traversing met with the secondary lane which led into the dining area, the long staircase coming down from above to meet it.

In the dining room, the fire seemed to be out. The smell of smoke and charred wood invaded Mark's nostrils.

He had hoped the flames would get out of control.

While it might have made it more difficult to get to Ally, he would have felt better knowing this place would not be standing when the sun rose.

But alas, that was not to be.

The Giants seemed to be milling around the remains of Hap's truck, which had not exploded along with the powder as they had hoped it might. Mark could hear the revving engine, slowly dying as it was shut off. From somewhere in the dining hall, Maru was shouting instructions Mark couldn't quite make out.

He heard a few creaks and pings as the truck was being moved by hand, while others cleared away broken furniture.

With the truck weighing more than 2000 pounds before the gun powder had been placed in it, Mark had hoped that if the truck didn't blow up, it might collapse the floor of the dining hall.

If it had done so, Ally might have been at risk again, if she was still down below, but it would be another distraction to their foes.

But that hadn't happened either.

The truck and the floor remained (more or less) intact. Mark moved closer, gun at the ready, pointing up the staircase, lest one of the giants or Frog-men, (or God only knew what else) might be lurking nearby.

As he moved toward the dining area, he began to understand the words being said in the dining room. One of the Giants was speaking to Maru.

"That's the end of Mr. Howard."

Oh no. Mark thought. What had gone wrong? Hap wasn't supposed to die in this. He was supposed to knock over the cinderblock on to the gas pedal, tie off the steering wheel, and jump out at the last possible moment. But the Giant's words left no doubt.

"Don't you understand you mindless fool? This was not the main attack. This was a distraction!"

Mark silently cursed to himself and wondered if there could have been some other way. And now it was all useless, Maru hadn't believed the lie that Mark had abandoned his wife to her fate and now Hap was dead.

What's more, Maru would be looking for him.

"... This goes much deeper than Mr. Howard or Mr. Thurston. With this power by their side, who knows what they might accomplish?"

Power? Mark thought silently, *What power? We don't have any magic.*

But Mark barely had time to worry about this, because a moment later Maru was shouting again, "I want the remaining two to continue the chanting but also to keep an eye on Ally. I do not want her to escape. I want the rest of you to scour the building! Thurston is here! I can feel it!"

Escape? Mark thought, had something happened? Had

Ally put up a resistance? Had she been able to somehow fight through the control that the "Sacred food" had foisted upon her? She was a strong-willed person and the best of women, surely if anyone could find their way back through the labyrinth of their own mind, and the invading will of a demon god, it was his Ally.

A wild hope leapt up within him.

Ally, *his* Ally was back. She was in her right mind and she was being held prisoner against her will. If she could be so strong, so could he.

By all that was good and right in this world, he would get her out of this accursed place!

He was drawn back to reality and the desperate nature of his situation, when Maru shouted out again, above the noise of the fire extinguishers, and the creaking metal of Hap's truck being moved by hand, "Nothing is more powerful than Dyondaygah! Now put me down. And gather The Children as I instructed you! We must find Thurston!"

Well, so much for being here without them knowing it.

Mark his back, literally and figuratively, against a wall wondered where could he hide.

He barely knew the layout of the building. He could try to make his way back down into the coal cellar, but there he would be trapped, no windows, and the only way in or out via a ladder.

Never mind that if one of the giants was familiar with the closet that led to the cellar, he might notice if the steel shelf was out away from the wall, and no longer covering the hatchway. A hatchway that now sported a broken lock.

Where to hide?

Where?

Where!

It was then that it came to him. He reached down in his pants pocket and found it; the key to the Honeymoon Suite. It was the last place they would expect, what's more, it was the only room that Mark knew of, he could be sure was uninhabited.

It was likely the place where they always sent their victims, a place to allow the changes that the sacred food would inflict to begin until they could be fully overtaken from within.

It would be the last place they might expect him to hide because of the horrible things that had happened to him in that room.

He knew that the giants and Maru could access it at any time and it offered no protection at all, but what it might offer him was time.

A place to hide until the search was called off. The time of the conjunction was growing near. They would have to call off the search so they could go and complete their meeting with the demon god. That would be his window.

But to wait so long, to wait until the time when Ally would be fully taken by Dyondaygah; could he afford to risk that?

Feet began to clomp around in the dining hall as the giants mobilized.

No time for wondering now. Hide. Find safety now. Think later.

Mark bolted up the stairs as quietly as he could. He stepped only on the edges of the stairs, at their (hopefully) strongest point, and had made it nearly halfway up before he heard them give a significant squeak.

No time for waiting to see if the sound had drawn attention, Mark continued his dash up the stairs, away from the first floor, away from the giants, but also further away from his goal; His wife.

He reached the top of the stairs and made a beeline for the door of the honeymoon suite. The handle of the doors to most of the rooms on this floor were not unlike the handle of the door to the Men's restroom downstairs, cast iron, twisted down into a curly-cue. But this time, above the handle, there was a small metal thumb plate, to withdraw the deadlatch, with a keyhole above it to open the bolt.

Mark withdrew the key as he approached the Suite door and was about to press down on the thumb plate, when his mind flashed back to the handle in the men's room, how he had seen it undulate and flex, ever so slightly.

There was no question in his mind now.

He *had* actually seen that happen.

He hesitated for a moment, it was a good thing he did because the handle immediately uncurled and lashed out to wrap around his arm, forcing the shotgun from his hand to thud quietly on the carpet.

Mark had tried to pull his hand away, but he wasn't fast enough. The handle, now an uncoiled tendril of metal, caught hold of his wrist, its cold grip holding him fast.

Mark feared it would suddenly become solid again, to hold him in place.

But it did not. It did something worse.

It began to pull him in, trying to draw his hand toward the wood of the door.

Mark pulled away with all his strength, and narrowed his hand, tucking his thumb in trying to slide free of the handle's vice-like strength.

He wanted to scream and let all of his terror flow out through that scream, but he couldn't.

Any noise, any sound, could draw the attention of the giants, they were already looking for him.

They might even now be at the base of the stairs.

But what good would it do him to be silent if this door held him here until they could arrive?

Was this some sort of security measure?

Would every door in the house now turn against him like this?

The handle pulled him closer, and now Mark looked, not at the tendril gripping his arm, but at the door itself.

The keyhole too had changed. The void where the key was meant to go was not a hole at all, but an eye. A multifaceted eye, almost like that of an insect, but rather than the facets being too small to see, Mark could make out that each facet had a pupil of its own. Fifteen or twenty irises stared hungrily at him.

The thing the eye belonged to had somehow taken possession of the door and was now using it to pull him in.

But just when he thought the horror was complete, the door had one more surprise left for him; the thumb plate began to wriggle and flex, up and down at first but then, it curled inwardly toward the middle, and Mark understood- It was now a tongue, a wriggling, writhing tongue reaching out toward his hand, wanting a taste.

Mark placed his feet against the wall next to the door jam and strained against it, but still, the metal arm crept up further, adhering around his wrist, and pulling ever tighter, until Mark was sure his hand would break.

Not knowing what else to do, nor where the thought came from, he took the key, which was still in his left hand and jammed it into the socket where the eye looked out at him.

He felt the pressure as the yielding squishy flesh first bent under the key's pressure, and then popped like a puss-filled balloon.

There was a quiet high pitched squeal of pain, like a tortured kitten, which emanated from the door, (or the thing in control of the door) as Mark continued to rack the key in the place where the keyhole should have been.

He could feel the teeth of the key squishing through the slimy muck of the creature's eye...

Making contact with the tumblers of the bolt.

He felt the metal tentacle react in pain, and so he turned the key in the lock, scooping the key's teeth through it, mangling the viscera of the eye.

The Metal recoiled from his arm, melting back into its previous form as the possessing influence abandoned it.

Free, Mark bolted away from the handle to the opposite side of the hall, backing into another door.

For a split second, Mark feared that this door two would

turn on him, but it didn't.

The door to the honeymoon suite was exactly as it had been before, nothing more than a piece of formed and shaved wood, with forged metal ironmongery.

Mark could see the door was now partly open; darkness beyond.

He was about to move away from the opposite side of the door when something darker in that darkness---Moved.

Flexed.

A muscle, or series of muscles, tightened and released.

Breathing.

Mark felt a rumble in the floor moving toward him, but he didn't even have time to curse before the door flew back on its hinge and a cyclonic wind bellowed up from within, sucking him into the void.

A tremendous wind that should have drawn the paintings from the walls and carpet from the floor began to pull on Mark and Mark alone, drawing him back toward the doorway.

Mark felt his feet being dragged into this "sideways tornado" and grabbed on to anything that he could, that thing being the door handle of the opposing room. He held on to the door with all his might, almost wishing that it too would wrap around his hand, as the other had moments before, but it remained a lifeless piece of metal, as Mark's feet were lifted off the ground and toward the blackness beyond.

A void, that was not void.

For now, with the door open, and the light from the hallway shining into that blackness, Mark could see what lay beyond.

Not a room, not the outside blackness of night, nothing that should have ever been behind that door awaited him.

The portal no longer opened on anything from this world at all. All that lay beyond was teeth. It was an endless tunnel of circling lamprey teeth and red muscle, like the esophagus of Hell.

The wind was the sucking in of some great beast, large

beyond understanding, trying to draw him in and down, down, down.

His right hand, already aching and possibly broken from its struggle with the living handle, Mark had only his left to rely on, and that had always been his weaker arm.

He felt his fingers slipping and before he could even try to change hands he had lost his grip.

He went flying toward the open doorway and felt the handle of the door scrape his back. He was drawn into the mouth of darkness and knew this was the end.

There wasn't time to think.

No time to pray.

No opportunity for salvation.

He was pulled out of this world and into the very throat of the devil-

-When something held him back.

He jolted against his sports bag. Miracle of miracles, the door handle that had moments ago been the tool of his foe, had now become his best friend in the world.

When he had been dragged horizontally across the handle of the door, his military-style sports bag, which had been draped around his shoulder had caught on the curly-cue and prevented Mark from being dragged away into the nightmare that awaited him.

He dangled only a few inches beyond the door, bobbing like a windsock.

Mark's impact against the bag had drawn the shoulder strap out to its full length, but it still held firm, with no signs of fraying.

Shocked to see that he still had a chance, Mark held tightly to the bag with his left arm, while reaching for the door handle with his right.

He felt his fingers glaze over the cold iron, but it was just out of reach, he couldn't... quite...

Suddenly, the force trying to pull him in relented. Mark felt gravity reassert itself, and in one final pull on the bag strap and with the loss of the opposing force, Mark was able to grab hold of the door handle from both sides.

The smooth knob of the door interior handle in his right hand and the iron bar in his left, but now he dangled directly over a row of wet, glistening, pointed teeth.

Somewhere hundreds of feet below him he could see them glinting in the darkness; they undulated hungrily.

Then he heard something, a slight rustling, gritty sound, like the sands of an hourglass spilling out. He looked and, in the light coming from the hallway, he could see a fine black powder drizzling down out of his sports bag.

The gunpowder.

The tree stump remover packet he had in his bag must have burst when his body had slammed against it, and the powder had found a small finger-sized hole and was spilling out.

From somewhere deep in the Hellmouth, there came a sound, a retching, irritated throat sound, like the distant deep bellow of a Mac Truck, only a thousand, thousand times bigger.

Mark heard and felt the wind begin to draw back again, but then it stopped.

Draw, and stop.

Draw and Stop, and the iteration between the drawing and the stopping grew shorter and shorter.

Mark was not idle, somehow he knew what was coming. He'd seen Pinocchio.

He thanked God for late nineteen-century ironwork, which seemed to have been made to withstand the assault of tanks, and began to swing his weight on the door, which was as nothing to its massive iron hinges.

The door began to swing toward the wooden floor and jam that lay beyond.

Out around the doorframe was nothing, it seemed to be suspended in midair, the red muscle and teeth of the Hellmouth going on somewhere beyond it, but Mark was beyond noticing such things, all that mattered was getting back into the Olde Towen Buffet; getting his feet back on solid ground before-

A great roar came from somewhere down in the gullet of the beast and Mark knew, as his shoe scraped the floorboards, trying to gain purchase that it was too late.

The black gun powder had irritated something in the creature and now there was one final massive and sharp backdraft, pulling Mark back toward the darkness, nearly dragging Hap's borrowed shoes from his feet, which was followed, just as suddenly and powerfully, by a complete reversal of its force with enough pressure to make Mark's eardrums burst.

He was thrown headlong back into the hotel, hitting the opposite wall like a load of bricks, as the Hellmouth sneezed.

The door slammed against the jam with all the percussive force of a fully-loaded garbage truck being dropped off the Empire State Building.

The entire hotel shook to its foundations as plaster, old and new cracked and became lined with gaps.

Mark's nose was bleeding, and his ears rang.

He was battered and bruised from being slammed against the wall, but he was alive. He felt the blood flowing in his veins as he saw the door opening again.

He scrabbled for the shotgun which lay at his feet, dreading what might come out of the room next.

But as the door swung back on its hinges he saw there was nothing behind the door, but a well-lit room.

The Honeymoon Suite, just as it had been when they'd left it earlier that night, their small suitcases, in disarray, on the now unmade bed.

He had feared that with all the massive changes in air pressure he had just undergone, that his eardrums might have been ruptured, but the sound of an approaching army's footsteps in the hallway below made it clear that his hearing was not only intact but as good as it had ever been.

But that also meant the giants were coming.

And as if he needed any more warning, he could hear Maru shouting at the top of his voice, *"THUUURRRRSTON!!!"*

Though it was the last thing he wanted to do now, and the last place he wanted to be, he had no choice. Grabbing up the end of his sports bag, as to stop leaving the black gunpowder trail behind, Mark dashed into the room, closing the door behind him as gently and silently as he could.

He was sure that, over the sound of the tromping feet, the gentle click of the latch had not been heard.

But he had to hide.

He was not safe.

He had only a moment before the giants would arrive.

16

Maru fumed as the Children of Dyondaygah milled around him.

It was annoying how much of their original personalities the Giants retained after being joined to their god.

If Maru would have had his way, they would have all been joined to a superior mind such as his own. While it was true that they often shared in a sort of collective, "hive mind" that was only at times of ceremony or worship, or the initiating of a new acolyte, such as when they had foisted their wills upon Mrs. Thurston.

Dyondaygah was growing more powerful by the day, both in this world of space and time and matter and his pocket dimension, with each new convert, and every square foot of ground he claimed, but when he was not directly connected to his people through the convergence, they seemed to have a good bit of free will.

They could question orders and think for themselves and in the latter days that was decidedly not a good thing.

Most people in the modern world didn't know how to think at all. More specifically they had no idea how to problem solve. When confronted with an issue, 200 years ago when Maru had been growing up, the average person was expected to solve it themselves, only calling for a specialist at the uttermost end of need.

If you needed a specific piece of iron, such as a horseshoe, you went to a farrier or blacksmith. If you needed a finely made suit, you went to a tailor. If you needed surgery, you went to a Doctor.

But for most things, you were expected to do for yourself.

It had been more or less that way until the end of World War II, but with the coming of *"The Push Button Era,"* humanity had become less and less capable as a whole. Then with the coming of the *"Digital Age"* the age of the Search engine and the smartphone, the disease had progressed significantly in a matter of just a few years. When the *"Pushbutton era"* and the "Digital Age" was too much work for the average person, the world was more than ready for a new master.

Humanity now only had two possible "best destinies;" Enslavement, or Extinction.

For whatever reason, it was from these "less capable people" that most of the Children of Dyondaygah were chosen.

Ally Thurston was an exception.

Maru felt certain that when she was fully joined to the Children of Dyondaygah she would rise quickly in the ranks, just as Brisco had. She might even become the de facto leader.... After himself of course.

But as a result of Brisco being out of commission, the children at the moment were very stupid and didn't seem to know how to do much of anything.

When Maru had bid them search, many of them had just stood around looking under tables and looking down hallways. A few of them had opened doors, glanced around and not seeing anything out of the ordinary, had closed them again.

Maru had to instruct them to search properly.

Look under the check-in desks and in the closets.

Listen for signs; breathing, things being out of place.

Sweep the hallways.

It was Ernest who had finally detected the oddity in the broom closet.

A steel shelf had been moved forward, away from the wall and beneath where it had been was a hatchway that Maru barely remembered seeing before. The wood of the hatch had been broken as someone forced their way in from below.

Climbing down into the room, Maru had discovered Mark's point of entry.

"Very clever Mr. Thurston," Maru said to himself. "Very clever indeed... But how did you know the location of this coal shoot, eh?"

"Maybe he scouted the building before he came, Master," Ernest said, rubbing his head after bumping the ceiling with it for the fourth time.

"No, he never had time for that." Maru said dismissively, "He and Ally have never been on this ground before tonight. I can tell when someone is on the Towen. I am connected to every square inch of it, and though I may not know where they are precisely, I know when they are here. Had I not been focused on Mr. Howard and his riotous music I would have known precisely when Mr. Thurston set foot again upon this land. Mr. Howard on the other hand. He has been here long enough to have made a study of the building. Perhaps with spyglasses and binoculars... He is a tech junkie, he may even have put a camera on a remote-controlled car or a drone. I would not have sensed that.... But we should have heard something."

"Maybe Carter had some blueprints in his books that you lost to Mr. Howard." Ernest said thoughtfully.

"Don't be ridiculous. I have the blueprints and they wouldn't have been sold with the books of the Old fool who built this place." Maru chided.

"I only thought maybe he, uh..." Ernest trailed off.

"What have I told you about thinking?" Maru said, "You and most of these other bumbling acolytes are not good at it! Let me do the thinking!"

"Yes, sir," Ernest said obediently.

"Now you bumbling beef-head, Lift me up and put me through the hatchway." Maru commanded and Ernest did as he was told, assisting Maru up and out of the Coal Cellar.

Once Ernest had crawled up back into the broom closet, he closed the hatchway, only to hear Maru give out a little cry of pain, as though he had been hit by something unseen.

"A doorway has just been opened in the house," Maru explained.

"The others are searching," Ernest observed, "I imagine they are opening and closing doors all the time."

"Not an actual doorway!" Maru groaned, "As the conjunction grows near, the worlds beyond this one start to collide, so that the Path to Dyondaygah may open. But others get opened along the way. Right now the Sarsen stones are powering up, drawing energy from the earth. But this is a strong connection... Such things only happen rarely. Usually its only doors to other times, and places, this was a door to something very old and powerful."

"Oh." Said Ernest, "Well that makes sense, one time I opened a door upstairs and I saw the body of a fat naked headless man stumbling around in what looked like a stone dungeon. He sensed me somehow and came running toward the door. Just barely closed it in time, I did. And he was pounding and hollering... Don't know how he managed to holler without ahead but he did it all the same... Then it suddenly stopped. When I opened the door, the dungeon and the Headless man were gone, Just a bedroom again."

"Hmm." Maru said thoughtfully, "Sounds like Y'golonac, the Defiler... Did he have a pair of mouths in his hands?"

"That was the one." Said Ernest, "The very one."

"If you should see him again, be sure to tell me immediately. He might be very useful to us."

Suddenly there was a deep rumble from somewhere above their heads. The rumble deepened and suddenly a great wind blew through the house from the upstairs.

The entire building shook as though hit with a wrecking ball from within. Maru saw the plaster crack and break, and a few large chunks fell out of the ceiling.

"He's upstairs!" Maru shrieked, "He has angered something! It might even be Yog Sothoth himself! Pick me up!"

Ernest obeyed, "Children of Dyondaygah!" Maru

shouted, and through whatever power he had been given, all of them, no matter where they were in the house heard their master's call, "The Intruder is upstairs! He has angered a great one! Bring him to me! Bring me Thurston! Alive!"

Immediately, all the giants dropped what they were doing and made for the nearest stairwell.

"Take me upstairs you fool!" Maru shouted even as Ernest was loping down the hallway, just barely avoiding hitting Maru's head on the support beams. As they turned the corner and raced up the stairs, Maru cried out like a man going to war, "*THUUURRRSTON*!!!" Ernest reached the top of the stairs, several of the giants directly behind him.

There they saw the empty hallway. Paintings now hanging askew, and a few of the doors sitting ajar. "I want him!" Maru shouted. "Thurston is somewhere on this floor! Find him! Find him now! Focus on finding him! Nothing else matters!"

From opposite ends of the hall, several more of the giants appeared, climbing out of the stairwells.

They all stood there looking at each other up and down the hall from the three points of entry, as though they expected to see Thurston somehow materialize out of the ether.

"The Rooms, you fools! Look in the rooms!" Maru explained, "I want two of you guarding each of the stairwells! Let no one pass! The rest of you, search the rooms! Do I have to explain everything??!!"

This seemed to lead to some debate amongst the giants as to who should do which of the jobs they had been assigned. But within moments it was resolved, and the giants began to open several doors in the long corridor, a corridor that, as Maru looked at it, now seemed longer than he remembered.

This was not unusual for the Towen. Sometimes, especially when the conjunction was near, the house would not only connect to other realities, but the strange geometry of those worlds would foist themselves upon this world.

As a result.... Well, anything could result...

The most common reaction of the Towen was that it would become "dimensionally transcendental" or more simply "its inside would become bigger than its outside". But why, oh why, did it have to be happening now?

Because the Old Ones were the gods of chaos, of course. They thrived upon it, they preferred it to be the natural state of the Universe, void and without form.

It had been the very undoing of chaos, the "order" of time and space and matter, being imposed on the Universe, which had driven the Old Ones into the outer reaches in the first place.

Giants disappeared into several of the rooms at once, but quickly after from the rooms there followed screams of terror and even a few gouts of blood and viscera, while others came running back out into the hallway, with looks of sheer terror on their faces, slamming the doors behind them.

Maru knew what had happened of course. The doors were not opening up on the hotel rooms, but on to other planes of existence. There the giants were being attacked by whatever inhabited that nearby world.

Some of them made it back, others didn't.

It was of little importance to Maru.

He had plenty of giants, and for whatever reason, once Dyondaygah had linked with a human body, it made little difference whether or not that Servant lived or died.

Once Dyondaygah's circle of influence in this world had grown it would stay the same, and only continue to grow, as Dyondaygah himself would continue to grow until he encompassed both Earth and sky and sea.

His tentacles would reach out to the rest of the solar system and beyond.

Perhaps it was even the will of Dyondaygah that these giants die or be taken away, so that the sacred food within them would become part of those other places and he might gain a foothold in them as well.

And so be it.

But Maru couldn't allow this to go on.

"Close those doors!" He shouted, and the giants obeyed. "From now on only open doors that have a number on them! The doors that don't have numbers on them are not from this plane!"

The giants obeyed and began skipping over unmarked doors. From up and down the hall, Maru could now hear the sounds of beds being overturned and closets being ransacked.

"You can't hide forever." Maru thought, still sitting on Ernest's shoulder, "I know every inch of this building and when it snaps back to its normal form, there will be no place for you to hide."

From somewhere to his left a strange golden light, a light Maru had seen before, pulsed. Looking in that direction, he saw one of the giants standing before an open door, the light pulsed and beamed and undulated over her.

"Look away you fool!" Maru shouted, but his words were lost in the ear-piercing scream the giantess let out, as she grabbed the sides of her head, unable to take her eyes away from what lay beyond.

"I don't want to see!" she screamed, her sonorous voice echoing strangely.

While Maru did not "know" what she was looking at, he knew what she must be seeing, the cosmic nature of the universe, that in seeing, immediately became part of you.

Some fools in the ancient writings had posited that by seeing what the light revealed, it was overwhelming your brain with concepts that it could never fully grasp.

The reality was that as you stared into that knowledge you became that knowledge, your body was transmuted into pure energy.

When others had been pulled away from it prematurely, and bodies where autopsied, some of what should have been within was missing altogether, while other parts, the brain, in particular, had become crystalline, able to transcend and compute faster and more efficiently than mere flesh ever could.

It was the fact that the process had been interrupted that had ultimately killed the victim, leaving them an irreconcilable mesh of human and whatever they were becoming.

Now Maru had an opportunity to watch first hand as the woman's body began to glow from within, first her brain began to glow out through the frail matter of her bones and skin, making every blood vein beneath visible as her body was changed, and she continued to shout over and over again, "I don't want to see! I don't want to see! Make it stop!"

Soon light was pouring out of her, and her eyes turned into columns of flame bursting out from her skull.

"I can still see!" she shouted, in a wail of despair and horror, that even moved what remained of Maru's shriveled heart, "I CAN STILL SEEEEEEEE!"

Her body was a column of flame, white-hot intense light.

The Paint on the walls around her began to liquefy, the plaster to melt and the carpet beneath her burned.

Suddenly the flame was sucked into the doorway, in a rush of power, and the door slammed home, leaving behind only the scorched surroundings where she had once stood.

The light underneath the door, faded...

Faded.

And went out.

The door reopened, whatever pressure had closed it in the first place, now gone, and beyond there was nothing but an empty room.

"Well," said Maru, "That was educational."

Ernest stood with mouth agape as did several other giants in the hall who had witnessed the Giantess's transcendence, or evisceration... Whatever you wanted to call it.

"What are you all standing around for?" Maru asked, "Continue the search!"

The giants obeyed.

17

"Oi. That was a good one." Said, William.

"What was?" Asked Tom.

"This'n over here in the hallway." William answered, "The Woman what got burned alive from the inside out and turned into light.

"Should have seen the one over here." Answered Burt, looking down through another set of eye holes that had been placed on the floor of the crawl space between the attic and the ceilings of the rooms and hallway below, "This one opened up into a jungle, and in the Jungle there was a spiny thing, had arms like a man all over it, like a big ball of walking muscley man arms all growing out of each other, with one big eye in the middle."

"Ate him up did it?" Asked Tom hopefully.

"Nau." Bert said disappointed, "The Giant saws it and he runs away, lick-ity split, fast as you please."

"That's a rum go." Said William, "I'd have liked to seen him torn apart piece by piece by a large show of hands."

"That's a good one, William." Said Tom laughing.

"Thank'ee matey."

"Ooow, Take a look at this'n over-'ere." Said Bert. "It's a sunken city. It's all wet and underwater-like. With seaweed and moss growin' everywhere between the stones."

"Is it R'lyeh?" Asked Tom, "Where great dead Cthulhu lies a-dreaming? I'd like to get a look at him."

"Nau." Said Bert, "But it might be Relex."

"Ain't they one in the same thing?" asked William.

"Best hope one of the giants don't be opening that door

while it's connected." Said Tom, "Otherwise we'll have an awful mess to be cleaning up, water everywhere."

"Should be alright," Said William, "As long as no one is stupid enough to breach the barrier."

"Anyone want to see the Lost City of Carcosa in its prime?" Tom asked after waddling over to look into another knothole.

"Nau." Said William, "Seen it. And the King in Yellow is a right git, he is."

"Oi?" Asked Bert, "Where's Thurston, did he survive?"

"Oh yeah." Said Tom, "He's still kicking. Over there in Room 4, the Honeymoon Suite."

"Maybe not so safe as you think." Said William, "The Honeymoon Sweet is back to being that great Gullet. The one what he made sneeze afore."

"Nau, you great cuttlefish." Said Tom, "That's what *they* sees when the opens the door. But right now far as Thurston knows he's hiding in the closet of the Honeymoon suite. He's in his pocket dimension while the real world is actually at the door.... Or is it the other way around?"

"I don't see how it matters." Said Bert, "Either way he's safe at the moment, and I pity them what opens that door, a-looking for him."

"He's doing awful good mischief, all the same." Said Tom, "Living up to his word, he is, says I."

"He ain't done no mischief at all yet." Said William, "He's just opened a door or two and done a lot of hiding."

"But they's looking for him ain't they?" said Tom, "If I'd turned him over right away like you two muttonheads might have, we wouldn't be having all this fun, now would we? Wouldn't have gotten a look at The Defiler neither, and he was quite fun to watch, trying to figure out where our voices was coming from."

"Aye, what with his gibbering and wailing. That was quite the comedy. And to think we might have missed it, had we been doing the work the master assigned instead of "helping" them look for Thurston." Bert chortled deep in his throat.

"Kaw! Look over here!" said William. "We've got a lively one!" I hope someone opens this door. Looks to me like *"The Star Eater"* himself!"

"Oooh! Let me see!" Said Tom and Bert together.

18

Deep down, below the restaurant, below the corridor of inter-dimensional gateways that had once been a simple hallway of guest rooms, at the very heart of the Towen itself, two figures danced.

One man and one woman continued, per their master's orders, to chant the name of their god, over and over again.

Every once in awhile the female would let out a loud, ululating sound, such as might have been given by an ancient tribeswoman, either in the darkest jungles of Africa or by a native American woman on the warpath. But then she would return to speaking the strange guttural language of the dark realms, always punctuated by the name of Dyondaygah.

In the corner, in a hollow of one of the Sarsen stones, Ally stood her eyes half-closed, one eye twitching just slightly. That twitch, that slight movement of one eye, was all she could muster. She felt as though she were caught in a dreamy twilight, trying desperately to wake up but somehow not quite able to do it. She had been that way since she had been led down here by the Children.

They had placed her in this hollow and left her to stand, unmoving while they danced and sang for hours.

She thought back to her time in that room when she had tossed Mark against the wall and on to the bed, as easily as a careless child might toss a rag doll; her heart pounding in her chest, not with exertion but with power, and something like joy. It was a rush, a thrill like nothing she had ever known, feeling like she could do anything, be anything.

It was strength and power and exhilaration and rage all at once.

She thought of every time she had been mistreated in her life. The million jabs about her height and ugliness, and her weight that she had endured during her young school days.

Every moment she had struggled to improve herself and fit into what the girls and boys at school expected her to be, and she knew deep down she was not.

Made fun of because she wasn't pretty enough.

Made fun of because she was a cheerleader.

The Whispers behind her back about being the only girl who had been injured so badly in a Cheerleading routine that she couldn't continue, losing her place on the team. Teachers, Students, and coaches talking about her, and how she had failed.

Being a cheerleader had been her one big chance, her opportunity to break free of the "loser" reputation that had followed her all her young life. To not be the "nerd" with her nose buried in a book.

The Team Captain; a "mean girl" through and through; had not wanted to give her a chance in the first place. She had been dismissed from the auditions, sight unseen.

But when she had gone to the head coach and begged for a real opportunity to show she could do the routines, it had been granted and somehow she had made the team.

Somehow...

She knew exactly how and why.

She was small and light.

She could be the one at the top of the pyramid.

She could be the one the others tossed through the air, and it wouldn't hurt them because she weighed next to nothing compared with the other taller, stronger girls.

But it didn't matter, she was there!

She was on the team!

... For three weeks.

Then the accident had happened.

Her right ankle had snapped like a twig and it was over.

In the years that followed she wondered if it had been on purpose.

She wondered if the other girls who had never wanted her there in the first place had meant to injure her and get her off the squad.

She could never be sure.

She had limped for months and by the time she could walk properly again the school year was nearly over.

The next year, her leg had not completely healed, (and would continue to give her pain for the rest of her life) and the staff of both the school and Cheerleading squad had changed.

The people in charge wanted to get into competitions, meaning they would only accept the prettiest and most athletic of girls. (Despite all the claims to the contrary.)

Which ensured she would never get another chance to be on the team.

Then there was college.

And nothing had changed.

She was mocked because she didn't party enough. Then she had begun to attend the parties and she was mocked because she partied too much, and had been called (among other things) a poser and a fraud.

She remembered every embarrassing moment of her life when she couldn't lift something others thought she should have been able to. From not being able to climb the rope in school to having to ask for help, again and again, seeing the others roll their eyes at her; thinking her lazy or useless.

Mark, classmates, teammates, and co-workers, they had all literally looked down upon her.

At some time or another, she had been mistreated by everyone in her life because of her weakness and size.

It all came rushing back into her mind, moments that had seemed petty and childish for years were experienced anew, with all the pain and sorrow they had caused her, long healed over wounds reopened with a vicious sharpness.

Then there was Mark.
Mark with his constant teasing.
He thought it was cute.
He thought it was funny.
To him, it was all a big joke.
"At least now you'll be able to reach the top shelf."
All the times he had humiliated her, all the times he made her the butt of his jokes.

Now when she was going through something he couldn't even begin to understand, he had the nerve to poke fun at her.

Then the loss of control had come.

Not the moment when she had picked him up with one arm and thrown him across the room. That had felt incredible at the moment, although she had regretted it the next.

It was when she had been on the floor sobbing, all that hate and regret and power pulsing through her when she had felt her mouth begin to move of its own accord.

She had tried to stop it, stop the repeating of the nonsense words coming out of her, but she could not, and somehow the chanting made her feel better.

While the strength and energy were not diminished in the least, it seemed that they were being focused.

No longer shooting off in wild tangents like that of a hyperactive child who had no thought or control of the energies throbbing within, but the extreme focus of a martial arts master, who knows exactly what every muscle is doing inside of them.

And she too was aware. She could feel the changes being wrought in herself, and she both loved and hated them at the same time. She felt herself standing to her feet. Her mouth and voice calling out the name of something she didn't understand but knew that it was helping her channel her energy at the same time, feeling more like a conduit through which energy was flowing, rather than a fallen sparking power line.

Then the other Giants had entered the room, and she had felt a great kinship with them.

She could see their minds.

Hear their thoughts.

Somehow, in a manner that she could never have explained, all of their experiences that mirrored her own were imprinted on her mind. All the times they had felt weak and powerless, abused and forlorn.

Sports teams they hadn't been accepted on, being picked last every time.

Being slapped down by a father or mother, they were too weak to overcome.

Being unable to retaliate in schoolyard fights, or stand up to a competitor.

Barroom fights avoided because they feared the pain and shame of being soundly thumped by an opponent that was too big for them.

Being called a coward.

Over and over again, the impressions of:

Coward.
Weakling.
Fraud. Fool.
Not strong enough.
Not fast enough.
Not good enough.
No hand/eye coordination.
Can't run.
Can't aim.
Can't throw.
Can't shoot.
Can't dance.

They all came flooding into her mind.

She knew that all of these people had been just like her at some point and that they were that way no longer.

They, all of them, herself now included, had once been weak, powerless and overwhelmed, and they were no longer.

They had been saved.

They had been given everything they had always wanted, and who had given all this to them?

Who had made them everything they had always wanted to be?

Who was the great one who alone could give them all they had ever wanted, if they would only serve him?

His name was coming out of her mouth even at that very moment.

She knew she would have given anything for this.

While, yes, the moments *the changing* had been frightening, had this choice been given to her, had she known what the eating of (what she would later learn was called the) Sacred food of Dyondaygah would do to her, and the power it would bestow, she would have accepted it without hesitation.

Without a moment's apprehension.

Ally had said to Mark moments before "I don't want to be eight feet tall."

But now she did want it.

Oh how she wanted it! The power, the strength, the agility, she could feel she was more herself now than she had ever been.

Her body, now matched her soul.

Then Brisco had stepped to the fore and welcomed her as his sister. And she felt a warmth and compassion from them that she had never felt or understood was possible until that moment.

The words were given to her, and yet they were also the words she would have chosen: *"I am honored."* Ally said, *"May Dyondaygah's coming be made manifest in me."*

Brisco had declared Mark a weak mortal, and that he was

to be made a sacrifice, and Ally had repeated the word, "*Sacrifice.*" Mulling it over.

She loved Mark. She did! But if he was the price for this, she would pay it.

After all, hadn't he been part of the reason for her grief? All of his teasing and humiliation, all of his emphasizing her weakness, her lack of size and power, he had kept dredging up all of that hurt, and sadness, he was just as guilty as the others.

She had felt next to nothing when he was dragged away, unconscious, by two of the giants.

Maru had reached up and taken her hand, "*Have no fear, my dear.*" He said with great sincerity, "*He was part of your old life, and he was holding you back, as the entire world has held you back until now. Your new life, your real life, begins tonight at the coming of the conjunction.*"

A single tear may have rolled down her face at that, but whether it was sadness for the loss of Mark, or joy at the prospect of all she could become, she did not know.

Hours had passed by, and now the power that filled her limbs was pure ecstasy.

She felt as though she could lift a train engine single-handedly.

She could run with wild horses and stand astride two of them while chasing down her foes.

She could go to war. Not with guns, and tanks and trucks doing all the work, but real war. A sword in one hand a shield in the other, her foes would fall before her and anyone who would not submit would die on her blade.

She could rip them apart with her bare hands if need be, for all of mankind was weak and useless compared with her might.

She stood there in the chamber below The Towen, while the acolytes danced around the fire and performed their dark ceremonies.

Then had come the rhythmic pounding of music from outside.

The chant had stopped, and for a moment the trance was broken. Her mind awoke from the dream.

It was all ridiculous!

Yes, she felt powerful and strong. Yes, all those feelings had come back to her as though they were new but it was all so petty. All so stupid and childish. Greedy. Envious. Bitter. Spiteful.

And power?

Power at what cost?

Of being a slave to an evil beyond human imagining?

Being stuck here at the Towen and in the middle of nowhere Kansas?

Stuck staying nearby only to aid the entrance of a creature bent, not even on world domination, but annihilation?

To never again see her friends or family or Mark?

Mark.

Oh dear God in Heaven, Mark!

What had she said? What had she done? Was Mark still alive?...

Yes... Yes, he was alive...

Somewhere in the haze of the last few hours she remembered hearing one of the giants come to Maru, who was seated on that ugly, gaudy throne of his, and saying that Mark had escaped.

Maru had returned to his throne in a huff, saying something about Brisco being damaged, and that the giants were going to bring back Mark, and this time he would be bound in the chamber.

He had complained to himself about those *"miserable Frog-men"* as the chant resumed. It was all jumbled in her mind.

She had to think.

Had to escape.

Had to... What?...

What did she have to do?

Serve.

Yes. She had to serve her Lords, Maru, and the Great Dyondaygah. The great Masters who had fulfilled her dearest wishes made the life she wanted most, possible. All would kneel before them as Dyondaygah engulfed the world. All would be devoured in-

The Mound shook beneath her feet and around her. The sound of a great explosion somewhere overhead, followed by an impact that rocked the ceiling directly above her.

Once more the spell was broken.

Once more her thoughts turned to Mark.

Sweet, loving, compassionate, handsome, strong, beautiful Mark! The man she wanted to spend the rest of her life with.

Yes, he was a pain in the neck.

Prideful, and a fibber, like all men.

Yes, she had days she wanted to kill him, but that was what marriage was all about, choosing each other and committing to a life together!

Being strong for each other.

Even when you couldn't stand to look at them another moment you had to be strong...

Strong...

Strong...

Stronger now than he would ever be, she didn't need him anymore, she had NEVER needed him.

She had always been the strong one and he was a weak simpering fool.

She had supported *his* dreams, his wants, *his* "needs."

Who had it been that decided she couldn't follow her parents to Florida when they had left Chicago? Mark.

Who was deciding now that she had to leave Chicago and go to Los Angeles so he could follow his dreams, forcing her to leave behind her life, her friends?

But who had given her strength? Who had given her his own body for sustenance that she might be strong?

Strong.

STRONG! Dyondaygah! The great one! The Great Master who's tentacles would-

"Thurston is somewhere on this floor! Find him! Find him now! Focus on finding him! Nothing else matters!"

And suddenly her mind was her own again.

The hive mind of the Children of Dyondaygah was no longer controlling her.

They, following their master's orders, had turned all of their focus on finding her Husband.

Somehow it was them, who had been holding her to this single repeating chain of thought.

The power might come from the demon god beyond the world, but it was the unified mind and will of the Children that kept her locked in, that was holding her down until she could make the final commitment to the *"Great Old One."*

She remembered Maru standing on the throne next to her, caressing her face, *"The conjunction is not just in the stars, and here in the Towen, it is in you, my beauty. Once the Conjunction has occurred, you will be in the presence of the mind of Dyondaygah, not just his body. Then he will join himself to you and you shall be his forever. His and mine."*

Her skin crawled at the memory of his touch, even though it had not been so when it had occurred.

She had to get out of here.

Had to get this thing out of her.

Had to resist.

She could not let herself be taken again.

She had to save herself.

She had to save Mark.

He was somewhere in the building over her head. He was standing alone against Giants; men, and women twice his size, and at least double his strength.

If this power was for anything, it was useless if she could

not use it to save Mark. Silently she prayed, *"Dear God, I know I don't talk to you as often as I should but please, get us out of here. Please save us and above all let me save my husband. Whatever else happens, even if I am enslaved to this thing, let me save Mark first!"*

Before her, two of the Children still danced around the fire at the center of the Towen. Around her, the wall sconces blazed with light.

There had to be something she could do to escape; to get out.

The two Giants before her were still focused on the adoration of the Old One. She could feel that while they were still trying to exert the bond that had held her in place all these hours, the two of them alone were not strong enough, and suddenly, they knew it too.

They stopped their chanting and turned to face her.

It had been more than 15 years since Ally had been in a Karate class.

But some things got into your DNA.

It had been the training she received in the Karate classes that had made being on the cheerleading team a possibility in the first place.

Without the coordination and agility, she had learned there, she might never have had a chance.

In Junior High School, Ally had been one of the shortest girls in the whole school, and things didn't get much better in High School and beyond.

She knew she would need to be able to take care of herself. Counting on one of her friends to be there to defend her was a crapshoot at best, and counting on a teacher to come to the rescue, much less hold her blameless in a fight was a joke.

In elementary school, she had gotten into more than a few fights, and usually ended up not only battered and bruised but with a 3-day suspension as well.

"It takes two to tango." The teachers and principal would

always say, (in essence) which anyone who's ever gone through the public school system knows is one of the biggest lies ever told.

Several times she had been attacked seemingly out of nowhere. A person could attack you for any slight, real or imagined and according to the teachers, you were supposed to just lie there and take it.

And even if you did, you still ended up on suspension.

Then for the rest of the school year, you had a Sword of Damocles hanging over you.

You were marked as an easy target.

After 5th grade, Ally had decided, *"No More."*

It crossed Ally's mind now to fake that she was still under the sway of the spell and to wait for the moment when one of the two remaining giants was off their guard, but she knew such action would be pointless. They knew it and she knew they knew it. The only thing left to do was confront them.

"Come on!" Ally challenged, and the nearly seven and a half foot tall female, who under other circumstances might have been quite pretty, came at her, her nostrils flared and her teeth bared in a snarl.

The Giantess had never had a day of training in her life.

She lumbered at Ally trusting in her strength to overpower.

Running, she leapt at Ally, who made a quick sidestep to the right and grabbed hold of her by the neck and right arm.

Ally pushed the Giantess hard, and drove her forward into the space where Ally had just been standing, flinging her into a plastered dirt wall.

"Best Defense, No be there."

The Giantess impacted the stone with all the force of an oncoming train. Her head smacked into a spot in the uneven horsehair plaster and it fell away, leaving a massive gap in the space between stones, a glint of dented metal showing out from beneath.

The male giant, meanwhile, was not idle but approached Ally with more caution while his partner recovered.

He seemed to think a bear hug was the best approach for dealing with her and held both arms out in (what her Sensei had always humorously called) the *Zombie Frankenstein Pose*.

Ally didn't try to hide the smirk that came to her lips when she thought of this.

Taunted by that smirk the giant lunged and tried to wrap his arms around Ally...

Leaving his face completely exposed.

"*Closed hand, busted knuckles. Heal of hand, busted nose.*"

Using her newly powerful arms and hands, Ally raised her right arm to block the Giant's incoming left, while the heal of her left hand sailed right between the giant's arms and into her attacker's nose, which exploded in a gout of blood.

The Giant, (who had clearly not experienced real pain in quite some time and perhaps had never expected to feel it again since signing on with the Children of Dyondaygah,) reeled back and bellowed in agony.

With her heightened senses, Ally knew another attack was coming from behind.

It really wouldn't have taken heightened senses to know though, the Giantess announced her attack with a cry and the gritty sound of heavy feet on sandy stone.

This time, Ally tried a move she had always had trouble with; flipping the opponent.

Because of her short stature, before now, she had always had trouble getting her enemy off the ground, even using their force against them.

This time it was nothing, both because of her increased size and strength, but also because of the speed at which the Giantess had hurtled at her.

"*All Force, no control.*"

As soon as she saw the Giantess' long arm go out to the side of her head, Ally grabbed it, and pulled her adversary's weight forward, over her back and down, slamming the Giantess' head into the stones beneath their feet.

Following through with the force, she had tucked her head down and rolled with the Amazon, landing with her one leg under her, and the other across her chest.

Still holding tightly to her thoroughly muscled arm, she wrapped both legs together and pulled backward with all of her force, she heard the tendons stretch, as the Giantess's shoulder dislocated.

The Giantess' scream was more than a match for her partner's and was nearly as deep. But Ally didn't allow her opponent time to recover.

She released her hold and jumped to her feet, only to kick the Giantess in the face, breaking her nose as well.

The pain was too much and the Giantess passed out.

Ally looked around the room, ready for a secondary attack from the Male, but was surprised to see him passed out on the floor as well. Or maybe worse than passed out.

Not knowing her strength, and in the heat of the moment, she had hit the giant's nose, not from the side, but from below, pushing the Giant's nasal cartilage up into his skull.

Ally wasn't about to get close enough to check, but it might well have been that the cartilage had gone straight up into his brain and killed him.

In any event, they were both out for the count. Ally didn't let herself dwell on the fact that she may have just killed someone, and told herself even if she had, *"It was him or me."*

From somewhere up above came a cry of pain.

A male voice...

Was it Mark?

"Hang on Baby." Ally said to Mark, somewhere above, "I'm coming."

19

The plan had worked beautifully.
At least on his end.
Whatever happened now it was up to Mark.

Dressed entirely in black and with the giants focused on the truck, (aided by the fact that they all seemed to be a rather stupid lot as a whole, probably an effect of the "Sacred food,") none of the giants had noticed that Hap had slipped out of the truck at the last moment, before it went tearing across the parking lot and in, through the front doors of the Towen.

His knee, elbow and shoulder pads had served him well, (despite the pain in all of his joints which betrayed the fact that he was now considerably older than he would like to admit.)

He had been virtually unharmed...

Except for the one curly cued seed pod from the Razor Devil's Claw which had sliced through both his clothing and flesh to lodge in his leg.

That had hurt like a.... well Vestal didn't like him to use such language, but you can imagine.

After the truck had rammed through the building and exploded its cargo, Hap had used the distraction to crawl on his (admittedly far too large) belly, off of the blacktop and down into the path he had made through the Devils Claw.

There he had no choice, but to get up and do a crouching run down the hill. He had been sure any moment, one of the giants would spot him and the game would be up.

But somehow, by the grace of God the giants hadn't even been looking in his direction.

He wondered if he had killed any of them.

Distraction was the main objective, but if there were a few less of Maru's giants in the world that would be no great loss. None of them could have been saved. That he was certain of.

He wasn't entirely sure that Ally could be saved at this point, but they had to try. But that wasn't even what all this was about. It might be for Mark, but the whole world depended on what the two of them were trying to do.

If they didn't put a stop to this, soon, possibly even tonight, Maru would be able to draw forth into this world a power beyond the understanding of man; A power that no one could stand against, older than the stars, a cancer from beyond the world. And that's what these things were; make no mistake.

When God had flung the Universe into being; it had displaced these things. It may have even been one of his chief motivations for creating space and time and matter in the first place.

Who knew, except God himself of course, what the "Old Ones" had been before the creation of the Universe?

Creatures meant to go out into the void places and make them not void?

Some, like Dyondaygah, seemed to be meant to fill up the emptiness, while others seemed bent on ordering the cosmos according to their will.

Evil was not an original thing.

Evil has no imagination and can not create, it can only corrupt.

These beings must have had some purpose long ago in the depths before time, and then had turned away from that purpose, breeding their own form of hideous and mutated life.

Just as when cells went bad in the human body, deviating from the genetic code that they were meant to follow, these creatures and their offspring, their *"Star Spawn"* had turned away from their code and become monsters.

It was the only thing that made sense to Hap... If anything about creatures beyond the understanding of man could be said to *"make sense."* And all of that hardly seemed to matter now. What Hap had to focus on was how to deny it entry to the human world; the world of Light and flesh.

He approached the stump where he had hidden his supplies, well beyond where the noise from the daisy-chained speakers still played that ghastly, no talent, excuse for music. He had only programmed eight songs into the "On the Go" playlist of the iPod and it was approaching the end of the last song...

Thank God.

Up on the Mound, the fire seemed to be nearly out and he could hear Maru's screams of anger and shouted commands, and he had to admit that brought a smile to his heart and a quiet chuckle to his lips.

"Let's see how you like that, Rumpelstiltskin." He thought.

He tended to his wound, which despite the enormous pain it had caused was not half as bad as he had feared, barely more than a minor gash, and then began to take out the supplies he had brought along, for the second phase of the plan.

He had given Mark a single bag of the gunpowder/ tree stump remover. He had told Mark to wait as long as he could, then take the bag somewhere far away from the Dining Hall and its entrance to the Towen's Circle of Sarsen stones. Then he should punch a small hole in the bag, leaving a short trail behind him, light the trail and run as far and fast as he could.

The bag would explode and draw all the giants as far away from the Sarsen ring as possible.

If by that point, things seemed serious enough, they would have drawn away all but perhaps one or two of the giants, Ally included.

This would allow Hap to sneak in undetected and place explosive charges on at least one of the Sarsens.

"If we can do that, from what I've read in the journal, we might be able to... I don't know, "*short-circuit?*" the doorway." Hap had explained.

"What makes you think that would work?" Mark had asked. "See here in the Journal," Hap said pointing to a particular passage, "The Sarsens had to have the dirt cleared away to be fully functional. With the dirt in the way, the most they could manage was a few strange events once in a while; the lights over the Towen, a few noises and strange sights here and there, and whatever mental hook up Carter developed with Dy- ... the Demon god, seems to have taken years to develop, and only because he stayed in that place. But once the stones were exposed, and facing each other once more they were able to act as a ... doorway, a nexus. Destroy the stones, destroy the nexus. One alone might do it... Two or more would be better just for safety."

The plan was going to work.

The plan had to work.

Even if it meant all of their lives, (His, Mark's and Ally's) it simply had to work.

And if it didn't, there was always Aaron, his bright boy; the good son who had chosen to stay behind when his mother left.

He could only hope it wouldn't come down to that.

Now he had the gunpowder he would need, there was nothing for him to do but sit and wait until Mark gave him the signal.

But no signal ever came.

Fifteen minutes passed.
Then Twenty-five.
Then Thirty-five...

Surely Mark was not planning to wait the whole hour. If he had forgone part of the plan while the Giants and Maru were distracted with the truck, and managed to sneak down into the basement and secure Ally, he would have emerged by now.

The sedative he had given Mark would only last for about half an hour, to an hour, if he had given her the full dose. And that was on a normal person, let alone someone whose metabolism was redlining.

Something must have-

And that was when Hap saw it. Not the explosion he had been waiting for, but the Hellish Aurora Borealis.

It had actually gone away almost all together before. Every once in a while a star might turn red or pink, if you knew where to look, but now it had flared up again, possibly more bright and powerful than Hap had ever seen it before.

It was a rippling curtain in the sky over the Towen, nearly so thick and visible it might have been a physical veil, rather than a disturbance of electromagnetism.

Hap had to wonder if that was even what it was at all.

Within a few moments of its appearance, Hap was making his way up the Hill toward the Towen.

Either Mark had done something much more effective than the gunpowder, or he had failed and it was now up to Hap to complete the mission.

He was halfway up the mound when there was a sudden roar from within, as a gust of wind burst forth from the space in the building his car had left in it, while all the windows burst forth in a rain of glass shards.

Hap just barely had time to hold the sports bag up in front of his face, before he was sprayed with a conflagration of flying glass, and more than a few of the shards actually stuck in the bag.

Hap had thrown his back to the exterior wall of the Towen when he heard Maru's unmistakable voice cry out *"THURSTON!"* and a parade of heavy feet moving away from him and up the stairs.

Maybe Mark hadn't failed just yet after all.

He waited until the last of the clomping feet faded away, and then he turned the corner, only to hear cries from up above.

Multiple cries of horror and pain.

Maybe it wasn't Mark after all...

Oh well, never look a gift horse in the mouth.

Hap had one major problem. He didn't know how to get down into the Towen Circle, the Alter of Dyondaygah.

He had never actually been in the Towen before. He had very little idea of the building's actual layout.

From what he had read in Carter's diary and what Mark had been able to tell him, he knew the entrance to the circle had to be in the rear of the building, somewhere beyond the now wrecked food bar and the entrance to the Kitchens, where Mark had warned him the Frog-men might be waiting.

Not knowing who might be nearby he stepped carefully through the wreckage his truck had wrought. Avoiding every piece of shattered glass and doing his best to step over broken tables and chairs.

Finally, he was past the majority of the damage, and while there was still some debris around, it was easily avoided...

Until he stepped on a piece of glass that he hadn't been able to see, and it exploded underfoot with a crumpling *CRUNCH*, that was far louder than its tiny size would have been expected to make. From somewhere down the Hall, Hap could hear the sound of heavy boots on a wooden floor, pounding down the hall pell-mell.

Hap reached inside his bag and pulled out a rifle. He would have preferred to have had his shotgun, but he had figured Mark would need that more than he. Rifles had to be precise, Shotguns, just pull the trigger and you were bound to hit something, and having had no formal training with a gun, it was the better option.

Hap got down behind one of the knocked over tables, and waited for his adversary to come around the corner.

Suddenly, the heavy clomping stopped as if the enemy knew something was waiting for it. Hap waited, and after a long moment, called it out, "Alright! Come on out! I know you are there!"

"Hap?" asked a feminine voice, that while slightly deeper, was familiar. A dark silhouette, its hands up, moved into the hallway and down toward him into the light.

Ally dressed in (what Hap could only assume were) Mark's sweat clothes, was now considerably taller than Hap himself.

Hap was about six foot tall, and Alley must have had that and another couple inches on him, she was pushing 6'5, but she still looked as beautiful as when she had walked into the store that evening... if considerably broader under the previously baggy clothes.

"Ally!" he said standing up, "Is that you? Really you?"

"For the moment." She said, lowering her hands, "Where's Mark?"

"I have a feeling he's upstairs. I don't know what is going on up there, but it doesn't sound good." Hap explained.

"Whatever it is, got me out from under their control." Ally explained, "I only woke up a couple of minutes ago... I had to fight my way out. I don't-"

Another high pitched cry of pain came from up the stairs, *"I CAN STILL SEE!"*

"I need to get up there!" Ally said, taking a stride toward the entrance to the kitchens.

"Wait!" Hap said, "I think you'd do better for Mark if you just got out of here. If you are not here, they can't use you against him. If Mark was standing here, he would tell you to run. And if I can get downstairs and blow up one of the stones, we might be able to put an end to this."

"If I leave, he could die!" Ally said, "He wouldn't abandon me! I won't abandon him! Besides, I can't run from this. Whatever is happening is happening inside of me."

"If you stay, and they reassert control over you, you

might never regain your mind again, think of what that would do to Mark. Think of what you might do to Mark under their power!"

"If Mark dies because I ran away, and I lived, I would never be able to forgive myself, and whatever life I have from now on wouldn't be worth the living... I mean look at me! Do you think I can go back to the people I used to know? What would I tell them? Either Mark and I leave here together, or not at all."

Without another word, she started off again. "You two are too much alike you know that?!"

Hap shouted after, shaking his head, but then he realized something, "Wait!" He shouted, "How do I get down there?"

"End of the Hall," Ally called back not stopping, "Only door on the left." And with that she was gone; out of the dining room and (from the sound of it) heading up a flight of stairs.

"Kids." Hap said thinking back to his own youth, "Crazy love-struck kids."

Carefully, Hap moved down the long hallway, he had not missed the fact that Ally said she had to fight her way out, and a defeated enemy was not necessarily a dead one.

Whether it was the way John Carter had devised it, or whether it was some strange addition of Maru's, the door to the basement where the Alter of Dyondaygah lay, was a large structure. A single Oaken door made up of large, heavy slats, bolted and held together by cast-iron hinges that ran the width of the door.

On the center of the door was a smaller version of the symbol of Dyondaygah, which adorned the ceiling of the Dining hall. Above and below the symbol, there were two large bolts, to seal the room shut, as though anything that came from that room could have been contained by something as small and simple as a thick iron bolt or two.

This confirmed to Hap, that the door had been a construction of John Carter's.

Not that Carter had done a bad job. The door was much like those found at the main entrance to the Towen had been, before Hap's truck had smashed into them.

Even though there was now a gaping hole in the front of the Towen, the oak panels of the double doors had been largely undamaged.

But this single large door was built twice as thick, and very wide.

It was a vault door.

Hap was certain that if this door was locked against intrusion, it would require something with the force of a train to break through it.

Fortunately, the door was not locked, and was perfectly balanced and oiled so that the hinges did not even squeak and the door moved as gracefully as though it weighed no more than a feather.

Hap thought about it for a moment and decided that he would lock the door behind him. It would prevent one or more of the giants from sneaking in without his notice... At the very least, Maru would have to get the key.

But of course, that meant that he was also locked in with whatever lay down below.

He could hear the sound of the wall sconces, flickering with flame.

Of course, Maru wouldn't have installed modern electric lights. That would have been not in keeping with the old ways, and far too convenient.

Hap doubted the Great Old Ones much cared about how the room they were being worshiped in was lit.

Quietly, rifle at the ready, Hap eased down the stairs, which hardly made a sound beneath his feet.

At the bottom of the staircase, was another door identical to the one above, but it had been left wide open, swinging into the Sarsen Circle, away from the staircase. Hap thought that these doors and the earth on either side of the walls, probably made the staircase, the strongest, and most defensible place in the Buffet.

If one had to hunker down, this would be the spot.

As he entered the chamber, he saw two bodies lying in the center of the room. They were both giants of incredible stature. Hap had only ever seen one or two of the giants up close before.

Once when Maru had come into his shop to threaten him, and another time a couple of years before, when one of the female giants had come into the shop. Of all things, she had been sent to Hap's store to purchase a couple of pounds of sugar. She had even paid for it in cash. And while she had still been very tall for a woman, she was not nearly as tall as the two bodies that lay on the ground before him. She had been as tall as Ally was now.

These two were both nearly eight feet tall, and Ally had taken out both of them.

But there was no time to examine her handiwork; he had a job to do. Take out the Sarsens. Placing the bag on the floor, Hap knelt on one knee. He unzipped the bag and pulled out his secret weapon, a bar of plastique explosives and a detonator.

He hadn't even told Mark that he had this.

First, it was illegal for him to own without certain licenses he did not possess, and second, he only had a small amount. But this one brick should be all he would need. Taking out a pocket knife, he opened the paper coated brick and sliced off nearly half of it. Cutting the half of the brick in half again, made it into two smaller pieces. Stepping up to the stones, he jammed one of the two smaller bricks into a large fisher that ran across it.

The fisher was not exactly a crack, but it was a deep place in the stone that could be exploited to bring it down.

Hap packed the explosive deep into the stone, filling better than half the gap. Then Hap took the other quarter of the brick and did the same, making sure the two pieces were smooshed together to form a solid line of explosive.

Then he did the same with the other half of the brick on

a second stone, which lay nearby.

All of this takes time to tell and explain, but Hap had it done in a matter of moments. He then withdrew two long lengths of orange PETN primer cord, and placed blasting caps on the end of each, and sunk them into the putty-like explosives, smoothing the gunk over the caps, so that they would be fully encased.

Then he linked both of the cords into the detonator. He looked at his watch and figured five minutes would be more than enough time to escape... Then he thought it might be too much time, so he made it three.

He had warned Mark that if he was successful in destroying the stones, there was a good possibility, a large part of the house above could collapse as well, being that the stones were the foundation.

"If you hear a big boom," he had told Mark, "Be ready to run."

This, quite frankly, was good advice at any time.

He was just about to press the Start Button when he felt a massive arm take him by the throat, cutting off his air and the circulation to his brain.

"*Ah, ah, ah.*" Tut-ed a deep matronly voice in his ear, correctively, "None of that now."

He stretched out his hand trying to punch the button, which would override the counter and detonate the explosive, but his fingers just couldn't make contact, and then he was dragged further away, hopelessly out of reach.

As the world went black and fuzzy around the edges, his own thoughts came back to him, "*A defeated enemy, is not necessarily a dead one.*"

The last thing Hap saw before everything went black was the flickering flame of the wall sconces, and he knew he had failed.

20

Mark sat huddled in the closet of the Honeymoon suite.

He could barely hear the screams of the giants, being attacked by whatever strange forces from other dimensions had found their way in the hall beyond his door. He wondered if that was because of the fantastic "insulation" Maru had spoken of or if it was because he was somewhere else altogether from where they were; his own *"pocket dimension."*

Oh sure he thought he was in "reality", the Real-world, Earth 616, Keystone Earth, whatever... But how could he know that?

For all he knew he was sitting in the closet of a room he'd actually never been in before and any moment the phone receiver would grow legs, lift itself off the hook and start shouting random numbers at him, all the while telling him that all of his friends were dead, and *"Even if you leave this room, you will never leave this room!"*

Fortunately, nothing like that had happened yet. If not for the cries and screams outside he would have hardly known anything was a miss.

Once he thought he heard his room door open and a dying scream sounding right next to his ear, but there had been nothing there when he peeked out into the room through the slat covered door.

The main door remained completely closed.

Given everything he had seen already that night, a few mild auditory hallucinations were a small price to pay for the relative safety he seemed to be enjoying at the moment, but it didn't change the fact that if one of the Giants found their way into this room, on this plane of existence, he would be trapped.

He wondered if Hap had gotten inside yet.

While he hadn't been able to set off the gunpowder, he had certainly managed to cause a distraction, and get most, if not all of the Giant's attention.

He hoped that somewhere below him he would suddenly feel the building buck as one or more of the Sarsen stones were… if not blown to smithereens, at least cracked enough to disrupt the Nexus.

He didn't think the gunpowder bombs would be enough but Hap, who knew more about explosives than he, seemed quite confident.

Perhaps he-

At that moment, the door to the room, less than five feet in front of Mark, flew open, slamming against the wall. A male giant stepped into the room. Threw the slatted door, Mark could see he seemed to be pushing something aside with his hands.

Curtains? Palm fronds?

Mark couldn't be sure, but unless the giant was crazy, or had some kind of irresistible "tick" caused by Tourette's syndrome, he was seeing something Mark could not.

Looking a bit like Marcel Marceau, the Giant held the imaginary curtains back and looked around, "Thurston!" It called in a surprisingly high voice for a man of his size, "Are you lost in the Jungle? Did you get lost in here?"

Mark forced himself to breathe slowly and through his nose, as quietly as possible, and because he had not been running or exerting himself it was relatively easy to maintain.

Still panic tried to overwhelm him.

In and out.
In and out.
Keep calm.

Keep breathing.

"Is he in there?" Came Maru's piping, shrill voice. "No. Sir. Leastways not, so I can see him." Said the giant, now not even a foot away, "If he's here, he's run off into the Jungle and we may never see the likes of him again."

"Looks like Darkest Peru to me." Said Maru, stepping into the doorway.

"Maybe we'll get lucky and he's been eaten by some bears. No...Come on, Ernest. He's not here... But he's still on the property. I can feel him... Just like I can still feel that Old Man Howard."

"Howard? I thought he was dead." Said Ernest, "Burned up with the truck."

"No." Said Maru, as Ernest closed the door, "He made it out. I don't know how. Someone is protecting these interlopers, and I don't like it!"

That was the last thing he could hear, as Maru continued to move down the hall and away from the Honeymoon Suite.

Now was the time.

Mark could feel it.

He had to get up and move, NOW! Maru and Ernest had gone left so he would go right. If there were other Giants in the way he would just have to risk it and trust to fate, but now that they had finally checked the honeymoon suite, he needed to get downstairs to Ally.

Hap was still alive, and if he was, he would be heading for the Sarsen circle where Ally most likely would be located.

He had to get her out of the building.

Standing to his feet, he opened the slatted door of the closet. He half expected to get pushed back against by trees or Palm fronds that he couldn't see, so he kept his hands out in front of him, so he wouldn't break his nose on something.

But no sensation of unseen plants met his fingertips,

and he found his way to the door of the room quite easily.

He put his ear to the door and listened, he could hear Maru barking orders somewhere down the hall to his left as well as the sound of doors opening and closing.

Slowly he opened his door and looked to the left and the right.

No one was in sight.

The hallways must have gone down much further to the left than he had suspected.

Just how big was this place?

He stepped out into the hallway, quietly as he could.

When they weren't stealing away your wife, or making food that could damn you to everlasting slavery, the slaves of Maru must have spent a good deal of time maintaining and shoring up the Towen.

One would have expected a place this old to have so many squeaks and creaks that it would be virtually impossible to move silently, but upstairs, unlike the lobby, Mark could have been moving on the rock of Gibraltar and made more noise.

He made a quick move toward the staircase and...

He didn't make it...

It had just been across the hall... and it still was...

But he had run to the wall and it hadn't been there...

He seemed to still be on the other side of the hall, next to the door frame, as though he hadn't moved.

He did it again...

And still, he could not reach the staircase.

He ran for it, full tilt, as fast as he could go, and the stairs only got further and further away.

The hall was expanding right before his eyes. He stopped running and it shrunk back to normal size.

He saw the hallway snap back, like a rubber band.

If he had not been doing his best to stay silent and not alert the giants to his presence, he might have cursed aloud.

Was this, like the dimensions behind the doors, the result of the warping of time and space as the conjunction grew near? Or was it some sort of security measure, something Maru had deployed after Mark had entered the Honeymoon suite?

A Space-Warping Mobius Strip, that would not allow enemies to move through the Towen until Maru himself came and plucked them out of it?

He tried it once more, knowing it was futile, and he ran until he couldn't anymore. He saw the space between himself and the stairs grow further and further away. He saw the opening of the stairwell disappear beyond the curve of some neverending loop, and that was when he gave up. Slowed his run, and saw the stairwell reappear growing closer and closer as he slowed. Eventually returning to the space where it had been, only five feet away, as he came to a stop.

It was like being stuck on a treadmill you couldn't see.

But there had to be away out of it.

What if Maru or one of the giants got caught in it? If it was a defense mechanism Maru would want a way out.

If it was a "natural" phenomenon, something caused randomly by the Conjunction, then it would stop at some point, right?

Yeah, once the conjunction was completed and Maru had turned his wife into a lumbering behemoth of a slave, with no mind of her own.

No.

He wouldn't think of that.

There must be a way out.

He turned around toward the room he had just come out of, and the door was still within reach. As he moved his feet toward it, he saw the hall begin to stretch again.

He stopped, allowing the room to retain its shape, and

reached out for the door handle.

He tried not to think of the tendril and tongue it had been just a few minutes before, and indeed it was nothing but cold dead iron in his hand. Holding fast, he began to move his legs toward the door.

He felt the door and its handle pulling away from him, but he would not let go. He ran, seemingly in place as the door moved further and further away from him, he stretched his arms to hold on to it as he ran, to the point when he was sure one or both of them would soon dislocate from his shoulders, and finally the door handle slipped from his grasp, only to move further down the Mobius Strip away from him.

He stopped, and space snapped back.

It was hopeless.

In despair, ready to faint, he closed his eyes and stepped backward. When he opened his eyes, he was standing still, but the door was further away from him.

He turned to see that he was in the middle of the hallway, equidistant from the door and stairwell.

Something had changed.

He moved toward the stairs and saw it move away from him again. He turned toward the door, and it did the same.

He closed his eyes and took a step backward, then another, and he felt the corner of the wall that led down into the stairwell.

Eyes still closed, he reached back and felt the handrail.

As long as he kept his eyes closed and moved backward, the strip seemed to have no hold on him.

Carefully he stepped down on to the stairs, one step at a time. The voices of Maru and the giants were still far off.

He was safe for the moment. He took another step down, and another.

"*Mark!*" shouted a deep voice behind him, and a strong hand took hold of his shoulder. Mark didn't even have time to inwardly curse before he was forcibly spun around, and pulled forward.

And... kissed?

Not just any kiss, a forceful, deep, passionate kiss, with wet tears rolling on to his face that were not his own.

He hadn't felt such a kiss in years, not since... Not since the minister had said, "You may now kiss the bride."

He opened his eyes and saw Ally, his Ally.

All other thoughts were lost as he wrapped his arms around her increased form. He didn't mark the strangeness of holding his arms tightly against her newly powerful neck and shoulders, or that the position in which they normally hugged each other was now basically reversed.

The wrapper didn't matter, Ally was no more her body than he was his shoes.

All that mattered was that they had found each other. She was in his arms again.

"Where did you come from, baby?" Ally asked through her tears, "I was coming up the stairs and you were just suddenly there; walking backward."

Mark forced himself to pull away, and look her in the face, "I'll explain later, there's no time for that now. We need to get out of-"

"Leaving so soon—Little Man?" asked a deeply resonant and all too familiar voice from the bottom of the stairs.

The voice chilled Mark to his core.

But it wasn't possible.

It could not be!

But it was exactly as he had feared.

Letting go of Ally, who was face to face with him because she stood one step lower than he, the two of them turned to see Brisco, standing at the foot of the stairs, already beginning to make his way up toward them.

"How do you like my eeeye patch?" He asked, "Makes me look like a piraaate, doesn't it?"

The "eye patch" was little more than a small black leather belt wrapped around his head, the buckle of which hung above his right ear and with a black piece of felt, covering where the eye had been.

"Don't woooorry." Said the Ogre his words now more slurred and drawn out than they had been before, "The eeeye will grow back, pieces taken from the Childrennnn of Dyondaygaaaah aaalways grow baaaack."

"*Run!*" Ally said, and Mark didn't have to be told twice.

Together the two of them turned tail and ran back up the stairs.

21

"*Not that way!*" Mark shouted as quietly as he could. As they reached the top of the stairs, Ally had acted if she was about to turn to the right, "They are all down that way!" he explained, and took her by her hand.

Formerly, small and thin, her fingers were now heavy and considerably broader, though still retaining the form of their previous narrowness. It was still her hand, just twice the size and strength.

Mark had to resist the urge to wince and cry out at the strength of her grip, but at the same time, it felt so good to hold her hand again, any amount of pain would have been worth it.

Together they ran down the hall to the left, directly over the dining area, the sound of Brisco's heavy boots pounding the wooden floor beneath them.

They heard him call out to Maru, "*Maaasterrr, they've gone this way!*" His words sounded "out of tune" pitching up and down in the wrong places as if he were only now learning English and putting the emphasis on the wrong syllables. That and the slur seemed to be the results of the damage Mark had done with his knife.

"Why didn't you leave?" Mark asked between gasps, since being quiet was now no longer a concern.

"Knew you were up here!" Ally said almost as casually, as if she were on a Sunday jog, "Wasn't about to leave you."

"You should have gone!" Mark said, "*I* left you!"

"But you came back." Ally replied, and there seemed to be nothing more to say on that subject.

"How long does this hall go on?" She asked, "It is too big. We should have reached the end by now."

"Other dimensions," Mark gasped, "Maru said. Heard. Him. Through. The door. Intruding on ours. Makes bigger inside! Don't open the doors! Different places and times! Monsters!"

From in front of them, they heard Maru shouting their last name, but they didn't see him or the other giants yet.

"I thought you said, they were down to the right!" Ally said skidding to a stop. Mark grabbed his knees, and looked up at her, "I'm sorry. If being caught in a mobius loop. Might have. Made me. Lose track."

"Why hasn't Hap blown the Sarsens yet?" Ally asked no one.

Mark gasped, "You saw Hap?"

"Yes, he was going downstairs to blow the stones up. I assume you knew that was the plan? But if he hasn't blown them yet something must have gone wrong. I should have made sure both those Giants were dead. I won't make that mistake again."

Out of everything that had happened so far tonight, From Frog-men and Giants, dimensional shifts and being sucked into a throat that could have swallowed New Jersey, hearing his wife talk about murdering two people, and leaving no doubt that she was completely serious and was ready to kill even now, might just have been the one that confused Mark the most.

She had always been feisty, and quick-witted. Her comebacks had silenced many a Troll on the internet (or at least left no doubt to anyone reading, that she knew what she was talking about, and she was in the right.)

But now she was different, and this was not something the Sacred Food had done to her. Mark was sure of that. This was something that had been buried deep inside, underlying all the wit and wisdom.

This was what she had been all along and only now had the ability to express, and do something about it.

The warrior was set loose.

"Where aare you running, Little Man?" came Brisco's deep rumble. From down the hallway behind them, "There's no way oooout, up here."

"Rock and a hard place," Mark said.

"I have an idea." Ally said, looking around. "You're not going to like it."

Maru and the Giants had been standing in the hallway looking for Mark when they had heard Brisco thumping down the hallway away from them, shouting out *"Maaasterrr, they've gone this way!"*

"They?" Ernest asked.

Maru thought for a moment. He reached out for the connection to the Towen and all that lay within it and understood.

While he couldn't lock down everything to an absolute certainty, especially this close to the Conjunction, each of the fully taken Children of Dyondaygah, was like a radar beacon to him, he might not know everything, but he had a few "pings" to work with.

The two Giants below had ceased their chanting, and Hap was near them. He must have tried something. He had penetrated the heart of the Towen, and Maru could sense him clearly, and that he was unconscious.

He would have found Mark much sooner, but the fracturing of dimensions taking place above the Towen was messing with his abilities.

Mark had been nearby, but nearby in what dimension?

And when a separate dimension was intruding there was no way into the rooms of the Towen, until that connection was broken.

Mark could have been two feet away from one of his

Giants and neither they nor Maru would have ever been able to see or touch him, they could have walked right through him like so much invisible gas.

But now Mark was back in the Towen; truly in Maru's world. He sensed this through Ally.

While not yet taken fully into the fold, the Sacred Food within her, which was even now reforming itself into one of the many arms of Dyondaygah, had reached the point where it could give off a *"fuzzy signal"*. It was like listening in to a radio station when you were just beyond the range of its tower. You would catch a few notes here and there, and you just might be able to pick out the song that was being played if you knew it well enough.

Ally was running down the hall and Mark was by her side. But Maru could tell that the shortest way around to where they were was actually down the opposite direction from where the voice of Brisco had come.

The second floor of the Towen was a circle, even when it was not Dimensionally Transcendental. But someone coming into the Towen for the first time would not know that.

A secret passage at the end of the Hall connected both the seemingly unconnected "forks" of the hall. This passage was something Carter had built into the house long ago, and Maru had discovered it while making repairs.

Whether the passage was meant for some nefarious purpose, hiding secret lovers from his wife, or if it had been planned as a stop on the underground railroad, Maru did not know.

But as luck would have it, they, (the Giants and He,) were standing next to the passage when they heard Brisco's cry.

Maru had instructed Ernest on how to open the passage and the next moment all the giants were passing through it, single file.

Once out of the passage, which didn't seem to be much longer than it normally was, Maru had given his soldiers their orders.

"Take Thurston alive! He will be sacrificed! Do not harm the girl! Bring her back under our sway! I want her! She is mine! It is the will of Dyondaygah!"

As long as the Giants had been chanting the name of their god, and focusing their collective energies on holding Ally within the circle of control, Ally had not been able to resist their will. But Maru had made what he now recognized as a major mistake, by telling the Giants to focus on nothing else but finding Thurston. They had obeyed his command with every fiber of their minds. The two Giants he had left below had not been enough to hold her. But that was a problem that would be easily rectified.

Before the conjunction, he would need to have a word with her. The real her, mind to mind. He would warn her not to resist. She would see what he had seen of the one who had (possibly) resisted the communion with Dyondaygah, and his sticky end.

That memory alone would surely convince her.

Even the few moments of full consciousness she had experienced since The Children had let her slip through their grasp might have convinced her already.

She was no doubt feeling the power. The Strength. The rejuvenation and rebirth.

If she'd had any injuries, a bad knee, shoulder or joint, that had once been damaged and never fully healed, it now most certainly would be.

One of the Gifts of Dyondaygah was physical perfection.

Not always "beauty" perhaps, he didn't seem to be worried about such petty constructs as "prettiness" and "attractiveness," which were extraordinarily transient by even human standards, but the human body at the peak of its performance and potential.

That alone, most people would be willing to give up not only their souls but that of their, so-called "loved ones", to possess.

Who knew, they might come around the corner and find Mark already gift-wrapped for them, Ally begging, willing to do anything, to be admitted into the communion of the Children.... But he doubted that.

As one, Maru and the giants rounded the corner. Before them lay a long hallway, at the end of which was the hulking form of Brisco.

"Where are they?!" Maru shouted. "You had them! You let them get away!"

"They are here maaasst-eeer." Brisco groveled, his slur seeming to increase with his frustration, "There was nowhere for them to go. The rooms. They must be in one of the rooms."

"Oh not this again!" Maru groused. "This is ridiculous."

"Why not just wait until the Convergence is over Master?" asked Ernest. "Then the building will be itself again, and they will be easy to find."

"Because, you fool," Maru explained, "they might escape through one of the portals. If they end up in London in the 1890s they will be beyond our reach! What's more, the Sacred food can only last a single night without the aid of our collective will. If it does not reconnect with Dyondaygah, it will simply be vomited up like so much bad suet and dissolve in the light of the sun. She and her Lover will be set loose, we know not when or where! It may be on another world altogether for all we know!"

"Why not let them go then?" Asked Ernest again, "They will be gone. There will be others and the great Lord will emerge another night."

Maru struck Ernest across the face hard with his Scepter, "After what they've done to my building? After the brothers and sisters, they've caused to be lost to us forever? After the damage, they've done to Brisco, my best servant? After the way, they have mocked not only the will of Dyondaygah but me also?!"

"An insult to Dyondaygaaaah may not go unanswered!" Replied Brisco.

"I will have the girl for my own!" Maru shouted, "She is mine!!"

The Giants looked at each other, confused and even slightly amazed. Maru had never expressed such a desire before, at least not to them. There were a number of females in the children of Dyondaygah whom he might have chosen before now.

What was so special about this one?

Maru seemed to realize his foible and attempted to cover it up, "It is the will of Dyondaygah! Now, find them!"

But they didn't have to look at all. The next moment, one of the doors exploded open, and Mark ran into the hallway.

"Get him!" Maru shouted at the top of his piping voice, but there was no time for anyone to make a move toward him.

In less than a second after Mark came through the door, the Children found themselves in full out battle.

22

Mark had been standing by the door for nearly an hour. He couldn't understand it. The Giants and Brisco had been right behind them.

He had seen their shadows rounding the corner just before he and Ally had ducked into the room.

He had heard and felt the vibration of their footsteps coming down the hall. He knew it was too late and they would be on him in a moment.

Still, there he stood, in the middle of a forest, with his hand on a door frame attached to nothing. It stood there in the middle of the woods, the most ridiculous thing anyone ever saw.

Mark hadn't dared to take his hand away, for fear the door might disappear, leaving them stranded… wherever they were, but he had looked around to the other side of the door, peeking his head around the corner, and had seen nothing, no door, no knob, no frame, not even his legs or any part of him, just the empty forest around him. The door only existed on this side and seemed to be paper-thin, if that.

Ally had told him to wait and she would be back with help. "If they come through the door, just run into the forest. Climb a tree. Hide. I will find you."

Mark had tried to ask, *what help*, or where she was going, how she would find her way back, and about fifteen other questions, but she was long gone before he could ask a single one, and his words had come out as nothing but a weak stumbling blither.

Now it was at least an hour later, Mark had listened

closely, trying to hear what he could through the wooden door, which seemed just as firm as ever, yet he dared not let go.

He had heard a few sounds from beyond the door. Strange sounds that gave Mark the impression of a conversation taking place at an incredibly slow speed, as though someone had taken an old 78-speed record, and was playing it at 33 1/3 RPMs if not slower.

Suddenly amid the sounds of the forest, there was the sound of trampling feet, not just one, but tens of them.

It was then he heard his wife calling his name, and he shouted back to her.

They went back and forth calling each other's name for a moment and then Ally exploded up and over the hillside.

Mark only had time to realize that she was holding a long heavy sword, a Claymore, in one hand, and a large round shield in the other, before she was shouting, "Mark! Open the door! Open the door and run inside!"

Mark didn't wait for an explanation, because he could see that just a few yards behind her, a small army of men dressed in kilts, (if they were dressed at all,) and covered in mud, was running up the hill behind her.

Not in solidarity, but in chase.

Mark cursed, wondering what Ally had gotten them into now, and opened the door.

He half expected to find himself still in the woods, the door gone behind him, but instead, he was back in the hallway of the Towen, surrounded by giants.

Maru was perched atop the shoulder of one of the bigger men, and Brisco off to Mark's left.

"*Get Him!*" Maru shouted. But then Ally, sword in hand and shouting a battle cry, exploded through the door, followed by a pack of raving madmen, all of them holding their swords ahead of them.

Ally plowed into the Giants, while Mark, unable to stop his run, found himself falling into one of the other doors across the hall. He tried to stop but found that he couldn't in time, and the door hung loose on its hinges. As he rolled through the unnumbered door, he felt the sports bag roll off his shoulder and away from him, taking the shotgun with it.

Unable to stop his momentum, the next thing he knew he had landed on a hard cobblestone floor.

He had hit the door so hard that it bounced off its frame and slammed shut.

Before he even had a chance to stand up, the door had disappeared. It had not faded into the darkness but completely atomized into nothing.

Leaving only a cold stone wall where it had once been.

"Qu'est-ce que c'est?" Asked a voice behind him in the darkness.

Above his head, lights slammed on with a blinding flash and a *bang-hum* of electricity.

"Qu'est-ce que cet homme fait dans la chambre?" A male voice asked in the rafters above him. He could not see the man who had spoken but he could hear several people walking around on an unseen metal catwalk, just beyond the glare of the lights.

"Please!" Mark shouted, "Let me out! I have to get out of here! My wife is in danger!"

"Qui est cet homme?" asked a female voice, "Il est assez beau."

"Il parle Anglais." Replied the Male voice, "Qui fait de Lui notre ennemi."

Mark hadn't spoken any French since High School but he caught the words English and Enemy.

Apparently in whatever future, past, or alternate world he had found himself in, the French speakers above were not friendly toward those who spoke English.

"Please." Mark said, "I don't know where I am, or how I got here, but I need to get out! Does anyone speak English? Parlez-vous Anglais?"

That was the one phrase he could remember from his time in school, *"Do you speak English?"* and he had probably mispronounced it.

"Put these on Englishman!" Said the male voice from above, in English, and something hit the cobbles near his feet. Mark bent down and picked up the two metal circles. Because of their shape, he had to hold one in each hand.

Before he could react, they bucked in his hand. He almost threw them, and might have, had they not suddenly sprouted what Mark could only think of as "legs" and adhered themselves to his wrists.

"What the-" Mark started, but suddenly he was spun and yanked across the room by a powerful invisible force.

A large metal pole shot up out of the floor and the metal circlets pulled him toward it irresistibly. It was either move with the force or be pulled on to the floor face first, so he had no choice in the matter.

He heard and felt the metallic clang and a bit of a "zap" as the circlets locked on to the poll, holding wrists to them.

"You can't do this!" Mark shouted idiotically, "I've done nothing wrong! Let me go!"

Mark heard the voices, several of them now, laughing at him from above.

Then he felt something crawling on his pants leg.

His hands were held to the poll, and strain as he might, he could not remove them. He could make them slide around the poll, quite effortlessly in fact, but he could not remove his arms from the cuffs, nor could he lower them beyond a certain point on the pole.

He looked down at his leg and saw something small and red, about the size of a cherry, with legs similar to those the cuffs had emitted.

It reminded mark of drawings he had seen of a virus, a large crystalline head, with a pole at its center and several legs moving out from that pole.

It was crawling up his pants leg.

Mark freaked out.

He didn't have many phobias, he was not afraid of

spiders, snakes or rats, beyond reason. He was not prone to fits of panic but the site of this thing, crawling rapidly up his body, his hands unable to get at it, was enough to make him feel like a panicking little girl who had just seen her first real live mouse running across the kitchen floor.

The thing crawled up his leg and up his side, around the back of his arm almost as if it knew just where to go so Mark couldn't stop it.

He heard someone shrieking and was simultaneously mortified and horrified to realize the sound had been coming from his own throat.

He hadn't made sounds like that since he was a child, but that was how he felt now. Powerless.

After all that had come before on this night of insanity, he was utterly powerless to stop the red, legged thing from crawling up his collarbone and into his ear.

He thought of every horrific thing that had ever been placed in someone's ears or eyes during a horror movie; From the Earwig of *Night Gallery* to the Worms in *Wrath of Khan*.

He knew whatever was entering his body was going to tear up his brain from the inside, put him under the control of these new masters and bend his will do their own.

He would be tortured to death, when, somewhere long ago and far away, Ally was fighting for their lives as his life was already ending here and now! He-

... He felt the red thing "snuggle down" into his ear, and form fit. There was a slight "whirring sound" as something was knitted into Mark's inner ear canal like a pencil being moved over paper very quickly. Mark was afraid it was some sort of "shock collar, like device, or that he was now going to be deaf as the thing bore out his eardrum.

But there was no pain. It felt like nothing more than an "earbud" headphone...

The most comfortable and custom fitted earbud ever.

The whirring stopped and the red thing, some sort of robot, then dismounted from his ear and scuttled away.

"What's wrong with the man?" said a voice from above, in English, "You'd think he never saw a Universal Translator installer before." He realized that while there was a voice speaking above him, it was speaking French.

He was hearing English only in his right ear. It was perfect and had all the effect of distance that his other ear was picking up.

"Eh," said the Male voice, "That's the way the Englishmen are. Savages. They can't even make a good cup of coffee let alone a decent translator."

The future.... Oh yes. This was some version of the future.

Mark's heart was still pounding in his ears, but he was beginning to be able to think straight again.

"Can you understand me now, Englishman?" Said the Male voice.

"Yes." Mark said, "You have to let me go!"

"Name, Rank, and Serial Number."

"I don't have a Rank or a Serial Number!" Mark explained, "I'm a civilian, I'm not even English! I'm an American."

Laughter rang out above his head, "Well, that makes a lot of sense." Said the woman, but not to him, "A person who speaks three languages is Trilingual, a person who speaks two languages is bilingual, and a person who only speaks one language is an American."

This sent up more gales of laughter, but then the Male voice repeated, "Name, Rank and Serial Number, soldier."

"I'm not a soldier," Mark explained.

"Nonsense." Said the woman, "There's no such thing as a civilian, anymore. Don't you know that, Soldier? Just as there's no such thing as An American, hasn't been for nearly forty years, since the bombs on New York, Chicago, and Los Angeles, October 23rd, 2077. Tell the truth Soldier. Which faction do you belong to? The Legion? The Snakes? The Railroad? The Steel Brotherhood?"

"I don't know what any of that means!" Mark said truthfully.

"He's a liar." Said the male voice as something above made a notification sound, that sounded quite a bit like the digital trumpet *"ta-da!"* Mark remembered from Windows 95, "He is not an American. He has never even been to the Wastelands." The man said looking over something. "He doesn't have a trace of radiation on him. It's surprisingly low even for this country. It's like he was never exposed to anything worse than a battery of Chest X-rays."

"Is there anyone from an American Embassy I could speak too?" Mark asked.

"It's useless." Said the man, "He's sticking to this stupid story. I've seen it before." The man addressed him, "You will sit here, my friend, until you are willing to talk. No food or water will be given to you. We'll leave you here for a few hours and see how you feel about it then."

"No!" Mark shouted, "You can't leave me! My wife! I have to get back to her!"

"Barmy." Said the translation of the man above in his ear, "Simply Barmy."

Mark could hear the voices moving away. "Too bad he's English." said the woman. "He was quite cute."

Somewhere above him, a large metal door slammed home.

Mark called *"Hello?"* a few times, but he knew it was useless, he was truly alone. He slumped to his knees and put his legs out to either side of the pole, the only way he could sit, semi comfortably, with the hard cobbled stone pressing into his backside. He leaned forward and rested his head against the cold metal of the pole, which felt quite soothing, and to what would have been his great surprise, had he been aware of it, Mark fell immediately to sleep.

23

Ally was having a great time, all things considered.

"Fun" was not something she would have expected to call the last few hours considering the lurking horror that was forming and gaining strength within her, even as she grew stronger and taller because of it.

Both she and her husband were probably in the greatest danger of their lives.

Being surrounded by giants (and the Frog-men that she had only seen once or twice as they came and went between the Sarsen stones and the building above), and now they were running from a reanimated Cyclops, down a corridor, in which, behind every door, was the potential of being lost in time, or devoured by strange beasts the mind of man was never meant to comprehend, would not have been her idea of a good time.

And yet, while it may have been the "Sacred Food" affecting her mindset, she had also never felt more alive. Her husband was beside her and together they would beat this thing.

They would escape the Towen and never again be bound to the confines of an ordinary work-a-day existence, for now, they both knew the world was bigger and far stranger than anyone could imagine.

But she was getting ahead of herself, first things first, as they say. And the first thing was escaping the Towen and if possible destroying that little Goblin that had put them through all of this in the first place.

"Where aare you running, Little Man? There's no way oooout, up here." The Cyclops called after them.

Little man? Ally thought *You were never half the man he is.*

Mark, clearly exhausted, was panting like a racehorse, he couldn't go on much longer without rest.

"Rock and a hard place." He said, grabbing his knees.

Ally thought about what Mark had told her, other times and dimensions intruding on this one, a new world dialed at random through every door...

Or was it random?

Could it be controlled?

Her mind went back to her days in college, all this talk about time and space had dredged up something. A theory, more of a thought experiment than anything else, on the nature of reality and causality.

It was something about a Cat.

Pavlov's Cat?

No.

It was like that little kid that played the piano for Charlie Brown.

Schroeder's Cat?

Something like that...

Basically, it came down to that if you didn't know what was going on in an unseen space, it was like there was no reality in the box. The cat could be alive or dead, or both at the same time, and then by viewing what was inside the box, you forced reality to take on the most likely construct.

It had all sounded like a bunch of hogwash to her at the time, but what if, in this place, where all rules of physics and time were being bent, if not outright broken, what if she could force her will on the doors?

What if she made the time and place she wanted to appear?

If you opened a door at random, with no idea what might be, or want you wanted to see on the other side, you might end up just about anywhere, it was a crap-shoot.

But if you had a destination, if you had something in mind that you expected to see, forced reality into *your* construct... It might just work.

Was it crazy?

Yes.

Was it stupid?

Most likely.

But with the giants approaching from both ends of this absurdly long hallway, in a space that was larger than the building that contained it, anything seemed possible.

"I have an idea. You're not going to like it." Ally said, placing her hand on the nearest door, and thinking of Scotland.

Scotland in the 17th Century.

Still focusing on that thought, she grabbed hold of the doorknob and pushed. Before them stood a lush forest in the summertime.

They couldn't see very far in any direction for all the trees and greenery. She couldn't be one hundred percent certain but this seemed as close to what she had been focusing on as she could hope for.

"Come on!" She said, quietly grabbing hold of Mark and pulling him through the door before he could object.

They emerged into the forest, just as several ponderous shadows began to make their way around the corner of the hallway.

Ally pulled the door shut, and placed her ear against it, listening.

All around her were the sounds of nature a rushing wind, with a door frame standing in the middle of it all.

One moment for them, it had been the dark of the night, in a possessed Tudor style mansion in the middle of nowhere Kansas, with several hours before dawn.

The next moment, the sun was high above them, and they were surrounded by more green than Ally had ever seen before.

"Where are we?" Mark asked, clearly not expecting an answer.

"17th Century Scotland, I think." Ally said almost matter-of-factly.

"What?" Mark asked confused, "How could you possibly know that?"

"Never mind, there's no time for that." Ally said in lieu of an explanation, "What matters is that The Children could come through that door at any moment."

"The Children?" Mark asked, blinking. Ally rolled her eyes, "That's what they call themselves *The Children of Dyondaygah*", don't worry about it."

Mark cringed at Ally's casual use of the name of the demon, but Ally continued, "I want you to stay here, keep a hand on the door."

Ally reached down and grabbed Mark's arm as if he were a child, "Think about the Towen every once in a while and don't let go of that door. If you do it could disappear and we might be stuck here forever. If they come through, just run, get as far away from here as possible. I'll find you. But until they come through don't take your hand off that door. I love you, and I'll be back soon!"

She turned on her heel and ran down the path that lay before her.

"Path" was generous, it was a gap between most of the trees. There was no path to speak of. But there was a stream nearby and she figured that if she followed that she would come to something eventually.

She needed a town.

A town or a maybe some farmers armed with Pitchforks.

Anything.

She needed to find a way to get the villagers to follow her, any form of help would do in this pinch.

She ran along the stream, and at first, she almost didn't realize what she was doing, it felt so natural, it felt like something she had always done, as though she had been born to do it.

She was running through the woods. Not a cleared path

or a grassy mowed lawn, but the woods. Downed tree limbs everywhere, uneven soil and muddy patches; she glided over them, jumped fallen trees as thick around as a barrel, she lept over large stones and boulders and used low hanging branches as props to swing herself over obstacles.

It was like being Tarzan, if there had been any real vines hanging around she might just have tried swinging from one of them.

She felt like screaming *"I am youth! I am Joy! I am a little bird that has broken out of the egg!"*

And she knew she had read those words somewhere before, but couldn't be sure where. But whoever wrote them, they must have been talking about her and the way she felt at this moment.

But not knowing who or what could be around, she managed to contain her exuberance.

She wasn't free yet. She was still bound to the Towen, both because of that monstrous thing forming inside of her, and because the door that led back to the Towen was her only way back to her own time.

But there was even more than that and she had to admit it: there was some part of her that wanted revenge. Revenge on Maru and his "Children" who had tried to take the world from her.

It seemed a contradiction to hate the person and situation which had given her this power and this ability something she had never had on her own, far beyond what she had been capable of even at her zenith in High School and College.

But it was not a free gift, they had wanted to take from her, her life, her husband, and her free will.

The given strength and ability were meant to be used in the service of a being who would devour the world if he could.

"He will be your food and you shall give him sustenance."

A fatted Calf.

A beast of burden.

That was all Dyondaygah wanted her for.

And Maru... Well, she shuddered to think about what he might want with her.

Now the trees parted and gave way to rolling grasslands, studded with boulders and moss. She was at one of the higher points around and could see where the stream ran down into the meadow.

It was exhilarating.

The blood sang in her veins, her heart pounded like a drum, and her breathing was only slightly heavier than normal.

Her run had been no more stressful than climbing a short flight of stairs with nothing to weigh her down. She was looking at some of the most beautiful country on God's Green Earth.

And green it was.

The trees had put the green over and around her, but now it all lay before her.

She had to fight the urge to spin around like a mental patient in the mountains, fall to the grass and roll down the hill.

There was no time for it.

At that moment as she stood looking down into the valley, she saw exactly what she needed, and it was better than she could have hoped.

Down there in that valley was a group of men, clearly on the march.

They had set up camp for the night, though the sun was still high in the sky. They rested in the crook of the valley, where the sun could not reach, and there they bathed in the stream that even now was falling into the camp over a slight impediment.

It couldn't really be called a "waterfall" in the common way of thinking, it wasn't nearly powerful, or fast enough for that, but the water did take an immediate dive straight into the valley below and emptied into a small pool, before once again forming a stream and moving further down into the valley.

If any of those men had looked up they might have seen her, and she couldn't risk that just yet.

She needed a few things first.

She backed up on the cliff, knelt at the spring, and took a drink of cold clear water, the freshest and most delicious water she had ever taken in, in her whole life.

Once she had recovered a little bit, she began to make her way down into the valley.

She had feared she might end up on a rocky crag or two, and have to run the risk of actually climbing a bit, and while she knew she'd be able to do it, she wasn't quite so sure about the unsuspecting men who were about to go on a run they had not been planning on.

But fortunately the path down into the valley was relatively smooth and even-keeled. Stones and brambles and tall grass would be no impediment to her, and if it slowed her boys down a little bit, so much the better.

Before long she was down in the valley, approaching the camp from the south. She hunkered down in the tall grass. She didn't quite "crawl" so much as she "crab-walked". Her hands touched the ground to steady herself, as she moved them, one over the other.

She didn't need to worry about disturbing the grass too much because a breeze was constantly blowing through the valley, making the top of the grass play in the wind, disguising most of her movement.

She felt like a panther, only one at play, rather than on the hunt.

As she approached the tents she could hear the men talking to each other. Some were bathing in the stream, while others, sat in the sun, drying off, while others were wrapped in their "kilts" which were not anything like the traditional uniform most people associated with the "*Scottish look.*" They were nothing more than big long scarves which were wrapped several times about the waist and once over the shoulder.

The look reminded her more of a "Toga" than the "Traditional Highland Dress" she was used to seeing. She snuck around the one big tent the men had put up, most likely as a sleeping den, since they didn't seem to be all that worried about being without attire around each other.

They had laid all their weapons down opposite to the place where they were now bathing which gave her the perfect opportunity to steal a few things.

A large dagger, a broad "claymore" sword, and a shield, just what she wanted…

They seemed to have plenty and to spare. From what she could tell there had only been between twenty-five or thirty men at the most. They were all milling about in the water and by the shore so getting a perfect headcount while trying to hide and move down the hill at the same time was nearly impossible.

There were nearly fifty swords in the pile and various weapons strune about, and she thought that might be a pretty good gage, assuming two swords per-man.

Then, when she was sure she was ready, she strapped the sword in its scabbard to her waist, over her (*Mark's*) sweat pants, and the shield over her shoulder, (There was a small leather strap, more of a thong really, that was tied to metal loops inside the shield and made it easier to carry when not in use).

Holding the large dagger in her hands she walked to the edge of the tent, and stood up to her full height, and shouted to the men, "Balaich! Bha do mhàthair leannan nan gobhar!"

The men on the shore stood to their feet, while the men in the water began to make their way to the shore.

One of the men called back, "Co thu agus de' a tha thu ag iarraid bean bhoidheach?"

Shoot… This wasn't having the desired effect…

The insult she had slung at the men was the only phrase she knew in Gaelic.

She had learned it years ago from one of the boys in school, who was part of a student exchange program. He had used it once to insult a couple of other boys who had been in the program, and they had come to blows over it.

When she asked him what it meant he had been hesitant to tell her, but once she knew, she had insisted that he teach her how to say it.

Suffice to say it was a very nasty thing to say about someone's mother.

But that had been so long ago...

Had she mispronounced it?

She tried shouting it again.

One of the men laughed and said something that she couldn't understand, and pointing at one of the hairiest of the men, and all the others began to laugh loudly. And the meaning was pretty clear, *"You must be talking about this man over here!"*

"Come on you, Scottish idiots!" She shouted, "Be insulted! What the heck is wrong with you?!"

All of a sudden all the men's eyes locked on her with hatred and contempt. And they said something to each other. Somewhere in their words, she caught the word *"Anglish?"*

Perfect. She thought, *The one time knowing that stupid phrase could have helped me and instead it's the fact that I speak English that gets the reaction I wanted.*

"Yeah, you're darn right I speak English," she shouted back, and then in a perfectly awful British accent, she started to sing Supercalifragilisticexpialidocious at top volume.

"Because I was afraid to speak when I was just a lad, me father gave me nose a tweak and told me I was bad!..."

"ANG-LISH!" They shouted almost as one and began to charge after her.

"Well," she thought, turning tail and running as fast as she could, "That worked!"

◆ ◆ ◆

She had run more than two miles uphill, but she barely felt she needed the drink of water she drew from the stream. The water had looked so clear and good, that she couldn't resist.

And she had the time.

The Scotts were still following, but a long way behind her. She had stopped once or twice on her way up the hill, pretending to need a breather, but in actuality, she had been giving the Scotts a chance to catch up.

The one thing the "magic" (she didn't know what else to call it,) of Dyondaygah had not improved was her sense of direction. She had always navigated more by street signs than landmarks.

Here there were no signs and while the stream was as good of a guide as one could ask for, it had taken her a little while to find it once she'd left Mark to guard the door.

She hoped it had all worked the way she imagined. She prayed the power of the Towen worked the way she thought.

It had to have been at least an hour since she'd left Mark and the Children had been right around the corner.

If the cat theory had worked the way she thought, and she had to some degree forced reality into her construct, time on her side of the door would move differently than time in the Towen.

All she had done was to *wish* really, really hard, when all was said and done.

She had tried to pull Scotland to her through the doorway.

She did her best to believe that when she opened that door, it would be there. She couldn't be sure if it had worked exactly as she had imagined, though she'd managed the most important bit.

But if she had in anyway "shaped reality" she felt certain that they would have all the time they needed.

In the Towen, little or no time at all would pass, while hours or even days could pass in Scotland, so long as the door remained shut.

Thank you C. S. Lewis. She thought as she moved over the terrain, the Scots closing the distance. As she had hoped they would, most of the Scots had stopped to pick up swords and shields, and various other weapons along the way. She could see them glinting in the sunlight as she had run up the hill. And now in the near darkness of the canopied forest, the weapons glittered as they reflected the stray beams of light that broke through the trees.

She began to call out for Mark, shouting his name over and over again, until she heard him respond.

He was closer than she would have thought. She could pinpoint the exact direction of the sounds he made. With her improved senses, she could almost see the sound waves his voice made disrupting the air as they came to her.

This is so cool! She thought, almost like a child discovering video games for the first time. So many possibilities were now open to her, so many opportunities she'd never had before, and would never have had but for this night of horrors.

But she still had to survive the Towen to have any of that. She knew she was heading back into danger. Just as surely as she knew she had no choice. Much as she would have loved to explore the new world and time she was in, there was no way of knowing if she and Mark would ever have another opportunity to return home.

And who was to say what might happen if they stayed, and the connection to the Towen was broken?

Would they just pop out of existence as the timeline corrected itself? Would they suddenly reappear back in the Towen?

Who knew?

Being stuck in the past intact might be the least of the bad things that could happen to them here.

No, they had to go back. They had to escape the Towen, *through* the Towen. And maybe if they were lucky, they'd have the opportunity to destroy it.

Hap was still in play so far as she knew. Any moment, the floors of the Towen might buckle under the force of an explosion.

That thought gave extra speed to her feet and she shouted to Mark who had just come into view, "Mark! Open the door! Open the door and run inside!"

Mark didn't need to be told twice, (a quality in him she had always admired,) and he bolted in through the doorway.

There was just enough time to see him trip over the carpet and fall headlong into another room, but she didn't have time to worry about that now, and perhaps it was for the best.

Shouting a battle cry that surprised even her with its fierceness, she raised her Claymore with both hands and swung it down and to the side, hacking into the neck of one of the Giants.

Any normal person, hit with that much force would have been cut in two. But the Children of Dyondaygah were not regular people. The sword did a lot of damage, but only managed to sink to the mid-chest of the giant, but it was enough.

He fell to his knees, just as the Scotts broke through into the room hunting their prey.

They seemed temporarily stunned by the sight of the Children, all of which were between seven and ten feet tall or more, but then they saw one of them falling to the ground, wounded and for all they knew, dying.

Their swords were already in hand and when Ally yelled back to them, "*Attack!*" they needed no translation. (Ally had no way of knowing it but as it turned out she had chosen precisely the right word, as they were the same in both languages.)

The men, their blood already up from the long run, were battle-ready and waded into the Children, swords in hand and screaming war cries that would have chilled the heart of the bravest warrior.

Ally meanwhile, had withdrawn her sword from her first conquest, by placing a foot on his chest and pushing, while she drew back with her arms.

Once the sword was free, she lunged forward to sink her blade's tip deep into the side of another of the Children of Dyondaygah.

The children did not have weapons, and so at first, they were taken aback by the unexpected assault.

But they soon recovered, putting themselves between Ally and her warriors, and Maru.

"Kill them! Kill all of them!" Maru shouted, "But I want the Girl alive!"

The Girl? Ally managed to think, as she skewered another of the giants on her blade. In other times it might have been less offensive to her. It might even have been taken as a compliment (as it indicated youthfulness), but here it was completely devoid of the respect not only for the Woman she had always been, but for the power she now wielded, and the threat she represented. Her anger redoubled at those words and she once again buried her claymore in the body of one of the Slaves of Maru.

The Scotts swords were singing with the joy of battle and slaughter, the landed blows would have un-armed and taken the heads of most men. But male or female the Giants were ultimately too powerful for the Scotts.

They were falling, one by one to the hands of the enemy.

Ally had to focus on the Giants that stood before her, and could not come to the aid of any of her brave warriors. She watched unable to stop it as one by one, the Scotts were taken and overwhelmed by two or three Giants.

Even wounded as he was, Brisco was chief among the slaughterers.

With one hand he picked up a man by the neck, and squeezed, snapping off the man's head like a cap with a bottle opener.

Red exploded across the room as the man's still-beating heart forced blood up and out of the man's body like a fountain.

Brisco picked up another man with both hands and crushed his rib cage, like a man cracking a lobster claw.

Every man of the Scotts who had unwittingly followed Ally into battle was a brave and valiant person. But as it's often been said, *discretion is the better part of valor.* All of them fought, and none of them had retreated until that moment. But when they saw their leader, a man who had fought in countless battles and come through with little more than a few scratches, broken nearly in twain by the hands of but a single one of these giants, they're courage abandoned them.

This was not their fight.

This was not their war.

Whatever this was, it was not something they were prepared to die for.

And so it was that of nearly thirty men, only four passed alive back through the doorway by which they had come.

When the last stepped through, he closed the door and saw the frame vanish from before him.

For many years to come the tale of the Lost Legion, who had been ripped apart by the hands of Giants would haunt the countryside.

The tale changed as the years past, and the Giants in the story grew larger and larger in the retelling. But in the end, it was all dismissed as a fable.

While the battle raged, Maru perched on Ernest's shoulder, had somehow made it to the back of the horde, and continued to scream orders at his Slaves, which they dutifully obeyed, and Ally saw what lay in store for her if she did not escape, did not win: A life of endless servitude to that little goblin, unable to resist, with no will of her own, willing to die to protect the one man she currently hated, and would always hate more than any other.

She drove her sword deep into one of the females and Ally pushed her backward with all her force, laying the giantess out as a diagonal ramp, pressed against the bodies of the other unwounded giants.

Then with agility like none she had ever known, she ran up the body of the one she had just stabbed, feeling the flesh slide, jiggle and give under her feet like snow, she ascended above the other Giants and brought her sword down.

She was aiming for Maru, and she did hit him, but instead of slicing into him, her blade merely glanced off him, knocking him to the floor.

The same could not be said for Ernest.

The claymore sunk through him like a hot knife through butter. It didn't just cut through his body, it eviscerated him. The blade entered his right shoulder and exited through his left side at the waist. The whole top half of him fell left while his legs went right. The tentacle inside of him exploded out and up. Its suckers and orifices squelching and slithering, covered in the bloody remnants of the man whose body it had inhabited. As the legs of Ernest fell to the ground, the tentacle flopped around groping at the legs and feet, seeming to search for the top half of Ernest, as if it would say, *"Where's the rest of me? No! No! NO! Where's the rest of me!?"*

Ally saw all of this very clearly, for as the body had fallen, so had she.

Even with her new strength and power, there was no immediate recovery from what she had just done.

"Get her!" Maru shouted, "She is down! Get her! Hold her back!"

But she could not be held back.

Not now when she was so close to putting Maru down.

As the hands of the giants reached toward her, she began to crawl toward Maru, and nothing could stop her, not the bloody hands that reached for her, and took hold of her clothes and hair. Not the flopping slithering horror that even now was crawling out of the remains of Ernest.

Maru would be hers.

She drew the dagger from its scabbard on her belt, and stuck it into the floor, pulling herself loose from hand after grasping hand.

Maru, unable to stand himself, scooted away from her inch by inch on his tiny backside, like a child trying to keep away from an angry parent.

Ally drew the dagger point from the floor and raised her arm to strike.

It was only then that she became aware of something that had been happening for nearly a minute now. It had registered only as a low thrum in her ears, but now it grew stronger and clearer, and against her own will, and the natural movement of her arm, she hesitated.

It had been Brisco who started it, seeing that his master was in danger, but soon one by one, the giants who were still standing, and some of those who had fallen took up the chant. *"Dy-on-day-gah! Dy-on-day-gah! Dy-on-day-gah! Dy-on-day-gah!"*

Maru grinned beneath her as she found herself unable to move.

No!... NO! She would not allow this to happen! Not now! Not ever again! Not when she was so close!

Ally struggled to bring her arm down, even as she felt a squirming movement in her jaw, and realized that the words were once again coming from her lips, against her will. *"Dy-on-day-gah! Dy-on-day-gah!"*

Her mouth betrayed her, adding to the power of the chant.

She felt a squirming movement within her stomach and felt her arms drop to the floor, as she was overcome with a feeling of relief, and then relaxation, and even something like joy.

This was who she really was, who she had always been.

What had she been so angry about, just now?

What did it matter?

She was with her true family.

She would be embraced by the tentacles of Dyondaygah, and nothing else mattered.

Except for Mark!

Mark! I can't leave Mark!

What was Mark?

He was weak; he was just another man like any other, a worthless waste of flesh. He had betrayed her over and over again. Hadn't he even left her alone this very night to fend for herself when he should have stayed with her no matter what?

But he came back!

Did he? Did he really? Or did you just dream all of that? Was it for you he came back or was it to claim something he had lost? Like a man reclaiming a forgotten umbrella. Love was just a possession to him as it was to all men, and yes they got upset if it was stolen away but it was no worse than losing a sock, or an old glove.

Yes. He had thought of her that way. She was nothing but another possession to him.

He's not here now, is he? Where is this man who claims to care so much? Is he by your side even now? No. He's run off again.

Ally felt the dagger drop from her hand, as the hands of the Children grasped her shoulders and stood her to her feet.

Around her, the Children continued to chant. Maru walked up to her and signaled her to kneel before him on one knee, which she did obediently.

He climbed up her on to her thigh like a cat, both of his feet able to stand across the width of her thickly muscled quadriceps, and looked her full in the face.

"Welcome back to the Children, my love." He said, and with that he kissed her full on the lips, and she did not withdraw.

"Now," he said, "Place me on Brisco's shoulder."

The crowd of still chanting Giants parted as Brisco made his way to them, and just as she had been instructed, she placed Maru on Brisco's shoulder.

"Now," Said Maru satisfied, "Open that door and get me,

WESLEY CRITCHFIELD

Thurston. The time of the conjunction is at hand!

24

Mark sat alone in the chamber.
It had been that way for hours.
He had slept for a little while...
Which might have been eight hours or more.
There was no way to tell in this place.

Mark had given up wearing a watch years ago and had been used to using his cell phone to tell time, set alarms and keep appointments. Who knew where that was now?

The last time he'd seen it was when he'd left it on the nightstand in the honeymoon suite playing music.

He'd looked for it when he came back to the room, but it was gone along with all of the things he and Ally had brought along with them.

It made sense.

Why leave a bunch of personal effects lying around, especially something as personal as a cell phone?

If a missing person's report was filed, one of the first things law enforcement would likely do is activate your cell phone and try to lock on to the built-in GPS.

If movies had taught him anything it was that if you didn't want to be found the first thing to do was destroy (or give away) your credit cards and cell phone.

So now he sat there, promising himself that if he ever got back to reality, (his reality) he would always wear a watch from now on.

He had tried to escape of course. He could move the circlets around the pole and over and under each other, he just couldn't get them off of the pole itself.

He had thought to attempt picking the locks on the manacles, but there didn't seem to be any locks or even seams in the metal.

When the rings had come in contact with his wrists, it was almost like they had become endless. But that was impossible, right?

They were not uncomfortable and were it not for the fact that he couldn't remove his hands from the pole they would have been no more annoying than wearing a watch or a bracelet.

He had tried working his way up the pole, by wrapping his legs around it and shimmying upward. He thought the pull might be lessened at the top and he could slide it up and over, but alas all that did was to cause one of the cuffs to stick to the flat top, while the other sat to the side, and because they stuck in place so well, he had to fight to get the one on top back over to the smooth rounded part so he could slide back to the ground again.

Mark knew they had to be watching, whether by camera or from an unseen area nearby. But it could be worse.

It could be so much worse.

Doubtless, his sudden appearance had left them wondering where he had come from, and since they didn't know what he could tell them, or likely even what to ask, other than his name rank and favorite cereal....

Serial number...

Really?

Could he ever be serious about anything? Ally was right. She'd often told him he could make a joke out of anything no matter how inappropriate or ill-timed it was.

"Life isn't that stupid show with the guy and the two puppets making fun of bad movies." Ally had said often enough, "This isn't funny. Can't you take anything seriously?"

Apparently not.

Even here at the end of all he'd seen and being held prisoner here in (what he had begun to think of as) *The Château D'if* he couldn't stop making jokes and movie references.

Well, he didn't feel funny now.

After another hour of sitting on the hard stones, his backside began to hurt again so he stood up. Even though it had been uncomfortable he had to admit he had been grateful for the sleep he had gotten. He'd nearly been at the end of his strength. Now he felt only half as bad as before.

If he could have about five gallons of coffee and a decent breakfast he might even feel human again. But no food or coffee was likely to be forthcoming. They hadn't even offered him water yet.

He tried yelling up at the ceiling again, "Is anyone there?" Hello? I'd really like some water, please! Aqua s'il vous plait?"

That wasn't the French word for water, but Mark couldn't remember it, but if they had these stupid universal translators, (which Mark still couldn't get off of his ear,) and knew what anything meant, surely they would understand.

He thought about Ally.

What had happened to her?

When Mark had gone through that door, he had entered another time and place, and when the door closed, that connection had been broken, but when they had been in Scotland, moments before, nearly no time at all had passed before they came back out again, did it work that way every time? Or was it just certain portals?

Just thinking about it made his head hurt.

There seemed to be no rules, no constants.

One moment he was in the Honeymoon Suite and could hear Maru screeching through the wall, the next a Giant had come in, seemingly seeing an altogether different place, yet Mark could see him plain as day, and time was moving at the same rate, for both of them.

The next moment, he was whisked away to Scotland, and hours had passed for Ally and him.

But when they had reentered the Towen, hardly any time at all had passed. They had been back before Maru could even make it down the hallway. Then he had stumbled into wherever / whenever this place was, and now he might never get back. It was madness. Humans tended to think of time as linear, *"This happened and this happened, and then this."* But everything in the Towen seemed to subvert that, and became Doctor Who's *"Big ball of Wibbly-Wobbley-Timey-Wimey... Stuff."*

It was just as he came to this revelation, this "way of thinking," that he looked up and saw that the door frame to the Towen had returned.

Even if it was the Giants who answered, he had to risk it.

"Hey!" He called, "Over here! Please!! Someone help me! I'm in here!! Open the door! Please! Help me! I'm trapped in here! You've got to help! Can anyone hear me? Please!!"

He called out over and over again, but still, the door did not move. But he could see a light underneath of it. A pale candle-like light sat and quivered in one place.

He shouted and raved and fumed, he called out again and again. Someone had to hear him! They simply had too!

Then another light appeared under the door, moving, coming from the left side.

Mark shouted even louder, "Help, please! You must help me! I have to get out of here!"

And the door opened.

In front of him was the strangest thing he could have imagined.

Okay, well... Not the strangest, not after this night, but strange enough to cause him to pause to take it in.

Standing in the doorway was a little young woman, not much taller than Ally... At least not much taller than she had been before partaking of the Sacred food.

She was dressed in a pretty little flower-patterned dress, the skirt of which came all the way to the floor, all but hiding her shoes.

She had on a white apron and a small headband, little more than a ribbon of lace, that marked her as a house servant. In her left hand was a large oil lamp with a handle, so that it could be carried around the house like a flashlight.

Mark was so happy to see someone he shouted out to her before he could stop himself. "Please, you've got to help me! I've got to get back to the Towen! My wife... They are coming for her and me! They are going to make her one of them! Help me, please! No! Don't shut the-"

The Girl, (for a girl she was) was terrified by what she saw and screamed at the top of her lungs, pulling the door shut behind her, her light moving away from the door and then disappearing as the door itself quickly faded away to nothing again.

"No! NO!!" Mark shouted, "Come back! Please! I need your help! You can't leave me!"

But it was no good.

She was gone, as was the door.

Mark wanted to slam his head against the metal pole, but he didn't need any more pain, so he laid his head against it and all but cried.

He slumped to his backside.

That might have been it. His one chance.

His only opportunity to get out of here and he had missed it. If he hadn't been stuck against the pole, he might have kicked himself. The words came back to him as he sat there as clearly as if Hap were reading them in his ear at that very moment: "Maggie has claimed that she found herself in a room of the house she didn't recognize.... within the room was a man, tied to a metal stake, as he would be burned, and he pleaded with her to cut him loose before someone came."

So that was what it had been about.

It had been *him* all along. It was he who frightened Maggie to the point of madness.

He who had sent her running out into the night of May 2, 1891. Not some monstrous horror that the mind could barely fathom… Just *"little old"* him, tied to a metal pole, somewhere in an alternate timeline years and years in the future. Why there was nothing to be frightened of at all.

Yeah right.

And he hadn't exactly been the picture of composure either. If he had walked into an unexpected room and seen a man acting the way he had, he likely would have run away calling for help too.

He sat there staring at his feet, when he heard an old piece of metal scrape against another and a mechanism slide, as a door creaked on large iron hinges.

He looked up to see that the door had reappeared once again, and standing in it was a haggard old man, dressed in a very old fashioned suit, holding aloft a lantern. "Are you the man Maggie saw?" said the man stepping into the room.

To his surprise, Mark answered very calmly, "I guess so. Are you John Carter?"

25

"Don't just stand there!" Maru shouted, "Open the door and get him!"

The Giants stood around looking at each other, not sure which of them should open the door... Or perhaps none of them wanted to, afraid of what might come out, or worse still, what might drag them in.

They were saved the trouble of fighting about it when all of a sudden, from behind the door, there came a loud buzzing sound. Like a submarine preparing to dive.

The next moment, Mark burst through the door, right into the arms of the waiting Giants.

"Oh Mr. Thurston, how good of you to join us!" Maru said looking down at Mark from Brisco's shoulders.

One of the smaller giants, who was still a good head and shoulders over Mark, held Mark's arms down to his sides, as if he were a child, and turned him to face his master.

"By the sound of it, you have been a naughty boy, Mr. Thurston." Maru said listening as the klaxon in the place beyond the doorway sounded, loud and long, "It would seem you cause trouble wherever you go. That's a bad habit Mr. Thurston, and it's going to get you into hot water someday."

Maru looked back at the bodies lining the hallway, both giants and men alike.

Aside from Ernest, only one of Maru's giants had been slain beyond repair, one of the Female giants who had been rather old when she had first come to Maru.

The power of the Sacred Food had been able to undo some of her aging and certainly gave her much of the strength she had, no doubt desired all her life, but ultimately she had been a poor servant to Maru and little more than another conquest to Dyondaygah. She was no great loss.

Ernest, on the other hand, had been considerably more useful, which was why he was selected to take Brisco's place while he healed.

Brisco was still not completely 100% back to his old self and had acquired a slight "drawl" and slur to his speech which might become annoying rather quickly. If Dyondaygah could not repair that damage, in time, Brisco might become considerably less well-favored in Maru's eyes.

But in all likelihood Ally would soon be taking Brisco's place as his most well-loved servant, whether Brisco healed completely or not.

"Throw the bodies into the prison Mr. Thurston seems to have just escaped," Maru said, we'll clean up the rest of the mess later, once the Towen has compressed to its true form. Who knows, there may be considerably less of a mess than we think."

Two or three of the giants, wounded but not disabled, and closest to the dead bodies obeyed the command.

"Where is Ally?" Mark asked, his voice a little constricted because of the way the giant's strong hands restrained him.

"Not so tight Charlie." Maru said, "Mr. Thurston is the honored guest of Dyondaygah and we wouldn't want to harm him unnecessarily."

"Where's my wife?!" Mark demanded.

"Oh, I wouldn't worry about her, Mr. Thurston. I'd be much more concerned about myself at the moment, if I were you. But there's nothing to fear for her, she is quite comfortable. Aren't you, my dear?"

Maru signaled with a kingly wave of the hand, and the Giants parted as Ally stepped forward, belt and sword in its scabbard at her hip, the large dagger still in her hand.

"Ally, no!" Mark said, hands flexing as he tried to reach out for her, but could not.

"Yes Mr. Thurston, as you see your influence has worn off. She has once again achieved her true mind as a servant of Dyondaygah. See? I have not even had to take the weapons away from her for fear of them being used against us."

Ally looked back at Mark. She was not "dead-eyed" like a zombie, or disoriented as one who had been drugged. She looked at him as a soldier looks at a potential threat, which has not yet been realized.

She looked as Mark imagined the British Beefeater might when he was standing at attention, watching the passersby with a mixture of disinterest and solemn distrust.

There was no love in her gaze, nor hate. It was almost as if she had never seen him before.

Maru laughed inwardly as he saw something in Mark twist and break, most likely it was his will to continue the fight, a fight which he had now so clearly lost.

The Chanting would now continue for the rest of the night, (indeed a few of the giants had returned to the Sarsen Circle below, both to investigate and to resume the rituals,) and the control of Ally would not be so easily broken again.

After the night's conjunction Maru would never have to worry about Ally trying to "break free" again.

"She is beautiful, is she not; more so now than when you brought her to us. Wait until she has achieved full induction into the Children of Dyondaygah, Mr. Thurston. Then she will receive her true power. She may even be one of our tallest."

Maru tapped Brisco on the shoulder, a signal he wanted to be lowered to the ground.

Brisco put out one of his big meaty mitts and Maru stepped off into his hand. Brisco put his hand on the floor and Maru stepped off like a man stepping off an elevator.

"It is so sad you will not be with us to see that, Mr. Thurston. Or at least the part of your mind that allows you to think rationally will not be. It is a possibility Dyondaygah will leave your body behind when he takes your mind. He has done that before. Sometimes it leaves a mess for us to clean up but the

Frog-men enjoy a tasty treat now and again. So it is, how you would say, *"No big deal."* Maru laughed, "But I will make you a promise Mr. Thurston, if your living body is still with us after tonight, I will make sure that you stay alive long enough to see Ally's final beauty and perhaps I will even let you be an usher at the ceremony, when I wed your wife before Dyondaygah and all the Great Old Ones."

Maru had expected Mark to try to lash out at him, to try and break free of Charles' grip to get at him. But he only slumped in Charles grip, to the point where the giant had to readjust his grip on the substantially smaller man just to keep him from falling to the floor.

"That's right Mr. Thurston, just give in." Maru said with a toothy grin to match Brisco's, "There is no point in resistance. Save your strength for Dyondaygah, he likes it when the prey fights back."

Mark raised his eyes from the floor, to look at Maru, "You had better hope your god is everything you think he is. Because if I have one ounce of life left in my body, you will be dead before sunrise."

Maru chuckled softly, "You are so obsessed with winning Mr. Thurston, you do not perceive that you have already lost."

Maru turned away from Mark back toward Brisco. "You really are a little man aren't you?" Mark said, not bothering to lift his head.

"What was that?" Maru asked, through clenched teeth. "You are a little person," Mark explained almost flaccidly, barely bothering to raise his head or lift his voice much higher than a whisper, "In the mind, and in the heart. You're consumed by your hatred and envy, and desire for power over the lives of others. It's not your height. Height and strength, they mean nothing. They all come to most human beings as a pure gift. It's like being proud of the color of your hair. So few are remembered for their height and strength Mr. Maru, they are remembered for their heart and what they gave, not the power they wielded or what they took. You think that by taking people, and making them slaves to your will and that of your Dark Master, you will become *"Big and Important."* But as it turns out, with every life you take, with every person you rob of their freedom, you only grow that much smaller. And as it turns out, when all is said and done, there will be nothing left of you at all."

As Mark spoke, rage filled Maru. His fists clenched and his arms grew ramrod stiff at his side, his nostrils flared and his lips curled into a snarl.

"You think you have held me back?" Maru asked, not waiting for an answer, "You've accomplished nothing. I have my giants. I have the Towen and I have Dyondaygah, together we will raise a race of Giants! Superhumans! Who will march out from this place and Conquer the world! And when the stars grow right, and the time of the Great Old Ones, at last, comes round again, Dyondaygah will rule this Universe! I will be by his side!"

Maru turned back toward Mark and looked up at him, with all the fury of a wild animal; a hyena or a wolverine, "You think me small?" he said, "When the Great Ones have dominion on this pitiful mudball I shall be bigger than you can imagine. I shall have power beyond that of a god! I will crush solar systems in my fists as though they were peanut shells! My true essence will explode out of this flimsy clod of clay, and all the stars will tremble before my power! They will melt in the glow of my glory and I... I..."

Maru closed his eyes, and took a deep breath in and out, "Well played Mr. Thurston. When you knew you couldn't win, you appealed to my vanity. And I'm sorry you got to see that... While every word I said is true, I... prefer to keep such thoughts to myself."

He turned back toward Brisco, who carefully picked him up and put him back on his shoulder.

"Take him downstairs to the Circle," Maru instructed. "Dyondaygah will have his way, and whatever is left, will be ours to have fun with. Take him and tie him to a chair, have his mouth gagged. But make sure his eyes are open. I want him to see every moment of what is coming for him."

Maru watched as two of his giants carried Mark away.

Had the two been of average height, Mark's legs would have been dragging behind them as the hauled him off to his doom. But the size and strength of his warriors could not be denied or resisted.

Mark was more than a foot off the ground as the procession made its way down the hall toward the main lobby stairs.

A little man indeed. Maru thought to himself, but it would not always be so. His father had told him as much as he was growing up, so to speak.

"The ancients have prepared for your coming from time immemorial, my son. They have studied the stars and dreamed the dreams that the Old Ones prescribed for them. You will be the one who will finally open the door to Dyondaygah." Maru could hear his father's musical Irish voice repeating those words nearly every day, *"The stars will grow right in your time, and you will not die as men understand death. When the time comes for your transcendence, you will be like the Old Ones themselves, new and just as powerful in their greatness. The ceremonies and procedures your mother and I performed before your birth may have robbed you of stature in this world. But when the Great Old Ones, Dyondaygah above all, have reclaimed this pocket of existence, where matter and time have dared to form, in defiance of their will, all will be restored to the great void."*

Yes, the ceremonies. They had been tried before many times, but always to disastrous effect, and always as servants to different gods in the pantheon of the Old Ones.

Perhaps the most well known had been when Wizard Whateley had brought forth his two Monstrous sons to Yog Sothoth. The first of which had been reasonably human in appearance and the second... The second had been a secret horror and by all accounts mostly invisible, kept in a barn until both his earthly father and his brother were dead. Then it had ravaged the countryside for a while, but it was so much like, (and some said a part of) Yog Sothoth, that it had not been able to sustain itself very well in the world of matter. It was easily destroyed by simple country folk with only the simplest and superstitious view of "Magic".

Yog Sothoth himself might be great, but his followers were nothing compared with Maru's parents, the servants of Dyondaygah. His father and mother had provided a great deal of the resources he would eventually need, including their willing sacrifice, which had been necessary according to the documents, so that Maru might have no father but the demon god himself. It had taken nearly another hundred years before Maru had found the Towen of course, but that didn't mean their slaughter had been for nothing. Dyondaygah was outside of time and thus time held very little meaning for him.

Maru only now wondered why his parents' sacrifice had never been mentioned by the Great One.

Not that he had cared for them very much, but when they had done so much for Dyondaygah, you might expect an "honorable mention." But such things were not for a truly faithful servant to question, especially now.

Had it not been for Maru's extraordinarily long life and relative retention of youth and vitality he might have doubted his father's words, and the very existence of the Old Ones, as he often had during his younger, more foolish years, prior to his eightieth birthday.

While others had grown old and died, Maru continued. He had often expected, much like Wilbur Whateley himself, that some element of the strangeness that had birthed him would become manifest in time.

Wilbur had been able to hide away most of the glorious manifestations of his heritage by wearing simple if baggy clothing. But Maru, other than his height had nothing strange about him physically whatsoever.

It was almost disappointing.

He'd had a few "skin tags" over the years which he had hoped might be the beginning of some powerful transformation, but alas, it was nothing at all and easily removed with a scalpel, never to return.

But then had come the finding of the Towen, and coming face to face, as it were, with the great Old One himself.

From that day forward there had been no doubt whatsoever in his mind and heart.

All the Promises of his father and his father's master would come true.

Power beyond imagining.

Size beyond understanding.

Already he knew some of that power, in the sway he held over the Children. Once fully joined to Dyondaygah they could not reject any demand he made of them.

Were he to tell them to slit their own throats, they must obey. (This he had done more than a few times in the beginning, not only to test his power but to watch as they were rapidly healed from within.)

That extreme devotion and obedience had nearly been his undoing tonight when it came to Mr. Thurston.

He had ordered the Children to focus on nothing else but finding Thurston, which had led to a loss of control over Ally. Had she managed to get away all might have been lost, but it seemed *"Love and devotion"* were almost as good as fences and whips when it came to methods of control. He would have to remember that lesson in the future.

But now it was time to put an end to Mr. Thurston and to claim his newest servant.

The Thurstons had cost him a few bodies tonight, from those who had been lost in the search of the building and even one Hap or Thurston had managed to blow a hole through her with the shotgun during Thurston's initial escape. But this was of little concern.

While Dyondaygah might not come into the world tonight, as Maru had hoped, it would be no different from other days. And eventually, he would acquire more giants. It was

simply a matter of time.
> *And after all. From what I'm told, the Calamari here is delicious.*

26

A second giant, a female, took Mark's right arm, while Charlie took his left.

Mark refused to give them any help and remained "boneless" as they carried him back down, a now considerably shorter hallway, down the stairs, through the dining hall, through a second hallway, down another flight of stairs, and finally into the center of the Towen.

The Sarsen stones were lit from below, by the glow of a natural gas-powered trench of fire, that lined the walls.

A small iron grid prevented a hand being placed directly into the flame, but if one were to touch that grid, it would, no doubt be the same as touching a hot grill.

As Maru had instructed, Mark was tied to the chair, and a gag was placed over his mouth.

One of the giants brought forth Mark's sports bag, and took out the contents, making a circle of handyman tools around him; screwdrivers, knives, and a hammer, all tools Mark had brought with him, just in case he needed them.

With his mouth gagged, it was not possible to laugh out loud, but he nearly laughed inwardly when he saw that among the belongings, they had included his car keys and his cell phone.

It seemed that nearly everything he had brought into the Towen with him, excluding clothes, was laid at his feet.

Noticeably absent was the bag of Tree Stump Remover, and he wasn't sure if that was due to the fact that he had lost most of it when he had been sucked into the throat of that impossibly large beast, or if the giants had wisely realized bringing a bag of gunpowder into a room with a mostly open flame was not the best of ideas.

They also lay before him the weapons Ally had taken out of the past: The sword, the shield, and the long dagger, Ally had intended to use to kill Maru. Then a third Giant brought forth Hap's shotgun and laid it at Mark's feet to taunt him.

That was the purpose of the tool circle after all.

"Even with all your weapons close to hand, you can not defeat us." They said silently.

Before him at the center of the circle, was a large raised dais, (clearly some form of Altar). At its center lay a great circle, with strange symbols carved into the stones around it. Some of the symbols looked familiar, ranging from Celtic runes to the Arabian, to ancient Egyptian, but none of them seemed to tell a coherent narrative that Mark could understand.

Looking around him Mark could see the various Giants who did not have an assigned task, had resumed the "Dance" or march around the circle, which he had only heard about until now. Two of the giants stood in the corner, keeping rhythm with a drum.

The 1, 2, 3, 4, beat coincided with the syllables of the demon god's name.

"Dy-On-Day-Gah! Dy-On-Day-Gah!" They repeated over and over again.

Then at a forty-five-degree angle to his left Mark saw Hap, on his knees, tied wrist to ankles, with another bit of rope between his feet and neck, making a sort of self strangling noose.

At least he was alive.

Mark had feared that Hap might have been killed in his attempt to get at the sarsen stones. He had hoped that at the very least Hap had been unable to reach the stones and had managed to escape The Towen, and might even now be planning some sort of rescue, but alas, here he was, just as helpless as Mark found himself.

Across the dais, at the opposite forty-five-degree angle from Mark's right the Giants were directing Ally into an alcove in one of the Sarsens, and they were lifting great chains with manacles at the ends to her wrists.

These were not just simple small linked stainless steel chains such as you might see on a large garage door. They were old and solid iron chains, each one as thick as a man's thumb and each link must have weighed half a pound or more. They were connected to a small iron plate, bolted into the cobblestone floor by four large iron bolts.

The manacles themselves, were not handcuffs, but circlets of iron, (the primitive ancestors of the circlets Mark still wore on his wrists), clamped down and held together, but another iron bolt with a nut on the other side, which was twisted home by a modern ratcheting wrench.

The two Giants preparing Ally stepped away, their work done.

Ally stood there stoically, as though she were waiting in line at the DMV. There was no sign of resistance in her, nor was there any mark of expectation in her face. No fear, no love, no hate. Simply bland acceptance and indifference.

She had been free, had been herself, (though a more powerful and courageous version of herself than Mark had ever seen before,) and he knew that deep down inside her, she did not want this. "*The Choice*" Maru spoke of was a lie.

"Remove the gag." Maru said, walking on his tiny legs toward the chair where Mark sat, "I want to hear his screams when he confronts the great old one. I want to see his mind break. I want him to see his wife become one of The Children, now and forever."

The gag was removed, and Mark said nothing.

He spit on the ground, not in defiance but to get the taste of the stale cotton rag out of his mouth.

He didn't try to spit on Maru or give him the "evil eye." He simply looked at the floor and refused to even acknowledge the little man.

"Now Mr. Thurston," Said Maru, "You will know what it truly means to be little. You will see that in the grand scheme of things, you are nothing compared to the might of Dyondaygah. You are nothing compared with his children, and you are nothing compared with me. You may exceed me in height but you can never exceed me in power. There is no force in this universe or beyond it that can contest with my will. Compared to Zeus, I am a mountain; compared to Thor, I am Yggdrasil! Compared to Me, the petty Hebrew God is no more powerful than a rat, and the Christian God is but an ant beneath my boot! Where are they? Eh? Mr. Howard has no doubt been praying to them all this time, have you not?"

He looked at Hap, who like Mark refused to make eye contact, "Yahweh is not here Mr. Howard, and Christ is as dead as the Pharaohs. If they ever actually existed, they have no power here. Here, I am a god and I submit my will only to Dyondaygah and he will not refuse me anything."

Mark still said nothing. What was there to say?

"Cut the rope between Mr. Howard's legs and neck and bring him to the stone bowl." Maru said to the Giants standing on either side of Hap, "But make sure the gag is good and tight."

The Giants obeyed and brought Hap to the bowl, which stood on top of the Stone pillar. "Place his head over the bowl," Maru instructed, making his way to the stone Pillar, and starting up a small set of wooden steps, which were brought over by another Giant who had acted without being ordered. This was her recurring function in Maru's nightly rites.

The Giants placed Hap's neck over the lip of the bowl holding him face down in it. The bowl nearly encompassed his whole head.

"Maru!" Mark shouted lamely from his chair, "Stop! You can't do this!"

Maru mounted the steps and looked past the top of Hap's head, "Oh Mr. Thurston, I can do whatever I want. It's one of the perks of being a god."

He brought the knife in, underneath the place where Hap's head lay, and drew back quickly. Mark heard Hap scream threw his gag as the knife cut into him, the Giants holding him in the air by his still bound hands and feet. Hap tried to buck against them but all his efforts amounted to was little more than a slight jitter.

"Oh Mr. Howard, look what you've done, you've made the cut more jagged than it needed to be." Maru tisked, "I prefer my work to be neat and tidy and you've ruined it, now hold still this will only take a moment."

Mark watched as blood began to leak down out of the bowl on to the pillar below through some unseen trough. It traced down the center of each side of the stone and down into a channel below.

"That's it, just a bit more," Maru said as the blood flowed.

Finally, the blood reached the floor and filled in several small lines around the altar.

Mark might have tried to break his bonds but he knew it would have been in vain, unlike the chair he had been tied to upstairs in the kitchen, this chair was no factory-made flimsy, post the year 2000, mass-produced chair, made from pressed wood only slightly firmer than cardboard, (which had been bad enough).

This chair was handmade, the arms and legs were hewn from four by four beams, with iron brackets meant to hold the ropes which now bound him to the chair.

It was a chair meant for the work it was now doing. The rope was thick and strong, and no amount of struggling would have broken through it; certainly not in the time that he would have had to rush to the altar, even if they had simply fallen away like sand.

Mark could do nothing but sit and watch as Hap's lifeblood bled out on to the floor.

"Now just a bit more into the cup, if you please," Maru said affecting the same mannerisms he had used to seem so congenial earlier that evening while Mark and Ally had sat down to their demon contaminated dinner.

He lifted a small goblet and placed it on a small pedestal within the bowl. The giants shifted Hap's body to compensate, lifting his face above the rim of the bowl.

Mark could now see that it was not Hap's throat that had been cut, but his forehead. The blood pooling through the wound was deep, and might have bitten into the muscles above the eyebrows a bit, but not enough to do any real lasting harm.

"Dyondaygah likes to break his enemies before they die Mr. Thurston." Maru explained, "He will not accept any, but a living sacrifice. Normally, a bit of my blood or the blood of one of the Children would be sufficient to open the doorway. But tonight is special, and it would not do to let such a lovely treat as the blood of an enemy such as Mr. Howard to go un-tasted by his greatness. Don't fear Mr. Howard, you have only lost somewhere in the neighborhood of five hundred Milliliters of blood, no worse than a trip to the blood bank."

Maru then withdrew a rag and placed it to Hap's forehead, "Apply the pressure, but do not damage him." He instructed the giant, "Stand him up and put his feet on the ground."

Maru then withdrew, from somewhere in his little Red suit with black lapels the last thing Mark would have expected, a tube of Super Glue.

"Bring him here," Maru said, annoyed, and the giants obeyed. He was on the level with Hap and reached up with the tube, smearing glue over the wound, "This would have gone better for you Mr. Howard, had you not resisted, but now there will likely be a scar.... Not that you will be sane long enough for that to be a concern but all the same..." He trailed off and then resumed, "In fact, that could be said of much of what you have done since we met. It seems to be in your nature." Maru tisked again, "Some people will never learn."

Maru capped the glue and rubbed the remainder of the glue off on a handkerchief he withdrew from an interior pocket, "That's my bit done." He said, "Now its time for me to sit back and enjoy the show. Brisco!"

Brisco came to his master and picked him up, carrying him over to his large throne, glinting gold in the firelight, and placing him upon it.

Maru put out his hand, a scepter of some sort was placed in it. Above the stone altar, a dim, reddish light began to glow, seemingly out of nowhere.

It was very like the red aurora Mark had seen hovering above the Towen earlier that night, but this was thicker, more solid, and it was lined with electric trails of gold and blue and green.

As it grew more solid, it began to look more like a curtain, suspended in mid-air, than a light pattern.

Then the curtain, as though pulled from the center, shot down into the stone bowl where Hap's blood had been spilt, and disappeared into it.

The chanting from the giants, which had never stopped until that moment, ceased, and all the giants faced inward, facing the altar.

To Mark's surprise, the stone altar itself, began to lower into the ground. First, the movement was barely perceptible, but then it sank faster and faster.

From its base, a golden light began to shine out from underneath through the widening cracks in the stone floor.

Soon the pillar was gone and the light shot up in a shaft of dazzling energy.

Then more of the stones in the floor began to fall away; the Majority of them disappeared into the Earth (or the illuminated void that had opened up in the Earth), others rising above the growing pit, were suspended by an invisible force.

Mark's view of Ally was now unobstructed. She stood there her hands splayed, arms rigid at her side, her eyes half-closed, but whether it was against the light, or if she was now locked into a trance, Mark couldn't tell.

"Ally!" He shouted, "Ally don't give in! Fight them! Remember that I love you! Fight for your mind Ally! Fight for your soul!"

He didn't know if Ally could hear him or not and the words seemed pitifully weak and pointless even as he said them. He could barely hear the words coming out of his mouth and if not for the vibrations in his head he might not have been sure he was saying anything at all.

There was no "sound" coming from the glowing pit, nothing over which to shout, but there was a silence that the pit seemed to enforce. It was as if the light and power from the pit, was not allowing the air to vibrate, blocking the sound waves in a void. Yet Mark did not have any trouble breathing in and out.

The light from below seemed to become more liquid than light, and it seeped into all the markings around the chamber, filling in the lines on the floor, and the sarsen stones with its radiance. It moved through the empty lines left in the stone by the carver's chisel-like a bead of mercury, tracing the markings and filling them in.

The pit had opened up to the iron hoop at Mark's feet and seemed to stop there, but light showed up through the stones beyond it, as though it might open further at any moment. Mark had feared that the chair might fall into the pit and that would be the end of him, but it had come no further.

On the edge of his consciousness, barely able to hear it, Mark could hear the voices of the Giants surrounding them.

They were once again chanting the name of the demon god, but now it was not the tribal rhythm it had once been, it was more of a long drawn out mantra. Their deep tones sounding more like grinding stones than human voices.

"*Dyyyyyyyy-ooooooon. Daaaaaaaaaay-gaaaaah. Dyyyyy-yyy-ooooooon. Daaaaaaaaaay-gaaaaah.*"

From the center of the golden light below a darkness, a shadow, grew in a widening circle from within.

Up out of the pit rose a column of flesh, cutting off Mark's view of Maru on his golden throne. It was like an elephant's trunk, only much thicker and wider, more muscular.

It was like a tentacle, but like no tentacle that had ever existed on an earthbound creature. And while it might have borne some resemblance to the tentacle that had exploded from Brisco earlier in the night, Mark had only seen that against the backdrop of the Buffet and the starlit night. Here, every aspect of its unearthly vileness was highlighted by the light from below.

It was covered over with "suckers" and teeth and organelles, and eyes. Hundreds of eyes. Some like that of a human, others like those of horses or goats. Some contained multiple pupils, while others were multifaceted.

That alone was enough to make Mark shriek involuntarily in horror, but there was more to come.

Around the single column more tentacles reached out. These were more like those of octopuses or squid, and less horrifying, but it was clear all were joined to the whole; many arms, but only one mind behind them.

Ally, off to his right, had drawn rigid as the tentacle had exploded out of the hole, nearly touching the ceiling, as though a jolt of electricity had passed through her, her head and neck had arched back and her fists clenched.

Her strong shoulders strained against the fabric of Mark's increasingly too small sweatshirt.

Hap, to Mark's left, merely stared in slack-jawed amazement, with his gag filling his mouth; he could have had no other reaction.

"Mark." A voice said, "Mark, darling."

Darling? Mark thought as he saw the tentacle seem to slacken and decrease, into another form. All of the eyes seemed to sink away into the fleshy column, except for two. The tentacle changed, reducing in some places, becoming wider in others.

The black haze that drifted around the tentacles, became more solid and took on the form of clothes or a billowing robe. The shape before him became a woman in a black hood and cape. It reminded Mark of a black wedding dress.

The face was hidden, but out from behind a thin veil of dark smoke, two beautiful golden eyes shown through.

"Mark Thurston." Said the voice, now decidedly more feminine, "You have done well this evening. You have withstood challenges that would make most men cower in fear. You have shown yourself to be faithful, worthy, and true. You shall be my most honored servant. For *I* am the Great Dyondaygah. I have seen your great works with my many eyes. I have watched from my dark recluse as you have shown bravery and courage beyond measure. Now I call you to my service… to be my High Priest."

Mark couldn't be sure he was hearing all of this right.

Had he gone mad already?

Was this all something his broken mind had crafted, trying to make sense of the incomprehensible?

"You may speak to me freely." Dyondaygah said, "I, alone, shall hear you, my servants will not hinder you."

"High-Priest?" Mark asked, trying the words, not sure if his mouth could form them. "You want me to serve you?"

"Yes." Said the voice, almost girlishly, with a slight laugh, "Maru has had his time and plenty of it. He has grown complacent in my service. He thinks himself more than he is. He has always sought my favor out of a desire for power and the will to dominate others for his own ends. Maru was a useful tool, but now he begins to think himself an equal with me. But you Mark, you would never betray one to whom you have sworn your allegiance."

"My Allegiance?" Mark asked still confused. "You have stood by your friends and your wife this evening. You have called others to your side and they have followed. You are a great leader. Once you have set your hand to something you do not turn back."

"What I've done tonight, I did for love. Its something a thing like you could never understand." Mark said simply, not able to believe that he was talking to this thing as one might another person they had just past by on the street.

He had expected many things from the monstrosity before him. But it never even occurred to him that somehow this situation might become, of all things, a job interview.

"Love." Dyondaygah said, laughing out right now, in a pristine giggle, that reminded Mark of the stereotypical "Southern Belle", "Love," it repeated, "Mark, so many miserable little humans have passed through my clutches believing that Love in one form or another would save them; the love of a husband or a wife, the love of a mother or a child, even the love of other gods. But they all fell. No one as ever escaped my grasp and no god can withstand me. "Love" my dear servant Mark Thurston, is nothing but human emotion. A collection of chemicals and electric impulses in your miserable little coats of dust, designed to help perpetuate and protect the species. The most base of animals feel some version of it, but only humans are naïve enough to believe that it has some power beyond what they consider to be the physical realm."

The feminine phantom before him lifted a tutelary arm, "But loyalty, fealty and fidelity, those are the qualities you possess that so many lack. Not just in your world but in all the worlds. And that is what you have demonstrated here tonight. When you could have left Ally behind you came back. When your own life might have been forfeit, you returned to the one you had sworn your allegiance too. What are those lines that most humans in the English speaking world say when they are getting Married? *"To love, honor and cherish, till death do we part?"* For you those were not mere words, not simply a pie-crust promise, to be made and then abandoned when difficulty came, you meant them. You swore your fealty and you have kept your word. Maru knows nothing of this. He has only ever sought me out of his desire to be as great as I am. Take his place. Be my priest and you shall have control over Kings and Countries. You shall rule an unstoppable army and conquer this world in my name. Help me to enter your world by giving those I send to you my sacred food. While the Earth endures, you will have riches beyond the dreams of avarice, you will have power unlike the world has ever known. And when the stars grow right and I, at last, take this world, you shall sit beside me and have all that was promised to Maru."

Mark looked on at the form of Dyondaygah before him. He listened to the soft words, promising everything he could have ever dreamed of; ready to give him the world. Every world.

The voice in his mind was soft and seductive. He could do this. It would be worth it. Think of all the good he could do, right up until the moment Dyondaygah took the world.

He could have anything he wanted. He could take the reigns of power. The world would beat a path to his door. With all the money he could ever want, he could build and control empires, right from here, in this little corner of Kansas.

While the Children of Dyondaygah might be bound to the Circle of Influence for a time, Maru was not. He could come and go as he pleased. He had not partaken of the sacred food. Mark's mind would be his own.

Mind.
His mind.
No. Not his mind. *Hers.*

What about his wife's mind?

"And what of Ally?" Mark asked. "What will you do with her?"

"She will be one of my Children, but you may do with her as you will. She will no longer resist your commands as she has done in the past. She will be loyal to you above all else, save for me. No longer will you have to convince her of your rightness. She will be silent, loving, and obedient as a good wife should be. She will be everything you ever wanted in a woman."

He looked off to his left, where Ally still stood, rigid as a statue. Her powerful arms chained to the floor, and he realized that *this* was the truth of Dyondaygah's promises.

The victim was given power. Physical power. Strength. Wealth. Political or even ruling power, whatever they desired most, but then they were forever enslaved, chained to the will of the "god" they had sold their soul to and what did it get them?

Just as so many rulers down through the ages had done, promising *prosperity, peace, land, and bread, equal rights.* All this and more they promised and often delivered for a time, but in the end it always devolved into war, starvation, and death.

You got what you wanted.
But you lost what you had.
Your freedom.
Your-self.

"She could be everything I ever wanted," Mark repeated almost dreamily to himself. "But not the one thing I want her to be most; herself."

"What?" The voice replied, taken aback. Mark snarled viciously.

"Neither I nor Ally will ever serve you. Completely submissive? Doing just what she's told because I say it? No will or mind of her own? That's not love, devotion, fealty, fidelity or whatever you want to call it, its slavery. I swore an oath to her, to the woman I LOVE! Not to her body, not to a hollowed-out husk that simply does whatever I tell it to, I swore devotion to HER! I would sooner see her dead than to have her mind lost, and her will broken. I would sooner be dead myself than wield that kind of power over anyone. Is that what you think being a god is? You're not a god. You're nothing but a spider spinning your little webs, only thinking of ways to ensnare new victims."

"Silence!" The voice commanded, full of venom, "You will not speak so to me!"

"I haven't even begun!" Mark shouted. "You think you

can put on a little light show and convince me to betray not only my wife but the entire human race? To give my world up for a few years of "power" and control, just so you can bring your loathsome presence into a world you were cast out of long ago?"

"You will not speak to me so!"

The voice commanded, losing all façade of "femininity" or humanity, "You are nothing but an insect compared with me! I offered you power as a boon! You will serve me or you will die! But before you die, you will kneel to my power! You will see my glory! And you will worship me!"

"Your power." Mark said disdainfully, "Your kind has convinced generations that you are all-powerful and that mankind is nothing to you. You have made them believe this world is nothing but another conquest, not even a prize to be won, but a pebble beneath your boot. But I see the truth. If you were all-powerful, you would never have been cast out in the first place. Time and Space would hold no sway over you. Your "*unstoppable army*", would not be confined to a two miles radius of nothing, in the middle of nowhere! Not for a day, not for an hour, let alone twenty years! If you were really a god, you could claim this reality in a moment, as easily as waving a hand or snapping your fingers, but you can't! You need humans to try to invade this world. You require followers to open the door just so you can get a toe under it. A true god doesn't require worshipers to exist, but in this realm, you are powerless without them. You are little more than a ghost. You whisper in the minds of madmen to give them nightmares and make them promises you could never keep. A band of primitives with sticks and rocks defeated you here before in the middle of nowhere Kansas, and before that at the confluence of the three rivers, and how many times before that? You and your "Great Old Ones" try time and again to rape your way into this world but you can't. You fail again and again. If you ever did fully come into this world, you would be crushed beneath the burden of matter and time. You're not a god. You're nothing but bad dreams."

As Mark spoke the figure once again resumed its monstrous tentacle-like shape, and the golden light below turned crimson.

The voice now filled the chamber, no longer just in Mark's head but audible within the room, and it vibrated the very stones and timbers above them.

"You will now watch as I take from you everything you love." The voice of Dyondaygah shrieked, and Mark realized that the sound was coming from the mouths of all the giants around him, but not like a group of people speaking in chorus, it was one sound, one voice, that spoke with many mouths.

And somehow, it might have been where the giants were looking, it might have been a slight difference in the direction the ever-moving tentacles undulated, but Mark understood that the focus of the thing had left him and was now turned upon Ally.

The voices of the Giants continued to speak, "You will be my servant." They said.

"Yes." Ally answered, stoically.

"You will have the power and strength that you have always desired above all things."

"Yes." Ally repeated.

Mark tried to call out for her, but it seemed now that only he was affected by the forced silence, while the voice of Dyondaygah echoed from the mouths of his servants, and Ally's voice was un-muffled.

Mark's voice made no sound at all.

"You will conquer this world in my name and do my will, and that of my High Priest, Maru."

There was a long pause. Silence.

The voice repeated, "You will conquer this world in my name and do my-"

"No." Ally interrupted, and her voice rang through clear as a bell.

From across the room, Mark heard Maru shriek, "No?!"

"You will obey the will of Dyondaygah." The voice commanded. "I will…" Ally said.

"You will obey the will of Dyondaygah." The voice repeated. "I will…" Ally said. "I will… I will NOT."

And her declaration rang through the chamber.

Suddenly, Mark could hear his breathing again, and he shouted to her, "Yes Ally fight it! Fight them! Don't give in! I love you, Ally, fight your way back to me!"

But even as he said it, Ally fell to her knees, the chains on her wrists clanking as they hit the cobblestones and each other.

From deep within her there came a long bellow.

"No!" Maru shouted across the room, "Great one, do not kill her! I want her for my own!"

"She will submit, or she will die!" The voice of Dyondaygah said through the Children lining the walls of the chamber.

As Mark looked on, shouting his love to her, over and over again, he saw for the first time, a visible change shudder through Ally. She was becoming larger and filling out right before his eyes.

Until now, Mark had not been able to notice the changes as they were happening. They had been small and subtle, the same way a plant may grow very quickly, but not so much that you could notice it happening.

But now she seemed to swell before his eyes, as Dyondaygah accelerated her transformation.

Somehow Mark thought he understood the demon's reasoning, if he could accelerate the changes within her, perhaps he could gain more control, forcing the "Sacred food" to join with her as it had the other children, bringing her completely under his control.

No matter what Maru or the demon said, *"The Choice"* was a lie.

Mark could hear the fabric of his sweat clothes on Ally's body stretching, straining, and tearing. Seams and whole cloth alike failed in various places. Holes appeared in the pants and shirt as they gave way, allowing a peak at the flesh, and the swelling striated muscles and defined veins, as Ally's body expanded beneath the fabric.

"Fight it!" Mark shouted, "Fight back!"

"Silence!" The Voice of Dyondaygah commanded, but the muting force did not return.

Mark shouted to her more as the Voice of Dyondaygah repeated, "You will submit to Dyondaygah! You will submit!"

Suddenly Ally began to spasm. Every pronounced muscle in her body began to expand and contract violently. Her head flew forward and back like a "headbanger" at a rock concert, while her arms pumped next to her chest, her biceps straining as the holes in the fabric of the sweatshirt widened.

The shirt working its way further and further up her back as she quickly grew even taller.

Suddenly this "grand-mal seizure" stopped and from deep within her there came a loud gurgling sound.

"No! No!" Maru shouted.

"She is unworthy of the Glory of Dyondaygah!" The Children spoke as one, "She shall not be one with us!"

Mark knew this was the end for Ally.

She was about to die right in front of him and there was nothing he could do. But he held true to his word.

Better to see her die free than live forever as a slave.

It would be a fate worse than death. When men made slaves of other men, they could not control their minds. In their hearts and minds, they could always be free no matter what man did to them.

But in slavery to Dyondaygah, not even the mind was free.

Mark prayed it would be over for her quickly.

He expected to see the tentacle explode out of her stomach and chest. It would burst through the space that now existed between the bottom of the sweatshirt and the straining waistband of her sweatpants, as it had done with Brisco when he was wounded amid the Razor Devil's Claw outside.

But for her, there would be no healing.

She gurgled deeply once again, and out of her mouth came a black sludge, the same color as the tentacles that wriggled before Mark, in the fire-lit darkness of the chamber. She heaved again, and more black gunk exploded onto the floor beneath her, with all the force of a fire hose.

From the force and fury of her retching, it seemed as though she might be literally about to puke her guts up on to the floor of the Circle, but with one last almighty heave, she fell to the ground unconscious.

Maru jumped down from his golden throne and rushed toward Ally.

It angered Mark to no end that he could not do the same. But if he could have, he would likely have smashed the little hobgoblin to pieces, for daring to lay a hand on his wife.

Maru did not love her. How could he?

He loved no one and nothing but himself. Even Dyondaygah had known this.

Maru's little feet skittered across the stones until he came to Ally, and he lay on top of her back, reaching his little hand into the pinched space between her large deltoids and her neck, feeling for a pulse.

He looked at Ally like a pretty little smashed trinket, he had greatly desired for his own.

But even from his captivity on the chair, Mark could see that as he did so, Maru, rose and fell with Ally's breathing. She was alive.

Who knew what state her mind and body might be in after being juiced with growth hormones, her mind assaulted by the will of Dyondaygah, but for the moment, she was breathing and this was all that mattered.

Before her, on the ground, the puddle of slime she had

expelled began to move.

It seemed to sprout new little tendrils of its own, barely formed, and pulled itself forward towards, and then up the dais. Stair by stair, it gooped its way toward the writhing mass and then disappeared into the hole in the floor, leaving not a trace of itself behind.

"You have failed your master, Maru!" said Dyondaygah through the mouths of his children, "You did not maintain the sway. You allowed many hours to pass for Ally Thurston in which the chant of my name was not maintained! This is why Ally Thurston, who would have been among the greatest of my children, was not birthed into the new life. *You* allowed her body time and the natural defenses to take arms against the sacred food. It did not form within her. Now she will die as the sacred food, the arm of Dyondaygah, is not within her! *You* have robbed her of eternal union and *You* have failed your master!"

Maru seemed to panic, this had never happened before.

"Oh, truly tremendous one!" Maru said, pushing off of Ally's comparative bulk to stand to his feet, only to kneel again before the mass of writhing tentacles, "I have not failed you! It was Thurston! Thurston and Mr. Howard! They are the ones who have ruined everything, this night! They are your enemies! Destroy them, oh my Master! Show them your greatness! Break their minds with your majesty!"

"It is *you* that has failed me." The voice explained, "You have been tasked with the preparation and you are to maintain the sacred chant. You have not only allowed the endless adoration to be disrupted, you, disrupted it yourself, by ordering the children to focus solely on the search for your enemies. Did you not understand that when the Conjunction had ended all those who had entered the outer worlds by the Towen, would be returned to it, so long as they draw breath? No matter where in the Omniverse they might stray, their essence is tied to this place and time. Had you done as you were commanded Thurston would have been returned to you, and even now the

Woman would be among us. You have failed us and you will be punished for it."

The tentacles had been writhing rapidly and snapped like long whips in the air, but now their movement slowed and became more graceful and deliberate, as though the demon was bringing his rage under control.

"But that shall come later." Dyondaygah declared, "Now I would break the minds of those who oppose me. Bring forth the infidels. Bring forth, Mark Thurston!"

From behind him, Mark heard movement, and the next thing he knew he was being lifted on to the dais, chair and all, by two of the giants.

Mark's fists and toes clenched and stretched as he tried to resist, tried to fight back, but there was nothing he could do.

The chair was carried to the edge of the circle where the tentacles undulated above his head. Mark was certain that he was about to be crushed by their massive weight, but suddenly all but the outer most were drawn down and away from the hole, whiles some of the smaller outer tentacles, fell, severed, to the stone surrounding the circle.

For a moment Mark thought something had gone wrong. Had the conjunction ended sooner than anyone expected?

The golden light which had shown from below had gone out, though the symbols all around the pit continued to glow.

Then Maru spoke from his left, still standing near the comparatively hulking form of the unconscious Ally, "Children! Retrieve the Sacred Food of Dyondaygah!"

Maru's voice was subdued, no doubt with fear at what "punishment" he might expect, but also there seemed to be a sort of reverence at play as well.

Before him a black pit lay yawning, surrounded by ten or fifteen of the long trunks of black flesh that had once been part of the body of the Demon, and on some level, they still throbbed with his power.

Several of the giants, including the two that had brought him to the mouth of the pit began to collect up the black masses, which to Mark looked more and more like wet pulsating tumors than tentacles.

For a normal person picking up those slimy masses alone might have been difficult, but for each giant, it seemed as though they were lifting nothing heavier than a large sack of flour.

Each of the giants took the flesh and placed it in a large cooler.

An Igloo cooler.

And had he not been strapped down, about to be sacrificed on a Pagan altar, he might have found that funny, that something so mundane could be used in the preservation of something so sinister.

The coolers were taken away, by the giants, up and away into the halls of the Towen, and to the nearby Kitchen no doubt.

That made Mark think of the Frog-men.

Were they nearby?

Were they watching this?

Mark thought of Tom's threat, "…If me and my mates are not pleased by your performance, we will strip you to the bones and gnaw on the marrow for days to come, my lad."

He wondered what they thought. Had his "performance" been good enough for them? Might they come to his aid even now?

No.

If they were watching, they probably wanted to see what Dyondaygah was about to do to him. Well, he would do his best to give them a good show.

It was funny the thoughts that came into Mark's head, now that he was sure he was about to die, or worse.

He would have expected to be thinking about his mother. Or Ally. Or the chain of events that had led him to this fate...

But no, he was thinking about the Frog-men.

Then a light pulsed from below, and soon Mark was thinking about Nothing. Nothing at all.

27

Mark thought of the yawning blackness in front of him as a pit, but in reality, it was nothing like a pit. There was no tunnel. No tube, where light first shown on some rocky dirt surface, that gave way to blackness the further down you looked.

There was only a black void beyond the edge of the circle.

"A hole would have been something. But this was Nothing."

The words came unbidden to Mark from somewhere in the past, a book or a movie. They had been little more than words then, but now looking into that void he understood them perfectly.

But then the pulse of light returned and the void became full of stars.

Little points of white and gold and blue and green light filling his vision and the blackness below, far,--- far away but more brilliant and clear than Mark had ever seen. This must be what the stars looked like from space, with no atmosphere between the naked eye and the heavens.

Then the stars began to move.

They began to grow closer, and closer.

Mark felt as though he were moving forward toward the stars. He tried to close his eyes but he could not.

It was as if they weren't even there, or if there, not necessary for sight.

He was drawn further and further forward into the inky void, and when he tried to resist he found that he was no longer strapped down, but he was no less restrained as something pulled him forward, ever forward!

At first, he thought that the chair had been stripped from him, without his notice, but now he understood that not only the chair but his body itself was gone. He was no longer bound to that physical manifestation of his will.

He was moving as spirit. A ghost.

He might have been terrified, and to some degree he was.

Had he moved beyond death so quickly and easily? Had he died already and didn't even know it until it was already over? But more than anything he was in awe.

Now in the void large objects were moving past him.

Were they... planets?

Yes.

First, a large red one that he took to be Mars, then very quickly he had flown through a field of stones. Then he was passing a ringed planet, many times larger than the first.

Mark could feel the burning heat of the sun on his back. It did not harm him, but he couldn't turn to face it either.

The planets seemed large at first, but then again they were not.

They were like passing eighteen-wheelers, on the highway, that at first, were many times larger than him, but already he had a feeling that they were nothing, little more than specks of dust compared to what lay ahead of him.

Soon Pluto and a small array of stones covered in ice were behind him, and the wide-open sea of the stars lay beyond.

Quicker and quicker he sped forward, soon hundreds of stars were moving past and around him.

Not just planets, but stars.

Massive Gas giants, white dwarf stars, red dwarf stars, rings of light that only later would he understand had been black holes.

They all moved in and out of sight just as the planets had done, and yet still he was moving into the outer blackness at greater and greater speed.

Ally, Maru, Hap and the Giants were hundreds of light-years behind him and had he been able to turn around to look back, Earth would have been completely invisible, not even a glint of light in space.

Mark felt the darkness of space seeping into his soul, he was filled with despair.

What would become of him?
Was there any way back?
Was he now past all hope?

He could not control his movement forward, falling endlessly forward into the emptiness before him.

Now the stars were becoming fewer and fewer as he reached the edge of the Milky Way, and soon that too was far behind him, and he was out into the space between Galaxies.

He could see them shining and spinning all around him, but soon they too were passing him by as the planets had done, like bees or flies on the highway on a sunny day, he moved past them, and they passed him.

Soon he was beyond them all.

Eternities of light-years passed as he was drawn still deeper and into the void.

Then out of the blackness, there was just a hint of light, like the very first dim rays of sunlight in the desert.

The light increased and Mark suddenly realized there was something beneath him. He found that he was moving across a great red plain, almost a prairie.

Was he somehow back in Kansas?

Below him, there seemed to be dirt and sand, more like the wastelands of Arizona than Kansas. And yet it was all still so strange, and the sky was black as night. It was all so vast and empty. There were no signs that life was here, that it had ever been here.

No plants or vegetation of any kind marked that open flat vast plain.

No buildings, no ruins.

It was the definition of desolation.

As the plain moved beneath him there was no change.

No hills, no valleys, nor cliffs or crags, he alone moved over that flat arid waste, and deep within his soul, there was a feeling of profound loneliness such as no one had ever known before.

Off in the distance, which must have been light-years away at the speed he was moving, mark seemed to see a great wall rise on the horizon. It was a blacker spot against the blackness, dimly outlined by the faint bluish glow that seemed to come from beyond it.

But for it to be visible at this distance and to seem so far away at the speed he was traveling, the wall must be huge beyond understanding.

Compared to it The Great Wall of China was but an atom sitting atop the grain of sand that was the Earth. At this size and scale, the Universe itself might be little more than an atom.

Mark felt like the smallest of microbes who until now had thought himself a king of infinite space, and had somehow caught a glimpse of the world on which it dwelled.

He was overwhelmed with the scope of it all.

As the Wall drew nearer, Mark realized it was more like a mountain range than a wall, but it was high and flat-topped, as though it had been leveled, cut off smoothly by a capricious hand, and made uneven thereafter by the slow parade of years wearing away at its smoothness.

It was then that Mark understood he was moving forward into some sort of large natural amphitheater. The mountains rose up smoothly before him as if they were sand in a sandbox, raised and flattened by the hand of a child.

Now the wall drew nearer and Mark could make out figures perched atop the curved wall. Ancient stone statues taller than Galaxies were wide.

In the dim light, which was now steadily growing

brighter as he neared that distant horizon he could make out details which could barely be described.

Many of the figures were humanoid, having four main limbs and seemed to be standing erect, but none of them could have been mistaken for men.

Some had great heads of Dogs, and Horses and Eagles, others seemed more human but had multiple sets arms and legs.

Some looked like dragons, while others looked like great birds.

Suddenly Mark understood. These were all statues to the great heathen gods of the past. Ra, Seth, Anubis, Hathor, all stood together in one section, while Kali and Yama and Shiva stood in another.

There were many gods of all different religions represented, huge and powerful. But beyond them, a new and higher wall came into view as Mark soared over the Amphitheater, to the greater wall beyond. If the statues in the amphitheater had been large, the ones that stood before Mark now dwarfed them.

While the statues of the amphitheater had been horrible to behold, they had been things conceived and understandable by the mind of man.

These were not.

They looked down upon the gods of men as an adult looks upon a newborn child. Strange appendages reached out in all directions, some stood broad and bulky, while others seemed flat and spindly, but all of them were massive beyond understanding.

Broad bat-like wings stood out from some of the forms, the breadth of which must have been Mega-parsecs in length.

Hard carapaces like shells of giant insects or sea creatures reflected the dim morning light. Giant "Daddy longlegs" Spider legs, thick as Gas Giant Planets, stretched for the darkness above, fangs protruded from mouths, hundreds of slathering mouths coming out of every orifice.

They were horrifying beyond description.

Still, Mark flew on toward them. He had feared that they might come alive and reach out for him.

Where they statues or were they the Old Ones themselves, standing watch over the borders of the Universe?

Watching and waiting for a way in, immortal in a sleeping death?

And as he looked on he felt words rise within his spirit. He didn't know where he had heard them before, or even if he ever had, but he felt certain it was the truth of the strange beings he saw below:

"That is not dead which can eternal lie, and with strange aeons, even death may die."

But as he neared them something even stranger happened.

They all began to collapse.

The light behind them grew stronger and stronger now, becoming a green eldritch light, a dawning corpse light in the ancient sky.

Under the weight of this strange light, the statues began to break.

Legs snapped off like twigs, teeth crumbled to dust, as the green light seeped into the cracks in the stone and expanded them, breaking away metal armor and mortar.

The heads of the giant statues fell apart and the limbs were torn asunder.

With all the force and grinding catastrophe of stone planets being turned to dust, the statues crumbled before the light beyond the horizon.

Mark found himself flying between two of the figures, as first the statues and then the wall they stood on, crumbled away.

Felled and uprooted like a California redwood, one

statue fell over, smashed into dust on the plain below, while the other seemed to be crushed from above like a beer can, or a child's sand sculpture by the foot of a careless adult.

Then Mark was beyond the wall and into the light.

28

Mark found himself in pitch blackness.

He couldn't see his hand in front of his face.

He wasn't even sure if he had a hand to speak of.

During his whole strange journey to this place, he had not been able to move a muscle or control his flight, in any way. He had simply been falling horizontally, with nothing to hold on to.

The only thing he could be sure of was that he had been moving ever further away from the Earth.

Now, beyond the amphitheater wall and the wall of light, having traveled beyond all space and time, he was in the utter darkness, with no stars to light the way.

He wasn't sure if he was still moving or not.

With nothing around him to compare speed, movement, (if there was any) was meaningless.

Then in the dark, far, far away, there was a single pulse; a distant flash of green light, like a bolt of lightning in a far off cloud.

After what seemed an eternity it pulsed again, closer now, but still further way than words could explain.

Every time the light pulsed, with eternities passing between them, Mark found himself a little closer to it.

After a millennia, the light became a steady glow that every so often pulsed a hundred thousand times brighter, and suddenly before he knew it, in the space of a breath he was before the source.

And it was titanic.

All the space between stars, all the planets he had passed and the Giant statues that could have swallowed them all and finally the crumbling gods themselves were nothing compared to the scope of this.

It was a universe unto itself, it was a million Universes and counting.

His Galaxy and all those he had passed through were but grains of sand.

The Universe and the realm of the gods had been but outbuildings and changing tents....

This was the Ocean.

And the ocean was Dyondaygah.

From where Mark "stood" he could see the vastness of the demon god, and in seeing he felt his mind begin to expand like a balloon.

The Omniverse connected with his brain and funneled all its knowledge into him.

He was gazing into infinity and infinity could not be contained.

"See you now, the Glory and majesty of Dyondaygah!"

Mark didn't so much "hear" the words as he sensed them as part of the assault on his being.

Every thought he'd ever had from the moment of his birth to that very second rushed into his mind all at once with perfect clarity, as if it were happening again to him at that very moment.

It was like the most intense hyperactive sugar rush he'd ever experienced, jacked-up ten-thousand fold.

"The most merciful thing in the world, I think, is the inability of the human mind to correlate all its contents."

Someone had once written.

Mark alone knew now just how great of a mercy that fact

had been.

Mark felt himself swelling, expanding; inflating with information.

His being trying to contain all that was being foisted upon him.

He now had no physical form; no body of mud and clay could have withstood the onslaught.

As knowledge and understanding avalanched into him, he knew the exact position of every single molecule in the universe. He knew where its correlating photons where located across every dimension, in all the universes.

All the universes that had ever been or ever could be were part of his mind.

He knew the names, addresses, telephone numbers, passwords, social security numbers, credit cards, driver's license numbers, license plates and vin number of every man, woman and child, alien and everything in between, on every world.

He knew every sentient being's greatest hope and their greatest fear.

He knew the intimate details of their lives, and all the possible courses their lives might have taken.

Somewhere in the flood of data, that expanded his consciousness nearly to the size of Dyondaygah itself, the information that was coming before his "eyes" wormed its way in.

He saw the "body" of Dyondaygah; a constantly changing formless confluence of nebula and dust and stars, shaping, forming, and destroying itself, only to start the process all over again, endlessly creating and eviscerating itself.

He saw the placement of every claw and tentacle, eye and mandible, the trunks and tendrils and legs and feet by which it might move; all of it spiraling out from the central, undulating, mass of Dyondaygah.

Then from somewhere deep within him, just as his mind was about to explode into a hundred billion pieces and whatever Mark Thurston had been was nearly lost forever, Mark felt a rumbling.

A convulsion.

Then another.

And another… and still more, one after another, growing stronger and building in strength.

In this altered state of consciousness, filled up beyond capacity with all the information a universe could contain, larger than a hundred billion suns, ready to bust, Mark had trouble remembering what the sensation he was feeling somewhere in the middle of him was called, but eventually the word swam to the top of his consciousness:

Laughter.

He was laughing.

Not the shriek of a being, driven mad by too much understanding, but the chortling, ruckus laughter of a person, a human, who has just seen the funniest thing in the world.

Mark sensed puzzlement from Dyondaygah.

Puzzlement turned to anger.

The green eldritch hue of Dyondaygah changed. He was now pulsing with many different colors of light, greens, and reds, and purples and blues, all of them a swirl and mass of disorder.

Still, the laughter grew in Mark's head and being, and he wasn't quite sure even now why, but the laughter built in intensity and began to force out much of the other knowledge that had invaded his being.

"What is this?"

Mark felt the question being asked, somewhere in his being, but still, his laughter deepened and he felt himself shrinking, returning almost to himself.

Moment by moment, the force of the knowledge with which Dyondaygah had sought to destroy him was pushed away and the pressure was relieved.

"I'm sor- I'm sorry." Mark gasped between belts of laughter, hardly able to contain his glee, and confused to hear himself apologizing to the thing that was trying to kill him, "It's just that...."

Mark tried so hard to get it out, "You look like..." he laughed through his teeth, which he now discovered he had again, "You look like..."

"*STOP THIS!*" Dyondaygah commanded in Mark's head, "*YOU WILL NOT LAUGH AT THE GLORIOUS MIGHT OF DYONDAYGAH!!*"

This only caused Mark to laugh harder.

Cart-wheeling in the void, gales of laughter spewing forth from him, "Anything you say!" Mark guffawed. "All Hail The Great and Powerful Dyondaygah!"

Mark bellowed, "Dyondaygah! The Interstellar Amoeba!!"

Dyondaygah roared with fury! Every mouth, nose, and orifice capable of making sound bellowed in rage. The bright swirls of otherworldly colors undulated and flashed under the surface of the behemoth.

Lightning flashed over and around the place where Mark floated in the void.

Mark should have been terrified, he should have been overwhelmed with cosmic horror, beyond what any man should be able to endure.

He felt those things playing at the edges of his consciousness, but for some reason, none of it mattered...

Maybe it had worked, maybe he had gone insane, and his mind was broken by Dyondaygah after all, but he didn't think so.

When he was able to think, through the laughter all he was able to do was find the whole situation more and more hilarious.

His laughter rang through the spaceless place beyond time louder than the silent thunder from the bolts of lightning that swirled around Dyondayah.

"Oh look, honey!" Mark said to no one, "I made the living

gasoline puddle mad!" He found himself able to move in space, and in his ecstasy of hilarity, he did involuntary cartwheels in the void.

"*STOP!*" Dyondaygah commanded again.

"No-ooo you staahp!" Mark blurted, back, "You look so ridiculous!" And he returned to his laughter.

Looking at the demon god the impression of a giant amoeba was redoubled.

All the limbs, the tentacles and tendrils, and trunks of flesh, gave Mark the impression of the little hairs that single-celled organisms used to feel their way, searching for food or to move along.

The word came back from the depths of his mind "Cilia".

"Maru and his followers, your children, the ancient Indians that destroyed your temples and hunted your followers," Mark explained through his laughter, "They all made such big business out of you! And it turns out you are nothing more than a super-sized Paramecium!

"*I AM DYONDAYGAH!*" The Creature shouted back into Mark's mind, "*I AM THE STAR-EATER! I AM THE DESTROYER OF WORLDS! MY CHILDREN SHALL INHABIT THE WORLD, MY TENTACLES SHALL DEVOUR ALL THAT YOU HAVE KNOWN! I AM ANCIENT BEYOND YOUR UNDERSTANDING AND POWERFUL BEYOND WHAT YOUR MIND CAN CONCEIVE! AND I WILL NOT BE MOCKED!*"

Mark couldn't believe it, in all of the angry words, in all of the puff and bluster, Mark could tell, as easily as any playground bully, underneath it all… The demon god's feelings were hurt.

"*THE CREATURES YOU PERCEIVE AS SMALL AND INSIGNIFICANT ARE BUT REFLECTIONS OF MY GLORY!*" The monster continued, "*THE BRAVEST AND GREATEST BEINGS IN THE UNIVERSE COWER BEFORE MY MIGHT, MY WILL TO DOMINATE CAN NOT BE OVERCOME! I AM BEYOND ALL TIME AND SPACE, AS YOU HAVE SEEN! NOTHING IS BIGGER, STRONGER OR MORE*

POWERFUL THAN I!"

To Mark, the voice while powerful had taken on the sound of a hurt little child who's delusions were being expelled one by one.

"Whatever you say! Oh Mighty Dyondaygah!" Mark continued to mock, beyond all possibility of stopping, "Your little light show was really impressive! You could take that on the road! People might even pay fifteen bucks to see that at a sideshow carnival!"

Then Mark deepened his voice, and said like the announcer on a bad 1950s sci-fi movie trailer, "Can your mind withstand the inescapable horror that is Dyondaygah! The SPAAA-AAAAAAAACCE OCTOPUS!?!"

29

Hap stared on as Mark was taken up to the Altar of Dyondaygah, his chair placed at the edge of the black hole that had formed within the steel band, where the massive tentacles had once been.

Hap was proud of Mark and how brave he had been up until now. He could only hope to be so brave when it came to be his turn.

Mark was meant for better things, and certainly, a better end than this; sacrificed on a pagan altar to a being that cared no more for him than a man might an ant under his boot.

Light rose up from within the blackness below and Hap could see that whatever was happening in the light, Mark was in thrall to it.

Hap could see the reflection of the glow in Mark's eyes, and his mouth hung slack, a line of drool falling out of the corner of his mouth, his face blank.

He barely seemed conscious.

Had his mouth not been gagged, (it was all he could do to keep from throwing up in his mouth because of the cloth tickling the back of his throat,) Hap might have called out to Mark, just as Mark had to Ally.

Ally still lay passed out on the floor, but Hap could see she was breathing.

Oh if she could only wake up, right now, and use the power her body was now capable of, they just might have a chance to escape. But even if her mind was somehow intact (which frankly Hap doubted it would be) she most likely had been so devastated from within, that even with all that muscle she would likely be as weak as a baby.

Maru was pleased with the way things were going now, "Yes, oh my master!" Maru said, over and over again, "Break him. Break him! Take his mind and make it yours. Show him your glory, your power, your inevitability!"

The Children of Dyondaygah stood by watching silently. They no longer seemed to be acting as the voice of their demon god, and were now looking at Mark and occasionally at each other and Maru.

It seemed that they were currently as much, "themselves" as they were ever allowed to be. The controlling force was not exerting itself at the moment, all of its focus seemingly locked on Mark.

Then unexpectedly, Mark began to laugh. It started as a slight convulsion that might have been mistaken for a cold chill or gagging on his own spittle, but then it happened again... and again... He was definitely laughing.

First a slight chuckle, that built into a chortle, then a deep blast of a laugh, then outright hysterical laughing such as Hap had not heard in many a year.

Hap might have been concerned that this was it.

This was Mark losing his mind completely.

But this was clearly not what Maru or any of the Children had expected...

They had, no doubt, been expecting agonized screams of terror and horror beyond imagining as they had seen happen to all of the previous victims they had subjected to what Mark was seeing now.

Laughter, at least not laughter of this sort, was not part of the expected equation.

"What is he doing?" Maru asked no one, "What is so funny? What is he laughing at?"

But Mark's laugh was infectious. Hap himself had to resist the urge to laugh, even though he didn't know what the joke was, especially with the gag in his mouth, he couldn't allow himself to do something that might so easily lead to vomiting.

But the Giants too began to laugh. First one, then another, and another.

They laughed at his laugh. It was a merry and infectious sound that kept building and becoming more and more comedic.

"Silence!" Maru commanded the children, "You will not laugh! To laugh with this man is to blaspheme!" Most of the Giants grew silent, their deep croaking sounds subdued but not entirely suppressed.

Then through his gales of laughter, Mark started to speak, *"I'm sor- I'm sorry. It's just that you look like-"* He broke off again into hysterics.

"What is he laughing at?!" Maru demanded to know.

"Anything you say! All Hail The Great and Powerful Dyondaygah! Dyondaygah: The Interstellar Amoeba!!"

Around the circular room, from between the Sarsen stones, in that black hall lit only by the light of the fiery trough around its base, there was a sound that had not been made there in the over two thousand years, since other Children of Dyondaygah erected the Sarsens and consecrated it to the monster from beyond the stars.

There was the sound of laughter.

Not just one man laughing, but a whole score of men and women, not one of them under six feet, laughing a joyful hardy laugh.

Maru boiled with rage, "You will not laugh at My Master and your god! I am the high priest of Dyondaygah and you will be silent!"

Whether through the force of the power and control given to him by the dark one or for fear of what might come after, as one the giants stopped laughing... for a moment.

Still laughing his head off alone, Mark gasped out, "Oh look, honey! I made the living gasoline puddle mad!" and Mark gave off a shrill, *"He-he-heee!"* laugh.

Once again the room was filled with laughter, and Hap would have had to admit he was getting a kick out of it too. But then as Maru called for silence once again, Hap noticed movement from Ally.

Perhaps somewhere in her dreaming unconsciousness, she had heard what Mark had said, or perhaps nothing but his contagious laughter, because she seemed to shake with a cold chill or spasm with a bit of a laugh herself.

"Yes, Ally that's it!" Hap thought at her silently, "*Wake up! Please wake up and be sane enough to help! If Mark survives this we are going to need every ounce of your strength to survive.*"

Mark seemed to respond directly to Maru's command to Stop, "*No-ooo you staahp! You look so ridiculous!*"

Once more Mark's laughter filled the hall. Maru looked to Brisco, "Take me to Thurston!" and the giant obeyed.

Mark continued to laugh saying something about a *Parami-sum*.

Hap, and seemingly most of the giants, didn't know what that was, but Mark's intent was clear. He was mocking the demon god.

It jibed with everything that Hap knew about the Great Old Ones.

They were beings of immense power worshiped for centuries by civilizations on Earth older than the fossil record could record. If life existed on other worlds, they likely had worshipers there as well, for millennia they had known nothing but adoration and fear.

And now here sat Mark, one man armed with nothing but a sense of humor, blaspheming the loveless god. If it resulted in nothing more than a quick death for the three of them, it would be worth it.

Better to die quickly in a last gasp of defiance and hubris than to live insane and slowly rotting from the inside out, or torn apart while still living by the Children of Dyondaygah and the Frog-men.

But somehow Hap didn't think that was what was about

to happen.

Somehow Hap knew that something far more powerful was being done here.

He prayed.

He prayed with all his might that Mark would be given what he needed, even if that was more laughter.

He prayed that Ally would wake up whole and able to fight, and he prayed that if by his life or death he could put up even a temporary blockade against the coming of Dyondaygah, that he would have the courage to do what was necessary.

Still, Mark laughed and mocked, saying something about a carnival sideshow, and then Maru and Brisco were almost to the Altar, when Mark bellowed, *"Dyondaygah! The SPAAAAAA-AAAAACCE OCTOPUS!?!"*

Mark shook his head and face and jaw to make his voice quiver as though he were speaking through water or a tentacles, giving *"Space"* a gibbering sound, that made his words all the more hilarious, and with that the control Maru held over the Children was broken once again, and the Children burst into hysterics, laughing louder and more deeply than ever before.

Before Brisco could take another step, with Maru perched on his shoulder, a great roar of rage rumbled from the space beneath the Towen, shaking the whole building, the mound on which it sat and the earth itself for miles around.

Hap watched in awe as a new mass of tentacles, exploded up out of the Altar, and he was sure Mark was done for. He would be crushed like a bug beneath the weight of those massive, rubbery, fleshy, arms.

But instead he was only knocked backward, he and his chair pushed aside as the trunks of flesh pushed him away and reached out to grab hold of the giants around the room.

They were wrapped up in his ropey rubbery flesh, faster than the eye could see it. The giants who had laughed at their dark master were now experiencing the full fury of his wrath.

One Giant's bones cracked audibly, again and again, as

the tentacle squeezed and contracted around him, grinding him to a pulp.

Others were picked up and slammed against the walls and the floor and the ceiling.

All the while, Maru had fallen to the floor, brushed aside, as Brisco was slammed out from underneath him. Brisco was not a target for he had been faithful to both his masters, but he was in the way and as Mark had been, he was carelessly knocked aside.

Maru stayed on the ground, not dead, but not moving for fear of finding himself in the way of one of those massive swinging trunks of flesh.

Mark, meanwhile, seemed to be free of whatever hypnosis or "vision quest" he had been trapped in and now seemed to see what was going on around him.

When he had been thrown back, one of the leather straps which held his legs to the chair had broken off and Mark was working on getting one leg, then the other free, while the wriggling carousel of death swayed and spun over his head.

Hap watched as one of the Giants was picked up as he ran, but a tentacle seemed to bifurcate just to grip him and sling him against the wall. Hap saw as the already damaged plaster cracked and crumpled beneath the weight of his body with a metallic crunch.

Something shiny and metal shown out from the place where the plaster fell away, and a few grains of black powder fell out of it into the fire below, causing it to flare up just slightly.

It was something you had to be looking at to notice, and with all the chaos in the room it was unlikely anyone else had seen.

But Hap and Mark, (from his fallen position on the floor,) had both seen it, and that was enough.

Mark made eye contact with Hap, and shook his head. He pursed his lips as if to make a "shushing" sound, the message was clear, *"Don't say anything."*

Meanwhile, the violent onslaught seemed to quell as the tentacles retracted to the circle, but did not disappear within it.

On the ground around the circle, every Giant who had once laughed at Mark's mocking of Dyondaygah, lay motionless.

A shrill sound, ululating and squealing, that made Hap clench his teeth and want to place his hands over his ears, came forth from the pit, and seconds after it started, tentacles began to explode from the fallen Children.

All of them seemed to come from somewhere around the midsection, but some crawled out of the sides and others from the back, near the spine, and others from the stomach, but all of them slithered out on to the floor leaving the dead bodies of their hosts behind.

There had been nearly thirty giants in the room before the ceremony had begun, now there was less than ten.

The tentacles slithered across the floor and toward the altar like snakes on the hunt. Hap had seen video footage of Cobras and Black Mambas as they stalked their prey and it had looked almost the same.

Purpose-driven, they slunk up the stairs and down into the whole to rejoin themselves to Dyondaygah.

From the mouths of the eight or nine remaining giants, including Brisco, who was now returning to his feet came the voice of Dyondaygah,

"Blasphemers! Faithless ones! Unworthy! None shall live who mock my greatness!" Maru was picked up by Brisco, and placed on his shoulder.

"Oh mighty one!" he shouted, "Do not bring your wrath down upon your humble servant, Maru! You have rightly sentenced all those who do not adore your name to death and they have paid the price! Now take this one who has dared to defile your name, and your children by drawing them away from your worship and adoration!"

"Silence!" Dyondaygah said through his remaining

giants, "You will not dane to give orders to your master!"

Maru seemed both confused and cowed by the voice of his god. *"You will raise your hand to do my work."* The Giants continued, *"You and the Children must dispose of the infidels. I have taken my own, you will take the lives of those who would oppose me!"*

"Yes. Oh mighty one." Maru said, bowing, as best he could from Brisco's shoulder, putting his hands out to the sides, and lowering his head.

"Now conclude this night with the pouring of the blood sacrifice. Bring forth the chalice you have prepared!"

Hap could not believe his ears. The demon god, was trying to save face.

He had been defeated, not once, but several times.

Mark had clearly been tempted in some way, which Hap had not been able to hear or understand, but he could tell from Mark's reactions that he had first listened to and then rejected the advances of the demon.

Ally had fought off the union with the "Sacred Food" and instead of becoming one with Dyondaygah and the Children, had vomited forth the vile muck which had been transforming her body, marking another defeat for the god.

Finally, he had not only been unable to break Mark's mind, but in failing to do so, he had gone into a vengeful fury, killing his own followers, and undoing the years of work he and Maru had done together.

And now it seemed he was unable to kill Mark, and perhaps even Hap, himself.

The tentacles had been able to reach forth from the pit and take old of those members of the Children who had laughed at Mark's mockery of the demon god, but other than knocking him aside, the tentacles had not been able to touch Mark.

Several times Hap was certain he had seen one of the spongy columns of flesh reaching toward Mark, and himself, only to retract and reach out for some other nearby victim.

Given the writhing, seemingly indirect paths the tentacles had taken, Hap wasn't sure at first and thought he had been mistaken. But now the Old One had as much as openly admitted he could not touch them.

He could hold their minds in his sway and give them visions, but he could not bring physical harm to them.

Why?

Hap watched silently as Maru and Brisco, returned to the throne, where the chalice full of his blood was waiting. He looked toward the floor below, where Mark sat on his back, one leg free of the leather straps.

He could see that Mark's right hand was on the verge of freedom as well. If he could get that hand free, they might have a chance.

The strap had been damaged as the Chair was knocked aside by a passing tentacle.

Though he had not felt it himself, the skin of Dyondaygah's tentacles seemed to be more like a shark's skin than that of a squid or octopus; also his tentacles were lined with many sharp points and angles that reminded Hap of serrated teeth.

Whether it was the skin or the teeth, or something else, a gash had been made in Mark's chair, the leather strap holding Mark's right arm, and Mark himself had been damaged. A thin trickle of Mark's blood dripped down from his wrist. Hap had no way of telling how serious it was, but fortunately, it was currently being held up, over Mark's heart, so he would not bleed out so quickly.

But as he lay there, to Maru's eyes virtually unmoving, he was slowly straining and flexing the leather strap, and it was weakening.

Even as Hap watched, he saw the belt give way to one of the holes meant for the buckle.

Now Maru, sitting on Brisco's meaty shoulder, was approaching the dais. He was gently placed on the floor and took the last few steps to the iron ring out of which the tentacles of Dyondaygah still wriggled.

"Oh Mighty Dyondaygah, power behind the stars, Ruler of Branagag and Ralen, Father of Mor'tag and Roth'nel, receive now the blood of thy enemy, taken by force and offered by your servant's hand, take strength from it, oh Bane of Ken'taah'kee that you may one day cover this world with your greatness, and make the sky and the land one. *Albreh't Daggle Zalamond, Hegeth Igale Zale, Tarol Tarol, Zalamond, Nythleotep, Cthulhu, Asathoth, eg Yog-Sothoth, Dyondaygah F'tagahen za-hale!*"

The last part Hap couldn't understand, but he guessed it was a language meant only for the demon gods.

If he had to guess it might have been ancient Babylonian or even Atlantian.

He had caught the names of several of the Great Old Ones and Hap guessed he was invoking their names to give strength to his spell.

Then Maru poured forth the dark red blood on to a waiting outstretched tentacle, filling one of its suction cups.

As Mark's right hand broke free of the leather strap, a deep rumble filled the room, deeper and more powerful than any that had come before.

The Floor of the Towen circle began to buckle and break upward, cracking mortar and freeing many of the cobblestones in the floor.

Maru spun to look at the damage that was being wrought around them, while several of the giants fell to the floor, unconscious.

"Is this it!?" He shouted over the roar of the earthquake, "Is this the great coming of Dyondaygah at last?!"

But the roar that came from the pit was not one of triumph, it was rage; rage and pain.

"BETRAYED!!" Shouted the Children of Dyondaygah as one! "YOU HAVE BETRAYED YOUR MASTER!"

"What?" Maru shouted back, "No! Master, I would never betray you!"

"HAVE YOU SOUGHT TO DESTROY ME? ME? THE GREAT GOD WHOM YOU HAVE CLAIMED TO SERVE ALL YOUR DAYS?! FOR THIS TREACHERY, I TAKE FROM YOU THE CHILDREN OF DYONDAYGAH, I TAKE FROM YOU YOUR PRIESTHOOD! I TAKE FROM YOU YOUR POWER AND VITALITY!"

"What have I done, oh great one? What have I done to deserve your wrath?" Maru shouted.

But as he shouted, three things happened at once.

Mark, now free of the chair, rolled off of it and went for the shotgun which lay mere inches away.

Ally, who until now had been still, suddenly bolted to her feet and with a roar of rage to match that of Dyondaygah himself, began to strain against the chains, which were still fastened to the loosened cobblestones, beneath her. The two stones into which the chains were mounted, broke free of the ground, and now Ally was free, what's more, she had weapons.

And at the same moment, Hap heard Dyondaygah answer Maru's question, not through the mouth of the children, but through some sort of mental hook up. Somehow Hap's blood had connected him to the beast, and he sensed pain and anger.

But clear as day he heard the words, as perhaps no one else in the room could. "THE REDEEMED!" Dyondaygah shouted enraged, "YOU'VE SOUGHT TO DESTROY ME WITH THE POISONED BLOOD OF THE REDEEMED!"

30

Mark wasn't sure what was happening.

All he knew was the moment to act was upon him.

He had been all but free for a few moments and was waiting for the opportune moment to break the last shred of the leather straps that held his right arm and legs.

Suddenly that moment had arrived.

He had seen the powder fall from the steel box in the wall, and now knew exactly what he had to do, but not yet. It had to wait until Hap and Ally could make it to the stairs. If he did it now, it would be suicide. But if they could make it to the stairwell, they just might have a chance.

Of course, if Ally was dead or worse, there would be no point in trying to get out alive, not for him. But he owed Hap the possibility of escape, and if Maru could be distracted, just long enough for him to break free, he might be able to buy that opportunity.

Then Maru had dumped the chalice of Hap's blood onto one of the blobby masses of flesh protruding into his world from another dimension.

While Mark had expected some kind of a reaction, rage had not been in the catalogue. He didn't catch what some of the remaining children said as the earth began to shake and the floor of the Towen began to crinkle slightly upward, but he could tell The Amoeba was not happy.

He flexed hard and felt the straps on his legs and right wrist break free. It was only the work of half a second to undo the other strap around his left wrist, and Mark was loosed.

He threw his elevated legs backward and over his head,

flipping out of the heavy wooden chair and somersaulting toward the shotgun.

At the same moment, from the direction of the altar, there was another roar of anger he didn't understand, but there was no time to worry about that.

The remaining Giants would be on him in seconds.

He landed on the gun. It scraped across his midsection as he rolled over and as quickly as he could, he got the gun in hand and was ready to fire--- but there was no need.

The giants weren't coming after him.

At least not yet.

To his amazement, the giants were moving past and away from him. Had he been their target, he would have been dead already.

Most of the giants had moved past him in a single stride.

No, they were not after him, they were moving toward Ally.

As he had flipped, Ally had risen to her feet, she must have been able to quickly pry loose the two cobblestones that her chains were fixed into because she was swinging them at the nearest giants.

Mark stared in amazement at the warrior his wife had become, unable to reconcile her appearance with the memory of the cute little girl he'd seen on a park bench all those years ago.

She had been nothing like the tall scrapper he saw before him.

Yet, he knew that this was no alteration of her personality due to the infection of Dyondaygah.

This had always been who she was deep down, but now she had the means to express it.

Mark shook himself out of his thoughts and to the business at hand.

He checked the action of the shotgun, to his surprise all the shells were still inside. He ratcheted the pump-action and brought the first round up and into the chamber, but he did not intend to fire.

For one, Ally seemed to be handling things just fine. She swung the chains weighted with the stones at the giants who came nearest to her, with such force, they looked more like baseball bats than what they were.

When one giant got too close, she punched him in the face with her bare hands, and even though he stood a full three feet taller than her, (or perhaps because of it,) he went flying back, and Mark was pretty sure he had seen teeth flying out of the giant's mouth.

For a second, there was still the matter of Hap, and while the giants were distracted, he was going to take advantage of it.

Picking up his car keys and phone and stuffing them in his pockets, almost entirely out of habit, Mark picked up the big knife Ally had brought back from Ireland and made a dash for Hap.

He kept an eye on Ally, to make sure the giants weren't overtaking her but moved toward the old man, who was still tied up enough to prevent him from moving.

Using the knife, he went to work on the rope around Haps feet first. The knife must have been freshly sharpened because it felt like he had barely touched the ropes when they fell away. The hands were next and while Hap rubbed his wrists Mark removed the gag.

"Are you alright?" Mark asked as he helped pull the remnants of the ropes away.

"I'll be fine son." Hap said getting to his feet, "Did you see-"

"Yes," Mark said cutting him off, "I know all about it."

"How could you know-" Hap started again, but Mark cut him off once more.

"Don't worry about how I know, just make for the stairs. Get out of here." Mark ordered.

"But Ally-"

"Does it look like she needs our help?" Mark said, "You've

done your part, get out of here. I have to finish this and you'll only be another concern. Now go!"

Hap didn't need to be told again. He stood to his feet, a bit wobbly but his balance was returning. He made for the only exit.

As he did so, one of the giants came stumbling out of the horde, either thrown back by Ally or because he saw Hap making for the stairwell. Mark trained his gun on the giant and this time he remembered to hold the gun tight to his shoulder.

A chunk of flesh flew out of the giant's leg. Most of the leg was blown apart and the giant went down. Mark ran toward where the giant lay, racking the slide, as Hap continued his galloping limp toward the exit.

The giant reached out for him, but just as he was about to make contact, Mark pulled the trigger again, and the giant's head flew apart in a mass of gore.

Now, just as Mark had feared, he had drawn the attention of the other giants, and two of them came at him.

He was bought a few seconds while the giants made their way around the dais. The tentacles of Dyondaygah still wriggled up from below, lashing at the air.

In that time he managed to get a bead on the first giant, a female that was coming at him from the left.

Once again, he opted to blow the legs out from under her, but the giant was moving so fast he could barely pull the trigger before she was on top of him.

The shotgun blast took out her whole midsection. Mark just had time to see in the firelight the tentacle within her, blow backward out of her back, itself in pieces. She tumbled forward into him, and Mark had to roll out of the way to avoid being crushed by her mass.

Now he was covered in the blood of two of the giants and it was this alone that saved him from the third. The giant man was taking hold of Mark even as he moved to get out of the way of the falling woman, but the blood was coated on him so thickly that he was able to slide out of the roaring male's grip by continuing his spin.

As he turned he racked the slide again, and somehow managed to put the gun almost directly into the mouth of the giant.

He hadn't even aimed.

There was just enough time to see the large man's eyes widen before Mark found himself pulling the trigger, and the giant's head was no more.

Mark recoiled in horror at what he had done. How could he do this? This wasn't him at all. He had no skills with a shotgun and until tonight he had never considered himself a bloodthirsty man. He had never trained a day in his life for something like this. Where was this coming from?

But Mark was pulled out of his reverie, as all three of the giants he had killed began to move again. He saw their midsections writhe and pulse under their clothes and skin and watched as the tentacles burst out on to the ground.

He half expected them to start feeling their way towards him, unifying and becoming a wondering arm of the creature that still writhed up from the pit.

But instead, they began to drag themselves and the human bodies they were still attached to toward the dais.

The tentacle that had been in the female was actually in pieces and Mark saw the severed parts start making their separate ways to the pit as well.

"Well... That's just gross." Mark thought, but it was all the time he had to think because he then heard a scream from Ally's direction. Not the amplified and somewhat deepened voice of his wife, but the high pitched piping shriek of Maru!

"Protect me, Ally! You must defend me!" Mark mulled the words over in his mind... Ally... Not Brisco... Where was Brisco and why would Maru ever ask Ally (who was no longer under his power) to defend him? Mark ran back to the spot where the gym bag, the shotgun shells and the other weapons lay.

He was out of rounds and wanted to save the remaining

four in his pants pockets in case he needed them.

And as he opened the box and extracted them, flipping the gun over, to load the shells, he was finally able to see what was happening.

The giants were not coming after Ally, at least not directly. The whole time, they had been going after Maru.

Something strange had happened… Well, stranger.

Something had turned The Children, and presumably Dyondaygah himself, against the little man. Mark couldn't be sure if Ally was actually protecting him or if she was merely defending herself, unable to extract the little rat from her person, but he was certain that at this point it didn't matter.

Once they were done with Maru, Dyondaygah would no doubt turn his wrath upon them.

"Hey, Mark!" His wife shouted at him, as she continued to wrestle and punch and swing her stonemason blocks on chains at the approaching giants, "You want to get over here and help me or what? Bring the sword!"

"Coming Baby! I'm coming!" He said standing to his feet.

"I. Told. You!" Ally shouted picking up one of the female giants and throwing her into three others who were coming at her, knocking them all backward, "Don't call me baby!"

Mark couldn't help but smile, "Yes dear." He said as he racked the slide bringing the first round into the chamber.

31

Ally jolted awake.

She'd been having the worst nightmares; dreams in which she had not been herself; stuck out on the middle of an empty highway with a flat tire, having to walk for miles in Mark's oversized combat boots, arriving at some sort of restaurant. Being so hungry she couldn't stop eating, losing all sense of decorum, and hoovering up food at a ridiculous rate.

Then there had been some sort of goofy "Alice In Wonderland" episode where she had grown taller, and too big for her clothes, followed by throwing her husband across a room like a ragdoll.

Then she had become some sort of zombie, mind-controlled by a race of giants and a ridiculous little man, (straight out of that Ron Howard movie about the Witch who was hunting for a baby).

It was absolutely mad, as dreams often were.

Then there had been an incident where she was fighting against those same giants and had recruited a bunch of burly Scotsman from the 1700s to go to war with her, by calling them a bunch of goat children…

Children… The Children of Dy… Dyon… something… No matter. Then she had been a zombie again, chained to a pagan altar, like Fay Ray being sacrificed to King Kong.

Then she had vomited up a mountain of bad black sushi…

No not sushi… *Calamari.*

Tentacles.

"All Hail The Great and Powerful Dyondaygah! Dyondaygah: The Interstellar Amoeba!!"

She heard Mark's voice from far away, his laughing, joyful voice, and it all came flooding in.

It had all been real. It had all happened.

She became aware of laughing all around her. Others laughing at something her husband had said. He had always had a talent for making other people laugh, especially when he was laughing himself.

She could now feel the cold uneven stones beneath her and remembered she was in the Towen, at the heart of the Sarsen circle. She could feel the cold iron of the chains on her wrists.

She felt the urge to open her eyes, but resisted it. If she was still alive that must mean that the giants either thought her dead or not a threat. She would have only one shot at this... Whatever she was going to do, she needed to know what was happening, but she couldn't risk moving and giving herself away. The best thing to do now was to wait and listen.

Somewhere off to her right, Mark was laughing uproariously, *"Oh look, honey! I made the living gasoline puddle mad!"* Ally didn't know what Mark meant by that but she had to admit it was funny and combined with Mark's laugh it was so funny that she couldn't resist a slight shiver as she held back a laugh of her own.

Now that she had moved a little bit, however involuntarily, she was now more aware of her body.

She'd half expected to be back to normal, having vomited out the Calamari and rejected "union with Dyondaygah", (the very thought of which nearly made her sick all over again.) She had expected that she would revert to her previous, small self; the tiny girl.

But no, as she lay there on the cold stone she could feel that she was still tall and strong, perhaps more so than ever before.

She hadn't been aware of much physically when she had been resisting Dyondaygah.

She was aware of the pain.

She was aware of a feeling like when you had accidentally stretched too far and strained a joint, but that feeling was through her entire body.

But it had all been in the background. The main thing she recalled was a voice in her mind, first seductive, offering power, and strength; eternal life and youth. Everything she had ever dreamed of, abilities beyond that of the common woman, could be hers.

But then she resisted. Counted the cost. Remembered what was truly important.

Remembered that submission to Dyondaygah would mean the loss of her free will; the loss of freedom; the loss of Mark as well as her friends and family, everything in life that mattered.

Somewhere deep inside herself, she found the strength of will to fight back.

To say "*No.*"

The demon had lost all pretense of seduction and turned dark and angry, his words full of venom.

Dyondaygah was no longer asking for her consent, it was commanding, demanding that she give up her will and submit. That had been its primary mistake.

In college, she had once been taking a psychology class in which the professor had tried to train them on how to perform hypnosis. The female Professor had said it was important for each of them to be hypnotized themselves, at least once, so that they understood what it was like, and what a patient went through during the process.

She was a licensed Hypnotherapist and had a side practice where she helped people deal with their vices and offered to give each of her students one free session during which she would help them in the same way.

Later most of the girls would reveal they had asked for help with weight loss, while a few asked for help with smoking and other bad habits.

When it came to be Ally's turn, the Professor had asked what she wanted help with and Ally had answered that she wanted to be a better student, to not have such a short attention span. She wanted to be able to focus on her work instead of letting her mind drift so much.

But when the Professor had tried to induce the hypnotic state, Ally could not achieve it. The Professor kept using words and phrases like *"You have no will of your own. My words become your thoughts, and your thoughts become my words. You will submit your will to mine, and do as I tell you."*

Over and over again she said it, and over and over again Ally had resisted.

The mere thought of giving her will over to someone else was abhorrent to her being. Down to the very last ounce of what she was inside, every drop trembled with rebellion at those words.

When she had been a child, teachers would complain to her parents that they had never met a more disobedient and resistant child. She had been more compliant with her parents because she knew on some level, that even when they corrected her, they were doing it out of love. But if she sensed that she was being given orders by a person who felt they should be obeyed just because they were older or because *"they had the authority"*... Oh, she would resist them like a rabid dog.

The hypnotherapist Professor had given up after nearly two hours, *"I don't think you need my help."* She had said, *"You just need to apply that indomitable will to your studies. In all my years of doing this, I've only met three people who I couldn't put under in a session. You are the third."*

When Dyondaygah had commanded her to submit, to deliberately hand her will over to him, it had been the end of his control over her. Even if it had killed her, she would never have submitted.

Dyondaygah had tried to sound her soul from its highest to its lowest note, and every iota of it had resisted.

Now she lay on the floor listening as Mark laughed uproariously, "*Can your mind withstand the inescapable horror that is Dyondaygah! The SPAAAAAAAAAACCE OCTOPUS!?!*"

All around her, laughter redoubled and she felt the wind of something large and powerful moving mere inches above her head. Suddenly the laughter was replaced by screams.

Ally had to fight with every inch of her will not to move as she heard the heavy thud of giant bodies hitting stone, bones crunching and flesh ripping.

She took the opportunity to take an assessment of her body. As surreptitiously as possible, she flexed one part of her body after another, starting with her hands, and toes, working her way down and up to her wrists and ankles.

She was afraid to move her elbows and knees because that would be difficult to hide so she flexed her calves and biceps to see if any pain registered, instead, it was quite the opposite.

She could feel the strength in her limbs, far more than she had ever known. She had to resist the urge to jump up and try it out, to "*run it off*" figuratively and literally.

She felt like she could not only run, she could fly.

The earlier exhilaration of running through the Forrest of Scotland was like a dull sugar rush, a single cup of coffee, compared with this. She squeezed the muscles in her neck and shoulders, testing them for mobility, and found that she was completely unharmed.

She still felt queasy in her stomach, and her clothes felt snug, but it was certainly not the worst she had ever felt.

She then realized the queasiness was hunger. More than anything, she felt hungry. A thought which disturbed her, considering that was what had gotten them into this mess in the first place. But it was something that she would have to deal with until they got out of here…

If they got out of here.

She expected any moment that one of the massive tentacles swinging over her head, as it reached out for the children would come after her next.

The Children and Maru might be deceived by her act of unconsciousness but surely Dyondaygah was not. He would no doubt want revenge on her for her resistance.

Her and Mark.

Mark also had resisted some temptation or another, what had it been? What had the demon offered him?

But the blow she expected never came. Dyondaygah had been more enraged by the laughter of his followers than he had at the woman who had resisted union with him, at least for the moment.

"Blasphemers! Faithless ones! Unworthy! None shall live who mock my greatness!" Ally heard the chorus of the Children speaking for Dyondaygah, but now it was greatly reduced, where once there had been many voices, there were only a few.

She wanted desperately to open her eyes and see how many were left, but she didn't dare, and it was a good thing because, a moment later, she felt a large boot vibrate the stones beneath her, and heard Maru's voice almost directly above her.

"Oh mighty one! Do not bring your wrath down upon your humble servant, Maru! You have rightly sentenced all those who do not adore your name to death and they have paid the price! Now take this one who has dared to defile your name, and your children by drawing them away from your worship and adoration!"

"Well done, Mark." Ally thought, "Whatever happens after this, you have won." She prayed silently that whatever end Dyondaygah had for them it would be quick.

"Silence! You will not dane to give orders to your master! You will raise your hand to do my work. You and the Children must dispose of the infidels. I have taken my own, you will take the lives of those who would oppose me!"

Ally couldn't believe their luck... If it was luck.

Dyondaygah was not going to do his own dirty work. He had killed many of his children and now wanted Maru and the remaining giants to finish off the three infidels.

She had been overwhelmed by the sheer number of giants in the hallway upstairs. With the aid of the Scots, she had gotten pretty close to victory and might have even had it, if not for the control Dyondaygah had been able to exert over her with part of him literally inside of her, overloading her brain with chemicals.

But now that control was gone.

From the sound, there couldn't be more than fifteen of the giants left. Thirty had been too many, but fifteen, she might just have a chance.

It was clear none, (or very few) of the giants had much training in martial arts, and they likely had not done much fighting, even in training among themselves.

They had expected to overwhelm their enemies with mere size and brute strength. Perhaps that was enough in the dark days when Dyondaygah first encountered humanity, and it certainly had been enough until today.

But now they would have her to deal with, and maybe Mark too if she could free him.

Hadn't there been a shotgun among the items they had placed before Mark? He must have gotten that from Hap. She knew all too well that it could indeed do serious harm to the children.

After Mark had escaped, she had seen several of the Children with massive damage done to their bodies. It had healed quickly, within a matter of hours or even minutes depending on the severity of the wounds but a few moments of severe damage might be all they needed.

"Now conclude this night with the pouring of the blood sacrifice. Bring forth the chalice you have prepared!"

Ally felt Brisco moving away from her. Why couldn't that big lummox have laughed at Dyondaygah just once? He was damaged now, but she could tell that he alone would be formidable in a fight, and might have been unbeatable if not for Mark's knife being shoved through his eye. Now his movements were slow and deliberate, where once they had been quick and sure.

Was this the time? Should she make her move now?

But then she heard the chains next to her rattle. She had forgotten about them.

Drat. Even when she had not been resisting Dyondaygah, (because of the Giant's controlling chant,) the chains had been secured to the brick and mortar floor. She hadn't exactly been pulling against them at that point, but she was certain that no matter how strong she was now, there was no way she could break those iron chains.

It didn't cross her mind to think about what had rattled the chain at first. If anything it was likely some movement of Brisco's as he had passed... But no, he was beyond her feet, and the chains were anchored by her sides. So what had...

Ally felt something lithe and slimy crawl up on to her. She felt it slither across Mark's sweatshirt, and make contact with her skin through the holes in it.

She heard and felt the slight sucking, popping, squelching sound as the suction cups on one of the tentacles slimed its way over her.

Was this it? Was this the moment when Dyondaygah would drag her down into the pit to be lost forever in whatever place he dwelt in? He had said that her death and Hap and Mark's was to be dealt with by Maru and the Children, had he changed his mind?

But then the tentacle retracted, drew back as if it had touched something too cold or too hot, painful to its touch. It oozed away and continued on its path toward the dais.

It was not connected to the main mass, it was a loose piece of Dyondaygah that had once been inside one of the Children and was making it's way back to the demon.

Ally shuddered at the thought that something that had just been inside of someone else had just crawled over her, and that something similar had been in her as well, trying to take root, latching on to her spine.

As she listened now, she could hear the sound of multiple tentacles eking their ways across the floor, and up on to the dais. She hoped they were crawling down into the pit and they would be no further trouble, but she couldn't be sure.

Now Brisco was approaching again and she felt him brush her chains as he mounted the stairs. She heard Maru above her speaking some kind of invocation, *"Oh Mighty Dyondaygah, power behind the stars, Ruler of Branagag and Ralen, Father of Mor'tag and Roth'nel..."*

Ally heard the sticky flow of Blood pouring out of a cup, but then from below, she felt something happening...

The earth began to shake, as though something massive was moving beneath it, heaving itself upward and thrusting against the ground beneath the Towen. The Stones began to shift and the mortar between them began to crack. Ally felt a couple of the stones press upward into her side and felt the others beneath her head shift.

"Is this it!? Is this the great coming of Dyondaygah at last?!" Maru shouted.

"Oh, I don't think so." Ally thought.

She could tell even before a roar of pain and frustration exploded out of the pit, this was no triumph. It was defeat. It was the thrashing temper tantrum of an impudent child who had not only, not gotten his way but was now determined to break everything he could get his hands on.

"BETRAYED!! YOU HAVE BETRAYED YOUR MASTER!"

"What? No! Master, I would never betray you!"

"Oh yes, you would Maru." Ally thought to herself, still not moving, *"You would betray anyone and anything if you thought it would get you what you wanted."*

"HAVE YOU SOUGHT TO DESTROY ME?..."

While Dyondaygah was bewailing his defeat and Maru pleaded with the demon, Ally dared to open one eye, to take in what was happening around her.

When she was able to focus, she saw that Mark was on his back, still strapped to the chair, but breaking free.

She could not see Hap at all, because he was directly opposite of her, on the other side of the mass of swaying tentacles.

If she had been standing, or even on her knees, she might have been able to see him. She hoped he was alright.

Then she looked beyond, at the giants. On each of their faces was a grimace of hatred. Whether it was a reflection of the emotion of Dyondaygah at the moment or their own feelings, there could be little doubt who the emotion was meant for.

She watched as their lips made the words of their master, *"I TAKE FROM YOU THE CHILDREN OF DYONDAYGAH, I TAKE FROM YOU YOUR PRIESTHOOD! I TAKE FROM YOU YOUR POWER AND VITALITY!"*

Then Ally looked at the floor, where her chains were mounted, and she saw that the stones were all but free. They were still large and heavy and had gone unbroken in the earthquake, but she was certain she could pull them out of what remained of the broken mortar.

Brisco's back was too her. This was her chance.

"What have I done, oh great one? What have I done to deserve your wrath?" Maru shouted into the forest of massive tentacles that writhed before him, completely oblivious to Ally's sudden movement.

She jumped to her feet and began to pull on the chains which were linked to the stones. She felt them give a little but not much at first.

She leaned back against them.

She pulled with all her strength, unable to stop herself from giving off a sound that was somewhere between a roar and a growl.

Her mighty arms strained against the mason work which had held firm for nearly two hundred years, but it could not withstand her awesome strength now that the very dirt beneath them had shifted upward.

She felt one stone give way and then another. His attention drawn by Ally's roar, Brisco was in the process of turning around to see what was happening.

But already it was too late, as Ally, joining her hands together and taking hold of the chains, swung the stones around, up and over her head.

They slammed directly into the Chest of Brisco who fell backward into the tentacles. At the same time, Maru fell forward, toward her, hitting the ground beneath where Brisco had stood, hard, like a small sack of potatoes.

Brisco disappeared into the squirmy mass, trying to swim back up through the tentacles, but in an instant, he was gone from sight.

Maru, hurt, but not severely damaged, rose to his feet and made a move to run, but Ally was too quick for him.

Catching him by the back of his red suit jacket she hoisted him into the air and made him look in to her face, "And as for you, you little worm!"

She started, but then was taken aback, as a shock of gray hair suddenly appeared on his head. She saw it change, from coal black, to white as snow, as quickly and efficiently as a row of two colored dominos. The hairs did not grow or change, the color was simply sucked out of them, from the roots to the tips, in an instant.

Whatever was happening Maru felt it, but there was no time for questions, because at that moment Maru shouted, "Behind you!"

Ally turned to see the fist of a male giant, fully ten feet tall, coming down on her, whipping her torso violently back, and dropping Maru to the ground.

Once more she managed to dodge the blow, and taking hold of the chain, which was still attached to her wrist, she brought her left arm up and smacked the giant in the head with the cobblestone.

He fell back. But already a second giant, a female, only

slightly taller than Ally, was coming at her. Ally spun through her swing with the stone and came in low, letting go of the chain, she used the Giantess's momentum against her and flipped her over on to her back.

Out of the corner of her eye, Ally saw that Mark was free and moving toward Hap, shotgun in hand.

Then she heard Maru screaming.

It took her aback for a second, as she watched more of the giants closing in, surely they were coming to protect their master.

But no, they seemed to not even be focusing on her. Their anger was focused on Maru. Their downcast eyes left no room for doubt.

"Help me, Ally!" Maru shouted, "You must help me! You must protect me from the Children!"

It made no sense, but there was no time to worry about it. Whatever had happened, he had lost his control over them, and something more besides.

As one of the bigger females made her move to take hold of Maru, Ally brought the chain and stone around the female's neck. Taking hold of the stone end, Ally pulled it tight, climbing up The Giantess's back at the same time.

The Giantess, who was still more than three feet taller than Ally, strained and gurgled, simultaneously, she seemed more concerned with getting at Maru, than she was with Ally's stranglehold.

Now, practically riding on the Giantess's shoulders, Ally pulled tight on the chain and felt it snap under the pressure.

Suddenly her right arm was free of the stone, only four or five links still attached. At the same time, her hold on the giantess was broken.

Thinking quickly, she used her now freed hand, placing one on the back of the giantess's head, and one up under her chin, and without a second thought, she yanked as hard as she could.

She heard the bones snap, the tendons and cartilage giving way.

One down. But there was no time to revel in her victory for the next moment, she felt two sets of strong arms take hold of her from either side, pulling her backward as the giantess fell away.

Two of the big men had grabbed hold of her arms and were now pulling on her.

Fortunately, both of them had taken hold of Mark's sweatshirt, which had till now covered both of her arms, clear down to the wrist. The material was slick and didn't afford either of the giants a firm grip. It was also old, from Mark's days in college, and the seams were not as strong as they had once been.

The shoulder seam on the right was the first to go and it tore away cleanly, leaving the giant with nothing but a piece of cloth in his hand.

Making use of her freedom, Ally balled up her fist and punched the giant holding her left arm straight in the gut.

That blow, might have actually torn through a normal person, exploding *"Mortal Kombat"* style out the other side, but because it was one of Dyondaygah's giants, with nearly triple the muscle mass and bone density of a normal man, it only served to knock the wind out of him, but that was enough.

Ally followed through on the momentum of her punch and shoved the giant back into his fellows, including the one who still dumbly held her sleeve in his hand.

As they rose, Ally heard one shotgun blast, followed quickly by a second.

Mark was taking care of business.

The sound drew off two of the giants that had just been knocked away, and Ally smiled to herself, even as she took a swing at the next giant who was coming in toward her.

"Thanks, Mark." She thought, "It's about time you got in the game."

Still, Maru was lying on the ground, against one of the stairs of the dais, cowering like a child, "You must help me!" he shouted over and over, "You must protect me! I can't control them!"

Ally wondered if there was a way she could just get away from the little weasel. Let the giants have him, and let justice be served.

But she also knew that once they had made short work of him, they would simply turn on her, Mark, and Hap. And perhaps while Maru still lived, she could use him as a distraction.

So despite everything she wanted to do, she kept doing her best to keep the giants away from the little coward.

As one of the bigger Giants had made their way toward him Ally used her remaining Chain-stone like a hammer to take him out at the legs, breaking both knee caps, first one then the other.

As he fell to the ground both broken knees slamming into the stones eliciting a bellow of agony, Ally swung the stone one-handed like a baseball bat, bashed the giant upside the head, blood and hair flying.

She then swung the chain stone around clockwise, like David's slingshot of old, and made contact with several of the giants, (hitting one particularly obstinate one several times,) before he got out of the way.

Then bringing the helicoptering chain over her head, she made a perimeter, they dared not try to breach, and then brought it down on the head of the nearest, (and one of the smallest giants,) knocking him unconscious.

From somewhere off to her left she heard two more shots ring out in the echo chamber of the Towen Circle. She was surrounded now by five giants, with Maru toward her rear, whimpering like a whipped cur.

Where once there had been nearly thirty now there were only six, including the one who lay unconscious but breathing, on the ground, but they were still very dangerous.

If Dyondaygah hadn't lost his temper and killed better than two-thirds of his forces himself, all three of the "Infidels" might have been dead by now.

She saw now that the count was back up to six, as the giant who's knee caps she had decimated was back on his feet, damaged, but healing quickly.

Too quickly.

She knew she didn't have that, not now, with the tentacle of Dyondaygah expelled from her body. It might only be possible after the Star-spawn's Union with its host was complete, thankfully she'd not had the opportunity to find out.

"Let's see," She thought, *"radical healing factor, at the price of losing my free will and personality, and freedom? No contest."*

Ally got tired of waiting. "Well?" she asked, looking at one of the fatter male giants, speaking full words for the first time since she woke up on the cobblestone floor, "Come on big boy! What did you do, eat half of Dyondaygah yourself?"

Like a great galumphing moose, the fat one took the bait and charged at her. She ducked in low, and lifted the large squishy man, across her shoulders.

In a move right out of studio wrestling, she went spinning into the middle of the circle of the surrounding giants, hitting several of them with his head and feet.

Then she let him go, so that he flew off her back, forcing four of the giants to jump quickly back.

Now, she saw that Mark had made his way back to the weapons the Children had so unwisely brought down into the chamber.

In the dim firelight, she could see her sword glinting.

She wound up with the chain stone once again and smacked the living daylights out of one of the female giants who tried to sneak in from behind, caving in her (particularly large and ugly) nose, and the side of her face.

"Hey, Mark! You want to get over here and help me or what? Bring my sword!" She shouted to her husband.

"Coming baby!" He shouted, clearly overjoyed to see she was still alive and fighting.

Ally groaned inwardly, "I. Told. You!" She shouted picking up the female, who was bemoaning her smashed face, and throwing her like a small log, "Don't call me baby!"

As she continued to fight, she saw Mark pick up the sword with two hands and throw it toward her, between two of the six remaining giants.

While Ally had been able to fend off each of them as they came, and despite what should have been massive damage, she had only been able to permanently fell one of the giants, who's neck she had broken, and while she wasn't by any means fatigued, she was getting tired of fighting them off. She was also running out of moves they might not suspect. But as the handle of the blade slipped into her hand, she felt as if her right arm was suddenly whole.

She had a good sharp weapon in her right hand and the chain stone in her left. And she knew just were to put both of them!

She charged one of the giants, which were nearest to her, and rammed the sword home into his guts. She twisted it and pulled out to the right, drawing the sword out through his left side.

He fell to his knees in front of her, hands clasping his middle to try and keep his guts, (and presumably the tentacle within) from escaping. But with the backslash of her sword, she took off the head of the giant, his body falling over, and bleeding out on to the cold stone.

The tentacle immediately seemed to know its host was dead, because it exploded out of the wound in his side, nearly chopped in half itself, and started making its way back toward the pit.

Meanwhile, Mark had gone to work with his shotgun. He had blown several large holes into one of the giants, one in the guts, another in his leg, and as the giant was falling to the ground, Mark was just about to fire a third shell into its head when the earth began to shake once more.

"STOP!" The giants all shouted as one, and taking three steps back from the pair, arms at rest by their sides, "KILL NO

MORE OF MY SERVANTS!"

Taken aback, to hear the giants once again speaking for the Demon, both Ally and Mark moved toward each other, putting their backs against each other, Mark's head between her shoulder blades.

"YOU HAVE SHOWN YOURSELVES TO BE GREAT WARRIORS." The Voices continued, speaking as one, *"GO NOW IN PEACE AND LEAVE BEHIND MY TOWEN. LEAVE ME THE TRAITOR, MARU AND I, THE MIGHTY DYONDAYGAH WILL GRANT YOU YOUR LIVES. YOU HAVE EARNED THE RESPECT OF ONE OF THE GREAT ANCIENT RACE. THE GLORY YOU HAVE HERE ACHIEVED WILL BE A LEGEND AMONG US DOWN THROUGH THE AGES AND YOU WILL LIVE WITH MY BLESSING IN PEACE AND RICHES. BUT DEFY ME NOW AND YOUR LIVES ARE FORFEIT! YOU WILL DIE HERE AND NOW, UNREMEMBERED AND UNSUNG, NOTHING MORE THAN TWO MORE FOOLS WHO COULD NOT WITHSTAND MY GREATNESS AND MY MIGHT! LEAVE! NOW!"*

Mark turned his head to be closer to Ally's ear and whispered, "Are you buying this garbage?"

Ally laughed, "Not for a second, he's afraid."

"He should be." Mark said, "On 'three' grab Maru, and make for the stairs."

"What are you going to do?" Ally asked, whispering.

"I'm going to send Dyondaygah back to Hell, what do you think? Just be ready to close the door."

"SPEAK!" Demanded Dyondaygah through his remaining Children, and somehow the desperation and fear in his voice were clear, *"WILL YOU YIELD?"*

"You're supposed to be above all time and space! But you didn't foresee the Seneca Indians who defeated you and your children at the confluence of the Three Rivers. You drew Ally and me here, but you didn't foresee that we would be able to resist you! You used John Carter to build the Towen and uncover the Sarsen Circle, but you didn't see the preparations he made against you! You are no god. You are a prideful brat who got too big for his britches." Mark shouted back, and then he added in a low voice, "And you never saw *this* coming."

And then once more shouting he added, *"Three!"*

As one Mark and Ally moved in opposite directions, he toward the broken remains, of a steel box in the wall, and she toward the spot where Maru still lay curled up in the fetal position.

The tentacles, laced with eyes, reached out toward her, as she ran and jumped over them. They came one after another, but she never stopped. Using some of them as a ladder, while ducking beneath others as they wheeled over her head, she made her way forward.

No gauntlet devised by men could have been as arduous and yet she took it like a child running over a playground "Castle bridge". She felt her shoed feet squish down into the tentacles, as though they were beanbag chairs. She slid underneath one of the bigger wrinkled masses of elephant-like flesh, as it tried to come down on her head. She dodged and ducked and wove her way through the fleshy nightmare.

Within seconds, of leaving Mark on the opposite side of the chamber, Maru tucked under one arm, she made it to the stairway.

It was only then, as she turned to look back into the Towen Chamber, she realized, she and Mark were not Dyondaygah's target.

The giants were.

The tentacles reached out toward the five remaining giants, including the one whom Mark had not quite killed, and engulfed them.

Not to crush and break, but to encircle and protect.

As Ally continued her forward progress toward the doorway, she saw six masses of tentacles slam up into the ceiling, wood, and steel, cracking and exploding outward as the protected giants were hurled up and out into the building above.

Ally turned back into the stairwell and tried to throw

Maru up the stairs, but he clung to her forearm like a leech, refusing to be let go, all the while, continuing his chant of *"Help me! You must protect me!"*

"Shut up you little weasel!" Ally shouted and slammed Maru against the wooden cellar stairway wall.

Maru gasped in pain, but did not let go and gripped her bicep even tighter. Ally turned toward the chamber, sword at the ready in her right hand, and looking for Mark when she heard something go *"BANG!"*

32

"Are you John Carter?"

"You know my name?" John Carter asked, stepping into the dark dungeon of the *Château D'If*.

"Process of elimination." Mark said, "Don't close the door." He added.

"Wouldn't think of it, my Boy," Carter said, holding the lantern in front of him. As he neared and the lights from above shown on his face, Mark could see that Carter was not nearly as old as he had thought at first.

His hair was white, white as snow, and his face was lined with care and possibly madness, but he was probably not much more than forty-five or fifty. But people aged faster back in Carter's time, and given what little he had read of John's diary, what he had been through could make any man age prematurely.

"Process of elimination, you say?" Carter repeated.

"There's only ever been one person who has lived in the Towen longer than a year or two before Maru, and you seemed the most likely candidate," Mark explained.

"The Towen?" Carter asked astonished, "You know about the Towen?"

Mark sighed, "The Towen, the Sarsen stones in the basement, Dyondaygah, and The Northern Lights that are probably going crazy over the building right now. I probably know more about it than you do."

Carter had flinched at the mention of the name of the Demon god, "How could you know that name? No one has ever heard that name mentioned aloud in my house."

Mark laughed, "Oh my dear Mr. Carter, that name has been, or rather will be, said in your house so many times it would make your head spin."

"Then... I've failed." Carter said dejected, "If you know about the Towen it means that it still stands."

"Yep. At least one hundred and fifty years later, that puppy is still alive and well, and stronger than ever." Mark said, standing to his feet, running his circlet cuffs up the pole and sliding around it.

He put his legs out to either side of the pole and hung back on his wrists, and spun around the pole like a child on the playground, "Maru owns the place now. He's a dwarf."

"A dwarf?" Carter asked confused.

"A little person." Mark explained, "But oh, he's got big plans for the little mess you made, by digging up the Sarsen stones, Mr. Carter."

"I... I had no choice," Carter said, looking at the floor. "You don't understand what it's been like. That voice in my head, night and day, day and night, never a moment's peace." Tears welled in his eyes, "I had no choice but to dig up the stones, can you understand that?"

Mark continued to spin around the Maypole, not answering, what was there to say? He couldn't hold this man responsible for what an entity older and more powerful than any force in the Universe had made him do, and he truly was not responsible for what Maru had done years later.

Assuming the Stones had still been there 100 years later, Maru would have simply dug them up himself.

"I want to destroy them, the stones. I've made away." John Carter continued, "But I can't do it. I've tried and tried. But Dy-... The Confluence... he... he won't let me. I've been in this house too long, he..." John trailed off. "Anything I try to do that could damage the stones... I can't even lift my hand against them. That's why you need to do it."

"Me?" Mark said flippantly, "I can't do it. I can't even take my wrists off this pole, how am I supposed to damage stones that are just as big and heavy as the ones at Stonehenge?"

"Half the size." Carter corrected, "They are half the size of most of the ones as Stonehenge. They are only 15 feet tall."

"Yay!" Mark said deliberately sounding like a child, "Then I can just knock them over like Lincoln logs!"

Seeing that Carter was confused by the comment, Mark clarified, "That doesn't make it any easier Mr. Carter. It is still impossible."

"Black Powder, and dynamite," Carter answered without hesitation. "It's all prepared."

Mark stopped swinging on the cuffs, magnetically connected to the pole, "Come again?"

"When I was clearing away the dirt for the Sarsen stones we had to support the dirt around them with brick and mortar to hold back the dirt like any other basement, I had the workers do the digging, but I did most of the stonework myself. I started life as a bricklayer, did you know that? I made my fortune on the railroads, but I was laying brick when I was twelve years old, alongside my father."

"Fascinating," Mark said, sarcastically.

"When they dug them out, they dug to the outer edge of the stones, but I dug in further. I placed a Pittsburgh steel, waterproof box on either side of each of the stones and loaded them with enough high explosive to destroy each of them. I placed lead pipes in the dirt to protect the fuse cords running to a central box in between the seventh and eighth stone. All the bricks were covered with horsehair plaster. And the central box as well. It is loaded with black powder, ignite that and there won't be a stone left standing."

"How am I supposed to get at that?" Mark said dismissively, "You aren't aware but right now there's probably twenty giants marching around in the midst of those stones, chanting."

"Giants?" Carter asked his eyes widening. "Like Goliath?"

"Goliath." Mark laughed, "Goliath was only seven feet tall. My wife is probably that tall by now. Only the shortest of them is that tall Mr. Carter, some of these giants are nearly ten feet tall. One or two might even be twelve; I didn't exactly bring out my yardstick to measure them. They eat the body of Dyondaygah and the next thing you know they are shooting up like corn *"high as an elephant's eye!"* Mark explained, affecting a southern twang.

"Giants." John Carter said, "Eating the flesh of that... that thing!"

"Yup." Mark said simply, "What am I supposed to do, come in there with a sledgehammer and say *Pardon me, boys and girls, I'm just going to do a little light demolition over here. You go ahead and continue your worship of an ancient Demon, don't mind me!* It's hopeless Mr. Carter."

Carter did the last thing Mark would have expected, he fell to his knees and wept. "You must! You must find a way! I can't do it. God knows I've tried, but I just can't do it! I'd be more than happy to die if that would destroy this fell house and all that lies within it, but I can't! I've tried to burn it down and I can't even drop the match. I've burned my fingers so many times, trying to do it, but he makes me hold it until it goes out."

"If Dy—" Mark started but then Carter cringed and Mark corrected himself, "This thing is some sort of all knowing being, wouldn't he have known about your explosives and had them removed?"

"He's not all knowing. He only makes demands." Carter explained. "Maybe he knows more in your time, because he sees through the eyes of those who have eaten of him, but if he knew everything I wouldn't have even been able to place the explosives in the first place."

"Then why can't you drop the match?" Mark asked.

"I don't know." Carter said, starting to wail again, "Anything I do that could actually destroy the place he stops. Its almost as though he has placed a wall in my mind. I can pile the kindling, but I can't light the fire. I can load the gun, but I can't pull the trigger, not even to destroy myself. I've tried to write letters demanding that the house be demolished, and

I can't move the pen over the page! I try to speak, to give commands that would result in the Towen's destruction, and no sound comes out. Or if it does, no one can understand me! I can barely even leave the building. I can't leave the hill, the mound. Everyone thinks I am mad! But I'm not mad! I know it. You know it! You are the only one who can do it. The mere fact that it is still standing in your time proves that I will never succeed. And by the God we both adore, you must find a way!"

"I don't know if I'll ever get back." Mark said, looking at his manacles, "Ally, my wife, she may be lost to me forever by now, and if she is there's no point in going back. These French people from another dimension can do whatever they want with me. It won't matter if there is no way back."

"Is there a way to release you, my boy?" Carter asked seriously, drying his eyes with a jacket sleeve. "Not that I can find, these cuffs are held to the pole with some kind of magnetism, but it's not even affecting your lantern, so I don't have even the slightest idea how it works," Mark said, doing his best to show off the cuffs.

"There must be some manner of release mechanism within this room." Said John, moving towards the walls. The light in his hand shone into the places that the bright illumination kept in shadow from Mark's perspective.

"You dream old man." Mark said once again placing his legs on opposite sides of the pole and swinging around, "There's no way that they are going to put a release button where one of the prisoners could get at it."

"A button you say?" Carter asked.

"Yeah," Mark sighed, "A button or a le-"

He had started to say *"Lever"* but never got it out as the cuffs suddenly let loose of the pole and the pole shot down into the floor, sending Mark crashing to the ground.

"Hey!" Mark said, rubbing his backside as he shot to his feet, "How did you-"

"This big red button right here, my boy. It says "LIBĚRATION" right here, in large friendly letters." He said *"Liberation"* with a French accent.

"Great." Mark said, still rubbing his sore spot, "Warn a guy next time will ya?"

"My apologies." Carter said, "Now quickly, you know what to do! Get back to the Towen in your own time and destroy those stones! You must!"

"How can I do that?" Mark asked, "As soon as you close that door it will disappear."

"Not if you are touching it. If the door remains open, or if you keep your hand upon it, the doors will not fade away. Then you must think of your own time, in the Towen, and if all goes well it should open to the place you wish to see."

"How can you be sure?" Mark said, thinking of the time, now so many hours ago when Ally had done something similar.

"Why my boy, how do you think I was able to open this door and find you?" Carter said, "I remembered what Maggie saw, and I wished to see the same thing. I've lived in this house long enough to know many of its secrets and how it works, especially when the Conjunction of worlds is near."

Carter started to walk back towards the open door, "And by the way, should you find yourself trapped and the walls keep getting further away from you, close your eyes and take ten steps backward. That always seems to do the trick for me!"

Mark rolled his eyes, "I'll keep that in mind." He said, following Carter and placing a hand on the door.

Carter turned and looked him in the eye, "God Bless you, my boy, I hope for all our sakes you find your wife, and put a stop to the evil I've unleashed on the world. Forgive me."

Then, not waiting for a response, Carter closed the door. Mark's hand kept contact with the wood, as it closed, and he thought of the hallway where Ally was fighting for her life, with a band of crazed Scotts at her side.

He pictured the place as clearly in his mind as he could, for about five seconds, until the alarm sounded.

"Prisonnier est hors de confinement! Signaler a la cellule

vingt-trois! Retiens-le!" said a female voice over the PA system. Mark didn't know if he was the prisoner of *cellule vingt-trois*, or not, but he wasn't about to stay here a moment longer.

Taking hold of the handle, he flung wide the door and ran into what lay beyond.

"Oh, Mr. Thurston!" Said Maru, looking down at him from atop Brisco's shoulders, "How good of you to join us!"

33

Mark shouted, *"Three!"* At the top of his voice, and pushed off from Ally.

He made for the stones, directly opposite the door, as she made for the stairwell, Maru clinging to her bicep.

When Mark had been lying on his back, tied to the chair as the Children of Dyondaygah were being smashed like bundles of sticks, he had seen one of the giants slammed into the wall.

Part of the plaster had fallen away, revealing one of the steel boxes John Carter had placed there.

Mark looked to where the body of the dead Giant still lay.

Glinting in the flickering light of the fire ring, the corner of the box was now clearly exposed.

The cobblestones that lay on the ground until tonight had been relatively smooth and evenly laid, now they were uprooted and in total disarray.

Mark had to watch every step, lifting his feet high, to avoid tripping.

In addition, within a few steps of pushing away from Ally, Mark found himself dodging and ducking the approaching tentacles of Dyondaygah.

He was certain he was about to be wrapped up in them and squashed like a bug, but instead, he saw that the tentacles were going around him.

They would engulf a giant, bundling them up and explode up through the wooden ceiling of the Sarsen pit.

The sounds of exploding wood and crumbling plaster behind him told Mark that all six of the remaining giants had been evacuated from the Pit.

Then he was clear of the tentacles and a few more steps brought him to the wall, where the crumpled edge of the steel box stuck out from the horsehair plaster all around it. It was dented in and large cracks ran through the plaster, which Mark immediately began to use to his advantage. But even with all that, the box remained largely hidden.

John Carter had been a bricklayer and a wall maker, and he had been good at his job. More than one hundred years after he had laid down the brick walls and covered them with plaster, no water had seeped through. The plaster was as solid as shale bedrock, and only after several intense hits, had the box underneath begun to show through.

Large flat pieces of plaster came away in Mark's hands, but still, it was not enough. He needed to get into that box! Using the gun butt as a hammer, Mark began to smash away at the still sturdy cement-like plaster.

Suddenly the gun bucked in his hands as he impacted the box.

The pellets from the gun blasted up into the already damaged ceiling.

The added impact of the fired round was channeled into the steel box.

Some of the black powder began to spill out.

The flame in the fire ring in front of Mark lept up, just as it had before when it had drawn both his and Hap's attention.

Mark could have kicked himself.
He could have done this from fifty yards away!

Quickly he reached into his back pockets and loaded the last four shells he had brought with him into the holding tube on the shotgun. Hap had made him practice loading and unloading nearly fifteen times before he would let him have the use of the shotgun.

Now Mark was very grateful for it. In less than three seconds, the gun was ready.

Now he had to make it back through the tentacles, their sharp tooth-like extrusions gleaming like serrated knife blades.

Mark crept along the wall, keeping as far away from the dais as possible, but the tentacles were longer.

Now finished with the work of protecting the last of its children, Dyondaygah was reaching out toward Mark. One after another those long columns of flesh smashed into the stones and brick walls between, trying to crush Mark, but somehow, every time, they missed.

It was almost as though they couldn't touch him, but that was impossible, wasn't it?

Dyondaygah had been able to lock on to the giants twice Marks size who had mocked him, breaking them like twigs.

He had just shoved his five remaining giants through the thick beamed ceiling as if it were tissue paper.

At least within the confines of the Towen, and the Sarsen Circle, he was real, he was physical, and he was dangerous.

But still, the tentacles seemed to deflect around Mark. Twice he was certain he was about to be skewered like a fish on a pike. But the tentacle missed, went around him, and even cracked deeply into one of the Sarsen stones.

Then, with the door less than twenty feet away, he saw his doom coming. A massive white Lamprey mouthed tentacle came toward him out of the black squirming mass.

Unlike the tentacles around it, it seemed to be chambered, and "ribbed" like the body of a worm, though still connected to the main mass of the Demon. It reared up above Mark's head, ready to engulf him like a sock around a foot.

The mouth was covered with eyes both within and without, and it seemed that Dyondaygah, tired of missing the target had prepared this horror especially for him.

On his left three massive tentacles smashed into the wall, followed by another three on his right, blocking his path completely as the Lamprey's circle of wet slimy muck glistened above him.

Mark racked the slide, drawing a fresh round into the chamber. If he was going to die, he was going to make this Alien pay for it, from the inside if need be.

The mouth opened wider and wider, as it prepared to strike. But suddenly it shrieked and bucked in midair.

Mark looked beyond and saw Ally, who had leapt from relative safety in the stairwell, her sword held in both hands, and plunged it deep into the white worm upon landing, and was now holding on to the sword for purchase as the thing bucked.

Ally was riding the slimy mass like it was a bull in a rodeo. Wielding the Chain Stone, still attached to her wrist, like a mace, she struck the White Worm again and again.

The tentacles withdrew from around Mark and went after Ally.

But she was ready.

Ally, still grasping the sword, forced all her weight to the left, and unzipped the Worm's flesh like a sandwich baggie.

In what must have been agonizing pain, it wailed loud enough to burst eardrums, and whipped itself hard causing the "head" to fly off as Ally, landed in front of Mark, sword still in hand.

"What are you waiting for?" She asked Mark, who had merely stood there, mouth agape, "Get to the stairs!"

And together they ran...

That is to say, Ally ran, and Mark was caught up under both his arms and carried, like a toddler, to the doorway, gun in hand.

Ally practically threw him into the stairwell, as she had Maru. Ally turned quickly to shut the door behind them, and slam the bolt home, but Mark shouted, "Not yet!"

"What do you mean?" Ally asked dumbfounded, "We have to get out of here!"

"Not yet!" Mark repeated, bringing the shotgun to his shoulder, I need a clear shot!" And as the tentacles began to race toward the doorway where they stood, Mark raised the site and looked down the length of the gun.

It was so far away. The tentacles were blocking the shot...

He should have stayed at the box, he should have finished this when he had the chance; saved Ally even if it meant he would be lost. He never should have...

And then suddenly, he had it, a clear line of sight, between the steel box and the stairway door, the tentacles seemed to part like the red sea.

They may have been trying to block off a route of escape, (or perhaps they had moved that way for reasons Mark couldn't even fathom,) but now he could see the shiny corner of the box sticking out from behind the wall, and he knew his aim would be true. It had to be.

"Say goodnight to Dyondaygah!" Mark shouted as he pulled the trigger. The next few moments seemed to happen in slow motion. The gun bucked in Mark's hands, and the tentacles wormed their way toward where he stood in the stairwell.

Ally pushed hard on the big vault door, catching a single tentacle and chopping it off to flop on the floor.

It was the first, but more had been milliseconds away.

Ally slammed the big metal slide bolt (practically a steel girder,) home, into the catch.

And nothing happened.

The wet fish *"plop, plop, plop,"* of the tentacles slimed on the other side of the door, as they impacted it, searching for a way in.

"What the blazes were you thinking?" Ally asked, panting, "Was something supposed to happen?"

"Wait for it." Mark had hit his target. He knew it.

Within the chamber, behind the flailing arms of Dyondaygah, there came a loud "fizzling" like an hourglass, at the end of its run, as the black powder stored within the steel box fell out into the fire ring beneath it, fast and faster.

It was a sparse and slow trickle at first. Hardly noticeable by the ears, (hairs, feelers and other sensory organs that couldn't even be guessed at,) embedded on the tentacles of Dyondaygah.

But quickly the powder began to pour out into the fire. Gaining speed and solidarity until it created a solid stream of black sand flowing from the box.

This lasted for less than a millisecond, as fire shot up the stream, from the trough below, and hit the ancient brown paper bag from which it flowed. Fire flew into the steel box, igniting all the powder within it and ancient primer cords, protected by tubes of copper and iron.

Now, at long last their purpose was fullfilled as they turned to ash, leading the fire deep behind the Sarsen stones, one after another, to the cores of black powder and dynamite.

Dynamite, it is well known, when it becomes old, can nearly double in strength and it sweats pure nitroglycerine. But John Carter had prepared for such an eventuality, encasing many large sticks of dynamite behind the stones, wrapped in brown paper, which kept all of the nitro closely held to the sticks of explosive material.

The coolness of the underground chamber and the stones themselves had preserved the dynamite as well as a modern refrigerator might have done.

Carter had been a master of his craft, and more than 100 years after they had been placed behind the wall, the fire from the dynamite was just as effective as it would have been when it was first placed.

Within milliseconds, large pieces of stone and fire exploded up through the dining hall, and into the upper levels of the building beyond.

One by one, the slabs of stone first disintegrated from the middle, then blew outward into the center of the Circle, fire and dust and ash rocketing debris everywhere, striking tentacles and crushing the rubbery flesh.

The Towen and the Sarsen stones were no more.

34

Hap made his way up the stairs from the Sarsen Circle. He felt bad about leaving Mark and Ally behind, but he had done all he could without a gun. He didn't know what had happened to his rifle.

Unlike they had done for Mark, the Giants had not foolishly laid out all of Hap's weapons before him.

Dern fools.

How could they be so stupid, and so arrogant?

By rights and any sort of common sense, you'd want to keep such tools as far out of the hands of your enemies as possible, and yet there they were. So proud and secure in their hubris, that they had placed the means of their own destruction in the hands of the enemy.

Of course, they couldn't have predicted how Dyondaygah would be harmed, one might even say defeated, by the two young people who seemed to have nothing in their favor.

When was the last time laughter, of all things, had actually wounded an enemy?

But it had.

Whether just his pride, or in some kind of physical sense, the laughter of Mark had been first insulting, and then directly harmful to the Demon god, and it had caused him to lash out in rage, and destroy all those who had mocked him...

Except for the source of the insult, Mark himself...

"*I have taken my own.*" Dyondaygah had said, "*You and the Children must take care of the infidels.*"

Did that mean that for some reason he was not allowed to touch them?

Was other rule at play here; something beyond the power and scope of even Dyondaygah?

The Universe had rules, some of which man had only begun to guess at.

Perhaps unless one had made the "choice", to accept Dyondaygah as their master, he couldn't touch them...

He could invade their minds, rob them of their sanity, and turn them into slathering madmen, but he could not bring physical harm to their bodies...

Or perhaps he merely considered it "taking out the trash", and wanted to leave such work to "the help."

Even as he ran down the hall, and through the red dining room Hap pondered these things, looking for an explanation, a "grip", something he could use to explain what he had just seen.

But then he thought about the blood that had been given to the Demon.

His blood.

And he thought about the words that it seemed he and Maru alone had heard, and he was pretty sure he knew exactly what had happened.

From beneath his feet, Hap could hear the sound of raised voices, several shotgun blasts and a number of loud thuds and thumps.

More than anything he heard the sound of the tentacles of Dyondaygah, writhing, and wriggling, tickling the support beams below him. He wasn't about to stay in this building a second longer.

As he darted out onto the blacktop he heard several small, popping, and breaking sounds behind him, but he did not turn back to see what had made them... not yet.

Then as he made it to the end of the blacktop, where the line of the now atrophied Razor Devils Claw began, he saw the burnt-out remains of his dear old truck, and darted behind it, for safety and to hide.

Only now did he dare look back at the building to see

what had made the breaking sound, and there he saw five giants, all on different sides of the Towen coming together and running down the hill, away from the building.

Just as he had done more than a thousand years ago, Dyondaygah had saved the last of his children to go running off into the night, to preserve some trace of his followers upon the earth.

Hap wanted so much to run after them, to put them down, one by one, even if it meant giving up his own life in the attempt, but he knew it would be useless.

They were all too tall, and strong and fast for him, even if he'd managed to catch up to one of them, with no gun, and no weapons he would be sacrificing his life for nothing.

"He who fights and runs away lives to fight another day. But he that dies, in battle slain, will never rise to fight again."

Hap recited to himself, shaking his head, wondering if he was talking about the giant Children of Dyondaygah, or about himself.

Then Hap saw something moving out through several of the windows of the Towen.

In the growing light, they were visible as darker, more solid shapes wriggling within the darkness.

The figures at first looked like huge undulating snakes.

But as they burst out through the windows, it became clear what they were; the tentacles of Dyondaygah.

They were still extending outward and upward, reaching around the Towen breaking through wooden joists, plaster, thatching, and iron girders.

Had the moment Maru had so long tried to bring about finally come?

Was the Demon god about to truly emerge into the world?

The tentacles, thick undulating tree trunks, and rubbery as a garden hose, glinted in the early morning light.

They seemed to creep out through all the windows and

doorways of the buffet, shattering glass and cracking through already broken wood. Straining, groping upward and outward as though trying to gain some foothold in the world of life and matter, the tentacles reached up toward the lightening sky.

Hap heard a loud pop from within the Towen and he was sure that he saw several pieces of wood break out from the floor in the dining hall, through the double doorway, that was now missing both of its doors.

"*Come on Mark.*" Hap chanted to himself, "*You can do it, just get out of there.*" Behind the Towen, the sun was rising.

The fireball of that constant nuclear explosion in the sky, which gave light and life to the earth was not quite over the horizon, but with no hills or mountains in the way, its light shot out through the few withered and dead trees that still lay rooted in the ground around the Towen.

Hap kept praying it would rise.

Perhaps if it did, even now the doorway to Dyondaygah would shut for another night, giving the world a chance for even one more day.

It was then that the explosion of light came, not from behind the flat prairie, but from within the Towen.

First, one fiery explosion burst through the floor of the dining room, and then another and another. Eight massive explosions bucked the earth, chain-firing. The noise of the first not barely dying away before the next rocked the earth beneath Haps feet, until they seemed to be one long continuous noise Hap had to cover his ears against.

As the explosions detonated, Hap could see the Towen caving in, both from the destruction wrought by the dynamite, which undermined its foundation, and from the twisted tentacles that pulled the burning wreckage back in and down toward the center, as if trying desperately to hold it's temple together, and yet further destroying it at the same time.

Hap watched as the tentacles simultaneously pulled downward and sliced through the roof and the walls.

He could do nothing but stare as the fire rose up through

the structure, bringing it all crashing down, mixing the wreckage like some enormous blender.

In that moment, as the sun rose over the horizon, and the last of the Sarsen stones were destroyed, the doorway to Dyondaygah, at the Olde Towen Buffet closed for the last time.

Hap watched in awe as the massive tentacles first curled up and in on themselves, like the legs of a dead spider, and then hardening, as if into stone, they crystallized, solidified, and then collapsed to dust, driven away by the wind.

The flames still rose from the twisted wreckage, but in the light of the sun, every vestige of Dyondaygah was blown away.

As the dust began to drift away and the smoke rose higher and higher from what remained of the Towen, Hap began to call out for Mark and Ally.

Nearly half of the Building, the part that had sat on the Sarsen Circle, (which was mostly the "Grand Hall" which Maru had made into the dining area and kitchens,) was completely demolished.

The other half, the part in which most of the guest rooms had been, still stood, cleanly sliced off like an artist's cutaway of a house's interior.

Hap could see the places where the crossbeams of the Sarsen Circle had once stood, but even they had fallen into the pit and cracked amid the destruction.

Toward the rear of the pit, stood a section of the house which had clearly been an add-on. The remains of an added roof covered the long hallway, which had run from the dining hall, into a stairwell, leading down into the Circle.

It was from this back area that Hap first heard the thumping.

"Mark!?" Hap cried, rushing toward the solid Oak structure, "Ally?! Are you in there?"

Three more loud thumps and cries came from within, someone had survived!

"Stay there kids!" Hap called, I'm going to go get an Axe,

I'll be right back!"

The Door on the interior side had opened outward and into the hall, and was now covered, and blocked by the fallen roof.

The only way in now lay over the pit, there was no way Hap could get to it. So the best plan was to go through the wall, which while thick, lay exposed.

Hap could see the heavy steel, vault-like door John Carter had placed at the base of the stairs, covered by heavy timbers, and now Hap thanked God for John's foresight.

Carter had hoped to try and destroy the Sarsen Circle himself but had never been able to bring himself to do it, he had prepared this door as a protective shield, to give himself a chance to survive, and more than one hundred years later it had served its purpose.

But now it too was blocked, covered with the remains of the restaurant above.

Had the hallway and stairwell been part of the original design of the House it might not have survived at all, but because it was an add-on, and there was nothing but dirt surrounding the stairwell, it must have shielded them from the majority of the blast, and it was not pulled down with the rest.

As Hap ran back toward his burnt-out truck, hoping he could find something, anything at all, to make a hole in the wall, he heard a loud bang from where he had been standing only moments before, this was followed by a second.

Two shotgun blasts sounded, as bits of wood and plaster went flying out from the wall, weakening it. A moment later, the side of the structure was bowing out, failing.

Then with a loud crack, Hap saw a large blade pop out through the side of the wall, glistening in spite of the plaster dust which now covered it.

Twice it retracted, and reemerged, only to be followed by another loud crack, as a large arm stuck out through the hole, breaking away wooden lathing.

Ally's arm.

Her now, very large, arm.

Hap ran back to the spot.

"Kids! Are you alright?" Ally coughed, "Kids? Really, old man?"

Hap laughed, "I'm so glad you're still alive! Is Mark in there too?"

"I'm here Hap!" Mark called from within, "Here, you want to take this little rat for us?"

Ally handed up something in a Dark red suit, but it couldn't have been Maru. Maru had been short, yes, but he could only have been about thirty-five or forty at the oldest.

Covered with ashes and soot, Hap was handed a very little old man, who looked to be in his sixties at the youngest. His hair was grey and his face was lined with wrinkles, not just dirt and ash, but deep creases in his skin, with several severe blemishes on his face, that had only been freckles on Maru's.

The little old man did not resist being handed through the hole, head first.

"Don't let him get away," Mark added from within.

"I don't think he'll be running anywhere any time soon." Ally said from within, "Stand back Hap, I'm going to see if I can break through the wall."

"Don't hurt yourself now," Hap said, holding Maru by the waist like a large toddler, and moving away from the wall.

Ally gave a solid push and Hap could see it was cracking where the second shotgun blast had weakened it. Then with a mighty groan of effort, Ally came crashing through the wall and fell on her face with the force of the momentum.

Mark stepped out behind her, "You alright?" He asked, almost laughing.

Still lying face-first on the grass, sword beside her, Alley put a thumb up in the air, "Positively K-O." She said her words muffled.

She rolled over on to her back and looked up at the red light of the dawn, and sighed, "I never thought I'd be so happy to see the sky."

Mark handed the shotgun over to Hap and offered his wife a hand. She looked at him and then at it.

"Do I have too?" she asked like a little girl.

"Yeah. I think so." Mark laughed, "If only so we can avoid smoke inhalation when the wind changes.

"Fine." Ally said, moping, taking Mark's hand, and nearly pulling him down, as she pulled herself up.

"Sorry," she said, rising to her feet, "I'm still not quite used to being like this. I'll have to learn how to be gentle again."

Mark chuckled, "There's never been anything gentle or subtle about you, now it's just more obvious."

Ally chuffed, "Oh you mean *thing*, you."

"What do we do with this one?" Hap asked, turning Maru toward them.

"I don't think he can hurt anyone anymore." Mark said, "Look at him, he's wasting away."

And it was true, just in the time since Mark had handed Maru through the wall, Hap could see Maru had aged considerably. He now felt thin and brittle in Hap's arms, as though one wrong move might snap him like a twig.

"Here, let me take him." Ally said, taking Maru as gently as though he were a baby, and once more he did not resist.

The three of them, (Ally carrying Maru) walked across the broken blacktop and began the long trek down the mound from the burnt-out remains of the Towen, the wind blowing the smoke away from them to the west.

At the bottom of the mound, Ally sat Maru down on the road. "You're... You're not going to kill me?" Maru asked.

"I would love to." Mark said, "But it would just soil my hands unnecessarily."

"For what you wanted to do to me, I could crush you like a bug, but now it would just be cruel." Ally said, sword at her side.

"Vengeance is mine saith the Lord," Hap added, "And from the looks of things, you are going to be meeting him soon.

If I were you, I'd use whatever time you have left to make your peace. You are going to have a lot to answer for."

Maru seemed stunned, as though he could barely understand what the three of them were saying. Then his wrinkling eyes narrowed, and he spat on the ground in front of them.

"That for your mercy!" he shouted, and spat again, "And that for your God." He said looking at Hap, "This is not the end. You haven't heard the last of me, there are other Great Ones looking for servants, they will gladly take me in. I will reclaim my youth and I will find you. You should kill me now and be done with it!"

"No," said Mark. "I don't think you will."

Maru's expression of hatred deepened, but then he turned and ran from them, down the road, and away, cackling like an idiot.

"Don't go past my house!" Hap called after, "My boy has orders to shoot you or any of the giants if he sees them!"

"I doubt he'll make it that far," Mark said, almost to himself.

Something chirruped in his pocket.

Mark reached his hand inside and pulled out his cell phone, which he had reclaimed with his car keys.

"Will you look at that." Mark said, "Four bars, almost full signal."

Ally snorted, "Oh sure. *Now*."

Hap laughed, "It must have been the stones themselves, which were disrupting the signal. If we needed any other sign the power of Dyondaygah was broken here, that would be it.

"You think we should call the fire department?" Mark asked, looking down at the phone.

"Nah," Hap said with a grin, "It's confined to the pit. Let it burn."

Together they walked toward Hap's grocery store, as Mark played with his phone, "I have voicemail." He said, putting the phone to his ear.

As he listened his face fell with disappointment,

"There's three of them from the auto club, they said they couldn't find our car."

"I don't think I could fit in that thing anymore." Ally said, looking down at her arms and hands. She flexed them as if she were breaking in a new set of gloves.

"I'm sure you'll get used to it." Hap said, "We all grew up as children and adapted to it as it happened, it just happened a little quick for you. But maybe it needed to. Mother always said, *"All things serve the will of God."*

Mark snorted, "Yeah right. God. Hah. Where was God through all this?"

Hap looked at Mark disbelievingly, "You honestly don't think all this was the will of God?"

"Yeah, sure." Mark said derisively, "If your god is Dyondaygah."

"Don't be blasphemous." Hap said seriously, "God allowed you to be drawn here. The very people that were needed to defeat Maru and his little tin god. Think about it, all those people who came here unknowingly to join the Children, they couldn't resist the call, and they gave in, surrendering their wills to an evil they couldn't or wouldn't resist. All their friends and partners whose minds were broken and their bodies either tossed into the pit or devoured by the Frog-men. They couldn't survive, let alone win a blow against the evil of that place. You haven't been here. You haven't seen. I have. My son has. My wife did. It was the reason why she left. She couldn't stand to see another person disappear behind those doors forever. Then comes you. Two people, a husband, and wife, like any other, but the only people with the will to overcome.'

'First God gave you the courage and love necessary to fight for your wife. Then he afforded you the opportunity to escape, and come to me, where, now that you knew, I could finally tell someone the information they needed to fight back. Then God gave the will to fight. He gave you the love for your wife. A love so deep you were willing to march into the very temple of Dyondaygah, no matter what the cost."

"I was dragged in there. Carried by two people twice my size." Mark quipped trying to get Hap to stop, "I didn't have much choice in the matter."

But Hap was not to be contradicted, "God gave you the cleverness and the ability to survive, within the Towen. He made sure you would draw the attention of the Children so completely that Ally was able to break free of the mind control the Children were exerting on her.'

'Then at the end of it all, God gave you a sense of humor to see something in Dyondaygah that was funny. He gave you your infectious laugh, which made others laugh, bringing further harm to the Demon. And finally he..."

Hap broke off, and seemed to rethink what he was going to say, "He allowed you to find out what you needed to destroy the Towen... I'm still not sure how you managed that."

Mark shook his head, "My sense of humor. That's just who I've always been. God didn't have anything to do with that."

"And now look at Alley," Hap continued, "God gave her a rebellious spirit. He gave her a will strong enough to over come the Demon's prompting, even while he was dumping chemicals into her system designed to weaken her will. He caused euphoria, and fear, pleasure and pain. But still at the end, when it came down to it she had the ability from God to be the most important thing she could be: *Herself.*"

"How do you know so much about my rebellious nature?" Ally asked, somewhat perplexed. Had Mark told him that much about her?

"Knew it from the moment you walked in my shop." Hap laughed, "I spent time as a school teacher, and I've seen more than a few young people with that look in their eye. You must have been a real humdinger for teachers back in the day."

"Soldier. School Teacher. Medic," Mark listed, "Is there anything you haven't done?"

"Thought I'd try running a grocery store a few years

back." Hap said with a grin, "I hadn't done that yet. But this is not about me, its about you two. Ally has become something much greater than she was before, you both have. You don't honestly believe that all of this has been accomplished just so the two of you could survive the night? For your sole benefit? So that you can go on and live a life of quiet desperation in an office? So that she can be a housewife, and socialite?"

Hap shook his head and continued, "You are both very fine people, and I've grown quite fond of you, but something tells me this is only a beginning for you. There is much more to come, and much more that will be required of you. I suggest you be ready for it."

Mark looked up at Ally, (a sensation that would take some time to get used to,) and rolled his eyes, but Ally, he could see, was taking much of what the old man had said to heart.

An hour later, they had all gotten cleaned up considerably. Their cuts and bruises had been tended to, and Ally, while still wearing Mark's sweat pants, had removed the other sleeve of the sweatshirt, which was already torn in several places, including the shoulder seam, and which had been making her feel off balance. Not only that but also, (she hated to admit it,) the sleeve was too small for her arm and had felt restrictive.

She would have changed into something else altogether, but both of their clothes were likely piles of cinders somewhere in what remained of the Towen.

Most likely she was wearing the only thing of Mark's that would have fit by now, and even it was rather stretched out and tight over her form.

Hap had promised to get a hacksaw out of the back once he had finished calling his son to let him know what had happened, so they could cut off Ally's "Chainstone" and at least make an attempt at the high tech circlets that were still surrounding Mark's wrists.

Now the three of them sat on metal stools next to the counter drinking Cokes. Ally had surreptitiously snuck two of the stools underneath her bottom, trying not to make a big deal out of it, but Mark had noticed all the same.

He was also smart enough not to say anything about it.

"Boy's coming with the truck," Hap said, as he hung up the wired phone on the counter.

"I thought your truck got burned up." Ally said, taking a pull from the Coke. The Stone, chained to her left wrist resting on a third stool beside her.

"I have another one." Hap explained, "You didn't honestly think that Junker was my only one. That was my wife's actually... And boy is she going to be mad when she comes back and finds it gone."

"I think she'll forgive you when you tell her that it died in a good cause." Mark said laughing, "Killing Dyondaygah."

"That she will," Hap said with a smile.

"But is he dead?" Ally asked, "Can something like that be killed?"

Hap sighed, "Probably not. I don't think it was natural enough to die, at least not in any way we understand it. And if what Mark says about what he saw looking into the pit, only a small part of it was even in our world. If it really even harmed that thing, in any substantial way, its more in terms of setbacks rather than physical pain."

"But we did set it back." Said Mark, clinking his bottleneck on Ally's, who also lifted her drink, to toast, "It took something like 2000 years for him to find a doorway last time, hopefully, it will be another 2000 before it rears its ugly head again." Mark took a swig from his Coke bottle.

"Gosh. How am I going to explain this to my parents?" Ally said looking at her large hands, "And what about the girls?"

"I hate to say it," Hap said, "But you two are probably going to have to move away from wherever you live right now. It'll raise too many questions. I'm sure your parents, will accept you if they are the right sort, and judging by you I think they are; no matter what you'll always be their "little girl."

"Not so little anymore," Mark said, and immediately put his hands up to keep Ally from hitting him.

She had indeed already raised her hand, in a threatening fist.

"Two for flinching." She said, punching him hard, in both biceps.

"You gotta stop that," Mark said, not knowing went to quit, "Those two big Christmas hams, you call fists really hurt!"

"Maybe you'll remember that next time," Hap said laughing.

Probably not." Mark and Ally said at the same time. Hap laughed as he walked toward the door of the shop, "You kids are something else. Vestal would-"

But his words were cut off as a massive arm tore through the screen door and took him by the neck, and yanked him violently out of the store, like a fish on a line.

Mark and Ally both stood to their feet as a hulking form stepped in, under the door frame.

"Found you." Brisco growled, panting slowly, "Little man."

35

Ally picked up her sword and ran for the door.

Mark was right behind her, shotgun in hand.

Ally gave a battle cry and lifted the sword over her head with both hands as she charged at the giant, who, tall as she now was, still stood head and shoulders over her. In her rash rage and anger, she left her torso completely exposed, and Brisco came in with a quick jab to her gut, causing her to double over in pain.

Just as she had done before to others, he used her doubled over position to push on Ally's backside, making her lose her balance, falling through the doorway, gasping for breath.

Mark couldn't get a clear shot at Brisco while Ally had been in the way, but now he had the shotgun pressed to his shoulder and was ready to fire.

But with a quickness that belied his size, Brisco had reached out and pulled the gun away from Mark, quicker than he could see it, and the shot, Mark's twelfth and final round, missed, hitting nothing but a few tin signs on the wall behind Brisco.

"You're mine now, Little Man." Brisco said his voice now missing most of the slur it had acquired after Mark stabbed him in the eye, but still retaining its previous deep and "mushy" sound.

Brisco took the Shotgun and bent it with his bare hands.

It was like something out of an old Bugs Bunny cartoon.

The solid gun twisted like rubber hose, only the wood of the slide cracking as it was bent into a large knot.

As Brisco was showing off, Mark was not idle. He quickly reached back and grabbed one of the metal stools that he and Ally had been sitting on. Its top was made of wood, but the legs were sturdy metal poles.

Mark swung the stool feet up, aiming for Brisco's head. But the Jugernaught could not be stopped by something so puny.

The Metal thunked hollowly against his flesh, but it was as no more than a flea to Brisco.

"You killed my master." Brisco growled, "Tricked him into betraying Dyondaygah. Made his Children laugh at him."

Mark struck, again and again, backing away from the Ogre between swings but on the third blow, Brisco caught the stool and pulled it away.

He put it between two hands like a Beer can and crushed it just as pretty. He threw the remnants over his shoulder, as Mark ran down the center of the four narrow aisles, which were bolted into the floor. Brisco followed, wading through them, breaking the shelves and pulling up floorboards as easily as a man wades through water.

"Now you will know the full wrath of the Children of Dyondaygah!" Brisco called after him, destroying everything in his path, "Now you die. Your Ally dies. Your old man dies. I find your home. All of your friends die."

Halfway down the aisle, Mark climbed up and over the shelves, and jumped across it, even as Brisco's bulk began to tip it over.

Landing on his feet, but cut off by the dislocated line of shelves he climbed over the second aisle and was now between the wall and the aisle.

He ran back up the aisle toward the entrance. But even before he'd taken a step, Brisco was lifting the fallen wall of shelving and lifting it over his head to throw at Mark.

Mark saw what he was planning and kept moving but hunched down low, hoping the still standing row would serve as protection.

It didn't. As it flew through the air, all the items on that section of shelving seemed to stay in place until it smashed into the wall, a corner breaking through the plaster, while the other side rested on top of the undamaged aisle, dumping the entire contents on Mark's head.

"He couldn't have thrown the bread section!" Mark thought as a number of heavy objects rained down on him; bottles of oil, ratchets and wrenches, boxes of screws and nails and even a few cans of paint.

But that did not stop Mark.

Stopping meant certain death.

One fortunate thing about the way Brisco had wrought a path of destruction in his wake, was that he had to move through it again to go backward.

He tried to climb over the fallen shelves and everything that had been on them. He was having a difficult time moving through it all and that gave Mark the time he needed.

As he moved through the aisle, Mark picked up two bottles, one was a bottle of motor oil.

He screwed the cap off. Then, as he drew near the doorway, he dumped the contents of the bottle out behind him, in a zig-zag-ing pattern.

Running out the door, Mark knew Brisco would have to make it past the oil to come out of the shop after him, and he hoped that might by him a few seconds.

Darting through the gap where the screen had once been in the screen door, Mark tried to take an assessment of the situation before him.

Hap lay in the middle of the street, not moving.

Ally was only now recovering from having the wind knocked out of her, and she was limping back toward the store.

"Run!" Mark shouted, "Pick up Hap and run!"

"Not without you!" Ally insisted.

"I'll be right behind you, I can't carry Hap and run. you can!" Mark explained, "It's me he wants! Run!"

Just then behind him, in the store, they could hear the sound of Brisco roaring in anger as he slipped and fell.

They could feel the ground shake from the force of his body's impact with the ground.

Ally didn't need to be told again, throwing her sword, into the bushes, and taking hold of her Chainstone, so that it wouldn't hit her, or Hap, she was to the older man in just a couple strides.

Before Mark had even gotten down off the porch of the store, she had scooped Hap up like a baby and began to run.

Mark too was running away when it seemed like the whole front of Hap's store exploded, woodchips flying as Brisco smashed through it!

In his rage Brisco seemed to have lost all sentience. He was not a man anymore. He was a beast. He was the finger of Dyondaygah.

Within a few strides, he had caught up to Mark, seeming to put little more effort into his pursuit than a Sunday jogger at the start of his run.

Reaching out, he caught of hold Mark's clenched fist.

The high tech metal band refusing to yield was the only thing that kept Mark's wrist from snapping like a twig.

Lifting Mark into the air by his arm, like a fish on a line, he turned Mark to face him, "No knives this time, Little Man." He said, raising his fist in a long drawback, which would surely break open Mark's head like a cantaloupe. "Now you die!"

There was the sound of a grinding scrape from Mark's elevated hand. Brisco heard it and looked up. Suddenly, Brisco was sputtering and choking as clear gunk filled his mouth, stinging his nose and good eye.

The next thing he felt was heat, white searing heat, as the contents of the second bottle Mark had picked up on his way out was ignited.

The sticky napalm of hand sanitizer refused to be removed, as Brisco tried to scrape it away from his face, only managing to set his hair and shirt on fire.

Brisco let go of Mark completely now, unable to repress the animal instinct to get away from light and heat and pain.

Mark squeezed more of the clear goo from the bottle, which arched into Brisco's face, causing the flame to redouble.

But now the giant was coming for him again. With a bellow greater than before, the flaming torch that was now Brisco's head, came flying at him.

Mark got an up-close look at the melting skin of Brisco's face, and evaporating shirt, as Brisco took Mark by the neck with one hand and lifted him into the air.

The air around him seemed to roar with a mechanical fury growing louder by the millisecond.

He felt Brisco squeeze.

The world when black as he heard a bone-crunching thud, as he was thrown back through the air, to land limply on the hard ground.

Mark was dead.

He knew it.

Brisco had popped his neck like a tick and his brain was dying.

Was there supposed to be this much pain with a broken neck?

Didn't most of the nerves and neurons die very quickly once a person's spinal column and brainstem had been crushed?

Mark had always thought having your neck broken, or your head cut off would be a relatively quick and painless way to go.

Your brain would go into shock, and without lungs anymore you wouldn't even notice the lack of oxygen as the blood spilled out of your head, and on to the ground below.

There might be a few milliseconds of horror as your brain asked over and over again *"What happened? What the heck just happened?"*

But then it would be over...

A loud *"PING. PING. PING."* rent the air, again and again.

...This was nothing like that. Mark felt excruciating pain all over his body.

It must be a sort of "Phantom Limb Syndrome" because surely he had no body anymore, (at least not one that was connected to a nervous system).

Then horror of horrors, he found he was able to open his eyes. He couldn't move. He could only take in what was happening before him.

Ten yards away, lay the rear wheel of a truck.

A few feet in front of the now mangled front end of the truck, Brisco lay on the ground; still on fire, still moving, and not dead.

In one of those crazy moments that you only realize the significance of afterward, Mark noticed the disposable lighter he had used to light Brisco on fire lay on the ground between him and the truck.

He saw Aaron, Hap's son, step out of the Truck, rifle in hand.

He began to piece it together.

The snap and crunch he had heard, at not been the sound of his own neck breaking. It had been the sound of the truck smashing into Brisco's right side.

Aaron had seen what was happening from a distance, pushed the accelerator to the floor, and driven into the giant's back at full speed.

Mark had gone flying off to one side, and the burning torch that was Brisco had flown forward under the impact.

Now Aaron was pumping round after round into Brisco with a rifle. But it wasn't stopping him. Brisco was getting up.

The rifle was more accurate but the shotgun had been, more deadly and damaging at close range. But the comparatively small holes it left in Brisco, were more easily compensated for, and were healing quicker than the basketball-sized holes Mark had been able to punch in the other giants.

Mark, (head still attached,) was lying on one side painfully and found that he could now move. He rolled on to his face and tried to get a hand underneath himself.

He should have known he wasn't dead.

He wasn't that lucky.

Being dead couldn't possibly hurt this much. Brisco was on his feet now and walking towards the boy, Mark could hear him, amazed that he could still speak coherently through the damage that was still being wrought to his body by the flames and the impact of the truck and the bullets.

"You should have driven after your father and the cowardly woman." Brisco said in his mushy voice, through burning lips, "Now I make sure he dies too. You will all feel the wrath of Dyondaygah by my haaaaand."

Through the haze of pain, Mark heard the sickening *"Click. click. click."* of the rifle as it ran out of bullets.

Aaron turned the barrel of the gun around towards himself and prepared to use it as a club.

Brisco laughed. He actually laughed, as he reached out toward the boy.

Suddenly, all around them, there was a loud croaking groan and roar. It was a sound Mark imagined might have come from a dinosaur in the Jurassic period.

The sound caused both Brisco and Aaron to look up, even as the roar was joined by two more similar croaking calls.

From somewhere above, (possibly the top of Hap's store, or perhaps they just simply "hopped in") the three Frog-men came hurtling into the fray.

Their mouths were wide open as they attacked, fifty times wider than any man's, their rows and rows of sharp little teeth gleaming in the early morning light.

They chomped down hard on Brisco, latching on to him like iron bear traps. Brisco screamed at the top of his voice in pain, much like when Mark had stabbed him in the eye, and tore at the pint-sized monsters, tearing away the hunks of his flesh they had latched onto at the same time.

Mark grimaced as he saw one of them, Tom, make a big swallowing nod with his head, and then he made a wobbly run back toward them, his bare webbed feet slapping the ground, hungry for more.

Blood flowed from Brisco now, but even as it did, Mark could see that while the power of Dyondaygah over the Towen and the surrounding area had been broken, it was certainly not removed from Brisco.

In fact, Mark had to wonder if it was not redoubled, for even as the damage was done to Brisco, and blood poured forth, it seemed as though he was healing right before their eyes.

New Pink flesh was already replacing the burned and melted dead mush that slid off of Brisco's face.

The bullet holes no longer bled, and in the places where the Frog-men had bitten away skin and muscle, the holes were already closing up, the muscle mass replaced.

Perhaps somewhere in the depths of the ether beyond space-time, Dyondaygah knew that one of his few remaining children was locked in vengeful combat on his behalf, and was doing all that he could to help.

"Hold him!" Someone yelled from beyond the truck. Mark, stumbled to his feet, and started limping toward the tailgate. He couldn't see who had spoken at first, but the voice was familiar. As his head cleared further, he realized it was the most beautiful voice in the world; His Ally.

She was back. She was running back up the road toward them.

Mark tried idiotically, to move toward her, and the mass of Brisco and the Frog-men, but only found himself stumbling against the tailgate of the smoking truck.

Mark moved himself along the undamaged passenger side, by grabbing hold of the sides of the bed of the truck. But before he could even make it to the front, Ally was to the place where the Frog-men and Brisco continued to tussle, something was gleaming in her hand and only after she began to use it did

Mark recognize the long sharp dagger she had taken from the past.

He found time to wonder where she had gotten it, since the last time he'd seen it was when he was cutting Hap's bonds down in the Towen.

Had Hap brought it with him?

It hardly mattered at the moment, it was the same blade or one just like it.

"Hold him!" Ally shouted again, as she came in, "Hold him down."

The Frog-men obeyed, one of them, William went for the giant's throat while the others both simultaneously opened their impossibly wide mouths to chomp out both of Brisco's Achilles tendons, taking most of the rear calf muscles with it, the clods of meat disappearing down their gullets.

Brisco went down like a small landslide, screaming in his mushy growl all the way down.

Then Ally jumped in as the Frog-men took hold of his arms. She straddled the giant's waist, around the navel, while he tried to kick at her, but his legs being mostly gone he could only flop his thighs and try to twist away, as Ally raised the knife and plunged it deep into the right side of the giant's massive gut, and pulled hard to the left.

Without a moment's hesitation, Ally, jammed her hands inside the still squirming, screaming giant, raking through his guts with her bare hands, seeming to chase after something she couldn't see within the screaming Goliath.

Mark, his head still hazy had to wonder what she was doing, but then it became clear, as she took hold of something within, and with a mighty yank of her now, thickly muscled arm, she drew the tentacle, the sacred food of Dyondaygah up and out into the light.

Brisco wailed from the ground, knowing what was coming, powerless to stop it, "No! Stop! Don't! No! NO!" He cried over and over, as Ally went in deep with the knife and cut the tentacle out by the root.

The moment the last bit of gristle was separated from inside, Brisco's mangled body went limp and the tentacle, now free of its host, crystallized and solidified in the light of the rising sun and crumbled to dusty ash in Ally's hand.

Brisco was dead.

But that didn't stop Ally.

The tentacle gone, she didn't waste a second. Using the Chainstone, which still clung to her wrist, she began to smash what remained of Brisco's enormous head.

Up and down went the stone, again and again. Smashing through his face and cheekbones, and skull until there was nothing left but a bloody pulp mixed with a powder of shattered bone, peppered with bits of the cobblestone, which began to crack under the force of the repeated impacts.

As she struck, again and again, she was saying something Mark could barely make out as

"You killed him! You killed him! You killed him!" Along with a string of expletives that would have made a sailor blush. Mark had never heard such language coming from the mouth of his wife.

She only stopped when the cobblestone finally shattered, crumbling to dust in her hands, and breaking free of the chain.

Mark had a horrible moment. Again he felt that prescient feeling in his gut, he had felt when he had thought *"Alien."* just before the tentacle had exploded up and out of the newly Cyclop-ed Brisco.

"Ghost."

He thought as he turned around, fully expecting to see his own body lying somewhere behind the truck, his head, and neck spun at some horrifyingly wrong angle.

But there was nothing there.

No body, no soulless husk.

It was not him she was grieving.

"Oh. No." Mark said as the realization came slamming home.

WESLEY CRITCHFIELD

It was Hap.
Hap was dead.

36

"Pa?" Aaron asked, "Pa's dead?"

Ally looked up from where she sat, still straddling the lifeless corpse of Brisco.

She was covered in blood and viscera from inside the slain Giant, and much of the wildness and rage was fading out of her eyes, only to be replaced with guilt and sadness.

"I... I tried." Ally started, "He was barely breathing when I picked him up. I knew we shouldn't move him but I couldn't just leave him there. He kept telling me to turn around, to go back for Mark. But I just kept running. Then he started coughing hard. I had to put him down. I put his back against a tree and he reached behind his belt and drew out my knife. Told me to go back. To end it."

Ally looked at the knife in her hand and dropped it on the street. That seemed to draw her eyes toward the pavement, and the smashed body of Brisco.

She seemed to panic, almost as if until now she had not realized what she'd done. As though it were someone else who had taken over her body once again and they were only now returning control.

She seemed to realize what the muck that now covered her was, and she began to slap at it as if she could make it go away, but it only served to press it into the fabric and set the stain.

She looked around for Mark, only now realizing that she wasn't entirely sure what had happened to him.

"Ma... Maa... Mark!" She said only now truly able to weep.

Mark was still holding on to the front of the damaged truck.

Ally rushed to him, bent down on one knee, and buried her head into his shoulder. Her chest heaving in great racking sobs.

Mark was barely able to stand on his own, and Ally's greatly increased weight was not helping matters, but he stood there and took it, holding himself up with one arm, while he wrapped the other around her neck and shoulder, pulling her tight.

The Frog-men meanwhile were not idle. Once Ally had begun smashing Brisco's skull with the Chainstone they had let go of him and backed away, both to let her finish the job, and to avoid her wrath. But now that she had moved away from the body, they had moved back in.

"Right then, you two take the arms and I'll take the legs, what's left of 'em." Said Tom moving into position.

"It's a shame she killed 'im." Said William, "At the rate, he was regenerating, we could have had fresh meat for months, any time we wanted."

Bert snorted, "You think his body could have held up to that? Even with all that power a-flowin from Dyondaygah?"

"Suuuure." Said William, "Might have even gone insane, after a few days, and they always taste better when they's broken. Flavors the meat you might say."

Together the Frog-men lifted the remains out of the street and walked them off the road. Mark looked away from them, toward where Aaron had been standing, but he wasn't there.

Looking down the road, he could see the boy running toward where his father lay.

"Ally." Mark said, shaking her, "Come on. There will be time for tears later, but now we have work to do."

"Oh Mark," she sobbed, "I'm so tired."

It was true, she had not slept all night, (and while Mark had stolen a few hours rest in the *Château D'If*, he too was hurt and exhausted beyond words.)

The ordeal they had both been through was not something either of them had been prepared for.

God only knew what Ally's poor body had been through. Perhaps until the moment, she spewed the tentacle out on to the ground the Sacred Food had been powering her, giving her energy equal to and even beyond what a regular person could endure, supercharging her metabolism, and supplying a perfect blend of nutrition that dietitians could only dream of.

But now she was just herself.

A much larger, and powerful version of herself to be sure, but her body was now "merely" human. It needed food and sleep like any other.

"I know." Mark said, "I know, but Aaron's run off down the road and we have to go after him. We can't leave him alone in a moment like this. Come on. Let see what we can do about the truck."

Ally released Mark and shakily stood to her feet.

Mark, still using the metal of the car to steady himself, hopped around to the damaged side. The Front end and driver's side fender were smashed.

This truck too was not anything that could be considered new, but it was a closer year than the one Hap had slammed into the doors of the Towen.

"I think..." Mark said, looking around. I think the worst of it is the fender. It's up against the tire. May have scraped some of the tread, but it doesn't look like it popped the tire. Aaron must have only sideswiped Brisco because he was holding me up at the time. If we can get the fender off the tire, it might be able to run. How far down the road did you leave Hap?"

"I don't know." Ally said, tears still streaming down her face, "Maybe a mile and a half, maybe two... It was right by the place where the black plants were."

"That's more than three miles!" Mark said amazed, "How could you have..." Mark cut the question off.

There were probably a lot of athletic feats Ally was now capable of that would surprise him day after day. But she had only been gone for less than ten minutes. if that. It would mean she was literally running a mile a minute. (Three minutes there, three minutes back, and however much time she had spent with Hap before he'd died.)

"Do you think you can lift the hood?" Mark asked hopping around to the open driver's side door, (which had gone miraculously un-pinched by the bent fender,) and reaching inside to pull the hood release.

He heard it "thunk" as the primary latch let go.

Ally put her fingers into the gap that had opened up and lifted. "There's a release," Mark started, "You need to-"

Suddenly the roof was up, but not just up it was way up, and away, as Ally yanked it off of the front of the truck. Mark cursed, startled by the unexpected sight of the hood flying away from the car.

Ally herself was surprised, "Umm... Sorry." She said.

"Don't be." Mark said, now able to put a little more weight on his foot, as he hobbled back up to the front of the truck, "Do you know how many times I've wished I could do that?"

He looked under the hood, (or at least where it had been,) and a quick inspection told him that virtually no damage had been done. "Wow," he said to himself, "These old trucks. They knew how to build them."

"You think it will run?" Ally asked. "I think so if we can bend the fender up off of this tire... Would you... um..." Mark gestured to the tire.

"Oh great." Ally said, some of her typical snarkiness returning, "I'm going to have to open every jar for you now, is that it?"

Mark smiled, happy to see she was recovering even now, "If you'd be so kind." Ally reached inside the wheel well, and Mark could hear the crunch of bending metal.

"Look good?" Ally asked. Mark bent over and to his surprise saw the fender was nearly back in its original position, dented and creased but largely undamaged.

"Hop in the passenger seat!" Mark said, "We need to go after Aaron."

"I think I'll get in the bed if its all the same to you. Ally said as Mark hopped into the driver's seat, closing the door behind him.

He felt the truck bounce and shake as Ally climbed in, the rear end lowering considerably on the springs.

Even amid all this horror and the pain he was in, he found the ability to laugh at what Ally, even yesterday would have thought if he was to comment on it.

He put the truck in gear, and they were moving.

Ally opened the small transom window between the bed and the cabin, "Are you alright?" She asked.

Mark was taken aback, it was a strange question to ask, now of all times, when they were trying to catch up with Aaron.

"Depends on your definition," Mark said, not knowing how else to answer.

"I know your leg and side are hurt." She said, "What else? Any bruised ribs? What about your neck?"

Mark thought of how Brisco's hand had been squeezing him by the neck and realized that his neck was stiff, but not unusable, another two or three seconds and that might not have been the case.

Until now he hadn't been able to take a moment to assess his condition.

He could feel he had a few bumps and bruises, cuts and scrapes. His wrist and shoulder hurt like the Dickens.

But he realized to his surprise, he was reasonably unharmed. "I'm alright."

He announced, "I should probably be looked over by a doctor, especially for my neck and shoulder, but nothing that can't wait. What about you?" Mark asked out of true concern but he already knew, she was way better off than he.

"Physically, I'm perfect I think. Exhausted, but unharmed." She said, plainly unaware of the irony of that statement given her new condition. *"Perfect"* might just be the exact right word for what she was. "Emotionally," she continued, "I'm going to need a lot of therapy after all this."

"You and me both Honey," Mark said. "I can't help but wonder about what I just did back there." She continued, "I mean, I just killed a man. I mean… I really killed him. I stuck my hand in his living guts and ripped out apart of him."

She paused for a long moment, "My word, I've killed several men and women. And I don't feel one bit sorry for it. I'm worried Mark. What if it wasn't me? What if it was Dyondaygah? What if its something he put in my head? Worse still," she continued, "What if it really was me? Something I've been capable of all along, and just… didn't. If that's who I am, deep down, maybe I need to be locked away."

"For one," Mark said, "Brisco was hardly a man anymore. He had given into Dyondaygah a long time ago or was taken by him. The same goes for the rest of them. You kept your humanity. You fought the Devil and won. Personally, if that's who you are deep down, which I know it is, by the way, it's not only something I'm glad to see in you, it's the woman I married."

Ally put her hand through the transom and put it tenderly on Mark's shoulder, and he bent his elbow to grab hold of it.

He turned his head and brought her hand to his lips to kiss it.

"For another thing, Maru and his…" Mark trailed off.

"What is it?" Ally asked. "Hap," Mark said, quizzically.

Ally looked up and saw Aaron kneeling next to his father's body, he seemed to be praying or talking to it.

But then the body moved, turning its head toward the road and lifted an arm to point, and then made a pained wave to the oncoming truck.

The truck's brakes squealed a bit as Mark stepped on the pedal, slowing the truck down and bringing it to a halt.

Both Mark and Ally climbed out of the truck asking different versions of the same question, *"How are you alive?"*

"Well," Hap chuckled, instantly regretting it, "it's about time you two showed up."

"I thought you were dead." Ally said, still confused, "What the heck was that, Old Man?"

"You didn't know I had an A in acting class in High School, did you boy?" Hap said to Aaron, "I knew Mark was going to need help and Ally wouldn't put me down. So I gave her the old acting bit. Pretended everything was going dark, and I was in too much pain. Lungs collapsing, excruciating pain, and everything. Of course, I only had to play up the pain, didn't have to imagine that one too much. Same as I did when I played Hamlet. Even said, *"The rest is silence!"* As my last line before dying. Ally didn't get the reference. Kids don't know their Shakespeare anymore, all they know is Star Wars."

"So you're not hurt?" Mark asked.

"Oh I'm hurt alright." Hap said, "Hurt pretty good, but nothing fatal, leastways I don't think so, not if I see a doctor right soon. Few bruised ribs, maybe a broken ankle, and my neck is a bit sore, but I should be all right."

"I'd like to get Dad to the hospital," Aaron said, still kneeling next to his father.

"I'll get to the hospital in my own good time." Hap said, "Right now we need to talk about what we are going to tell the authorities."

"What do you mean Hap?" Ally asked. "Well, I for one am not about to tell them that two city folks came here and defeated an ancient Demon god, which I've known has been inhabiting the "Olde Towen Buffet" and turning people into giants for fifteen years but couldn't tell anyone because of magic. They'd throw me in the booby-hatch for sure!"

"Why do we have to tell them anything?" Mark asked.

"Because son, a very old building and business, that was known to be the dwelling place of a very rich Dwarf just burned to the ground, and there are at least several bodies of Ten-foot tall giants buried underneath it. What's more, my business has been torn up and I have to tell my insurance company something. On top of that, the police come through here at least twice a day, some of them to eat up there at the restaurant. And I think they are bound to notice that the bacon isn't being served." Hap laughed again, and once again winced at the pain.

Mark and Ally and Aaron had to laugh too, "What's more I've got two banged-up cars, one of them sitting up at the Buffet. If what the boy tells me is correct, those Froggy boys have taken away Brisco's body, and there's a big old bloodstain in the middle of the road."

"If the Frog-men haven't licked it up," Mark added, drawing a groan from Ally, who looked down at her gore smeared sweatshirt.

"So here's what we tell them. You kids were never here." Hap explained, "Maru and the other giants were killed by Brisco. He went insane and burned down the Towen. Then when he saw me coming in my truck he attacked me and threw me out of the car. In his madness, he drove the truck up into the Towen and that's why it's all burned out."

He looked at Aaron, "Then you were coming into work about an hour later, I had gotten up and limped my way into the store, where I called you for help. Brisco came down from the Towen and came after me again, wrecking the store. I ran out into the street again and you saw him coming after me, figured he was going to kill me. You rammed him with the truck, he had me in his arms and you knocked me free, breaking my ankle in the process and that's what happened to the front end. He was knocked out, and possibly dead. You helped me up into the truck and drove me to the hospital. When they go looking for the body, and wondering where it is, we just say he must have still been alive and walked away. They might have a manhunt for a few days but that will go away after a while, especially since he didn't have any family or friends. We'll have to stop at the store along the way and get the computer that records everything on my camera. Don't let me forget that. I might do some creative editing, or I just might delete everything, have to see."

"And what do *we* do?" Mark asked.

"Do I have to think of everything?" Hap asked, with a sly wink, "You kids go back to the highway, call the auto club, they said they couldn't find you last night, but you just tell them you slept in the car waiting, maybe you came down to my store got some supplies, but that was it. You were long gone before anything happened."

Hap looked over at Ally, "And you might want to give her your shirt before you get too far along. No matter how good our story is, blood on her like that will be a dead give away. You might want to clean off in the stream on the opposite side of the overpass before you go back to your car too."

"What about all the weird stuff under the Towen?" Ally asked.

"We don't know anything about that." Hap answered, "They didn't like us and we didn't like them, so we never went up there, all there is to it. Let the police worry about that and believe whatever they want to believe."

"You really have thought of everything," Mark said with a chuckle.

"Hardly, there will probably be a lot of questions I don't have answers for, but they won't matter. Pick a plausible story, stick to it verbatim no matter what, and they'll pretty much have to believe it. Even if they don't, that's none of your concern, but most people would rather believe a plausible story than dig for the truth. Now help me up into my truck."

Once Ally had lifted Hap carefully into the bed of the truck, placing him almost like a mother laying her child in bed, and even wrapping a blanket that had been stored in the back over him, Mark and Aaron exchanged contact information.

"We'll never forget what you've done for us," Mark said, shaking both the men's hands.

"You probably should forget, for at least a year." Hap

said, "Wait for all this to blow over and then if you think it's safe, give us a call. Mayhap be that Vestal well be back here by then, seeing as how the Towen is gone. And if we move up there with her, then we'll be the ones that call you."

Ally gently hugged the old man, and his son, and together Mark and she watched from the side of the road as they drove back toward Hap's store, knowing they would be bound for the hospital after that.

Mark took off his shirt, which while torn was definitely in better condition than Ally's. Ally stepped behind a tree so as not to be seen easily from the road, and got rid of the bloody sweatshirt.

Not knowing what else to do with the remains of the gore stained rag, they found a large gap under a tree and then buried it there, covering it with loose dirt.

If it was ever found it would be hard to explain why a bloody, sleeveless, gray sweatshirt had turned up more than three miles away from the Towen in the middle of nowhere, but hopefully they would be long gone without a trace before that happened.

"Well, there goes another nice shirt of mine." Mark said as Ally stepped out from behind the tree."

"You'll get it back." Ally said rolling back the sleeves, which were constricting her biceps and deltoids. The shirt was short on her and revealed her midriff.

"Eh, no." Mark said, "It's going to be all stretched out by the time we get home."

"Home." Ally said dreamily, "I can't wait to get home, and sleep for a year."

"It would probably be best for you to stay out of sight until the guy from the auto club leaves," Mark said, "There's still a good deal of blood on your pants, and that might raise some questions. Those manacles on your wrists would definitely stick in some poor tow truck driver's memory. And when he hears about the Towen, and bodies of several giants being found, he might think about the seven-foot-tall, blood-stained woman and her husband he changed a tire for, not five miles from where the place burned down."

Ally looked down and saw that he was right. While it was less noticeable than the shirt had been, the dark brown stains of Brisco's blood were quite obvious on the green of her sweatpants.

"Oh." She said simply; almost ashamed. "Do you really think I might be seven feet tall?" she asked.

"Did you notice something?" Mark said, changing the subject to make it less awkward for Ally, and knowing there was no right answer to her question, "All the blackened plants. They're gone."

It was true.

All the black grimy plants that had once infested the slight rise in the land near the overpass, marking the edge of Dyondaygah's circle of influence were nowhere to be seen as if they had never been. The land was barren and plant-less where the contaminated things had been, but Mark had little doubt the plain would soon turn green again, as the land before them, next to the highway was.

As they neared the overpass, Ally walked over toward the bushes and picked up something from the tall grass. It was the small plastic sign they had spotted on the way in, which read

**"The Olde Towen Buffet:
3 MILES THAT WAY! ▶
Carter's Hill, KS"**

Mark expected her to tear it in half, in a fit of triumphant rage.

Instead, she tucked it under her arm.

"Souvenir." She said, matter-of-factly. They walked under the overpass and quickly found the stream Hap had mentioned.

Washing their faces, and wounds as best they could,

they prepared for the long trek back to the car.

"At least you got to take a shower." Mark said, to Ally, "I was running all night and didn't have a moment to even spray on some deodorant.

"Yeah." Ally said teasing, "Don't think I didn't notice. Hope you have some in the car, otherwise, I'm going to have to invest in Old Spice."

"She's right, ya know." Said a familiar cockney accent from a few yards away, "My mates tracked your smell from all the way back at the Towen."

Ally instinctively unfurled the chain, which was still cuffed to her arm. While it was no longer weighted down with the cobblestone, it would still be a reasonably formidable weapon in a pinch.

"Nau need for that, Missy." Said Tom the Frog-man, "I were only coming to say goodbye and Thank you."

"Thank you?" Ally asked confused.

"You're 'usband, he made us a promise. Said we'd get to see some mischief. And 'ee kep his word. Means a lot to a poor Froggy when a man keeps his word."

"Well..." said Mark, taken aback, "You're welcome."

"And we thought you'd like to know," Said Bert, waddling down the hillside, "You won't be having to worry about Little Lord Maru anymore either."

"He weren't no Lord when he died." Said William, rising from the grass not ten feet away from them, "Dyondaygah done stripped him of his power. That's why he got real old all of a sudden and died into the dust."

"You mean he died and *turned into* dust!" Laughed Tom.

"That's what I said innit?" asked William.

"So Maru is dead?" Ally asked, "Well and truly dead?"

"Dead as Judas Iscariot," said Bert, flicking a stone with a long webbed finger.

"Sets us free to go and look for another master." Said Tom. Ally blinked, "Another master? Why would you want another master when you could be free?"

"Oh because that's what we do, us Froggies. We finds someone to serve." Answered Bert.

"Wouldn't have it any other way, would we boys?" asked William.

"Nau. Nau. Oh, nau." Tom and Bert agreed.

"Where will you go from here?" Mark asked, hoping it would prod the Frog-men on their way.

"I'm bound for Innsmouth." Said Bert, "I hear tell there might be some more of us up that way, or something near enough like us, might be nice to have a few new mates."

"Oi!" Said Tom, offended. "Are you a-sayin' we ain't good enough for you anymore?"

"I think he is." Said William, "I think he's going up to see Lord Dagon 'is self to make 'imself servile."

"Well, he's not going without me." Said Tom.

"Or me neither." Replied William.

"Just when I thought I was rid-a the two ou you." Said Bert, and then he started walking away, slouching toward Innsmouth, wherever that was.

"Well don't that beat all?" Tom asked Mark, "The little blighter is scarpering."

"Me too." Said Bert, starting off himself, his too-long apron dragging along the ground, between his widely gapped, high-kneed legs.

"Oh, just a word of warnin'." Tom said, "Don't think that this makes us friends. Us Froggies, we ain't got very long memories. Odds are we won't remember you or the Towen come this time next week. So if we was ever to meet up again, there's a fine chance we might eat you just for spite, and there's lots of other Froggies out there, not so nice as us. And we's only letting you go being as you kep your word. Just a reminder, to you and the big lady."

And with that, he too slunk off into the high grass that lined the road.

Mark didn't know what to say. "Um, we'll keep that in mind."

"See that you do." Said Tom.

Their *"clean up"* (such as it was) taken care of, Mark and Ally began the long walk back up the road to the place where they had left their car.

As they walked, he noted that Ally was still wearing his boots, which she must have put back on at some point during the night.

"When did you put those back on?" Mark asked.

"Not long after they took you away." Ally said after a moment's thought, "I guess the Children or Maru had me put them back on. They're really tight."

"Should have taken the socks out," Mark said, unthinkingly.

"I did." Ally said, "There's only one sock in there, and it's on my foot."

"Oh," Mark said. (Leaving the "oops" unspoken.)

Ally let him off easy, "I suppose it was because of the cobblestones down in the Stone Circle."

"*Sarsen Circle.*" Mark corrected.

"Yeah, like you would have known that before tonight." Ally said with a derisive snort.

"I might have." Said Mark, "We studied Stonehenge when I was in school."

"Like you ever paid attention to anything they taught." Ally said, pushing gently on Mark's shoulder so that he crossed over the white line that demarcated the berm from the rest of the road.

"Of course I did." Said Mark, "I studied anatomy very closely."

"I'm certain you did." Ally smirked, "The female variety

in particular."

"Very closely." Mark confirmed, "Before, during and after class."

"Yeah well, mine better be the only anatomy you study from now on."

"Definitely." Mark said, attempting to push her back, (and failing) "Especially since there's so much of it now."

"More of me to love, huh?"

"You know it." Mark said and then began to hum some old lascivious song, about exploring a *"Wonderland"* loaded with double entendre.

"Wait a minute." Mark said, breaking off his humming. He had taken a bad step which shot a wave of pain up through his leg. It wasn't unbearable, but it wasn't pleasant either, "Why am I walking?" he said, "You're the super-strong circus freak. Why aren't you carrying me?"

"Sure, I'll carry you." Ally said, amicably, her feet coming to a stop.

"Really?" Mark said, somewhat hopefully, surprising even himself, "You don't mind?"

"No problem, just let me break both you're legs first, so you'll have a good reason."

Mark put up a "wait a minute" finger in protest, "No… No… I think I'll walk." "You sure? I'd love to do it."

"No. I'm good," Mark said walking on.

"Darn." Ally said.

When they arrived at the car, Mark expected to need to call the auto club once again and try to explain to them in more detail where the car was located, but to his surprise, he could see as he approached that the tire was already changed.

New un-muddied black rubber gleamed in the mid-morning sun.

"I thought you said they couldn't find us?" Ally asked.

Mark nodded, "That's what the auto club said."

"There's something under the windshield wiper." Ally

said, pointing to the driver's side where Mark stood.

He picked up the piece of paper which was taped to a small book of some kind. He read the note aloud:

> *"Dear Sir or Madam, I noticed you were in a bit of distress, and that you had left the spare key under the gas door. I had the spare tire, and a jack, and replaced your damaged tire. No payment is necessary. As they say, please just, "Pay it forward."*
> *– A fellow passenger on life's journey."*

"Well isn't that something." Ally said, opening the back door, and placing one long leg into the backseat, and then another, hoisting herself in by holding on to the top of the car. She sat long ways across the back seat, her feet in the footwell of the rear driver's side, while her backside and torso were mostly on the passenger side.

Mark, jumped into the driver's seat of the Chevy Malibu, "This was attached to the note." Mark said handing back the little booklet, "Look at the front cover."

"Is it all Coincidence?" Ally said, reading the title and flipping pages, "Looks like a religious tract. Oh look, and they made it into a little comic book so you'd be sure to understand it."

"Yeah." Mark said, thoughtfully, "Reminds me of something Hap said, that our surviving the night here wasn't just for us, that there was a bigger plan in action."

"Well whatever the plan is, I hope it involves a bigger car for us because this is a very temporary situation." Ally said, squirming around a bit in her blood-stained sweat pants, "I still don't know how I'm going to explain this to my mother."

Mark laughed, sticking the key in the ignition and turning it. The engine roared to life.

Whoever had changed the tire, must have turned the car stereo on, because the audio cassette had looped back around and familiar music began to pour out of the speakers.

A soothing guitar played, and then a nasal voice sang:
"*Whenever I need to leave it all behind.*
I feel the need to get away.
I find a quiet place,
far from the human race,
Out in the country."

Mark stepped on the accelerator and the fields and meadows began to move past them, leaving the Towen and the whole nightmare far behind.

But of course, that wasn't true.

The repercussions of that long night would follow them for the rest of their lives.

Some good.

Some bad.

But as Mark drove he found for the first time in decades that he was beginning to believe there was something greater at work in the world. Not just the will of Dyondaygah, or Kings and Princes of men, or even the politicians in Washington.

"You know hun," Mark said, "I think we ought to.." But Mark's thought was cut off by a titanic snore from the backseat.

He looked in the rearview and saw that his wife was dead asleep, her mouth hanging open as her head leaned back against the rear dashboard.

Even with all the changes, she had undergone in the past twenty-four hours, and as "unattractive" as most people would have considered it, to Mark it was the most beautiful thing in the world to watch his wife sleep, even when she slept, "ugly", as she was doing now.

Mark laughed quietly to himself, turned down the music, and pushed a button to resume his historical audiobook where it had left off.

Whatever and whoever's "plan" lay before them it would have to wait until they got back home to Chicago.

EPILOGUE:

Mark and Ally arrived at home that evening under the cover of night and managed to sneak into their small apartment without anyone noticing them.

When Mark awoke, nearly two days later, there was a message waiting for him on his cell phone. He had gotten the job.

The two of them agreed it would be best to go to a hospital (out of town, where no one knew them,) and get themselves checked out.

Mark had several severe cuts and bruises from his fight(s) with Brisco. Now that he was home and not running for his life, he had noticed a slight pain in his side and he feared he might have a bruised or broken rib. Every time he breathed deeply it hurt considerably, but not unbearably.

The big cut on his leg which Mark had received when he fell on the knife, which Hap had field-dressed, was his most dangerous wound.

All things considered, it was holding up pretty well and didn't seem to be infected, though the doctors did decide to pull and reapply the stitches.

When asked about the injury to his leg, Mark told the doctor that they had spent a weekend with friends at a cabin in the woods in Indiana, and he had fallen on a hunting knife.

Mark told them his buddy had been a field medic in the army and had fixed him up, but told him to have it looked at when he got back home.

He explained that he had later, in a separate incident, lost his footing and fell down a long hill, thus explaining his other injuries.

The doctor admonished him for not getting to a professional sooner, but said that his "Buddy" had done a good job. Mark indeed had a bruised rib and several other small injuries including a strained neck, but the doctor told him all he could do was "stay off of them, and let them heal on their own."

He offered him a neck brace, but Mark turned it down.

Other than a battery of shots meant to prevent tetanus, lime disease and a few other conditions there was little the doctor could do for Mark, except telling him to give it time.

Ally, on the other hand, seemed virtually unscathed and felt better than ever. Once the horrors of that night were over, Ally realized that several old injuries, (including the damage she had done to her right ankle which had ended her career as a cheerleader, and a slight problem in her left hip which had caused it to pop like a finger joint when she stretched, as well as a tendon she had torn in her right shoulder when she was fifteen, helping her father move a couch, which had never quite healed properly, and restricted her movement slightly in that shoulder,) were all healed and better than perhaps they had ever been.

She too had a variety of cuts and bruises, but by that time most of them had healed up nicely.

While she didn't have the radical healing factor of one of the Children, (and probably never had, without the final joining to Dyondaygah) she seemed to be able to recover from small injuries quite quickly. Ally was given a clean bill of health, and told she was, "as healthy as a horse."

The female doctor noted that she seemed to be in peak physical condition but noted that there was a major mistake on her chart: She was listed at 5 foot tall and 125 pounds.

Silently cursing modern technology which made it virtually impossible to avoid being treated without it being known to every doctor in the United States who cared to know, Ally laughed to cover it up and said, "I haven't been 5 foot tall since middle school."

The doctor eyed her suspiciously but didn't say anything more about it. She also recommended that, since they didn't have too many tests for her on record, that she undergo a battery of stress and blood tests, as well as X-rays, to check the condition of her heart.

"Women, after all, suffer from heart disease at a rate nearly double that of men. For someone who works out as much as you do, we want to keep a check on such things."

Later, after all the tests, she was sat down in a room, to wait. The attending doctor said they had a specialist on call they wanted her to see.

When the man walked into the room, a nurse by his side, he identified himself as an Endocrinologist. He sat down and began to ask a battery of questions.

"Your chart said you were 5 foot tall, and you say that was a typo," The Endocrinologist explained, "but the weight ratio is also consistent with a woman of that height. We called your Primary Care Physician and she confirmed that according to her records you were 5 feet tall."

"I don't know what to tell you." Ally said, "Except that I've only been to see her twice and she probably doesn't remember me very well. She's probably just going off the same records."

"You seem like a very athletic young lady." The Doctor said, looking her up and down, "Too much so in fact."

"Whatever do you mean doctor?" Ally asked feigning ignorance, and then immediately kicked herself for sounding too much like she was covering something up.

The doctor looked at his computer screen, "We put you through a battery of tests, and you passed them all well. Too well. We've never seen anyone able to take a run on the treadmill at top speed, and have a heartbeat that never got over 95bpm. That's the kind of result we expect to see on a casual walk or a light jog on the average person Mrs. Thurston. You are also exceptionally tall and strong for your sex and age. We measured you at 6 foot 11 inches."

"Darn," Ally thought, *"Missed seven by an inch."*

"Yet you don't seem to have many of the signs of trouble a woman as tall as you would normally have by your age, particularly you have no signs of osteoporosis."

"So I'm in trouble for being too tall and healthy?" Ally asked sheepishly.

The Doctor cocked his head, "No one is, in trouble here Mrs. Thurston, but I do want the truth. You see, it's exceedingly rare, especially in someone over the age of 25, but some women, when they start using certain illicit substances have noticed a change in height as well as muscle mass. I was wondering if you were using such substances."

"Substances?" Ally asked, legitimately confused, "Like what?"

"Anabolic Steroids and Human Growth Hormones," The doctor said plainly, "It's the only thing that can explain your condition. Except in your case, it seems you have avoided some of the worst symptoms and side effects so far. No facial hair growth, or heart problems, and your voice doesn't have the deepened quality we might come to expect."

It was all Ally could do to keep a straight face, "I can assure you, doctor, I've not taken anything illegal."

"That's what I would expect you to say." He said seriously, "But let me warn you against taking any such substances in the future. Nature has programmed our DNA to reach a certain level of muscularity and height. When you start trying to go against nature, you run the risk of causing severe, even life-threatening conditions. Taking such substances can also cause severe damage to your ability to conceive and carry children. I have to tell you, I expected your blood, urine, and hair follicle tests to come back with definite positives for steroid use. But they were all negative."

The Doctor folded his clipboard against his chest and looked her dead in the eyes, to emphasize how serious he was, "I don't know if you come by it naturally, or if you've been using something we don't know how to test for, but I assure you, if you keep using it, it will catch up to you. That's all I'm going to say about it."

After a few more comments, and a *"Think about what I've said."* The Doctor left, and the two of them were free to go.

As they drove home, Mark looked back at Ally who was spread over the entire backseat. She was oddly quiet, and several attempts at conversation fell by the wayside, until Mark too was silent, letting the music on the radio break the tension.

Mark could tell Ally was thinking deeply about something, but he didn't press her on it. Now was not the time.

The two of them agreed it was for the best that they follow Hap's advice and completely uproot their lives, cutting off as many ties as possible, and Mark's new job was the perfect opportunity to do that.

Fortunately, Ally hadn't been working a job for several months prior to the night at the Towen, in preparation for when something finally came through for Mark, so for her at least there was no boss to report to or desk to cleanout.

Other than a small group of friends, who she planned to keep in contact with primarily over the internet, Ally didn't have too many stakes to pull up.

"Your face looks more or less the same as it ever did." Mark said, truthfully, "All the same, I'd avoid putting up any face pictures for a while. That way in a couple of months, if someone notices a difference on the web, you can say you've just been working out. But I'd avoid standing next to anything that would show off your height."

"I'm not going to hide." Ally said, firmly, "This is who I am now."

But she had to concede that not posting a few pictures for a while was a wise choice and a small price to pay.

Within a few days, the two of them had packed up their meager trappings, (which were greatly reduced after Ally gave most of her old wardrobe and shoes away because they no longer fit,) and they were on their way to Los Angeles.

As they unloaded their stuff, taking it into a new apartment building, Mark finally broached the subject, "What's the matter Ally?" he asked handing her a large box from off the flatbed handcart, "You've been depressed ever since we went to the hospital."

"It's just something the doctor said," Ally explained, "He said that people who use steroids often have trouble conceiving and carrying their babies to term."

"I thought you said quite firmly you didn't want to have any kids right now?" Mark asked.

"I don't." She explained, "But its one thing to not want kids, and quite another to be told you can't have them."

"You weren't taking steroids anyway." Mark reasoned, "This was something completely different. As far as I can tell, it is like Dyondaygah almost completely rewrote your DNA."

"That's what I'm really afraid of." Ally said, setting the box down, "What if in changing me, he may have damaged my ability to carry a child? Am I still a human or am I something else now? Is my DNA even compatible with humans anymore? What if we try to have a baby and its not just malformed, what if it some sort of horrible monster?"

"That's a little over the top don't you think?"

Ally gave him a withering stare, "Do you really think anything is beyond the realm of possibility after what we have seen?"

Mark didn't have an answer for that.

"Or, what if we have a baby and she seems normal at first, and then she turns out to be like me? What if that kicks in at an early age? She won't be able to have any friends or play with the normal kids."

"Honey," Mark almost laughed, "there are lots of girls who are tall in high school. Have you ever seen a women's basketball game? They've got girls nearly as tall as you at half your age. And if they are stupid enough to make fun of her, she'll be able to punch them in the nose. It might be one of the best things that could happen to her. Look how much *you've* taken to it."

"It's different, I'm an adult, I'm out of school. It's different in school, people are a lot crueler there." Ally said, thinking back.

Mark nodded, "In school, they will make fun of you for anything, too fat, too thin, too short, too tall, too smart, too dumb. You can't let that worry you. Our kid will take whatever they look like, and deal with the teasing, and we'll be there to support them when the time comes." Ally smiled, knowing Mark was right.

But then the little idiot had to add, "All the same you might want to go to a good gynecologist once our new insurance kicks in. At the very least it will ease your mind. And we can afford it now."

And it was true, they could afford it. They could afford a lot more than they used to. In addition to seeing new and better doctors, it wasn't long before they could afford a new car, (one that Ally could actually fit into and drive herself.) Ally was even able to afford a completely new wardrobe, (much of which had to be custom fitted.)

Ally went to a gynecologist and had a few tests done, both on her bodily organs and DNA.

As far as they could tell, in the office that day, physically she was in good condition, and nothing should inhibit her ability to have children. But the DNA tests would need a few weeks to come back.

On the day that she went to see the doctor about the test results, she was riding on the Purple Metro car, just after it had gone underground, when a man suddenly attacked a nearby woman, grabbing her purse.

The train was pulling into its first underground stop when he made his move, and the next thing anyone knew, he was off the train and running across the platform.

While other people on the train pulled the emergency cords and surrounded the woman, who had been punched in the face, and fallen to the ground, Ally was on him.

The Mugger had run across the platform and was already halfway up the stairs when Ally climbed up the metal railing next to the stairs, hopped over it and took him by the collar.

"Get your hands off me, you big Bi-" he started, but the next thing he knew a strong but boney fist was slamming into his face, knocking him, unconscious.

Taking hold of him under both arms as though he were a ragdoll, Ally carried him back down the stairs and placed him in front of a fat security guard who was only now coming out of his booth on to the platform.

"This man assaulted that woman and stole her purse." Ally explained as the woman was escorted off the train, by passengers, "I suggest you call an EMT for both of them and restrain this man before he wakes up."

"Who are you?" The Security guard asked. "Just a concerned citizen, trying to help." Ally said, stepping back on to the train, to thunderous applause.

The doors closed and she was on her way again, leaving the guard gobsmacked.

The DNA tests came back clean, it seemed there was nothing dangerous about Ally's DNA in the least, as far as the reproduction technicians were concerned.

"There's no reason not to expect that when you are ready to have a child. Assuming all goes well they will be quite healthy and normal."

The Doctor told her, much to her delight.

However, that was not the end of the DNA testing that Ally had performed. Unbeknownst to Mark, Ally had several more tests done by different doctors, and they determined that she did have certain markers for strange conditions that might have contributed to both her (seemingly natural) strength and height.

First, it seemed that her mitochondrial levels were exceptionally high.

Mitochondria are the energy powerhouse of cells, and therefore the body, and they tend to be found in higher numbers among more naturally athletic people, but Ally's numbers were more than double the highest numbers the doctors had ever seen.

While this didn't seem to pose much of a threat, so far as Ally could tell, it did seem to explain why she now found that she needed to eat so much more than before, and why she seldom felt tired after physically exerting herself.

Indeed, she would often need to go on a run several times during the day, to burn off the extra nervous energy that had built up.

Though she couldn't quite remember it, she felt certain this was what many little children probably felt when they *"just couldn't sit still"*.

Then, there was a known Mutation in her Lrp5 gene, which in a previous case in 1994 had led to a man having bones nearly eight times denser than a normal human male. It was a condition he had unknowingly lived with all his life until he was in a car accident that should have killed him.

After receiving this result Ally had a few X-rays done, which proved that yes, her bones were indeed at least four to six times denser than the average human woman's.

She might have gone further and gotten a more precise verification, but being that it would have involved painful and unnecessary bone biopsies, she opted not to pursue it.

Another test showed that she had a rather strange mutation in her MSTN gene and that this might account for both her strength and height.

She didn't understand it all, but the long and the short of it was that an abnormal level of myostatin protein could cause accelerated and tremendous muscle growth.

One condition she was glad to find she did not have was "Acromegaly"; a condition that had affected many tall people over time, including Andre the Giant.

Acromegaly was passable to children genetically and could have resulted, in time, in disfigurement by causing abnormal growth in the soft tissues.

Of course, this was only what human scientists had been able to pick up on at the moment. Whatever Dyondaygah had done to her, he had known exactly how to manipulate her body in a way that would cause all the benefits and "improvements" he wanted, and none of the unwanted side effects.

On the one hand, she was very happy, on the other hand, she was incredibly creeped out. To have someone, even a (lower case G) "god" messing around with her body, despite the improvements, was not a health plan she would by any means recommend.

Once Ally received this information, she realized she was never going to be "normal" again. While she knew doorways would almost always be an issue for her from now on, being so tall, Ally had expected and even hoped that her muscle mass and agility might decrease over time. She felt a little bulky and had very little chance of not standing out in a crowd.

Conspicuous was an understatement. So she had deliberately avoided lifting weights or doing anything that would normally be necessary to maintain such a condition, but it never changed.

Most athletes had to work hard to maintain such size and strength, and just a few weeks or months "time off" often led to a major loss.

But Ally's body maintained itself perfectly, and she didn't lose or gain an inch or a pound after nearly six months of virtual inactivity. So she decided to embrace it. While Mark worked at his desk job, Ally made a habit of walking around the city, and visiting different gyms to impress and shame the others who had to work so hard for their "gains".

She started a Pict-o-Gram account to document her feats of strength and heroics.

The incident on the subway had given her a purpose and a goal. She would walk through the streets of LA and be a protector.

"Defender of the weak," Mark had mocked when she told him her thoughts, *"Guardian of the oppressed!"*

"Haha." Ally said dismissively, "I'm serious Mark. Hap said there was a reason I've been given this, and I don't think it was so I could shame the boys at the local gyms or join a woman's powerlifting squad."

Mark took her hand, "I could never stop you from doing anything you wanted *before* this happened, and I certainly couldn't stop you now. Just promise me you'll be careful. No matter how powerful and fast you are, you are not bulletproof."

"I promise." She said solemnly.

"Good." Mark said mischievously, and then putting on his baby voice, "Because I still luv my widdle baby wifey!"

"That does it!" Ally shouted playfully and tackled him.

In the weeks that followed, Ally joined several self-defense and Martial arts classes.

She also eventually joined a "Historical European Martial Arts" group and learned how to better handle weapons, such as knives and daggers and swords. She took to all of them easily, and before long was at the top of her classes.

"Mark," Ally asked one day, nearly a year after they had moved to LA, "What's a Mary Sue?"

"I think it's a character that's too perfect." Mark explained, "Basically it's a woman in literature or a comic book, who has no imperfections and takes to everything too easily. Why?"

Ally smiled, "Oh nothing. It's just that someone at the gym today said I was a real-life "Mary Sue". I could tell it was meant as a compliment but I didn't know what it meant."

When Ally's folks finally did show up for a visit, Mark had to prepare them for the differences in their "little girl." He told them that Ally had acquired a lot of new skills and been "working out" a lot, which was not entirely untrue.

Had either of them engaged in social media they might have already had some idea, of what was in store for them.

Ally had become a pretty big deal on most of the platforms, and while she wasn't as famous as a movie star, (though they had started to receive a few calls from people in Hollywood, looking to recruit her for different projects,) she had become well known across the country in certain circles.

The muscle they were prepared for, (somewhat,) the height they were not.

Mark really couldn't find a way to mention it. Ally's father was quite impressed and happy about it in the long run, especially when they showed him all the pictures of people she had helped and people who just wanted to get a picture with her on the street.

Her mother, on the other hand, was not quite so understanding and wanted to know why she had done this to herself.

They tried to tell the truth, as best they could, giving them a brief account of what had happened over the course of that night, more than a year ago. And while her parents were doubtful, they couldn't deny the changes.

When they left, to return to Florida, it was with the understanding that Ally was still the same person she had always been, just with a lot more skill and ability.

"Well." Said Ally, "That's one awkward explanation out of the way."

"What's the other one?" Mark asked, "My parents are dead, have been for years. *And mama never would have liked you, under any circumstances.*" He added the last part with a fake southern drawl.

"The other is my High School reunion." Ally said.

"I thought you'd want to skip that," Mark asked confused.

"Are you kidding? Miss out on sticking it to all those girls who made fun of me for being short?" Ally said with a grin, and then added in a passable Jack Nicolson voice, "Wait until they get a load of me!"

It was a year and three months after the night at the Towen that The Thurstons once again made contact with Hap and his family.

Hap's wife Vestal had returned to Carter's Hill, and the three of them, (Hap, Vestal, and Aaron) were getting along well.

Hap didn't want to discuss the events of that night over the phone, but said that the three of them would get together soon.

A month later they met at a restaurant in Colorado. (Ally having no desire to ever even enter the state of Kansas again, and Mark couldn't exactly blame her.)

Together the five of them had a wonderful night. Vestal, who was a lovely, heavyset lady a few years younger than Hap, had been filled in on most of what had happened that night, and the truth of how the Olde Towen Buffet had burned to the ground.

Hap explained that in the days that followed police had been crawling all over the place. They had discovered the remains of the Sarsen Circle and several of the bodies of the giants below the Towen.

They had also discovered a small human-sized mound of dust and bones less than a mile away from the Towen itself. The dust was determined to contain human DNA but no one had any guess who it was, or how it had gotten to such a desiccated state. They were certain the body had not been burned, and the few bones were in an advanced state of decay.

The nearest anyone could figure was that a small child's body had been disinterred from a grave and dumped on the side of the road, possibly in some sort of Pagan ritual that had gotten out of hand at the Towen.

While Maru had been a figure known to local police and authorities, they determined that the remains could not be his because they were very old and had been decaying for some time. Maru was known to have been a living person only a few days before, and the remains were so decayed they had to have been rotting in the earth for at least 5 years before the day they were found by the side of the road.

The damage to Hap's shop and the destruction of the Towen had ultimately been blamed on the attacks of the insane giant, Brisco. While there had been some obvious doubt on the part of the police that Hap's story was entirely factual, in the long run, nothing better could be made of it than his side of the story. Especially when Hap "recovered some video from a corrupted file" on his "broken computer" which showed the giant pulling him out of the shop by the neck, and destroying the shop, breaking the camera in the process, there was little left to doubt.

While forensic experts had first determined that the destruction of the Towen itself had been arson of some kind, the final verdict was that Maru and his clan of tall people were actually drug runners and the explosion had been the result of something going wrong in a Meth Lab.

It was supposed that the disaster had occurred when Brisco had been testing some new experimental form of *"Bath Salts"* which had resulted in him killing his partners, burning the Towen to the ground, and attacking Hap's store.

It might have gone further, but since there were no known next of kin for any of the giants whose bodies were found, and because Maru had disappeared, making any insurance claims unlikely, (if not impossible since it was determined to be a drug lab gone wrong,) the case of the Towen had been closed.

The remains of the building had been bulldozed into the Sarsen pit and buried. The grass was already beginning to grow over the knoll where the building had once been.

When Mark tried to fill Hap in on what Ally and he had been doing, Hap laughed and said, "Oh, believe me, I already know a lot of it."

Drawing out his phone, he opened an app and flipped through a number of Ally's posted pictures. "There's finally a point in me having one of these since we have signal out by The Tow... I mean, in Carter's Hill..."

His attention turned once more to the phone, "You call this "laying low" for a year?" His voice was not angry, more incredulous than anything else.

"What's wrong with it Hap?" Mark asked, "There's nothing here that could lead back to the Towen, or you guys."

"Oh isn't there?" Hap asked, "It may have failed to come to your attention, but Maru wasn't the only one who knew about the secrets of Dy-...The Demon and the Towen. There may be things that we don't even know about. There might be signs on Ally's body that we might not even be able to see, which will stand out to followers of the Demon like a sore thumb."

Hap explained, "Imagine: You are a follower of the demon god, or one of the other "Old Ones" and all of a sudden you see their marks on a woman who has complete control of her own faculties when that shouldn't be possible. On top of that, she is causing mischief for the forces of evil in LA just a few months after The Towen was destroyed. You might be just a little interested. You might even have been told where to look by your masters. And here you are, making a celebrity out of yourself."

"Its just purse-snatchers and the like," Ally said, "We aren't going after anyone in power. Besides, the real bad guys are much harder to catch, they have lawyers."

"Maru had lawyers. He had money and connections. These are not things that are come by easily, or forgotten just because a man died. I could be off my nut about a mile and a half. I might be completely wrong and there's no one else out there, but what I do know is it's not worth the risk you've taken."

"So what should we do?" Ally asked, "Take down the accounts? Not make any more videos?"

"Nah," Hap said, easing back into his chair and putting the phone away, "Damage is done. It would be more suspicious if you just suddenly "went away" from the internet. Do whatever you want now."

Mark had been taken aback by the phrase, "*Causing mischief*" and remembered Tom the Frog-man saying more-or-less the same thing. Somewhere, they were out there too, and though they claimed they would forget about Ally and Mark and even the Towen and Maru himself... What if they did remember? What if "*having a short memory*" had only been hyperbole, and they remembered perfectly? Was it the kind of information they would give up willingly to their new masters? Whoever and wherever they were?

"I just can't believe none of that made the papers." Ally said.

"The papers?" Mark asked laughing, "What do you think this is, Lois Lane, 1938?"

"Fine." Said Ally mocking, "The interwebs! The news headlines! Whatever."

"Oh, it made the papers alright." Hap said bringing up a small folder, "The Papers are exactly what it hit. The supermarket tabloids. The ones in the *"Midnight Star"* and *"The National Supermarket Check-Out Examiner"* are particularly accurate."

He spread out several newspapers with extremely large type headlines that read:

"OLDE TOWEN BUFFET IN KANSAS
SECRET LAIR OF GIANTS!"

"MY STORE WAS DESTROYED
BY A MAN-EATING MONSTER!"

"ALTAR TO FORBIDDEN GODS

DISCOVERED UNDER HOTEL!"

"Someone did a lot of work and research. There were a couple that even talked to me. Though I never described Brisco as a *Man-Eater*." Hap explained. "But because these stories were surrounded by stories like *"Aliens From Outer Space Are Sleeping In My Car," "Eat Jelly Doughnuts and LOSE 20 Pounds a Day"* and ads promising you can *"You can use your ESP to learn to play guitar."* They mostly went overlooked. Fortunately, neither of you is mentioned. I was only mentioned once in the *"My store"* story. Oh and that reminds me!"

Hap brought out a large long box and handed it to Ally. She opened it and saw that within it, cleaned and polished, was the sword and knife she had taken from the past.

"I had Aaron go back after he dropped me off at the hospital, told him where to look for the sword, and he already had a rough idea where the knife had fallen. I thought you might want them back, especially when I saw you had taken up Medieval Martial Arts on the internet."

"Thanks, Hap that was awfully thoughtful of you." Ally said, looking at them lovingly, but keeping them in the box, so that others wouldn't see them too easily, or seeing them, consider them a threat.

"Oh by the way." Hap asked, "How did you ever manage to get those manacles off?"

"Hacksaw." Ally explained, "Just like we had planned before Brisco came busting in. I took them off that evening when we got home, while Mark was sleeping it off in the bedroom."

"I wasn't talking to you." Hap said, looking at Mark, "I meant yours, something told me those weren't going to be easily cut through."

"Still got them." Mark said, rolling back his sleeve, "Hacksaw didn't even leave a mark. I don't know what they are made out of but they aren't coming off any time soon. No big deal though really. They aren't uncomfortable, no worse than wearing a watch. I've been thinking about taking them to a metallurgist to see what they are made of, but I have a feeling they wouldn't be able to identify it, and they'd just want me to hand them over for study. They'd try to reproduce it, and make it into weapons. I think I'll just keep them for now. Then again, if times get tight, its always something to fall back on."

"Probably a wise decision, all things considered." Hap agreed. Might come in handy, you never know."

"Yeah and the universal translator is still in there too." Mark said pointing to his ear. "Its actually really helpful working with our foreign clients. And I can hear conversations clear on the other side of the restaurant just by looking at the speaker. That took some getting used to."

"The what?" Hap asked.

The rest of the evening passed quietly, with the five of them talking about all the things that had happened in the last year, and how different their lives were now, and how much better it was for Hap and Vestal now that they didn't have to watch people disappearing into the Towen ever again.

When the evening was over, everyone stayed in the same hotel Mark and Ally had spent the night in, just before arriving at the Towen, (a lovely place with a gigantic swimming pool,) and it was plain to see that for the time being, all was well.

Mark and Ally returned to LA, but not before determining that they had to meet up with Hap and his wife and son, the same time, the same place next year.

A couple of years passed that way.

Ally joined in a number of athletic competitions, a few of which she won but she made a point of losing every once in a while on purpose, (especially if the prize money was not needed or wasn't enough to worry about.) She needed to keep the full extent of her abilities a secret, but if she had so chosen, she could have one every single meet, hands down.

Mark, meanwhile, continued to work at his desk job, now quite happy in his work. And every year at the same time the five of them got together.

Until one year it was the six of them, Aaron brought along a girlfriend, and it was during that long weekend that he proposed to her.

Somewhere amid the talk and congratulations that followed, Hap mentioned that Kansas was once again changing its "Tourism Slogan" which was primarily an advertising campaign nearly every state had and was known to change from time to time.

Kansas had a number of previous slogans, including *"The Land of Aahhs"* playing off of its being the primary location in the real world of L. Frank Baum's fantasy OZ novels. Maybe the slogan *"Simply wonderful"* had been doing that as well, *"The *Wonderful* Wizard of Oz"*.

Finally a few years before, it had been changed to " Kansas, as big as you think." Seemingly leaving the OZ motif behind.

"They are changing it to "Kansas, On a Clear Day You Can See Forever!" Terrible if you ask me." Hap explained, "I liked the Wizard of Oz thing, it's all we've got in Kansas."

"No." Mark disagreed, "I think it is pretty good actually."

Mark knew the truth all too well. He had looked into the void of space and the space between spaces, where time and matter could not exist. He had seen the great ocean that was Dyondaygah. And yet behind all of that, even Dyondaygah himself, Mark now knew there was a power behind that power, something bigger and more awesome than even the demon god.

He had caught just the slightest glimpse of infinity and the eternal that lay beyond it. And he had seen it all while his body was in the state of Kansas. There really had been a place in Kansas where you could see, *"Forever."*

Completed, July 17, 2019

"Out in the Country"
Written by Paul Williams

CPSIA information can be obtained
at www.ICGtesting.com
Printed in the USA
LVHW031750270622
722210LV00023B/391